Too close

They stood, too clos bit too terse, the force or emotion behind them seeming to echo in the sudden silence. She found that it was difficult to be this close to him now. She wanted so much, and yet she was scared. She'd always been so scared. And confused. He confused her terribly.

But there was something in his eyes, his beautiful, dark eyes, that drew her to him, despite everything else. Something that had her swaying on her feet, her body moving almost imperceptibly closer to his and then drawing back again.

So this was it, she thought. For the first time in her life, she began to understand the true power of attraction between a man and a woman. She'd never been so torn, never wanted a man so badly even though she suspected, in the end, he would hurt her.

There is no Dublin, Kentucky, but people who know Central Kentucky will likely see that the town I made up is on the Kentucky River between Lexington, Winchester, and Richmond. They may also recognize the Winchester Public Library, in the old church complete with stained-glass windows, the old Corner Drug Store, and the Dairy Queen. I waited tables at Hall's Restaurant on the river and my husband-to-be had a way of convincing me to skip classes at Eastern to go to the horse races at Keeneland with him. Somehow all of those places made their way into this book.

When my characters Allie and Stephen talk about a bone-deep sense of recognition for a place, they're speaking for me and the way I feel about Kentucky.

Prologue

Nine-year-old Allie Bennett woke to a hand shaking her shoulder, a light shining in her eyes. "Allie?" Her mother's voice was odd and tense. "Come on. We have to get up now."

"Is it morning?" She squeezed her eyes shut and buried her face in her soft pillow. "Do I have school today?"

"No. No school. It's not morning. But we have to get up. Now."

"Why?" Allie said. Outside, it was dark. Inside, the only light came from the flashlight her mother held.

"You and I are going away. Tonight."

"Away?" she whispered, the first flickering of unease creeping in.

Her sister, Megan, went away. And never came back.

Megan *ran* away six months ago. Allie still missed her desperately. She sneaked into Megan's room sometimes and lay on Megan's bed with her knees drawn up to her chest, her arms clasped around them, and inside she just ached from missing her sister.

"Why are we going away?" Allie whispered, scared now. It seemed she'd been scared the whole time since Megan disappeared.

"We just have to. Be a good girl for me and hurry." Her mother went to Allie's closet and flung open the doors. "Get dressed while I pack your things."

Her mother handed her a pair of jeans and a sweater, socks and her favorite shoes. Still sleepy, she hurried to put them on, watching in growing fear as her mother hastily stuffed things from Allie's closet into two suitcases. Cold, Allie grabbed her favorite doll and sat on her bed wrapped up in her comforter.

Outside, the rain was loud. At times she heard the crackle and boom of thunder, saw a flash of lightning. Her mother, breathing hard and still wiping away tears, took Allie by the hand and led her down the big, curving staircase to the front door. Two more bags sat there, packed and waiting. From out front, Allie heard a car horn.

"There's the cab," her mother said, reaching down for the bags.

There were footsteps behind them. Allie turned and ran to her father. He lifted her into his arms and held her, something he rarely did now that she was so big.

She held on tight. "Daddy? We're going on a trip?"

"Oh, baby. I love you. Will you remember that? Always? I love you."

She nodded gravely. He put her down and went to her mother. There were whispers, strangely intense whispers. Something was terribly wrong. Sick with fear, Allie remembered the morning they woke up and found Megan gone. She wanted to be back upstairs safe in her bed.

Her mother and father began arguing. Her father said, "Don't do this, Janet. Don't take her away from me." Her mother, weeping, said, "I've already lost one daughter. I'm not going to lose another one."

And that was that. Her father turned away.

Allie ran to him and threw herself into his arms once again. "Daddy?" she said urgently. "You're not coming with us?"

"I'm sorry, baby." She saw tears in his eyes, thought his heart must hurt, just like hers did. "I'm so sorry."

"For what?" she said. Whatever it was, he'd said he was sorry. When someone said he was sorry, you were supposed to forgive him and be his friend again. Her mother taught her that.

"If I could go back and change things, I would, Allie," he said. "And I'll always love you."

There was a rush of air, and the sound of the rain grew louder. Someone must have opened the front door. She buried her face against her father's neck, the next moments a terrifying blur. She remembered screaming and holding onto her father, her mother pulling her away, her father wearing such an odd expression on his face as he watched them disappear into the night.

Chapter 1

It was just a house, Allie told herself as she climbed the front steps for the first time in fifteen years and paused outside the massive door of wood and beveled glass.

Of course, that was like saying this was merely a small town in Kentucky. That it held no power over her. It was like saying all the people now gone from her life were nothing more than her family, like claiming that finding herself virtually alone in the world didn't matter in the least.

It did.

So did this house.

A shiver started at the base of her skull and worked its way down her spine, chilling her through and through. Allie wasn't sure if she could open the door and walk across the threshold. She never expected it to be this hard to come back, never expected anything as ridiculous as an eerie feeling about a house to throw her so off balance. Especially after she'd read the letters and realized she had to come back.

She was a careful, cautious woman, with her feet planted firmly upon the ground, one who'd spent the past six months watching her last living relative— her mother—die. There wasn't a single, silly, fanciful notion in her head, and certainly not a superstitious one.

Still, the house seemed to have a power all its own. It stood three stories tall, a stately mass of white-washed stone with white columns on either side of the entrance. Statuesque oaks and broad, full willow trees—weeping willows, for which the road was named—shaded the entire area and hid most of the house from passersby. Rosebushes, azaleas, and all sorts of greenery had run amok throughout the yard, and she could smell the river from here, the scent achingly familiar.

Outwardly, there was nothing at all sinister about the house, just an air of abandonment, of loneliness, and of isolation. Yet Allie had felt a sense of dread building inside her from the moment she learned it was still standing, that it passed to her mother upon her father's death two and a half years ago, then to Allie at her own mother's death.

Until then, Allie hadn't even known her own father was dead and buried. She never had a chance to ask why a mother would keep such a thing a secret. Allie had written him letters for years, letters he never answered, letters she now suspected her mother never mailed. She'd found one among her mother's possessions, stamped, addressed, just lying in a box gathering dust, letters in which she'd poured out her heart to a father she believed hadn't cared enough about her to even take the time to write her back. And now there was this thing with her sister . . . Could her mother have lied to her about what really happened to Allie's sister, too? Why would she ever do that?

Allie sighed. Why indeed? Maybe for the same reason that fifteen years ago Allie and her mother had run off into the night and never returned. Maybe if she could solve that one mystery, she could solve them all.

A strong autumn breeze, surprisingly chilly for this early in the fall, whipped around the corner, hissing menacingly as it came and smelling of rain. The wind wrapped itself around Allie, sending shivers through her. It felt like an omen, like someone or something warning her, *Don't go inside.*

Unnerved, Allie was grateful to see a car pull into the circular driveway. A statuesque man with stark white hair and a kind smile climbed out of the car.

"Miss Bennett? I'm William Webster." The man in his sixties moved slowly up the walkway and held out a hand. "I'm so sorry I'm late."

Allie wasn't sorry at all. She didn't want to go inside. They shook hands, and she said, "I appreciate you meeting me here on such short notice."

"No problem at all, young lady," he said, smiling. "I'm awfully sorry to hear about your mother. And I'm glad someone's finally going to do something with this old place. It's a shame the way it sat empty all these years."

She smiled, knowing it was as obvious an opening as she was likely to get.

Ask him, she told herself. *Just ask.*

"I made copies of the keys for you." Mr. Webster pulled a set from the pocket of his overcoat. "Had the utilities turned on, too. Shall we go inside?"

"Of course."

She hadn't come all this way to cower on the front porch. After all, it was just a house, stone and mortar, wood and plasterboard. An inanimate object. It could not hurt her.

In fact, the few memories she had of this place

were happy ones—at least until that last summer. Until her sixteen-year-old sister ran off into the night and was never seen alive again. Somewhere on a rural highway in Georgia, Megan had died in a car accident. At least, that's what Allie had been told. To this day, Allie didn't know why her sister ran away, and she could no longer be certain how her sister died, either.

Glancing up at the stately white columns flanking the entranceway like the most stoic of sentinels, she wondered if the answers to that particular mystery were somewhere inside. She hoped so, because there was no one left to ask. There was no other place to go for answers. Except here.

The front door opened with an ominous creak. The lawyer stepped back to allow her to enter. Allie took that first step. And caught her heel on the antique rug just inside the doorway, nearly falling down.

"Careful." Mr. Webster's hand shot out to steady her. His other hand stretched past her left shoulder and found the light switch.

Nothing happened.

"Why am I not surprised?" Allie said.

"I'm so sorry," he said, flipping three wall switches in a row, all to no avail. "My secretary called the power company as soon as I hung up the phone with you yesterday. They assured her this would be taken care of by now."

"Oh, I didn't mean this is your fault. Just that I'm not surprised at any little glitches. It's been a difficult day."

She spared him her tale of flying through the storm. Now she found herself in something akin to a mausoleum with no electricity. Glancing outside the open doorway, she saw the faint light of day beginning to fade. Soon it would give way to full darkness, made even more ominous by the clouds that would obliterate the moon and the stars. She'd be alone with nothing but her memories and wild speculations about why she'd been so scared to come back.

Mr. Webster phoned the power company about her electricity. Allie hovered just inside the doorway thinking that perhaps this was a blessing. She didn't have to stay. It would have been silly to go to a hotel when she had a five-bedroom house sitting here empty. But she had no power. For one more night, she had an excuse not to be here. Relief flooded through her.

Just then the lights in the overhead chandelier flickered once, then again, then stayed on.

"Damn," Allie muttered. It would be a long night.

Mr. Webster graciously brought in her bags. In the big kitchen, he opened the refrigerator, showing her the casserole his own housekeeper had prepared and delivered earlier, along with a few other staples. A small welcome home, he explained. Surprised and touched, Allie thanked him.

She stopped him at the front door, knowing she couldn't let him go at this. "My father . . . All those years, he knew where my mother and I were?"

"I'm not sure he knew all along," the man said kindly. "But when he came to me eleven years ago to make out a will, he did. Your mother was his sole beneficiary. He told me then where to find her."

He rattled off the address and phone number.

Allie nodded, unable to deny it any longer. All along, her father had known. He could have been with them, if that's what he wanted.

She forced herself to go on. "He and my mother never divorced?"

"I've never seen anything to indicate they divorced."

It seemed impossible. They'd lived apart for fifteen years, yet Allie also had found no divorce decree when she went through her mother's things. Instead she'd found letters from William A. Webster, attorney at law, Dublin, Kentucky, the town of her birth. Letters addressed to *Mrs. John Bennett*, among them one notifying her that her *husband* had died, a letter dated more than two years ago. Allie had been sure it must be an awful mistake. What kind of mother didn't even tell her own daughter that her father was dead? One who hadn't told her daughter much of anything else, she supposed.

"What about custody? Of me?" Allie tried. "If they went to court, there should be a record of it somewhere, shouldn't there?"

"If there was a custody agreement, I'm not aware of it. The only thing I handled was the will and your father's estate."

"But . . . you could check?"

"Of course. I'll do anything I can to make this easier for you, my dear."

"Thank you," she said, so many questions running through her head. Allie settled on one. "All this time . . . My mother . . . she wouldn't come here?"

"No," he said simply.

"Why not?"

"I'm sorry. I don't know," he said. "The first time I called your house when I asked for Mrs. John Bennett, she hung up on me. I called back and got an answering machine. The next day the number had been disconnected."

Allie remembered her mother abruptly having the

phone number changed. She'd claimed she was getting crank calls.

"I wrote letters," Mr. Webster continued. "She never replied. I finally flew to Connecticut, thought she'd throw me out of her house. But she must have seen that I wouldn't give up, because we came to an agreement. She didn't want anything to do with the house. I offered to have it sold. She said she'd think about it. I told her there was some money from your father's estate. She didn't want it. So I paid taxes on the house, had somebody cut the grass, that sort of thing. I kept your mother informed all along. She never responded."

Allie could hardly believe it. All that time her mother had known.

"For what it's worth," Mr. Webster said, "I always liked your father. And he missed you, Allie. I could see it in his face whenever he talked about you and your mother. He missed you both."

"My mother said he didn't want to have anything to do with us," Allie whispered.

"I scarcely knew your mother. I couldn't say what might have given her that idea. But I knew your father. He missed you."

Allie thanked him for all his help. Once he left, she stood with her back pressed against the door, the house spread out before her like a mystery to solve. The first piece of the puzzle only left her with more questions.

Allie shouldn't have given in to her mother's wishes. She should have demanded answers years ago, no matter how much it upset her mother.

How could she have let her mother slip away without telling her anything? Allie knew, of course, but that didn't make it any easier to accept. She'd done it by refusing to accept that her mother was so close to dying. Janet Bennett had been diagnosed with breast cancer and seemed to respond well to chemotherapy. But she'd grown weak, her body worn down by the treatments. She needed the kind of care that could only be provided by someone with her day and night. As much as Allie hated to give up the independence she'd gained over the years, she quit her job and moved back into her mother's house.

In the end, it was nothing but a cold, which turned into pneumonia, that sent her mother slipping into a coma and dying. For so long, Allie had longed to be free of her mother, a master manipulator. Until she was free, and it didn't feel like freedom anymore. It simply felt like being left all alone.

She'd been sorting through her mother's things one day when she started finding letters. Not just the ones from Mr. Webster. There was the letter Allie wrote her father that had never been mailed. Stamped and addressed in her childish scrawl but never mailed. She'd found it in a box tucked into the corner of a drawer by her mother, who seldom threw anything away.

Allie had written many such letters, full of love and longing and sadness, and later, shortly before she'd simply given up, letters full of adolescent rage. Her father had never answered her. Her mother's face fell every time Allie asked about him, every time she asked her mother to send off another letter. She'd stopped writing around the time she was twelve. She'd started to believe her mother, who was all she had left then, and she'd never imagined her mother might not have even mailed those letters.

But it was the last letter she found that had sent her rushing back here.

It had arrived at their house in Connecticut after her mother's death, forwarded by Mr. Webster from their old address in Kentucky, from a man named Jason Getty, who lived in a suburb of Atlanta, Georgia. He wrote rather cryptically that he was trying to contact the parents of Megan Bennett, who had been killed in a car accident in Georgia nearly fifteen years ago. He had questions about the incident he hoped they could answer, and he might have information for them as well. He suggested they might help each other.

Allie tried to tell herself it really didn't matter, not after fifteen years. Her sister was dead and buried. Nothing could bring her back. The letter was probably someone's idea of a sick joke. But she simply hadn't been able to leave it alone.

There was indeed a man named Jason Getty at that address in Atlanta, Georgia. He was a forty-three-year-old stockbroker, with a wife and three children, a man who claimed he'd never heard of Megan Bennett or her mother and knew nothing about a fifteen-year-old accident. He couldn't imagine why anyone would think he would, and seemed genuinely baffled by the whole situation.

Allie had the man checked out by a private detective. He was well respected in his job and his personal life, paid his bills on time, had never been arrested, seldom missed being in church on Sunday. As far as they could tell, he'd never been to Dublin, Kentucky, or to the town in Georgia where Megan died.

He'd pointed out, quite reasonably, that anyone could use any return address they wanted on an envelope, and if the letter writer truly wanted answers about her sister's death, he wouldn't have Megan's family writing back to a false address. All of that was true. But why would anyone write such a letter in the first place all this time? Why use Jason Getty's address? Had they simply picked it from the phone book?

It had been so odd, and it had made Allie think. She really didn't know much about how her sister died, didn't even know why her sister ran away. She didn't know why her family fell apart all those years ago. It was her mother's way, of course. To avoid all things unpleasant, to pretend they didn't exist, to hope they might go away. Well, none of Allie's questions had ever disappeared. They'd always been there, hovering on the edges of her mind. And she'd decided it was time to stop wondering, time to go after the answers for herself.

She just hadn't realized how hard it would be to come here after all these years. Even this morning, at the airport, her bags packed, her plane ticket in her hand, she'd had the ridiculous urge to get up and walk away. The past might tease at her mind, like the half-forgotten lyrics of an old, familiar song. It might haunt her like a dream at times, a nightmare at others. But she'd lived with it for so long, the questions, the uncertainties, the odd sense of yearning for something she didn't even understand. It had taken all of her resolve simply to board the flight.

But now that she was here, she made a solemn promise to herself. No matter what happened, she wasn't leaving until she found out the truth. About her father, her sister, her life. She had to have those answers before she could ever really put this behind her and start fresh.

Which meant she had no business standing here with her back pressed against the front door as if she meant to escape at the first opportunity.

Outside, she heard the ominous roll of thunder, felt electricity in the air. At any moment it would come together in a blinding bolt of lightning. More than likely, she'd lose power again before the night was over. Interminable hours of darkness stretched before her.

It was that thought which finally propelled her through the first floor, past the graceful, swirling lines of the grand staircase in the front hall, through the living room—the furniture like ghostly mounds under fading white cloths—to the kitchen in back. In the walk-in pantry, she rummaged through the cabinets until she found several large candles and some matches. She lit three candles all around the kitchen, then had the oddest feeling of the past closing in on her, smothering her.

She'd been in this room so often, and the memories seemed to come rushing back, memories she thought she'd lost completely in the intervening years. Allie turned her head and could have sworn she saw . . .

Herself?

She blinked twice. The image before her remained stubbornly the same. For a moment, it was as if someone had turned one of the pages of time, and she was back in this room, fifteen years ago. Like she was two people—herself, as a grown-up, watching herself, as a child.

She sat on a high stool in the corner of the kitchen, using the wrapper from a stick of butter to give a baking pan a thin coat of butter, something she'd done a hundred times. Her mother never threw away a butter wrapper. She folded them neatly into rectangles and stored them on the shelf on the refrigerator door that held the butter dish. When it came time to bake, Allie got out one for each baking pan. There was just enough butter left on the wrapper to grease a pan.

"Almost done, dear?"

Allie whirled around. There was her mother, clad in a pristine white apron her hair without a speck of gray, her face not nearly as sad. She walked over to little Allie and dumped a quarter cup of flour into the pan. Allie worked it around the bottom and the sides, so nothing they baked would stick, and her mother smiled at her. There had been times when her mother smiled beautifully, when she'd been happy, as well. Allie had forgotten that.

"Can I lick the bowl?" little Allie said, looking unbelievably young and happy and innocent.

Allie knew why. This had been *before*.

Their lives together were inexorably separated into *before* and *after*.

Before Megan ran away, little Allie had been happy, unafraid, thinking life would go on just like that, that nothing would ever change.

Blinking to clear her eyes, the grown-up Allie now saw nothing but the flickering of candlelight in the corner where they'd been. A chill ran down her spine. Her own voice—hers as a child—seemed to echo in the room, the sound filtering through the house, like water flowing down a gently moving stream, until it was gone and silence remained.

"Oh, God," Allie whispered. Obviously, she was in dire need of a decent night's sleep and some food. Her stomach had twisted itself into knots, and she had a bad case of the shakes, which meant her blood sugar level was crashing. She always got the shakes when she waited too long to eat.

Allie turned on the stove, put the casserole inside, and set the timer. Coffee sounded good, too, and the caffeine didn't worry her in the least. She had no prayer of sleeping well tonight. She made a pot, stood there in the kitchen waiting for it to brew, finding her gaze darting this way and that at every little creak, every whine of the wind.

It didn't matter what happened here—what she thought she saw—she was staying. If the house didn't hold the answers she sought, the townspeople likely did. This was the kind of place where people were born, lived out their whole lives, and died. She'd find people who knew her father, remembered her mother and her sister. She'd ask her questions, have her answers, no matter how painful.

She was still standing there a moment later when the wind started screaming. Even though she was expecting it, she still gave a start when the thunder finally sounded and the lights flickered and died.

She was just starting to calm down a little when she heard another sound. Someone was knocking on the door. Her heart gave another painful lurch, thinking of that eerie vision of herself and her mother in the kitchen. But the noise persisted, and Allie hurried to the front door.

Without even looking to see who it was, she flung open the door, forgetting all about the candle in her hand. The wind came at her in a rush, the light dying abruptly. Lightning crashed around them, for a second providing dramatic backlighting for the man. She'd thought Mr. Webster might have returned for some reason, but this man was much younger, taller, broader through the shoulder, darkly handsome, and he looked as surprised to see her as she was to see him.

"Oh, my God," he said softly. "Megan?"

Chapter 2

A bit of light flared between them—from a cigarette lighter, she realized—and Allie gaped up at the tall, dark stranger. He reached for her, and it wasn't until she'd likely made a fool of herself that she figured out he only meant to light the candle she held in her hand. She was trembling so badly he put his hand over hers to steady it, then took the candle from her. He slipped the lighter into the pocket of his raincoat and carefully shielded the candle flame from the wind as he held it up to her face. The man stared at her for a long moment, as if he couldn't reconcile the image he saw with the truth—that the girl he remembered was dead. Surely he knew that.

"She died," Allie said. "Fifteen years ago, she ran away and never came back."

"I know. That's why I was so startled by the sight of you." He stared at her, his eyes narrowing, recognition dawning yet again. "Allie?"

"Yes." She gave him a tentative smile. "I'm afraid I don't remember you."

"I doubt you would. You were what? Six or seven years old? When you and your mother left town?"

"Nine," she corrected. She'd just finished third grade and had so few specific memories of that time. Struggling with multiplication tables. Watching with curiosity and envy as a few of the older girls started filling out in all the right places and gossiping about boys.

She didn't remember this man.

Just then, the rain came thundering down, running off the sides of the porch and blowing toward them. The man came one step closer. Allie hesitated only a moment. She dreaded the idea of being alone in this house, and he had known her sister.

"Would you like to come inside?" She would never have invited a stranger into her apartment in Connecticut, but this wasn't Connecticut, and he wasn't exactly a stranger.

"Yes, thank you."

As she closed the door she realized there was no other car in the driveway. He must have walked here before the rain started, and she wondered if he was a neighbor.

He set the candle on a small table at the bottom of the stairs, took off his obviously expensive and now very wet raincoat, and hung it over the banister. He was wearing a beautifully tailored suit in a rich brown color, the jacket showing off the wide expanse of his shoulders. He ran a hand through his hair, which was short and dark and wet, then stared at her once again.

"Sorry," he said. "I can't get over how much you look like your sister."

Allie found herself absurdly pleased by the idea, and she liked knowing someone still remembered Megan. Sometimes it had seemed she was the only one. Her mother hadn't so much as mentioned Megan's name in years, and Allie had learned not to, either, as she'd learned not to ask about so many things over the years.

She let the man take his time looking at her as she studied him. He was in his mid-thirties. Tall, trim, with the build of an athlete and an air of self-assurance and power. Money, too. It was evident in the cut and quality of the suit. He looked like a man used to having the best, to getting his way.

A second later, he turned his head a bit, and the light hit his face at just the right angle. Allie saw something there, something she recognized. The shape of his eyes, maybe the hint of gold in the dark green irises or the shape of his lips when they stretched into the barest hint of a smile.

"You used to live next door," she said.

"Still do."

"Stephen Whittaker?"

He nodded. "I'm surprised you remember."

"I'm surprised now that I forgot," Allie said. "Megan talked about you nonstop from as far back as I can remember. She watched from the window of my bedroom when you went out on your first date. Then she cried for days."

He looked surprised, then a bit embarrassed. "Megan was a sweet kid."

Allie nodded. Stephen, if she remembered correctly, had been a few years older than Megan. Allie wondered if he'd always viewed her sister as nothing but a sweet kid, if there had ever been anything more between them.

Allie's memories of the time she'd spent here had always been vague, but strangely, the closer she tried to get to her memories of that summer Megan ran away, the more difficult it was to recall anything at all. Was it merely the fact that she'd been so young? Or something else entirely that made it difficult to remember those last days with her sister?

Allie couldn't say. But Stephen would have been in high school or college. He'd always lived next door to her family. His mother did volunteer work at her parents' church, and his father was a judge. Surely she could trust him.

Impulsively, Allie said, "Someone was kind enough to leave me a casserole for dinner. I think it had enough time to heat before the power went out. I also made a pot of fresh coffee. Would you care to stay for dinner?"

"Coffee and a hot meal? In the middle of one of these storms? That's an offer I couldn't possibly refuse."

By the time she served the casserole, Stephen was sitting at the small table by the window in the kitchen, the flames of a half dozen candles dancing around the room. Outside, the thunder and the wind had subsided, but the rain still fell heavily, the wetness glistening against the windowpanes, the atmosphere suddenly intimate.

They ate hungrily. Stephen had her laughing as he came up with news of people and places she remembered. The food was warm and settled her stomach. She'd stopped shaking, was more relaxed than she'd been in weeks.

"I don't remember the last time I enjoyed a meal more," she said.

"Then the man in your life ought to be ashamed of himself."

He grinned as he said it, and there was power in the easy smile that rested so naturally on his lips, in the richness of his voice, the warmth in his tone, the mere hint of flirtation in his sparkling eyes. She couldn't help but admire the elegance infused within every move he made. Everything about the way he carried himself spoke of unfaltering self-confidence and an assurance of his place in the world and with women.

He had to know women found him charming. All women, she suspected. Allie suspected he could get most anything he wanted, simply by asking. She wondered exactly what was happening to her. If it was some trick of the soft, pretty light or her gratitude in having someone to keep her company tonight. Whatever it was, she was enchanted with him. And she found it was easy to sit there in the dark with him. She wasn't nervous or tongue-tied, as she often was around men like him, because she knew him. It seemed she'd always known him, and that at the core, the man was not so different from the boy. He'd always been kind to her and Megan.

"So, who is this man who's treating you so shabbily?" Stephen asked.

"There is no man," she said quickly.

No one at all. The thought sobered her faster than anything could have. She was all alone, missing her mother, missing her sister and her father more than she had in years, and she still had to face the night alone in this house.

"So what brings you back?" Stephen asked. "The house?"

He'd poured her another cup of coffee when he'd gotten up to refill his own cup. Even lukewarm, it still tasted good. They'd pushed their plates to the side, and Stephen was leaning back in his chair now, watching her intently in a way she didn't think she'd ever feel comfortable being watched. And he would be gone soon. If she had questions, she had to get to them.

"My mother died recently," she said.

"I'm sorry." His hand slid across the table to hers in a simple, eloquent offer of comfort.

"Thank you," she said, unable to remember the last time a man held her hand. "I miss her. More than I had imagined I would." Particularly given the fact that she'd been angry at her mother for most of her life.

"It was just the two of you? Once you left here?"

"Yes."

"You must have been close . . ."

"I wouldn't say that." Allie sighed. "We just never quite got it right, you know? The mother/daughter thing. I always thought one day we would, but we didn't, and I let her rob me of all those years with my father."

"Rob you?"

"We both acted as if my father didn't even exist. She wouldn't talk about him, except to say that he didn't want us anymore," Allie explained. "Of course, I did what she wanted. I can't blame it all on my mother."

Janet Bennett painted herself as a frail, wounded woman her whole life, and Allie had always known her biggest responsibility was not to upset her mother. That included not starting any conversations about her father. Not asking any questions. Giving up on the letters, and never trying to see him.

"Your mother was all you had left, Allie. You were just a little girl. It's natural for you to want to please her."

"Maybe when I was nine. I'm twenty-four now."

"You grow up a certain way, expected to do certain things for your family, and it's hard to break those habits. It's hard to stop wanting to please them, hard to do what's right when you know it's going to hurt them."

"You do things like that for your family, too?"

"We all have our little eccentricities." He laughed humorlessly. "Eccentricities is a generous word for the things that go on in some families. Don't beat yourself up because you didn't handle your mother's problems as well as you think you should have. She was the one with the problem, Allie."

"No. It was my life. I let her do this to me."

"What did she do?"

"I think the current psychology term would be that she had control issues. She liked having me under her thumb. She was unhappy and the biggest hypochondriac I've ever known. Every time I managed to pull away just a little bit, she came up with these mysterious little problems, vague weaknesses and complaints. It was like she couldn't stand the idea that I might actually be happy. If she wasn't happy, nobody was going to be happy. I feel guilty that I didn't stand up to her more often—especially when it came to my father. Even felt guilty because I didn't want to give up my job and my apartment to care for her in the end. I kept thinking she was willing to do anything to stop me from having a life of my own—even get cancer."

"Oh, Allie—"

"I know. It's crazy to even think it. Even crazier to miss her so much now that she's gone."

"You took care of her? All by yourself? In the end?"

"For a while. I quit my job. As an accountant," she said with what she thought was only a tad of distaste.

"You don't like being an accountant?"

"No." She grimaced. "It's so dull."

Stephen laughed.

"I suppose it was a good thing—that I quit, I mean. I should have figured it out long ago. I just . . . I've always been good with numbers, and accounting is so logical, so predictable. There was a time when that appealed to me." One place in her life where everything made sense. No surprises. No disappointments, just sheer logic. "But I've hated it. All except the last few months, at least."

"What was different about the last few months?"

"There was an organization in town that was very helpful to my mother and me when she was sick. A church group, sort of an umbrella organization that provided all sorts of services in town. They had a home health nurse who came once a week and a support group for women battling cancer. They brought my mother hot meals, before I moved back home, that sort of thing.

"They lived constantly on the verge of financial ruin, lived on sheer faith alone at times." She admired them for their nerve, their renegade do-gooder tactics. "I ended up doing volunteer work for them when I had the time, juggling funds as best I could to keep everything going."

"And you enjoyed that?"

"I did. Clients, to me, had always been a bunch of numbers in long rows on a computer screen. These people had records scattered from one end of the county to the other, so I ended up visiting a lot of the different sites where they provided services. Seeing all those people they helped . . . It made it all real. It made the job important in a way it never had been before."

"Sounds like you've found a career," Stephen said.

Allie nodded. "I think I did. If the group had any money, they would have hired me. They still may, once I go back."

"And if that doesn't work out?"

"I don't know. I'll probably look for another organization like that. I've found that I need the connection to people," Allie said, then forced herself to tell him what had really gotten to her about the whole organization. "They had a shelter for teenage runaways, a wonderful place. I ended up spending a lot of time there."

"Thinking of your sister?" Stephen guessed.

"Yes." Looking at the girls. Lost, scared girls who hid it all behind a wall of bravado a foot thick. Streetwise, old-before-their-time girls. She'd stared into all their faces and wanted to see a bit of her sister, wanted for one of them to make her understand why Megan ran away. "I couldn't help but think . . . Why couldn't Megan have found someplace like that, where she would have been safe? Maybe come home?"

"I remember when she was a little girl, she always seemed to be disappearing to one place or another," Stephen said. "I remember listening to your mother standing on the back porch calling to Megan, sometimes to the two of you to come inside. Threatening all sorts of dire consequences if you didn't show your faces."

Allie thought about it. She did remember that. "Megan always liked to run away and hide."

The minute she said it, Allie felt the muscles in her stomach tighten, felt her throat go tight as well. An image came to mind that she'd sooner forget. A young Megan in the backyard, crouched behind a tree, begging Allie to be quiet so they could stay hidden a while longer. Why did Megan love to run and hide? Why did she have to do it so well?

When Allie looked up, Stephen was watching her. She could have sworn he knew just what she was thinking. Did he, too, wonder why Megan ran away?

"I think this conversation's gotten too grim," he said, standing and walking across the room.

"I'm sorry." Allie couldn't believe she'd told him so much about her mother. She hadn't talked about any of these things to anyone.

"Don't be. I asked. And I'm willing to listen to anything you want to tell me, Allie." Leaning against the cabinets, his long legs stretched out in front of him, he look relaxed and perfectly at ease once again. "I just thought there must be something we could talk about that might make you smile again."

She found herself unexpectedly touched. That he'd listened. That he claimed to understand and even thought she should try to forgive herself. And that, as he claimed, he simply cared about making her smile.

"Let's talk about you," she suggested.

After all, it would be no hardship to listen to that low, soothing voice of his. Southern to the core, the sound of it was like an old familiar song, one she hadn't known she missed until she heard it again. She decided she'd been gone for too long when nothing but the sound of a man's voice could charm her so.

"What do you do?"

"I have a law degree I've never put to good use, much to my father's dismay," he said easily. "For the most part, I build things."

"You?" Allie doubted it. He certainly looked strong enough for manual labor, but that wasn't what he did. Not in a suit like that. Not with those hands. They were not the hands of a man who earned his living through hard labor.

"I rebuild things, actually. Old things. My company buys old buildings, restores them. Sometimes we keep them and manage them. Sometimes we sell them and buy more." Stephen took another drink of his coffee. "I find old buildings interesting. They have character, charm. I hate to see them torn down and replaced with modern ones that all look the same. I'd hate to see this town look like a cookie-cutter version of any other small town anywhere in America. Take this house, for instance. It's beautiful."

"I've missed it," she said, finding that she had and was happy to share this thing with him—a love of things old and solid and enduring. Did he see that in it, she wondered? That it had endured. That it had a history. That it no doubt held so many memories, so many secrets. She wondered if old buildings spoke to him, as she wished this one could speak to her.

"I haven't been inside in years," he said. "But from what I can see, the house seems to have held up well."

"I hope so. I haven't had a chance to explore yet, but Mr. Webster, the man who's handling my father's estate . . ."

"I've known him for years. He's a good man. You can trust him."

"Good. He said the place is basically sound."

"What are you going to do with it?"

"I'm not sure." Allie sighed. "What would you do with it?"

"If I inherited this house? I'd keep it. Sink a small fortune into restoring it."

Allie didn't have the luxury of that kind of money

or time. The house was mortgage-free, but it had also appreciated over the years until it was, unfortunately, worth a great deal of money. Her mother hadn't done anything that might have minimized inheritance taxes, and she'd left hefty medical bills. Allie's father hadn't died a pauper, but between her mother's medical bills and the inheritance taxes Allie faced, she was a classic example of someone house-rich and pocket-poor.

She could not afford to keep the house. But she was intrigued by Stephen's ideas, enough to ask, "And then what? Once you'd restored it?"

"Live in it."

"All by yourself?" Or at least, she assumed he lived alone. He wore no ring, and he hadn't needed to tell anyone he wouldn't be home for dinner.

"Until I found someone to share it with me," he said. "I've watched it sit empty for years and imagined what I'd do with it, if I had the chance."

"You have an amazing house next door," Allie said.

"No, my parents have an amazing house next door, and I'm in the embarrassing position of being thirty-five years old and still living in my parents' home."

He said it with such an easy grace, she couldn't help but smile. "Cushy deal, huh? A great house? A cook? Free maid service?"

He nodded. "I'd be a fool to leave."

"Somehow I can't quite see you as a freeloader."

"Actually, I have a town house in Lexington. The city's been booming in the last ten years, and most of the work my company's doing is there. But my parents are on an extended trip, and they didn't want to leave the house empty. It's not exactly a hardship to be back here. I've enjoyed the past few months more than I realized I would. And I've spent a lot of time staring at this house. It's the kind of place a man keeps. A place where he stays.''

Again, he'd touched a nerve. Allie found her throat suddenly too tight for her to even think about replying. She would love a place where she could stay, a place where she belonged. But that sense of belonging came not so much from the physical structure as from the people with whom one shared it, and by that definition, she'd never truly belonged anywhere. Except here, so long ago.

She wondered if Stephen could possibly feel that, too. That tugging of loneliness deep inside, that need to belong, not so much to a place but to someone. She would have never expected to find that in someone like him. She would have thought he was a man who wanted for nothing.

She looked up to find him watching her thoughtfully and tried to summon up a smile. He really had the most amazing smile. She wondered if he was consciously flirting with her or if he treated all women this way, if his natural inclination was to be polite and utterly disarming; wondered, too, if perhaps it wasn't a way of bringing people close to him but of keeping them away. A false kind of intimacy he used like a shield.

Did anyone ever truly get close to him, she wondered, and found herself wishing that she could. It was unsettling—to be so taken with him already, having spent so little time with him, to be so caught up in what she suspected was a flirtatious bit of nothing to him.

She was simply out of practice with the way things were between men and women. She'd been alone too long. The last few years had been busy, working her way through school, trying to take care of her mother. There hadn't been time for casual flirtations. Maybe that was why it felt so oddly sweet to be with him, why she was reluctant to let the moment end.

"So," Stephen said. "You never told me. What are you going to do with the house?"

"I haven't decided. It's one of the reasons I came back."

"What else brought you back?"

"I miss my father, I suppose. And my sister," she said, then admitted, "I don't even know why Megan ran away."

"What did your mother tell you?"

"It's so odd," she said, searching her memory, as she'd done a million times before. "I don't remember. Not exactly. I knew something was wrong that day we found her gone, but I didn't know what happened at first. My mother woke me up early and sent me to a neighbor's house. I think she must have worried about frightening me, because she was so frightened herself. She always tried to protect me."

Which was another way of saying she never told Allie much of anything.

"Megan didn't say anything to you before she left?" Stephen asked. "She didn't seem upset or angry?"

"My sister was always quiet and a little shy." At least, that's what Allie recalled. She looked up at Stephen. "You must remember her so much better than I do. You were . . . what? Eighteen? The summer she disappeared?"

"Nineteen," he said, carefully setting his coffee mug on the counter. "You're right. Megan was quiet. Serious. A little shy. I'd watched her grow up, and it was hard for me to think of her as anything but a little girl, which is not something a sixteen-year-old girl wants to hear from a boy. I'm afraid I hurt her feelings that summer."

"So the two of you were never . . . involved?"

"No." He laughed a bit. "Nothing more than friends."

She couldn't help but ask, "Did you ever want to be more than friends?"

Stephen went to the window and looked out into the rain once again. "I wish," he said carefully, "that I'd been a better friend to her."

"Why?"

"She ran away, Allie, and she never made it back. Whatever was going on with her that summer, it must have been bad for her to just take off like that. She must have felt so alone, like she didn't have anyone to turn to. I wish she'd come to me. Or to anyone who could have helped her."

Which made perfect sense. She imagined there must be dozens of people in town who knew Megan and felt the same way. And surely there was someone who did know what went so wrong for her sister that summer, someone who could tell Allie. Someone who might know why someone was looking for information about Megan's accident after all this time.

"It was just a car accident, wasn't it?" Allie asked. "You never heard anything else, except that she was involved in a car accident?"

"No. Allie, what's going on?"

"I don't know. I—I've just always had all of these questions, and none of the answers."

He took her hand in his. "You've lost too many people."

Yes, she had. Allie had to turn her face away, because all of a sudden the urge to cry was nearly overwhelming. Stephen pulled her to her feet, his hands running up and down her arms. They stood facing each other, watching the rain through the flickering light of a half-dozen candles. Allie was feeling cold and lonely and frustrated. She wanted the man who made her laugh over dinner to come back, wanted him to chase away the shadows a little longer and help her remember some of the good times she had while living in this house. So she wouldn't have to think about the bad just yet, about all the people she'd lost.

"I know what it's like to feel alone, Allie," he said softly, then looked honestly as surprised by his own admission as she was.

"You?"

He nodded, that sense of unease covered in a flash with the barest hint of a smile.

"You've lived in this town your whole life," she said. "Your whole family's here—"

"They are," he conceded.

"But . . . What? You're not close?"

"We have our differences," he said, like a born diplomat.

"Still, your family's wealthy. I'm sure you're successful, that you love having your own company—"

"I do."

"And that it keeps you busy."

"It does."

"And you're . . . You're . . ." she stammered, then blushed.

"What?" he said, the teasing tone back, the near-blinding smile.

"You know what you are," she said, irritated now. He was going to make her say it.

"You tell me," he prompted. "What am I, Allie?"

34

"Gorgeous," she shot back. "Charming. Confident. What more does a man need?"

He threw back his head and laughed, beautifully, and she found she wasn't cold at all, not anymore. And he still had hold of her arms.

"You want to know what else a man needs?" he said seductively.

"No," she said, a hint of self-preservation surfacing too late to save her. He really was beautiful.

"He needs not to feel so alone when he's sitting in his house late at night. Or even worse, when he has a woman in his arms—the wrong woman."

"You spend a lot of time with the wrong kind of woman?"

"Not anymore," he claimed.

"Oh? I suppose you're just sitting at home alone every night?"

He nodded. Sure, he was.

"Poor little rich boy," she teased. "And what exactly would be the wrong kind of woman?"

"You want a list—"

"Go through a lot of them, do you?"

"Not anymore," he repeated.

"Tell me, Stephen."

"The wrong woman is the kind who wants to be with me because of my bank balance or because my last name is Whittaker. Because she thinks she knows who I am and what's important to me, when she doesn't have a clue."

Oh, damn, she thought. He was either very, very good at this, or she truly had been alone much too long. She wanted to believe everything he said.

"What's important to you? Give me a hint."

"I may do that before we're through." He grinned

again, his gaze narrowing in on her. "How long are you going to be in town?"

"I'm not sure." She'd be here as long as it took to find the answers she needed.

"I think we're going to have to see each other again," he said.

Allie blushed. "Just like that?

"Just like that."

"You hit on all your neighbors?"

"I'm not hitting on you. Believe me, when I do, you'll know it."

She laughed herself and tried not to let the sadness creep in. He was leaving, and she didn't want to let him go.

"What is it?" he said softly, his hand warm along the side of her face.

"I don't remember the last time I laughed like this."

He turned serious, as well. "Allie?"

"Yes." She dipped her head so he couldn't see her face, the moment too intense, too touching, too personal.

"You don't have to be alone. Not while you're here."

Ridiculous tears flooded her eyes, and she was touched by the words. He was a stranger, and yet he wasn't. She could have sworn he truly cared about her, which was ridiculous given the fact that she'd spent maybe an hour and a half with him.

"You're a dangerous man," she said, finding the courage to look him in the eye once again.

"No, I'm not."

He tugged her to him, pulling her into a loose embrace. She fought the urge to snuggle against him, to bury her nose in the warm skin at that place where his neck melded into his shoulder. He was warm and solid and his mere presence reassured her like nothing had in years.

He most definitely was dangerous. He seemed to see right down to the lonely depths of her soul, and as much as she liked him, she truly had to back away, to remind herself she didn't know him. Not well enough that she should ever feel this close to him so quickly or tell him so many personal things about herself.

She was a cautious person, after all. A person who always thought things through carefully, who wanted always to do the right thing. She'd always feared that one little misstep might lead to out-and-out disaster, to utter chaos. She'd seen it happen, after all. She'd watched life as she'd once known it simply fall apart. And it could easily happen all over again.

Allie pulled away from him, while she still could.

He squeezed her hands one more time. "I suppose I should go."

She nodded.

"Thank you for dinner," he said as they headed for the door.

"You're welcome."

Allie was careful to shield the candle flame from the wind this time. The rain was finally slowing, but it was still pitch-black outside.

On the porch, he hesitated. "Will you be all right here by yourself?"

"I'm a grown woman, Stephen. I can take care of myself."

He smiled at her once again, took a business card out of his pocket, and scribbled something on the back of it, then handed it to her.

"I'm right next door. Here's the number. Home, work, cell phone. Call me if you need anything."

"I will." She took the card, then stood there watching until he disappeared into the rain.

Allie bedded down on the sofa in the family room because she wasn't ready to face the bedrooms on the second floor. There would be time for that later.

She lay there thinking that she liked Stephen Whittaker, certainly more than was prudent after what amounted to one brief meeting, and a few fifteen-year-old memories. Mostly memories of Megan watching him and talking about him with the kind of awe only a sixteen-year-old girl could have. Particularly for a boy who seemed utterly out of reach and not the least bit interested in her as anything more than a friend.

But Stephen had been a good friend, and Megan had always been sure he would grow to be an absolutely perfect man. Allie remembered Megan's litany of his attributes. Strength, a sense of purpose, of determination, a feeling that he was someone who knew what he wanted and how to get it. All of those qualities had been there inside of him, even at nineteen.

Allie thought she saw those same things in him now, and it worried her. She wasn't sixteen, but she was at a very vulnerable point in her life. Mourning her mother, her father, maybe even still mourning her sister. She had absolutely no one in her life now. She supposed it would be too easy to find anyone, simply to avoid feeling so alone. She'd seen women make terrible mistakes that way—by latching onto the first available man they saw, no matter how unsuitable, how undesirable.

Trouble was, she hadn't discovered anything at all undesirable about Stephen Whittaker. She couldn't imagine she ever would.

Still, she'd come here for one reason—to find out what happened to her family all those years ago, including what anyone might know about her sister's accident. She hadn't come here to find a man. No matter how appealing he might be.

That decided, Allie lay there, tired and restless and still too keyed up for sleep, feeling more edgy the later it got. Old houses spoke a language all their own, it seemed. Flooring creaked. Tree branches scratched against the side of the house. Wind whistled and moaned. For a while she could swear she heard all sorts of faint thumping and bumping sounds from overhead. The second floor? The third? What in the world could be up there?

She listened for a long time, hearing nothing now, telling herself it was nothing and that she desperately needed sleep.

Uneasy about sleeping with a burning candle, she blew it out. Darkness settled around her, smothering her. Suddenly, she had to remind herself that she could breathe freely and easily. There was nothing closing in around her except her own foolish fears, nothing at all sinister about this house. Still, at times she'd swear it wasn't the random creaking and settling she heard but . . .

Footsteps?

Overhead?

Allie caught her breath. She had the urge to go to the windows and look outside, to see if someone was watching her, had a fear at times that the next instant, if she turned her head, she'd catch a glimpse of someone.

She remembered being afraid of the dark when she was little, remembered the way she tried to make herself stay absolutely still, as if the illusion of sleep would somehow save her from whatever monsters lurked in the dark.

But she wasn't a little girl anymore. There were no real monsters, she reminded herself, merely things that had little girls curling up in tight balls in their beds at night. Still, the house seemed heartbreakingly empty now, hollow and sad, as she lay there, absolutely still, waiting to see if someone was going to jump out of the shadows and get her.

Chapter 3

Allie woke to sunlight shining in her eyes, stiff muscles in her neck, and a faint chill in the air. She glanced at her watch, saw that it was shortly after six, and felt as if she had barely closed her eyes all night.

She touched her bare feet to the cold floor and walked to the windows. The world outside was wet, the surfaces glistening with water. The birds were up, making all sorts of racket. Light was making a halo at the treetops. Soon the sun would come over the top of the hill behind the stream. It seemed foolish now to have sat here late into the night afraid of the dark and a bit of noise.

Allie headed for town. Now that she didn't have to fight to see through the rain, she found the area lushly green, especially near the river. Trees towered overhead, aglow with staggeringly vivid colors—burnt oranges, bloodreds, golden yellows. There were large, rolling, open fields on one side, houses old and far apart on the other, the lots heavily treed, covered with vines, bushes, and pretty, little flowers. The sky was finally clearing. It was a soft, lazy blue, the sun beaming down on the wet world, everything smelling fresh and new.

The road was narrow and winding, gently rising

from the river, taking her past farms, past horses galloping playfully through the open fields, white wooden fences, fancy barns with spires and trim work painted in colors to match the big, fancy houses. This was horse country, after all, even if a good bit of it had been lost to subdivisions.

Looking at the land now, recognition tugged at her heart in a way she simply didn't understand. Suddenly, it felt like home, as if it had been wrong of her to stay away so long.

Town was just as tiny as she remembered—not much more than four square blocks, old three- and four-story buildings with wide sidewalks and pretty black wrought-iron lampposts and trees planted within neat squares of grass cut out of the sidewalk. There were still only a few cars on the road, the downtown area filled with neat, well-tended shops, restaurants, and offices. She wondered if anything would be open for business at this hour, then saw from the looks of the grocery store parking lot that it was not.

Allie drove into the center of town, coming upon a little drugstore on the corner with a cluster of cars around it. It seemed odd to find so many people there at that hour until she saw a sign for a coffee shop in back. Obviously, she'd found a local gathering place.

She followed the aroma of bacon and no doubt homemade biscuits, the chatter of lively conversation, to the rear of the store, where red-topped stools encircled a counter, behind which three women were working frantically. The waitresses not only took the orders and served the food, they cooked it, as well. There were eggs sizzling on the grill, an old-fashioned soda fountain to the right, and a standing-room only crowd. It was a comfortable place, a familiar one. She suspected people came here as much to sit and talk as to satisfy their hunger.

Two men paid their bill and left. Allie slid onto one of their stools next to a little girl and a woman with a baby. A heavyset waitress in her forties, wearing street clothes largely covered by her plain white apron, breezed by, plopping down a coffee cup as she went.

"Decaf or regular?" she said, a pot of each in either of her hands.

"Decaf, please." Allie had already downed half a pot with caffeine at home.

The woman had dark hair with just a hint of gray, dark reddish lipstick, and a heavily lined face that spoke of a difficult life, but a kind smile. She was doing three things at once, and doing them quite well. She hardly looked at Allie's cup, but managed to fill it to the rim without spilling a drop.

"Cream?" the woman asked.

"Yes, please."

"Sugar's there next to the napkin holder." A tiny ceramic pitcher was deposited in front of her. "What'll you have?"

Someone at the other end of the counter called out to the woman to have a nice day. She turned to wave good-bye, then finally looked at Allie. Allie tried to work up a smile, because people seemed to smile at strangers and friends alike here, and she watched as the waitress's face went from open and friendly if a bit hurried, to cautious, to disbelief.

The woman opened her mouth to say something and brought the coffeepot in her hand crashing into the side of the counter. It shattered. The liquid pooled on the counter, then slid in Allie's direction.

She jumped up just in time. A little girl seated beside her squealed and jumped as well. The waitress cried out in pain, and every eye in the room turned toward the commotion.

For a second no one moved. Allie just stood there with all of them staring at her, hating that feeling, and then someone gasped. The whispers started, the looks growing more intense, openly curious.

Two other waitresses came rushing to help clean up the mess. "Good Lord, Martha," one of them said. "You never break anything."

Martha looked as if she still couldn't believe her eyes. She still gaped at Allie, as if she were looking at a ghost. Maybe she thought she had.

"It's all right." She tried to reassure the woman. "I'm Allie. Her sister."

"Good grief, child," she replied. "You just about gave me heart failure."

"I'm sorry." Allie sat back down. "I didn't realize the resemblance was so strong."

Stephen had thought so at first, but Allie had attributed that to the fact that he'd seen her for the first time in the dark standing inside the house where Megan once lived. This was morning, in a well-lit store in downtown. For Martha to react so strongly, Allie must indeed look very much like her sister.

She wondered now if that was one of the reasons her relationship with her mother had always been so difficult. If her mother had looked at her and seen Megan.

"Are you somebody famous?" the little girl next to her asked, wide-eyed.

"Missy," warned the woman beside the girl. She flashed Allie an apologetic look, then turned back to the fussy baby in her arms.

"No," Allie told the girl. "I'm not famous. I used to live here a long time ago, when I was your age."

"Really?"

"Yes."

"Dija like it here?"

"I . . . uhh," Allie sighed, ready to give a polite lie.

"You did," the woman next to the little girl said.

Allie looked at her more carefully, a woman in her mid-twenties, with long, blondish hair in a simple ponytail and wearing a fancy warm-up suit, the baby snuggled against her chest sucking his thumb and looking sleepy.

"You don't remember me, do you?"

"I'm sorry," Allie said. "There are a lot of things I don't remember."

"I'm Carolyn Simms. My maiden name was Grayson. My parents lived about a half mile from yours. You and your sister and I used to play together."

"Oh." Allie remembered. "Of course."

"Welcome back." Carolyn smiled, introducing her daughter, Missy, and her son, Andrew. "Are you here to stay, Allie?"

"Just to take care of my parents' house."

"Oh. Is your mother with you?"

"No. She died two months ago."

"Oh. I'm so sorry. With your father gone and your sister . . ." Carolyn broke off abruptly, her face flushed, her eyes averted.

You're all alone in the world now, Allie.

"I'd love to sit and talk to you sometime," Allie said, wondering what Carolyn might be able to tell her. "Maybe the next time you take Missy to her grandparents, you could stop by? I'll be here for the next few weeks, at least."

"All right," Carolyn said. "I'll do that."

Allie got to her feet, still able to feel people watching her, and said her good-byes to Carolyn and her daughter. She put two dollar bills on the counter for Martha, who could barely look at her, and left.

Why, she wondered, after all this time would Martha react so strongly to seeing her? Had she known Megan? Or their mother? Allie didn't remember anyone named Martha.

She sat in her car thinking she should have been here when her father was still alive to explain things to her, to tell her whether he still loved her, and if he did, why he'd stayed away for so long. She could have asked him why her sister ran away, and whether it had been a simple car accident or something else entirely. If she'd come then to find her answers, surely she wouldn't have felt so absolutely alone.

Martha had a pack-a-day habit, and normally she knew better than to sneak out the back door for a cigarette in the middle of the morning rush. But this morning was different. She was rattled, and Mary Lou McMahon, her boss, knew it. Mary Lou merely nodded when, with the counter still three-quarters full with customers, Martha said she was going outside for a smoke break.

Her hand trembled as she pulled out a pack of Camel Lights. She took a long, deep drag on the cigarette, which didn't steady her in the least, then headed for the pay phone on the corner. Tucker would be leaving any minute for work, and she wanted to catch him first. She wanted to be the one to tell him. She'd rather do it in person, so she could see his face and try to figure out how it made him feel, but she'd have to settle for calling. With the crowd at the diner this morning and the spectacle she'd made of herself over the girl, there was no way Tucker would make it home tonight without knowing.

Tucker answered with a gruff, impatient "hello." He didn't like to talk on the phone, didn't talk much at all. But he was a good man, the best she had ever had, and she didn't want anything to mess that up.

"It's me, Tuck," she said.

"What's wrong?"

He knew something was. Otherwise, she wouldn't have called him.

"I saw her," Martha said. "She walked right into the diner this morning."

They'd heard the first rumors of one of the Bennett's return three days ago, when Bill Webster's secretary called the power company to have the utilities turned on.

It had always been one of the great mysteries of Dublin, Kentucky—the house that stood empty year after year. Some people said it was haunted. Others said no one knew where Janet Bennett and her daughter were. But Martha heard at the diner—eventually she heard *everything* at the diner—that Webster knew all along, that they flat-out refused to come back. And no one had. Not for two and a half years.

"You sure it was her?" Tucker said finally.

"She said her name—Allie. Even if she hadn't, I would have known. When I turned around and saw her, I thought I was seeing things. She looks just like Megan," Martha said. "She's a pretty little thing, Tuck."

"And her mother?"

"She was by herself. But I told you yesterday, I heard her mother died. She said something to Carolyn Simms about her mother, but I wasn't close enough to hear."

Tucker waited a long time before he said, "Find out. Find out about her mother."

On her way to the grocery story, Allie passed the public library housed in what had obviously once been a church. She remembered that now. As a girl, she loved combing through the shelves for something new to read and looking up and seeing the pretty stained-glass windows, the sun shining through them.

Now she looked at the building and thought about old newspapers. Libraries kept old newspapers on file, and there had been newspaper stories about her sister's disappearance, copies of which were probably on their way to her in Connecticut right now.

Allie had hired a private detective, to investigate that mysterious letter from Georgia. After Greg Malone had checked out the letter writer, she'd decided to have him dig a little deeper, into the accident itself. One of the first things he mentioned was copies of the police reports and newspaper accounts of Megan's disappearance and death. He was supposed to be sending her copies of those things, but she'd impulsively flown to Kentucky before they arrived.

Allie knew the bare bones of it. Her sister, driving down a rain-slicked road, skidded off the pavement into a swollen creek and drowned. Glancing back at the library, she told herself there was no reason to wait for the rest of the details. She was capable of digging through back issues of the newspaper herself, and she was right here.

She turned around and parked her car. The librarian, who looked to be her mother's age, couldn't stop staring at her. Allie looked the woman right in the eye and asked to see newspapers from September of 1985 through March of 1986, from a few weeks before her sister ran away to a few weeks after her death. She found several stories and the obituary, made copies, and left.

Sitting in her car in the parking lot, she picked up the first article. It was small, but on the front page and included a photograph of Megan, sitting at the piano after a recital, Allie thought.

LOCAL GIRL MISSING

The Sheriff's Department is asking anyone with information on the whereabouts of sixteen-year-old Megan Bennett, of 307 Willow Lane, to please contact them immediately.

Megan, daughter of Mr. and Mrs. John Bennett, has been missing since Sunday morning. Deputy Lance Jacobs said Mrs. Bennett went to wake her daughter that morning and found her room empty.

There were no signs of forced entry into the house, Jacobs said, and bulletins were sent to sheriff departments all over Kentucky and in seven surrounding states asking people to be on the lookout for Megan.

"So far, every indication leads us to believe the girl is a runaway," Jacobs said.

Megan is 5'3", weighs approximately 100 pounds, has long brown hair and brown eyes. She was last seen Saturday evening at her home wearing a pair of jeans and a blue University of Kentucky sweatshirt. She is a sophomore at Dublin County High School and a member of the First Baptist Church.

The family requests prayers for their daughter's safe return.

The second article repeated much of the same information, adding that her father had offered a reward for information leading to the location of his daughter. The sheriff's department said it had traced Megan's whereabouts to a small town in Tennessee, near Nashville, the day of her disappearance, but had lost her trail there. The final two clippings were about Megan's death. Allie quickly skimmed the obituary, amazed at how anyone could sum up a life in so few words. It made Allie's stomach turn to read it.

Then she turned to the last article.

LOCAL TEENAGER, MISSING SINCE SEPTEMBER, FOUND DEAD FOLLOWING ACCIDENT IN GEORGIA

Sixteen-year-old Megan Bennett, missing from her home in Dublin since last September, was found dead last week following a car accident during torrential rains in Georgia.

The car, which had been reported stolen several months before, slid off a narrow, two-lane road near Macon, Ga., and into a creek that had overrun its banks. Rescue workers found several of her belongings in the car. Three days later, they found her body about a mile downstream.

Local police said heavy rain and high winds contributed to several accidents in the area over the weekend and that Miss Bennett may have swerved to avoid a downed tree limb or may have simply lost control of the car during the storm. Visibility was extremely poor and the area was not well-lit, Officer Bruce Davis told the Dublin Times.

Miss Bennett had been missing for the past five months. Believed to have run away from home, she

was the subject of an extensive search by the Dublin
Co. Sheriff's Department.

"We sure did hate to see things end this way,"
said Deputy Lance Jacobs, who headed the search for
Megan. "We wanted to bring that little girl home
safe and sound."

The girl's father, John Bennett, declined to com-
ment, except to thank everyone who had been praying
for his daughter's safe return.

Miss Bennett's body was returned to Dublin on
Monday. Funeral arrangements had not been final-
ized at press time.

Allie's hand shook as she read the starkly factual
account of her sister's death. She'd hoped for so
much more than this. It left her with nothing. What
was there to possibly question about a car running
off the road in the middle of a storm? What could
anyone possibly know? What could it matter to anyone now?

Glancing down the block, she saw the sheriff's office. She could go, but she wasn't sure how easy it
was to get a copy of a file on an old investigation.
She decided to make a quick run through the grocery
store for cleaning supplies and food. When she got
home, after putting away her supplies, she called
Greg Malone, but got his secretary, Beth, instead.

"He's wrapping up some business for another cli-
ent today, and he's heading for Macon tomorrow,"
Beth said.

Macon, where her sister died.

"Did he get the police report from Kentucky?"

"Sure. You didn't get your copies yet? I mailed
them two days ago."

"I'm not in Connecticut," she said. "That's the

other thing I wanted to tell Greg. I'm in Kentucky."
She rattled off the number at the house and the address, in case the detective needed to reach her.

"Okay, I'll send you another copy of what we found."

"Just the police reports," she said. "I went to the library myself and got the newspaper articles."

"Oh, okay. Allie, if you're there, there's something you should know. The researcher we hired to find the newspaper stories for us . . . I guess she's a good friend of the librarian, who told her it was the oddest thing. No one had asked about your sister's disappearance in years, and then in one week, the librarian had two different people come in looking for the records."

"Someone else *is* looking? No wonder the librarian looked so surprised when I asked for those issues of the paper."

"Greg said for you to be careful."

Allie felt a chill go all the way through her. She thanked the secretary and went outside, just wanting out of the house for a few moments, then stepped into the sunshine, needing its warmth.

Someone else was looking. . . .

Allie told herself to be calm. It wasn't working. She wasn't leaving, not without all the answers. But now she was afraid of what she'd find out, worried of what might happen to her while she was here.

Stephen worked like a demon that day, hoping he might grow so tired he could forget that once he got home, Megan Bennett's little sister would be right next door. It didn't seem to be working in the least.

Late that night, after he'd showered and dressed, he poured a shot of whiskey and took it to the back porch so he could smoke a cigarette. His mother didn't want anyone smoking in the house, and he respected his mother's wishes. Including staying here at her request while she and his father were gone. Although, as soon as he heard Megan Bennett's sister was coming back to town, he'd known it had been not his mother's idea for him to be here, but his father's. His father, who wanted someone close by to keep an eye on Allie.

Standing on the porch on the warm night, not a hundred yards from her house, he told himself not to even look in her direction, not to even think about going over there tonight, no matter what he'd told his father.

Already he'd spent countless hours with his thoughts drifting back to the way she looked, all lost and vulnerable and sad, standing in that empty house. Once he'd gotten over how startling it was to look up and see Megan's face, as she might have looked had she ever grown into a woman, he couldn't deny he'd enjoyed sitting there having dinner by candlelight with Allie. He found it painfully satisfying to bring a smile to her pretty face. He'd picked up on her loneliness right away and thought to forge a bond between them over it, by telling her he understood, that he was lonely himself. And damned if it didn't sound like the truth to him once he said the words. He'd told Allie about all those women, the ones who hadn't seen him for what he was, and now it seemed, he hadn't seen himself that clearly, either.

Lonely? Who would have thought . . .

He swore yet again, took a long, moderately satisfying drag on his cigarette. He'd told her that deliberately in hopes of provoking a certain reaction in her. Just the one he'd gotten, in fact. She'd been surprised, a little uneasy that he'd seen her own loneliness so clearly, but it had drawn her ever closer to him, as well. That's what he needed. For her to trust him.

Feeling as if they had something in common should help her trust him. He'd reasoned it out in his mind, nothing but cool logic, his goal firmly in place. But Allie was flesh and blood, vulnerable and so very alone, right next door.

He couldn't apologize for what he'd done, couldn't afford the regrets he felt, and somehow he had to find a way to stay away from her now. Before he did something really stupid. Like tell her the truth.

Stephen stood there for a long time, his first clue that she was very, very close the faint creaking of the glider on the back porch of her house. He hadn't heard that sound in years. John Bennett had never sat on the glider. Stephen had seldom seen him at all in the last few years before he died. The man had worked behind a closed door in his office at the bank and hid in his house, barely showing his face in public.

Standing there in the darkness, Stephen wondered just how much Allie knew about her father. He wondered what she'd done today, who she'd talked to, what sort of answers she'd already found. Would she look at him already with suspicions? Others certainly had after they found out what he'd done fifteen years ago.

She'd be angry with him for keeping his part in it from her. It would come out, if she stayed for any length of time. Stephen frowned, thinking he'd have to chance it, chance the fact that she'd either leave fairly quickly and it wouldn't matter what she thought of him. Or that he could forge some kind of bond between them before she started hearing rumors about him and her sister. Maybe then she would believe him when he told her his version of it. As distasteful as the idea of deceiving her was, he had no choice, if he was going to keep his father happy and some eighteen hundred miles away.

Stephen took one last drag off the cigarette, then flicked it into the big, stone flower pot on the porch that served as an ashtray. He was almost inside when he heard another sound from next door. It was so faint, at first he thought he was imagining it. Then he felt a chill work its way down his spine.

Next door, someone was crying.

Allie, he told himself. *Not Megan. Not this time.*

Megan was in a place where no one could hurt her ever again. He firmly believed that. But Allie . . .

He swore softly as the sound cut right through him. It haunted him, made him remember another night and a different girl.

He told himself one more time to stay away from Allie, to keep his hands off her. One day, she'd know the truth and hate him all the more for anything that happened between them from this point on. He fought with all he had in him to stay right there, because that was the smart thing to do, and he was normally a very smart man. But in the end, nothing else mattered, except that she was over there all by herself, sad and scared, just like her sister. And just like before, he couldn't leave her all alone with her tears.

Allie was so caught up in her own misery, she didn't hear the footsteps until they were very close. Turning to the right, she caught a glimpse of someone coming toward her. Her hand came up to her mouth to stifle a scream, and the man shifted slightly to the right, so that the light from inside fell against his face for an instant.

"Stephen?"

He frowned as he looked over her tearstained face and said softly, "Who else shows up at your house this late at night?"

"Oh, God." Allie groaned. "Tell me you didn't hear me. Not all the way over there?"

"Okay," he said gently. "I didn't hear a thing."

She groaned and fought the urge to bury her head in her hands. How could she let him catch her like this?

"I'll be okay," she claimed.

"Will you, Allie?" he said gravely.

"Of course."

She waited for him to leave. He didn't. Foolishly, she kept thinking of the promise she'd made herself. That if he came back, she simply wouldn't invite him in. She'd get him to leave and close the door firmly behind him. But here she was, utterly miserable and falling apart right in front of him, with no door to close between them.

"What happened?" he asked.

"Nothing. I just found some old photographs." She'd started in the kitchen, thinking how hard could it possibly be to clean out a kitchen? Who kept truly personal items in a kitchen? And then she'd found a cabinet with stacks of old photographs. " I uhh . . . I hadn't seen a picture of Megan in years."

"Your mother didn't have any?" he asked.

"I don't know. Maybe. Maybe I just haven't found her stash yet. But she didn't keep any in places where I could see them."

Allie supposed he found that odd. She certainly had. But maybe it was just too painful for her mother to bear. It seemed her father felt the same way. It looked as if he'd gone around the house one day and gathered up all the photographs there were of her and Megan and shoved them into a cabinet, closed the door, and left them there. For years, it seemed, piled haphazardly and gathering dust. That's how she'd found them. It had felt like he might have locked away some of his own pain within those piles of photographs, that it had all come spilling out when Allie opened the cabinet door.

"It just got to me for a minute," she said. "I didn't mean to . . . disturb you." And she certainly hadn't meant for him to hear her crying.

"It's all right. I was wondering what you'd done today, and . . . I worry about you, Allie."

"Why?"

"I don't like to think of you being all alone over here in this old house."

"I've been alone for a long time, Stephen. Even when my mother was alive . . ." She broke off, hating the bitter tone of her voice and all it revealed.

"You weren't happy at all?"

"I don't know," she said miserably. "How happy is anyone, really? Are you happy?"

"I'm . . . busy," he decided. "I like my work. It interests me. I like making money, especially on projects people say will never fly. I like this town. I like Lexington. I have a few good friends, so I'm not lonely. I have a comfortable lifestyle. Is that being happy?"

"I think that's just living."

He stood there for a moment, studying her, then seemed to reach a decision. Somewhat reluctantly, he settled in beside her, stretching his arm along the back of the cushion, his body warm and inviting against hers.

She sat there fighting the wordless comfort he offered, fighting and losing. She was so tired, so sad. She hadn't had anyone close to her in so long. Her head fell to his shoulder, and his arm came to her, telling her it was okay. She could lean on him. Just for tonight, she told herself. Just for a few minutes. She would be so much stronger tomorrow.

"Is that what you've been doing all these years with your mother?" he asked. "Just living?"

She winced. Because the truth hurt. And she'd never met anyone who saw inside of her so clearly. Or maybe . . . maybe she hadn't known any man who'd bothered to look as carefully as he did. Maybe no one had cared enough to try to see all the things going on inside of her. Allie wondered if that was it. If he saw because that was the kind of man he was and because he cared.

"I wondered what happened to the two of you after you left," he said. "I wish things had been different for you."

"Forget it, Stephen. Please." She'd said too much the first night. No matter how drawn to him she was, it was too soon to be pouring out her heart to him like this.

"I don't know how to do that, Allie. I don't know how to stay away. Especially not with you over here like this. . . ."

She took a breath, a quick, too-shallow breath, and felt tears threatening once again. He was going to be kind, and she wasn't sure if she could handle that, either.

"I really don't know you," she said, reminding herself, as much as him.

"I know."

"Which means . . ." That it was ridiculous to be so drawn to him, to need him so much. And yet she did.

"What?" he said, his hand at the nape of her neck, caressing gently and stealing her breath, every bit of her resolve. "What does it mean?"

That she didn't want him to see her this way, didn't want to need him this much, but she didn't want him to let her go, either.

One of his hands fell to her shoulders, and before she knew it, he pulled her into the circle of his arms. Allie couldn't remember the last time anyone but him held her. She remembered wishing someone would after her mother died, something that had seemed to suck every bit of energy and life out of her, too. She'd felt old and used up and so bitterly alone. Vulnerable, she reminded herself. She was way too vulnerable. But this . . . Oh, this was so nice.

"Stephen?" she protested, because she felt she must.

"Shh."

His hand made soft, slow circles against her back, leaving a trail of warmth in its wake. With her head tucked against his chest, his heart beating in a strong, steady rhythm beneath her ear, Allie couldn't help relaxing against him a little. He was warm and strong and solid, all things she wished she was.

"Go ahead," he urged. "Let it all out."

"I can't," she said.

"Why not?"

"Because . . ." He was a virtual stranger, and she'd been raised to keep everyone at a careful distance, to swallow her emotions and put on a pretty face for the world, even when she thought she was dying inside.

She'd lived her life virtually alone, trusting no one, remembering that the people she came to truly care about had a bad habit of disappearing from her life. It taught her to never let anyone close, to always guard her heart, which was a smart way to live. She'd always been so smart about things like this.

"Allie?"

He pulled away an inch, maybe two, and she shivered at the look on his face. So intense. So concerned. She had the feeling that this all meant something to him. That her being here and still being torn up over Megan's disappearance was important to him, too, though she couldn't understand why. Megan had been next to nothing to him.

"What is it?" she whispered. "Why is this so important to you? Why am I?"

"I knew a girl once, who was so sad and absolutely lost. Sometimes I heard her crying at night. I tried to help, but she told me she was okay. I'm not sure I believed her, but I didn't know her that well and I wasn't sure what to do. So I backed off. And that was a huge mistake. Because not long after that, she ran away and died. I feel guilty about that to this day—"

"So do I," she admitted. She felt so guilty.

"I don't ever want to feel that way again—like someone needed me, and I didn't do enough. So I don't think it matters that before last night, I hadn't seen you in fifteen years. I don't think it matters that you and I don't know each other that well. I can't sit over there knowing you're over here and upset and crying, and do nothing about it. I can't."

He pushed her face against his chest, and Allie felt

tears fill her eyes once again, felt the trembling she couldn't control start deep inside. He held on tight, as her shoulders shook and her tears fell unheeded and she struggled to breathe.

"Why don't you let me try to make up for that mistake? Why don't you let me help you now?"

She supposed she'd have to, because she didn't think she could have let him go if her very life depended on it, despite the fact that she simply didn't do this. She didn't cry all over virtual strangers or even what passed for close friends. She didn't let anyone see how the past still ripped her apart inside and sometimes came spewing out of her in a slew of desperate sobs and angry tears.

She'd been desperately lonely for so long, and all of that seemed to catch up with her tonight. Surprisingly, she found that it helped a great deal to not be so alone. If the price she had to pay for this kind of comfort was letting someone inside her life, maybe it would be worth it. With him here, she was no longer afraid. The darkness was like a cloak, curled around them, pushing out the rest of the world. Even the house lost its menacing presence, and for the moment, she thought she'd done the right thing in coming here.

He held on to her long after her tears stopped falling, even when she was thoroughly spent from crying and utterly drained. She lay there curled up against him, feeling every breath he took, feeling so in tune with him.

Something happened then. The comfort he'd so generously offered became something else entirely. His hand tangled in the hair at the back of her neck, and he bent his head down to hers. His soft lips settled against the side of her cheek, where he found what was left of a single tear and kissed it away.

One minute, the kiss was gentle and soothing, and the next it deepened into something more. Something hot and deep and slow that set her pulses to pounding. Something dangerous and enticing and real. It felt so real, despite the fact that it was over almost before it began.

"I'm sorry," he said, tucking her head against his chest. "Megan—"

His voice was raw. Low and strained and barely above a whisper, but the name was unmistakably clear. *Megan?*

Allie scrambled to her feet, all the pleasure she'd found in that kiss simply disappearing, overpowered by the feeling that she'd made a mistake. A terrible mistake.

"What did you say?"

"I know who you are, Allie. I was going to say that once, before your sister left, she asked me to watch out for you, and I doubt this was what she had in mind."

"I doubt it was." She wasn't sure she believed him, either. Not about what he was saying now. Maybe not what he'd told her last night. That he and her sister were never more than friends.

"Allie, I never kissed your sister like that."

"Why not?"

"Because I never wanted to."

He got to his feet and came to the edge of the porch where she stood. With him towering over her this way, Allie felt anew the differences between the two of them. He was so much bigger, so much stronger, so much more powerful than she was. But she wasn't afraid of him. Not exactly. She was afraid of the connection between them, the strength of her reaction to him. That so easily, he could hurt her.

He pulled her close and placed one quick, breath-robbing kiss on her lips again.

"God, Allie." He sounded as frustrated and confused as she felt. "This is the last thing either one of us needs right now."

She just stood there staring at him. No one had ever kissed her quite like that. Like he wanted to devour her whole in the next instant. Like he was fighting the impulse even now. Still . . . he'd called her Megan.

She cleared her throat, tried to find a no-nonsense tone. "I need to know about you and Megan."

"She lived next door. I'd known her my whole life, Allie. We were friends."

"You know something," she insisted. "Something about the reason she ran away."

Allie watched carefully. It happened so fast, she almost missed it. But for a second, the warm, charming man was gone. In his place was Stephen Whittaker, real estate tycoon, all steely determination and rock-hard resolve. She wondered how many other sides of him there were, sides that she hadn't yet seen. She wondered which, if any, of them were real.

"I wish I knew," he said, and just like that, Mr. Kind and Considerate was back.

"No," she insisted. "You *know* something."

"I don't think anyone but Megan knew for sure why she ran away, and as far as I know, she didn't tell anybody."

"You must have heard things. . . ." She tried. "Anything . . ."

"I heard every rumor in the world about Megan. I couldn't remember half of them, if I tried, and what would be the point anyway? It was nothing but gossip."

"I have to find out," Allie insisted. "I have to know. This was my family, the only one I ever had. It literally fell apart, and I don't even know why. I can't live with all the questions any longer, Stephen."

"Can you live with the answers?" he asked. "You don't know what you're going to find, and I'm sorry, Allie, but it's not going to change a thing. Nothing's going to bring your family back."

"I'll know," she said. "Finally, I'll know."

"And if the truth hurts?"

"I've been hurting for years and too much of a coward to insist on knowing what happened."

"Maybe you were just protecting yourself. Maybe you were being smart and trying not to be hurt anymore."

"No. That's not it," she said. "Are you really going to try to talk me out of this?"

"No, I'm going to try to help you."

"I changed your mind? Just like that?"

He swore softly and shook his head, but he started talking to her again, too.

"Megan never told me she was going to run away," he said, a touch of steel in his voice. "She never told me why. I don't know what else I can say to you, Allie, except that if you want, I'll ask some questions, see what I can find out."

"I can do it." She was right here, after all. This was the reason she came.

"I know people," he pointed out. "They'll talk to me."

"I'll get them to talk to me."

"All right." He gave in. "Whatever you want."

They stood, too close for comfort, their words a bit

too terse, the force of emotion behind them seeming to echo in the sudden silence. She found that it was difficult to be this close to him now. She wanted so much, and yet she was scared. She'd always been so scared. And confused. He confused her terribly.

But there was something in his eyes, his beautiful, dark eyes, that drew her to him, despite everything else. Something that had her swaying on her feet, her body moving almost imperceptibly closer to his and then drawing back again.

So this was it, she thought. For the first time in her life, she began to understand the true power of attraction between a man and a woman. She'd never been so torn, never wanted a man so badly even though she suspected, in the end, he would hurt her.

Stephen reached for her, his hand lingering on her cheek, so softly, so gently, making her think again of his kiss. The first, soft, sweet one, the long, slow, hungry one, the last, hard, fast one.

"You are so like her," he whispered.

There, she thought, pain arching through her. She knew it. He was thinking of Megan. "How?" she said. "How am I like her?"

"You're scared. You're hurting. You're all alone, and it's hard to see you here, feeling the way she felt, and not think of her. And not wish that . . ."

"What? What do you wish?"

"That everything had turned out differently for her. Allie, if I asked you to go back to Connecticut? To drop this . . ."

"I can't."

"All right." Obviously unhappy with that, he let his hands fall to his side and stepped away. "I'm not sure where that kiss came from. I should apologize for that, too. I don't make a habit of taking advantage of women that way."

"I'm not Megan," she said, because she hadn't felt taken advantage of in the least, just hurt thinking he was kissing her and remembering her sister. She'd tried for years to take her sister's place with her mother and failed miserably. She certainly wasn't going to do that for a man.

"I know who you are." He took her chin in hand, tilted her face up to his, watching her intently with dark, glittering eyes. "I know it doesn't make a lot of sense for me to find it nearly impossible to stand here beside you and not touch you. When we haven't seen each other for fifteen years and you've been back all of a day. What can I say, Allie? I want to touch you. To kiss you."

"Oh." She sighed, wishing she could just accept that, wishing she could forget that he'd called her Megan, that he might be looking at her and seeing her sister. Most of all, she wished she hadn't felt so much when he touched her.

"Try not to dislike me so much, Allie." His mouth was so close to hers that she felt his breath brush past her cheeks, her lips, before he gave in and kissed her once again, softly, so softly. "Try to trust me. Just a little."

More confused than ever, she promised nothing.

"Are you sure you're all right here?" he asked. "Don't be afraid of me. If anything happens . . . If you need me, for anything, I'll help you, Allie."

And then he was gone.

She lay on the sofa that night trying not to think about the kisses and remember instead that once more, he really hadn't told her anything about Megan. He'd given her a hint that their feelings might have been stronger than friendship, and Allie thought at one point Megan ended up crying in his arms. But that was it. He seemed to have a gift for seeming so open, like he was telling her his deepest, darkest secrets, which made her want to trust him even more, when he really hadn't told her anything at all.

She would think of Megan, she decided. If she was ever tempted to fall into Stephen Whittaker's arms again, she'd remember how much it hurt to believe he was holding her, kissing her, while thinking of her sister.

It wasn't until later, alone in the darkness, that she remembered what he'd said there at the end. *If anything happens . . .*

Why would he say that?

What did he think was going to happen to her here?

Chapter 4

Stephen was up before dawn, standing on the back porch of his parents' home, sipping his first cup of coffee and staring at the Bennett house. He didn't think he'd ever fumbled a situation quite as badly as the one last night with Allie.

He wasn't supposed to like her. She wasn't supposed to be so damned vulnerable, so absolutely alone, and he hadn't expected to feel so rotten about lying to her. But he did. He never planned to kiss her or to have his hands all over her, either, and he'd certainly done those things, as well.

She just kept surprising him, and he didn't like it. A simple conversation with her was like ripping a vein open, pouring out his heart, something he just didn't do with any woman.

That first night, all he'd intended was to keep her from feeling so alone, but she'd been so surprised by the idea that anyone else might feel the same way. What could he do? He'd told her he did and in the time since then figured out it was likely true. He'd just have to deal with it, after he dealt with her.

A nagging little voice inside told him she'd feel even more alone, more isolated, once she knew the truth about him. And she'd have nowhere to turn.

Everyone she had in the world was gone. He felt like even more of a louse than before.

The phone rang. Stephen picked it up knowing who it was—his father calling from a boat somewhere in the Mediterranean. They wasted no time on preliminaries.

"She's there?" his father demanded.

"Yes."

"You saw her."

"Of course. I told you I would."

"Did you find out what she wants?"

"I'm not sure she knows herself at this point."

His father laughed. "That should make it easier for you to help her come to the right decision."

"And what would that be?" Stephen asked. "The right decision?"

"She doesn't have any business being here."

"She owns a home here now."

"Not for long. Not if we have anything to say about it. And I hope she doesn't intend to do anything but dispose of the house. The mess with her sister is ancient history."

Stephen said nothing. He was finding that the past wasn't so very far away anymore, especially not once he saw Allie.

"You said you'd take care of this for me, Stephen," his father said.

"I will."

He'd offered, actually. He'd deliberately insinuated himself into the midst of this situation, thinking he could handle things just fine. He always handled things.

"The best thing for that little girl would be to go back to where she came from," his father said.

Stephen had told Allie that; his conscience was clear

on that point. Nothing would bring Megan Bennett back to life. Once Allie figured that out, he intended to make it easy for her to go.

"Did you make her an offer?" his father asked.

"Not yet. I thought I'd let her come to the decision to sell the house first, then make the offer."

"Stephen—"

"I bought and sold more than forty million dollars worth of real estate last year, Dad. I know what I'm doing."

"Still, why not help her along?" his father insisted. "Get her out of town a little faster. Whatever it takes."

Stephen bit back a curse. *Whatever it takes?* He suspected that would be his father's motto going into this situation. Stephen was ready to do whatever it took, as well, to keep his father from handling this in his own typically heavy-handed way.

"She's not going to stay in that house, Dad. She couldn't, even if she wanted to. Inheritance taxes will wipe out most all the cash her father left her. Even though the house is mortgage-free, the maintenance, the utilities, and the property taxes would be too much for her."

"You know that for certain?"

"Of course, I do. When I set out to buy a piece of property, I make it a priority to know who I'm dealing with and what assets that person has at his or her disposal," he said. "This woman hasn't had a paying job since before her mother died. She has a little in savings and a stack of medical bills of her mother's. Nothing that's going to allow her to stay in that house for long."

"Still, she's a woman. Women are sentimental, illogical—"

"She happens to be an accountant," he countered. "She knows she can't keep that house."

"Stephen—"

"I told you I'd take care of it, and I will."

"All right. In the meantime, stick close. I want to know what she's doing, who she's talking to, what she knows. All of that," his father said. "Turn on the charm, boy. It shouldn't be hard for you."

Stephen swore softly and got off the phone. When he and his father started thinking alike, he was in serious trouble. But the truth of his words couldn't be ignored. It would likely be very easy to find out what he needed to know when the woman in question was right next door. When she was all alone and very, very sad, and in need of someone in whom to confide.

She seemed surprised and pleased by the smallest of compliments that first night over dinner, seemed genuinely flattered and a bit shy. Before last night, he would have said it would be easy to talk to her, to flirt with her in the mildest of ways. To get her to open up to him as she decided what to do with the house, which fell perfectly into his father's request.

But it felt too personal now. He'd held her in his arms while she cried her eyes out. He began to realize the price she would pay simply for being here, for asking all those really hard questions about why her family fell apart. And he didn't like being the person standing between her and the answers she sought, even if he still believed she was likely better off not knowing.

He didn't like being attracted to her and knowing he shouldn't do anything about it. He hadn't quite figured out how he was going to stick close to her and not touch her again.

Stephen swore softly in the dark solitude of the morning. He should go back over there today because the quicker he wrapped this up, the better it would be for everyone, including her. He'd back up, he told himself. Start over. Surely he could charm her, without ever getting that close to her. Surely he could be with her and scarcely lay a hand on her.

He just had to get her to trust him and to leave. Before anything happened to her here.

Allie woke abruptly, pulled from sleep, by what she didn't know.

She lay absolutely still and listened. In her bleary, half-awake state she could swear she heard the sound of footsteps. Carefully, she worked to separate the sounds of her own pounding heart and labored breathing from the rest of the sounds around her.

There was something . . . Above her. On the second floor? The third?

It could be nothing but a mouse. Anything could have gotten in, she told herself. *Anyone.* It would be just her luck that the house sat here empty and undisturbed for two and a half years, and someone would pick the week she came back to break in.

She threw back the makeshift covers and padded into the hallway, turning on lights as she went. Upstairs, nothing moved, except a bit of dust floating on a ray of sunshine.

Dust didn't move by itself, did it?

She tried to fight off the sense of dread she felt at the thought of walking up those stairs and into any of the bedrooms.

She put her foot on the first step, had a death-grip on the banister. Her heart was thundering, drowning out everything else, and she felt feverish one minute, cold and clammy the next.

She couldn't go up there, she realized. She just couldn't.

Allie sat down instead on the bottom step, and then scooted down onto the floor. She was such a coward she just sat there until she realized that the noises overhead had ceased. She didn't have to go up there. Not yet.

She walked back into the family room, where she'd slept. Last night she'd been unnerved by the big, tall windows facing the backyard, bordered by a solid line of trees and vegetation. The house backed up to the creek that flowed into the river just past Stephen's house, and on the other side of the creek was an equally tall, thick stand of trees. No one lived back there. No one could see in the windows. But as she lay there trying to go to sleep, she felt as if she were being watched. As if someone was waiting to see what she would do. If she would run away in the middle of the night or if she would stick it out and finally find the answers she sought.

She'd double-checked all the locks on all of the doors and windows. One window in the family room had been unlatched. Of course, it could have been that way for years, but it left her feeling even more uneasy.

The moon had been out, shining through the trees in the backyard, casting all sorts of intriguing shadows through the room. There was a bit of wind, and every now and then she heard something thump up against the house, probably just a tree that needed pruning. Nothing more. She'd told herself quite firmly that she'd be fine in the morning, in the bright light of day, and what had she gotten? Footsteps.

Allie raked a hand through her hair and resolved to do better from here on out. To be calmer, more logical, and not so on-edge. She had to make a plan and stick to it. Even if it was merely to search the house room by room, starting with the first floor, packing and sorting as she went. It all had to be done. If there was something here—some clue as to what happened to them all, she would find it eventually. She wasn't leaving until she did. Maybe when the first floor was done, she'd find the courage to walk up those stairs and start on the second.

She felt calmer, more determined. Heading through the back hall toward the kitchen, she discovered the little piano tucked into the alcove under the grand staircase. She and Megan had spent hours here. Flipping back the lid, ignoring the cloud of dust rising from the keys, she softly played a scale, finding the instrument badly out of tune, the off-key notes echoing through the house.

Closing her eyes, she thought she could see her sister here, sitting on the piano bench. Her long brownish-blonde hair hanging down her back, her thin arms stretched out toward the keys, fingers spread wide to reach the notes of the last chords. She was smaller than Allie remembered, thinner, more delicate, looking as if a stiff breeze could pick her up and carry her away.

Allie sensed something in the memory that suddenly turned so vivid, something waiting for her. She looked at Megan's hands moving across the keyboard. Her hands were so small, her arms so pale. She'd lost weight, Allie remembered, realizing this must have happened that summer, right before Megan left. Allie had noticed her sister losing weight.

"Megan?" she whispered. "What's wrong?"

Megan hit a jarringly wrong note. She winced, and her hands fell to her lap. She turned briefly toward Allie, seeming to look right through her, and there were tears on her face. Megan was rubbing her hands together and shivering when Allie noticed the bruises on her sister's arm, as if someone had grabbed on to her and refused to let go.

"What happened?" Allie whispered. "Megan, please. Just tell me, what happened?"

But her sister didn't say a word. She brushed away tears, put her hands back on the keys, and started to play again.

Startled, Allie opened her eyes to find her own fingers on the keys, playing that same song she thought Megan had played that day. She felt a chill in the air, one that seemed to go right through her, and fought the urge to run screaming from the house. Instead, she closed her eyes, wanting one more look at her sister, and waited until the sound of the music faded completely away.

Five minutes later, Allie was still sitting with her back to the wall, still able to close her eyes and see the bruises on her sister's thin arm, when the phone rang, startling her yet again. She grabbed it like a lifeline and said, "Hello?"

"Hi," Stephen said. "I'm sorry, I know it's early, but I saw your lights on and thought I'd take a chance on calling. Tell me you were up."

"I was up," she said, wondering what he'd say if she told him, *I saw my dead sister playing the piano and begged her to tell me what was going on, but she wouldn't.*

"Are you all right?" he said.

"Yes," she lied, thinking *bruises.* Who had done that to Megan? Who had hurt her and made her cry?

"I was wondering if you'd like to get out of that house for a while."

She was trembling hard enough and was paranoid enough to think he knew everything, that he somehow just knew, but she managed to keep it to herself and simply ask, "Why?"

"I want to see you."

He'd said that the first night, and she'd wanted to believe it. It was harder now. Every bit as enticing, but harder to believe. She kept thinking about Megan. How awful it felt not to be Megan for the mother who had loved her. For the mother who could never love Allie as much as she had loved her sister. Allie didn't ever want to try to take her sister's place again, not in any way, no matter how little or how much Stephen might have felt for her sister.

"It's going to be beautiful today," he said. "Much too pretty to stay inside all day."

Allie frowned, thinking it wasn't fair that he could cast a spell over her, just with his voice. The familiarity of the cadence of his speech hit her again. It wasn't what she was used to from Connecticut, and yet she recognized it, much in the same way she felt a recognition of the place itself, of the trees, the grass, the sky, everything. The man could draw her to him with his voice alone.

"We were doing so well that first night over dinner," he coaxed.

Before she thought he was involved with her sister and that he was keeping something from her about Megan's disappearance.

Allie sighed. The saddest part was that despite all her doubts, all the reasons she had to be cautious around him, those moments in his arms had felt better than anything she'd experienced in months. More

likely years. How many men could chase away loneliness and bone-deep sadness with a kiss?

Even so, she couldn't let it happen again.

"Let's back up, all right?" he said. "Be friends. I was
wondering what you remember about Kentucky."

"Not much." And she didn't need to. She was
likely leaving never to return again. She was supposed to resist any excuses he came up with for them
to be together.

"I thought I could show you some of the sights."

"I don't have time for sight-seeing, Stephen. I have
so much to do . . ."

"And you will. Later. Just give me an hour."

"I've barely started sorting through everything and
packing. I only got half the kitchen done yesterday."
And found pictures of Megan. And fallen apart in
Stephen's arms.

"You can't mean to work every minute you're
here," he argued.

"Actually, I did." That was why she'd come. To
work. To find out what she needed to know and
leave. She could scarcely remember the time when
she thought it would be as simple as that.

"This is your home, Allie. There's no place in the
world as beautiful as Kentucky on a cool, misty
morning in the fall. I want to show it to you."

What did the beauty of anyplace have to do with
anything?

Megan, she thought, closing her eyes and hearing
her sister's name spoken with that deep Southern
voice of his. Seeing the haunted expression on her
sister's face as she sat playing the piano with bruises
on her arms.

God, the bruises.

"Allie?"

She closed her eyes and counted to ten, knowing she should stay away from him, particularly when he was acting this way. Like this was about her and him and nothing else.

It was more than that. Something else had him here, acting this way.

"Come with me," he said.

"It's six o'clock in the morning, Stephen."

"It's the best time of the day."

"I'm not even dressed," she protested, although she couldn't help but be curious. What could he possibly show her at this hour?

She sighed, already finding excuses for herself and what she wanted. Like, how was she going to find out what he was up to, what he knew? Spending time with him seemed to be the simplest way.

"Put on some jeans and a sweatshirt. I'll be there in fifteen minutes," he said. "I'll even bring coffee. Very good coffee."

Before she could say another word, he hung up.

Torn, Allie glanced at the now-silent piano and shivered yet again. The thought of getting out of the house, for any reason at all, seemed too good to pass up.

She wondered if years ago she'd *seen* Megan with bruises on her arms, if the image had been inside her head all this time waiting to come out? The sister she remembered had been a solemn soul, quiet, serious, secretive even. But not sad. Not crying. Not bruised. This was like trying to put together a puzzle without having all the pieces, without knowing what the picture was supposed to look like in the end. But pieces of her life were coming back to her, the memories too vivid to be anything but the truth, pieces of her old life.

And next door was a man who knew more than he was telling her about her sister's disappearance. Maybe he knew about the bruises, too. Surely that alone was enough of a reason to spend an hour with him this morning.

She didn't have to take anything he said seriously. Perhaps she'd been right that first night when she thought he wielded his charm like a weapon, disarming women completely with it, blinding them to anything except him and the way he could make a woman feel. Had she made it easy for him? Did he think she would just give in and give him whatever he wanted?

Allie frowned. He probably charmed every woman he met. It was probably second nature to him. But she wasn't going to let him do that to her. Surely she had a bit of common sense left and could use it with him.

Exactly fifteen minutes later, he parked in front of her house in a luxurious four-wheel-drive vehicle with leather seats and every convenience imaginable. It still smelled new, had a logo on the side, WHITTA-KER CONSTRUCTION.

"You take this to construction sites?" she said.

"I'm not that spoiled. Or that pretentious." He grinned at her as he helped her inside, then handed her a steaming cup of coffee. "I take very important people, like bankers, investors, and potential clients to construction sites in this. And when it's just me, I take a real truck."

She settled into the cushy, heated-leather seat and drank what had to be the best cup of coffee she'd ever had, as they drove through town and headed toward Lexington. She had to admit he didn't seem like a man who thought he was better than everyone else simply because he had money.

They skirted around the south side of town, past subdivisions and shopping centers and early-morning commuters. Allie recognized the route, the same one she'd taken from the airport. They went past it, then turned into a farm with what had to be miles of neat wooden fences painted white, fancy barns in white with dark blue trim. The entrance gate was made of fieldstone with scrolling iron arching overhead. They drove down a narrow, private road lined with towering trees.

"It's like something out of *Gone With the Wind*," she said as they drove through the canopy made by the branches.

"Not quite." He stopped in front of a huge house made of whitewashed stone, with towering columns lining the front porch. "It's only a hundred and ten years old."

"It's takes my breath away," she said because it was so beautiful, so obviously lovingly preserved. "Did you restore it?"

"No." He grinned. "This is my great-grandfather's farm."

"Oh." She felt foolish and a bit in awe. Spoiled or not, this was the way he'd grown up, surrounded by all this. And yet, despite all her misgivings, she felt comfortable with him. The charm, she told herself. He had it down to an art form—putting a woman at ease, maybe saying just what she wanted to hear. Why, she wondered, would he work so hard to put her at ease?

"The house isn't what I brought you here to see, Allie."

He drove around the side of the house and down

another narrow lane, and that's when Allie first saw the horses, sprinting along in the misty morning with their tails tilted up in the air. Two of them stopped to stare, but the babies kept right on playing. The sky was warming to the coming day, faintly lit with the palest of blues, the trees in the distance not much more than shadows. The pretty white fences did indeed go on for miles, pasture after pasture in the softly rolling hills, and up close she could see that the grass was an unusual, particularly deep shade of green.

"Is this the famed bluegrass?" she said.

"Some of the bluest." He stopped the vehicle and came around to her side to give her a hand out. "I'm going to sound like I'm bragging, but this is your home state and I promised to play tour guide. I think I'd be neglecting my duties if I failed to mention that you're standing in the middle of one of the most famous horse farms in the world."

"Oh," she said, noting the logo on the barn, an elaborately scripted W superimposed over an F, a logo quite similar to that he used in his construction firm. "Whittaker Farms?"

He nodded and steered her around the side of the big barn. There were a lot of horses, sleek, beautiful animals prancing in and out. The men leading the horses back and forth tipped their heads respectfully toward Stephen, and there was a track, a training facility she supposed, on the other side of the barn. He led her to the outside rail, and they leaned against it. On the dirt track, a tractor was pulling a device that carefully groomed the surface, and there were three horses that she could see working out. They walked behind lead ponies, galloped, sprinted, walked some more.

She couldn't believe they were this close to the city, because the farm obviously encompassed hundreds of acres, all so carefully tended, so pretty. The mist rising off the grass gave the whole scene a surreal air, and the sky to the east blushed in the softest of pinks. It was like being in another world, something wholly apart from anything else she'd ever known.

The horses snorted and pranced back and forth, as if daring her not to look at them, to admire them. They were tall and slender, their legs seeming much too dainty to ever support their weight, let alone send them streaking down the track.

She and Stephen watched for a long time without saying anything. He had brought a thermos, so there was more of the wonderful coffee. She could have sworn it tasted all the better on this breathtakingly beautiful misty morning, that her whole life seemed better in this moment. She'd been so tense for so long. Since she realized her mother was dying, since she found out all her mother had kept from her, since she decided to come back and found it so hard. She didn't remember the last time she felt this relaxed and wondered if this place did the same thing for him, if he'd somehow known she'd feel better just by being here.

She could have asked. How had he known? Why did he seem to find it so easy to look inside of her and know these things? But she didn't. She wanted the moment, wanted every bit of peace offered by this wonderfully soothing place.

"Did you somehow make the sky bluer here?" she said finally.

"We've been known to do that here. But it's a little secret. Only the people who are born here can see it."

"And the grass really is greener, I suppose? Or bluer?"

"Of course," he said.

It truly was an odd shade of green, odd in a nice way. Every now and then she'd catch sight of it in a certain way and think it was one of the most intense shades of green she'd ever seen, and there was something about the way the green grass blended into the startlingly blue sky that she found utterly pleasing.

"Look," he said, pointing to a spot over her left shoulder.

A horse came flying by, a shiny black colt with pretty white caps on his feet and a brush of white on his long nose. He seemed especially proud of himself. The jockey turned around in the middle of the track and looked to Stephen, who must have given him some kind of sign, because the man gave a salute and turned the horse and took off.

Stephen pulled out a stopwatch and set it to zero. The horse galloped easily around the far turn, and on the backside picked up speed gradually until he was flying even faster than before. Allie found herself fascinated by the way the horse moved, stretching out its long legs and dipping its head down low. It was a symphony of motion, of sleek muscles and strength and style.

She heard the click of the stopwatch. Stephen looked down at it and then looked at her and grinned.

"He's breathtaking," she said.

"He's fast and absolutely full of himself." Stephen took her by the arm and led her to a gap in the rail. "Come on, I'll introduce you to the arrogant little beast."

The rider slid off the tiny excuse for a saddle and walked over to them, leading the horse behind him.

Up close, Allie realized just how big the animal was and how small the rider. She wondered exactly what it took to control an animal this strong and this big.

"Lookin' good, Mr. Whittaker," said the man who might have been five feet tall and weighed a hundred pounds.

"He does, but is he behaving any better?" Stephen took the reins, and the horse, who had steam rising off his back, dipped his head to let Stephen rub that splash of white on his face.

"He's got his moments," the rider said.

Stephen introduced Allie to the rider. They talked about the horse for a minute, and then Stephen sent the man on his way, saying they'd deliver the horse back to the barn themselves. The horse danced around, as if he wanted to play and hadn't been allowed to expend enough energy yet.

Allie rubbed his nose and tried not to be overwhelmed by him. He snorted and shook his head. Stephen scolded him, stroking him the whole time, and the horse finally settled down.

"He misbehaves often?" she asked.

"More than we'd like. But he's still a juvenile."

"As in delinquent?"

"No," He laughed. "As in two-year-old. A two-year-old horse is called a juvenile. We're hoping he settles down when he grows up a bit."

"Oh. Is he going to run in the Derby?"

"It's too soon to tell."

"But it's only seven months away."

"Which is an eternity with a young horse. He's only run two races in his life, and anything could happen between now and Derby day."

Stephen tugged on the reins, and they headed back toward the barn.

Allie couldn't help but appreciate the moment. It was still quiet, save for the occasional pounding of hooves. The sun was almost up, the mist nearly gone, the day seeming absolutely perfect.

"It's like a painting," she said.

"Better," he insisted.

"So . . . the Whittakers raise horses?" she mused. She hadn't a clue until she saw this.

"Some of us."

"And the rest of you?"

"My great-grandfather used to say there are four main branches of the Whittaker family, four acceptable career paths: raising horses, raising tobacco, making bourbon, and going into politics."

"*The* industries of Kentucky?"

He nodded.

"And that would make you . . . the black sheep of the family?"

He nodded.

Allie forgot she wasn't supposed to be enjoying herself and laughed. "You must be such a disappointment to the family."

"Actually, I am."

He smiled as he said it, but there was an unmistakable undertone. He was serious, Allie realized. Maybe she'd thought from the image he projected that he was indeed perfect, strong and supremely confident and in absolute control of his life. She'd liked all of those things about him, envied him even. She'd like to possess all those qualities herself. She knew all about disappointing people, knew exactly how it felt. But him? How could he ever be a disappointment to anyone?

"I find that hard to believe," she said, finding him utterly fascinating and unable to keep from asking.

"It's true. To my father, I am."

"Why?"

"God, I could make you a list, but I doubt you have the time to hear all of it."

"You're kidding."

"No, I'm not."

"What have you done that's so disappointing?"

"I told you I have a law degree, but I'm not using it to practice law."

"But that's not on the list of acceptable professions."

"No, but the practice of law could lead to a judgeship, which he would understand and respect. Or a career in politics, which is on the list. Building things is much too common, as far as he's concerned."

She thought of what she knew about him already. No doubt, he was accustomed to being surrounded by beauty and elegance. He was appreciative of it, as he'd shown her by bringing her to this place.

"I can't believe you build common things," she said.

"Thank you." He looked genuinely pleased. "I don't. I build beautiful things, and I restore even more beautiful things, and I like it."

"So, your father thinks you're hopeless?"

"Most of the time." He grinned back at her. "Although I'm trying to redeem myself with Wish."

"What?"

"The horse. His name is Three Wishes, but I call him Wish. And I guess I'm not really trying to redeem myself. I don't have him to please my father. I happen to think he's beautiful, and he's provided me with much more pleasure than a stock certificate or most any piece of property I own."

"You own this horse?" she asked.

"Yes."

Allie felt so foolish. He *owned* the horse. A Thoroughbred. She didn't know anything about horses, except that they were surely very expensive. And he owned this one. Because Wish was beautiful and brought him pleasure. Allie might have bought a CD by one of her favorite musicians for the sheer pleasure of listening to it. Stephen, rather than a certificate of deposit or shares of stock had chosen to buy this horse, and obviously, she and this man were worlds apart.

Stephen frowned. "I really didn't bring you here to try to impress you with what I come from, with what my family has."

She forgot all about her own resolve to see him merely to find out what he knew about her sister, and asked, "Why did you bring me here?"

"For about a dozen different reasons," he said.

Damn. "That many?"

He nodded. "I'm afraid nothing between us is going to be simple, Allie."

No, she could see that it wouldn't be. Not if he'd turned her head so quickly yet again. And she simply couldn't leave it alone. She wanted to know what was happening between them.

"Name one reason," she said. "Just one."

"Because I don't want everything you see here to make you sad."

She tried to ignore that little tugging in the region of her heart, the one that said she was touched by the fact that he cared about her state of mind.

Helpless, she asked, "Another one?"

"Because I wanted to be with you, outside of that house where your family fell apart, where maybe you could forget for a little while about all the bad things that happened here."

"You did that," she told him, against her better judgment.

He grinned down at her, a sleek, powerful, beautiful man leading an equally beautiful and no doubt amazingly expensive animal, a man who most certainly lived in a completely different world.

Allie closed her eyes, ignoring the gap between them and all the doubts she had about him. Mesmerized, she said, "That's two reasons."

"Because this is one of the most beautiful places I know, and I wanted to share it with you."

Her heart gave another little lurch. She didn't think any man had ever found beauty in the world that he simply had to show her.

"I could help you, Allie," he said. "If you could trust me. Just a little."

"I'm not very good at that," she confessed, feeling totally inadequate at the moment. A part of her thought she should be able to simply open her mouth and let the words come tumbling out, telling him all her doubts, all her fears, all her inadequacies. Maybe other women could ignore what she thought was perfectly good sense and reason and a caution she was entitled to with him or with any man she'd known for so little time, and just trust. She'd never given her trust easily. Life had taught her not to. So had he.

"Tell me, Allie. Tell me why."

"It's just the way I am, the way I've always been. In my house, we didn't talk about the bad things. We closed our eyes and hoped they'd go away. We became quite adept at taking bad things and shoving them into little boxes in our heads and pounding the lids on tightly. Can you even begin to understand that?"

"Better than you know," he said.

"Really? I can't imagine anything truly bad ever happening to you."

"You'd be wrong," he insisted.

"My sister died, and I never saw my father again," she said softly, sadly. "That kind of bad?"

He frowned. "How is it that every conversation we have ends with you digging something out of me that I never tell anyone?"

No, that was what he did to her. "What have you told me that you never tell anyone? About being lonely?"

Grim-faced, he said, "Yes."

"I didn't believe you at the time."

He swore softly and shook his head.

"I'm sorry. I just didn't. I can't imagine any man like you ever being lonely."

"Did you think you'd cornered the market on that? Did you think you were the only one?"

She could scarcely breathe all of a sudden, and she thought that whatever she did to him, he did the same thing in return. She'd told him things she'd never told anyone. About the boxes full of hurt stashed in the corners of her mind.

"Sometimes I do," she said. "Sometimes I think I'm the loneliest person in the world."

"God," he said, taking her by the arms and turning her to face him. "Don't."

She dipped her head. It settled against his chest, and she decided this was why she didn't have conversations like this. Because it hurt to put her emotions out here for someone else to see. This was why people held things deep inside.

"More than you wanted to know?" she asked,

afraid she'd gone too far, that these were indeed feelings too raw to share with anyone.

"No. That's not it at all. I don't want you to feel like that, Allie. God, I hate the thought of that."

"And your family?" she asked, wanting to believe he wasn't simply saying what he thought she wanted to hear. "What happened to you that was so bad?"

"My brother despises me—a feeling that's mutual—and my father was here, physically at least, but I've been a disappointment to him his entire life. He barely tolerates me. He's a lousy father and husband who thinks he's somehow entitled to do exactly as he pleases because his last name is Whittaker. He thinks we're as good as royalty in Kentucky, and he treats most people that way," he said. "Believe me, I may have grown up in privileged surroundings, but my life hasn't been without its little problems."

"I'm sorry," she said. "I didn't mean to drag it out of you that way."

He waved off her apology, as if it had been nothing, what she'd pushed him into admitting.

They walked back to the barn in silence. He turned the horse over to a waiting groom, and after talking with the man for a few moments, led Allie back to his vehicle. He opened her door. She stepped forward to get in, but he stopped her and turned her around, pinning her between him and the door.

"Look beneath the surface, Allie," he said. "Look past the material things. You and I are not that different."

He lowered his mouth to hers. Lips smooth and warm and knowing settled over hers. She grabbed onto his shirt and held him there against her, not thinking of anything but the heat of his body and the way he smelled, so fresh and clean, the way he tasted, the way her knees threatened to buckle.

She knew he couldn't possibly want her. No man had ever truly wanted her. But there it was, that intriguing tug of awareness, that huge pool of need rising up inside of her. He was so big, so solid, and she felt absolutely safe with him and at the same time like they'd stepped off a skyscraper and found nothing but air beneath their feet. It was such a rush. So very unexpected and so powerful, it scared her. And thrilled her.

She could barely breathe by the time he lifted his head, and she noted with satisfaction that his shoulders rose and fell with every breath he took. He was not unaffected. This kiss, this wild need rushing between them, this at least was real.

Still, as confusing and exhilarating as it was, she had to remember why she was here. She had to remember he said her sister's name with what sounded like a world of pain.

"I came here to do something with the house and find out why my family fell apart," she protested. "I didn't come here looking for anything like this."

"Neither did I. Are we supposed to ignore it, just because it surprised us? Or because we didn't go looking for it?"

"I don't know."

"Give me a chance," he said in a way that made her want to give him anything, absolutely anything at all.

"I feel like it's going to be all I can do just to stay sane long enough to do what I came here for."

"Then I'll help you. Let me help."

She sighed, thinking it was much too difficult to refuse him and not liking the realization at all.

"Allie, I know these people. I know this town. I can make this easier for you."

Common sense waged a small war inside her, going up against age-old habits of trusting no one, depending on no one. When he told her things like he had this morning, she felt like they were two kindred spirits, two lost souls. Playing it safe, pushing him away seemed like an awful price to pay for her own innate cautiousness.

A woman had to take a risk at some point, Allie reasoned. Was she going to be alone her entire life? Scared and stubborn and sure that she knew what was best for herself?

And honestly, they weren't talking about anything except spending a bit of time together, him helping her sort through the mess of her past. She wasn't promising him any more than that, and she'd already agreed she should see him, to find out what he knew about her sister. Not to kiss him. Not to fall for him. To find out what he knew about Megan.

"All right," she said.

"Good." He grinned at her, lightly touching his mouth to hers.

The sun had risen behind him, and it hurt just to look at him this way.

Ah, damn, she thought. She was positively dizzy with the speed at which things were moving between them. When he took her into his arms, she had trouble remembering her own name, much less her sister's.

She looked up over his shoulder and saw his world, his life. She could never belong here, and honestly, all she'd ever wanted was a place to belong and people around her who loved her and never left her.

Which meant it was ridiculous to be here with him.

She couldn't imagine ever belonging to him, couldn't imagine him ever being the man who would love her and never leave her.

But he'd said they weren't so very different, and she wondered—foolishly no doubt—if he could be looking for the same thing.

Chapter 5

Stephen delivered her to her front door and asked, "What are you going to do with your day?"

"Finish packing up the kitchen, I hope," she said, a bit of her equilibrium restored now that he was no longer touching her. "Sort through things to give away, things to keep. Clean. See if anything needs to be repaired."

"So you can put the house on the market?"

"I have to," she said. "I hate admitting it, but the house is much too big for one person and much too expensive for me."

And she felt too much here. There were too many memories, memories that hurt. It seemed odd to abandon the house—the only tie to her past—but she didn't see how she could keep it, either. What in the world would she do with a house that size? What could anyone?

"It's a big job for one person," Stephen said. "There are people who could take care of this for you. They could pack up the whole house."

"I have to do it. My father's things are still there. Probably my things, my mother's, even Megan's. I may find things that tell me why she left." Allie looked up to find Stephen frowning. "You still don't think I should do this?"

arm. "Like someone grabbed her and wouldn't let her go."

"Did you ever see her with bruises?"

"I saw her sitting at the piano so many times. But I didn't remember anything about bruises. Not before today," she said. "It was the oddest thing. Like she was there in my mind for a reason. So I would see the bruises. It made me wonder if I know everything. If it's locked inside of me somewhere, and I just had to come here for all the memories to come back."

"God, Allie." He held onto her for a moment, his touch gentle and reassuring, not the kind that would ever leave marks on a woman. "This is going to be hell for you. You know that, don't you?"

"Maybe. But you said I had to move on, and this is the only way I know to do it. It's going to work, too. Being here has been good for me already. I know now that I could never live in this house. It's too full of memories."

It wasn't going to be the home she'd always longed for, not when it was full of such sorrow. And there was no reason to be upset about that. She'd known all along she wouldn't be able to keep the house, although she did hope that someone would find happiness there someday.

"Which means, I have to figure out what to do with it," she said.

"If you mean that . . ." Stephen stared down at her, hesitating. "If that's what you really want, I'm willing to buy the house from you."

"You want to live here?"

"I'm not sure. You said yourself, it's too big for one person. But I'd love to be able to restore it. It's one of the most beautiful houses in town."

She was tempted. It would be nice for just one

little part of this to be easy. She could just sell it to him and be done with it. "I'll think about it."

"Take your time," he said easily. "You're planning to be here for a while?"

"A few weeks, maybe a month," she said.

"You don't have to be back in Connecticut?"

"I don't have to be anywhere." She was as rootless as a person could be.

Stephen squeezed her hand reassuringly, and she stared up at the house. Perhaps for the first time she thought about truly giving up this last link to her former life, to her family. There was truly nothing left except her and a few faint memories, the possessions of theirs still to be found within the walls and the house itself.

Just a house, she'd told herself. But it wasn't, of course. As uncomfortable as she felt here, it was hard to imagine it belonging to someone else. She could sell it to Stephen, and he'd turn it into an even more beautiful place, but in the process, he'd wipe the slate clean. She might not even recognize it anymore, once he was done restoring it to its original beauty.

It would no longer exist except in the faint traces of her memory. But she couldn't hang onto it. She didn't have to run the numbers to know. This was simply beyond her means.

She was letting her emotions simply overwhelm her—to be even thinking of keeping it, trying to salvage something of her childhood, of her family, that was simply unsalvageable. Maybe she thought as long as the house was here, there was something of them all left. Maybe her sudden panic over the loss of the house was simply her inability to acknowledge that for all intents and purposes, her family had simply ceased to exist.

Which was foolish. They had lived and breathed within these walls. She would never forget them. Obviously she was having trouble letting go now because she was still trying to make sense of the losses they'd suffered.

It all seemed so wretchedly pointless. That they were born and lived, and died. All of them but her. Where was the logic in that? Had they merely been here to suffer? To have so many regrets? Or had they simply made all the wrong decisions? Taken all the wrong paths.

It seemed there had to be a lesson learned, a wrong to right. As if something had to come of all the tragedy. They talked about that at the runaway shelter in Connecticut. Allie happened to be there one day when a group-counseling session was starting, and she simply hadn't been able to pull herself away. They talked about refusing to give the things in the past the power to ruin the present. About mistakes, disappointments, and hurts making people stronger, smarter, more determined.

Allie had never thought of it like that. She'd tried to simply escape her mother and bury everything in her past, but she'd never thought there might have been some point to it all. That there might be something she should take away from the whole experience to make her a different person, a better one. She'd never imagined anything good coming of what happened to her family.

Until she looked up at her former home and had an idea.

To her, this would always be Megan's house. She'd believed mistakenly that it would always be the site of a tragedy—the place where her family fell apart.

But it didn't have to be that way. She had the

power to make it something else, something good. Genuine excitement surged through her veins, for what seemed to be the first time in years.

"A runaway shelter," she said. "That's what this should be. Something in my sister's memory, something that might help girls like her."

Megan's House, she thought, smiling broadly up at the stately old home. Stephen was right. It was time to look to the future, and this was exactly what she wanted to do with the house and with her time and energy.

"It's perfect," she said, feeling like she could fly, like she could do anything at all.

"Perfect?" Stephen began.

"Of course. I can't live here, and I'd been thinking of donating the money from the sale of the house to the organization that helped my mother. But this would be so much better."

"Money, yes. But this house?"

"Why not?"

"I could make you a list," he said.

"I don't want a list of reasons it might not work. I want to make it happen. That's what you told me to do," she reminded him. "Think of what I want and figure out how to make it happen."

"Allie—"

"I don't want everyone to forget her, Stephen. Sometimes it's like she never lived at all, like someone wiped a slate clean and she was gone. But if her death and her story can help other kids . . . If it can give them a safe place to stay or maybe help them get back home again, I can't think of anything better I could do in her memory."

"Allie, it would cost a fortune to fix up this house."

"Which you were perfectly willing to do five minutes ago."

"I have the money. You don't."

"I'll find it."

"You said yourself, the group you worked with in Connecticut lived on the edge financially. There was never enough money. There won't be enough to renovate this house." He frowned. "I admire you for what you want to do. But this isn't the way. Not here. Not with this house."

"Why not?"

"If not money, let's start with zoning. Do you know anything about zoning ordinances?"

"No," she said.

"I do. And I bet this whole area's zoned for single-family housing. That means one family living in one freestanding house. Communities protect their residential areas, and you won't find anything like a shelter for runaways specifically permitted in any zoning district in any town. It's going to be subject to more rules and special reviews than most anything you could build. Which means the zoning board will have a lot of discretion in deciding where it can or cannot go."

"I'll convince them it's a good idea," she said, ready to ignore all logic for once in her life. Where had logic gotten her anyway? It had kept her quiet and following a bunch of rules made by her mother, which had been a huge mistake. She was tired of playing by the rules, of dispassionately running through a list of variables and doing what she thought was safe and sensible.

For every reason he could cite to make this a bad idea, her heart said it was a good one, maybe even the real reason she'd come back here in the first place.

She'd always wanted to live in an orderly world, wanted to believe that in the end, things worked out the way they were supposed to. That there was a grand plan for the universe. Someone directed it, understood it all, even if Allie didn't. If for some reason her sister had to die, maybe Allie had finally found a way to make something good come of it.

"I don't think it's going to work," Stephen said.

"I do," she insisted. "And I thought you were going to help me."

"I am. I'm trying to talk some sense into you," he said. "Sell me the house, Allie. I'll pay you a good price for it. Take the money, then give it to the organization that helped your mother. With the kind of money we're talking about, they can build a new shelter. I'm sure they'd be happy to dedicate it to your sister's memory."

"It wouldn't be the same," she said. "This is where she lived."

"It doesn't matter," he argued. "This won't work."

Allie crossed her arms in front of her and glared at him. "Why are you so set against this?"

"I'm not. I'm being practical."

She paused. She was normally a very practical woman. She found she wasn't in this. "I can make it work."

"You'll never get the zoning approval."

"Never?" she asked, taking it as a personal challenge.

"Look around you," he said, annoyingly calm. "What do you see?"

"Rich people's houses," she guessed, seeing where he was going. Was he a snob after all? "And they shouldn't have to put up with something like a shelter for runaway teenagers in their neighborhood."

"I'm not going to argue the right or wrong in that. I'm telling you that your neighbors are some of the wealthiest and most influential people in this town, and they will not react favorably to having a shelter for troubled kids in their midst. They'll protest long and loud in front of the zoning board, most of whom are probably their friends, and you'll be dead in the water before you ever make it to the first meeting."

Allie looked back up at the house and thought of her sister. She pictured the house with a sign across the front that said MEGAN'S HOUSE, thought of other families escaping from the devastation that had rained down upon hers at her sister's death. She thought about the amazing potential within each and every person, the unimaginable losses to the world when life was cut cruelly short because young people lost themselves at times and felt like there was nowhere they could go, no one who would understand.

Allie could do something about that.

She thought about all the compromises she'd made in her life to date, all the seemingly safe paths she'd taken. The paths of least resistance, she realized, ashamed of what she'd always been.

But not anymore. She was through compromising, through running away from things because they were hard and they might seem impossible at first. She was here, she owned this house, and she knew exactly what she was meant to do with it.

"It's going to be a runaway shelter," she vowed. "I'm going to make it work."

Stephen's cell phone rang as he pulled out of Allie's driveway. It was his father, and Stephen knew what his father wanted.

"I made her an offer, Dad."

"And?"

"She's thinking it over."

"What else?"

"There's nothing else to tell. Unless you want to tell me something for a change?"

Like what was his father so afraid Allie was going to find out? Or remember? Bruises on her sister's arm, maybe? What else might still be locked in her memory after all this time?

"I just want her gone," his father said. "You checked the records, right? The newspapers? The police reports?"

"Yes. I had someone check."

"There's nothing for her to find?"

"Not much." But someone had gotten there before him. More than one person, in fact. He didn't like the sound of that at all. And he'd already heard Allie had been there herself.

"We should have pulled the records before she ever came back here."

Stephen was sure his father could have made that happen. Newspaper records disappearing, police reports. Still, he couldn't see how that would have helped.

"Having them disappear would have looked even more suspicious than what little she could find from the records," he argued.

"All right. I'll leave it to you," his father said reluctantly. "Is that it?"

"That's it," Stephen lied.

There was no way he was going to tell his father about Allie's newest idea. A shelter in her sister's name.

That's just what they needed. Something to get everyone in town talking about her sister's disappearance all over again. He didn't see how Allie would ever trust him once his part in Megan's disappearance came out, didn't see how he could keep his position—firmly between her and his father—once she knew.

He had to talk her out of the shelter. It was a bad idea all around.

So was the fact that he genuinely liked her, that he hated seeing her hurt, that he truly enjoyed having her in his arms.

He could lie to his father with hardly a twinge of conscience, but he was finding it hard as hell to keep the truth from her.

He wasn't capable of lying to himself, either. He'd called her this morning because he had to find out what she was doing, but he could have done that anywhere. Taking her to the farm had been a purely emotional choice. It *was* one of his most favorite places, one of the most beautiful he knew, and he'd wanted her to see it exactly as he did. As a special place, one where he could breathe, where he could forget all the little stresses of everyday life and be reminded that in most ways he was a very lucky man.

He could have sworn she'd seen all the things in it that he did. He'd felt a connection with her, felt a need to dig deeper into who she truly was. He was afraid the more he knew about her, the more he'd like her.

Which was impossible.

Stephen closed his eyes and swore softly. The whole situation was getting more complicated by the minute, and she'd only been here for a day and a half.

"Call me," his father grumbled. "Call me as soon as you know anything."

"I will," Stephen said, which was yet another lie.

Allie refused to let Stephen's skepticism bring her down. She was determined to make the shelter work. She hadn't felt this energetic, this enthusiastic about a project in a long, long time.

She spent an hour on the phone with Holly Rowe, the director of the runaway shelter in Connecticut. Holly promised to send her all kinds of information on organizing and funding a shelter. Holly was cautious, too, particularly about zoning troubles. She'd helped organize three shelters and discovered people were picky about where they'd allow a bunch of troubled teenagers to live.

Allie put that thought to the back of her mind and concentrated on the positive. Holly had gotten three shelters up and running. Surely Allie could do one.

She felt more energetic than she ever had in her life, felt a sense of purpose that had always been missing. She was ashamed to say she'd never found anything truly important she'd wanted to accomplish with her life. She'd drifted along, trying to take care of herself, trying not to get hurt, always looking inward—at herself—and never outward at what she might have to give to the world.

Her past was her past. She still wanted answers. But Stephen was right that in the end, there would be nothing gained by knowing what had happened, except she hoped peace of mind for herself.

This was different. This was real. A tribute to her sister's life that would help kids like Megan.

It was so much more than columns of numbers on

a page. How had she ever thought she could be happy doing something like that with her life?

Life was a gift, she'd decided today. Megan lost hers, but Allie hadn't. As she saw it, that meant she had an obligation to make something of her life.

Her first stop was town hall. The zoning office clerk confirmed that the area surrounding her house was indeed zoned for single-family housing. Anything else was permitted only by special exceptions granted by the zoning board, with even more stringent criteria for a shelter.

She left with a stack of papers explaining all the regulations—practically a whole book—and refused to be deterred. The rules didn't say absolutely no shelters for teenage runaways at 307 Willow Lane. It just said she needed special permission, and she'd get it.

What she'd told Stephen was true. Her own mother might as well have denied Megan ever existed, and after years of silence, Allie wanted to talk about her. She wanted everyone to know that she had a sister named Megan, a girl who thought she had no option but to run away from home, a decision that ultimately cost her her life. Allie didn't want anyone to ever forget that.

Part of the process would be telling her sister's story, telling the story of her own family. Allie knew a bit about raising money. People were most generous when the appeal was personal. She would use Megan's picture, would tell Megan's story. Which meant she had to have the whole story. It was all tied together now, a part of her end goal. Deal with the past, to move on to the future. Use Megan's story to help make the shelter work.

*   *   *

She was leaving town that morning when she drove right by the drugstore and remembered the waitress, Martha, who seemed to know something about Allie's sister. Allie was right there. Martha seemed like an obvious place to start.

Allie walked into the drugstore and sat down. Martha moved cautiously closer, another pot of coffee in her hand. She didn't spill or break anything this time, merely asked, "What can I get for you?"

"Answers," Allie said. "You knew my sister?"

Martha went still. In the entire time she'd been there the day before, Allie hadn't seen the woman hold still for an instant, except when she first looked at Allie's face.

"I knew all of you. Your mother and your sister and you used to come here." Martha's gaze narrowed on Allie. "You don't remember much, do you?"

"Bits and pieces. Seeing things is helping bring back more memories."

"I'm real sorry," Martha said. "About the other day. About everything."

Everything? She made it sound like a world of trouble had befallen Allie's family here.

"Did you know my father?" she tried. "What was he like?"

"Before you and your mother left? Or after?"

"After."

"He was quiet, kept to himself. He came in during off hours. He'd sit in the corner, order right away, hide behind his newspaper until his food came, then he'd eat and leave. I hardly ever saw him say a word to anybody."

Allie imagined him here hiding. She felt a little ache in her heart for this man she hardly knew, a man she'd both loved and resented her whole life, one she'd never understood.

"Why did he hide? Didn't people around here like him?"

"Oh, Lord, child." Martha looked concerned. "You don't know?"

Allie took a breath and thought, *How bad could it possibly be?* But her heart was racing and Martha was fiddling nervously.

"I never believed the gossip," Martha said. "Some people did, but I didn't. And nothin' ever came of it, so you'd think the whole story would have died down after a while. But you know how people like to talk, and the truth gets lost along the way sometimes. Still, when you and your mother disappeared so unexpectedly . . . No one knew where you were, and your father . . . he looked so . . ."

"What?" Allie said. "He looked so what?"

"Guilty," Martha said.

"Guilty of what?"

"Like I said, nobody knew for sure where you and your mother were. Or what might have happened to you. . . ."

Allie's mouth fell open. "People thought my father did something to me and my mother?"

Martha nodded.

"But he wouldn't hurt us," she said. "He didn't. We just left. My mother took me away. That's all. She took me; he knew that. Didn't he tell anyone? Didn't he explain?"

"I don't know, and even if he did . . . I'm not sure how many people believed him."

"Oh, my God." Allie thought for the first time about what his life might have been like here. They'd left him in the house where they'd once been so happy, left him all alone with nothing but his own memories and the town's suspicions. "How could anyone think he'd hurt us? He was a wonderful man."

"I really wouldn't know about that," Martha said in a way that had Allie thinking just the opposite, that Martha did indeed know more.

"Why would anyone believe he could do something like that?"

"It was the way he looked, child." Martha's face fell. It took on a look of concern, of compassion, or maybe reluctance to bring about any more hurt. "He looked guilty, even said as much to some people. They'd tell him how sorry they were about you and your sister being gone, and he'd say it was his own fault, that he deserved to lose you."

"Why?" Allie cried. "Why would he say that?"

"I couldn't say, child. I just couldn't."

Allie went straight from the drugstore to her father's attorney, who agreed to see her right away.

"After my mother and I left . . ." she began, having trouble even repeating what she'd heard. "Did people blame my father? Did they think he hurt us somehow?"

"I'm afraid so," Mr. Webster said kindly.

"Why?"

"Nothing but circumstances, I'd say," he explained. "It was all so odd, Allie. One minute you and your mother were here, and the next you were gone. Your father didn't tell anyone at first, but he looked awful. Megan had just died, so that wasn't unusual. But people would ask about where you and your mother were, and he'd make up some excuse. That you weren't feeling well. That you'd gone to visit relatives. I think he was hoping you'd come back before he had to tell anyone the truth. But the lying didn't help him later, when it all came out. You have to understand, it was like you'd disappeared off the face of the earth. Your mother didn't tell anyone she was going away or why. She hardly took anything with her. It looked suspicious."

"So what happened?"

"Eventually, the school came looking for you, and you weren't there. By then, all sorts of rumors were flying around town. Your father said you and your mother had moved away, and when the lady from school asked where you were, he wouldn't tell anyone. I'm not sure he knew at that point. That's when the sheriff's department got involved."

Allie winced. "They arrested him?"

"No, but they questioned him, and in some people's minds, that was enough to make him look guilty. The cabdriver who took you and your mother to the airport was the only person who could verify your father's story, and it took a while to track him down. His statement was enough for the sheriff, but you know how stories get started. . . ."

She imagined the whispers, the odd looks following her father wherever he went. "He must have suffered so much."

"He looked bad during that time."

"Someone told me he said it was his fault my mother and I left."

"He told me that. Every time I tried to tell him how sorry I was for everything that happened, he said he'd gotten what he deserved by ending up here all alone."

Allie shook her head, thinking of the bruises on her sister's arm and dismissing them just as quickly.

Her father hadn't done that. They weren't the source of his guilt.

"Every memory I have of him is a good one. Except for that night my mother and I left, and even then, he wasn't hurting us. He was just so sad."

"What do you remember of that night, Allie?"

"That we ran away," she said, thinking how odd it sounded when she said it out loud. But there was no other way to explain. They ran. Not like they were guilty of some crime and trying to escape. Like something terrible had happened, and they had to get away from it.

What terrible thing? she wondered, no closer now than she'd ever been to knowing.

"We were on the stairs when I realized my father wasn't going with us. I remember he hugged me. He begged me to always remember that he loved me, and that was it." That had always been her most vivid memory of him—standing on the stairs looking hurt. "Did he ever say anything about my mother?"

"I never heard him say a word against her. And I checked the family court records," the lawyer said. "Here and in Connecticut. There was never any formal custody agreement between them. She simply took you, and apparently he didn't fight her on that."

"Why?" she cried. "Why wouldn't he fight for me?"

"I don't mean to pry, but there aren't a lot of reasons mothers grab their daughters and run away. Allie, did you ever see him hit your mother?"

"No," she said. That was ridiculous. He wasn't that kind of man.

"Could he have touched you? In a way he wasn't supposed to?"

"No." Allie shook her head back and forth. "He loved me."

"People do terrible things to people they claim to love," Mr. Webster said gently. "Do you remember anytime he was in your room late at night? Anytime he touched you, and you felt uncomfortable?"

"No."

"Memories are fluid things. People can block out a lot of things that hurt them or frighten them."

"It didn't happen," she insisted. "I loved my father, and he loved me."

"What about your sister? Could he have hurt her?"

"He wasn't like that," Allie said, again seeing the bruises on her sister's arm. Just because Megan had bruises didn't mean they came from her father.

"All right." Mr. Webster backed away. "I had to ask. I want to help you, and I liked your father. But I had to ask."

Allie nodded, glad to have the questions out in the open, ready to put them behind her. The idea had flirted around the edges of her brain for so long. Not because she believed anything like that happened. But, as the lawyer said, there weren't a lot of reasons a woman took her child and ran away from her husband. These were the worst she could imagine—that a man was either abusing his wife or his children.

"It must have been tied to Megan's disappearance." Allie sighed, coming back to one single question. "Why did my sister run away?"

"I don't know, Allie. There are just so many things I don't know."

"Did you ever hear anything about her accident? Anything to indicate that it might not be an accident?"

"No. Never."

She nodded. "Well, thank you. I appreciate all your help."

"Anything else I can do?" he offered.

Allie thought of the shelter, the future, of leaving the painful past behind. It was time, long past time.

"What do you know about zoning issues?" she asked.

Martha called Tucker and said, "The girl came back."

"And?" Tucker said.

Standing at the end of the alley at the pay phone, sucking hard on the cigarette in her mouth, Martha said, "Janet *is* dead."

Tucker said nothing. Martha felt the life they'd shared slipping away, felt how unimportant she must have been to Tucker all these years if he could still be this torn up over Janet Bennett's death. She didn't make him ask for the details, she just wanted this to be out in the open and hopefully forgotten.

"It was cancer," she said. "Two months ago. She went kind of fast."

Tucker was still there. She could hear him breathing shakily. She nearly choked on the words, "I'm sorry, Tuck."

"And the daughter?" he said finally. "Allie? Does she . . ."

"I don't think she knows anything."

Chapter 6

Allie started shaking as she drove home, thinking again of the old rumors about her father. And she was ashamed to admit it, but her first impulse was to run to Stephen. As she got closer, she couldn't help but slow the car in front of his house. She wondered if he was home and what he would do if she just showed up there like this. Upset and uncertain and in need of a little reassurance.

She thought she knew. He'd make it all better somehow, would likely hold out his arms to her and draw her close, and she would indeed feel better just because she was with him. But the strength of the need she felt for him had her hesitating. She barely knew him, she reminded herself, and trusting people, depending on them, was dangerous. Life had taught her that. People left. They hurt you and lied to you, and they died.

Would he hurt her, too, in the end?

Allie squeezed her eyes shut, and when she opened them again, he was there, standing just outside his front door watching her and waiting. She thought about being smart; she thought about being alone. She thought of the kindness he'd shown her, the tenderness, and then she was lost. The morning and images of her father living with the suspicions of the whole community for the rest of his life.

She pulled into the drive in front of his house.

He opened her door for her, pulled her from the car, and held onto both her hands. "What's wrong?"

"Was I happy here, Stephen? When I was a little girl, was my family ever happy?" she said, her voice trembling.

"I think so," he said.

"And my father? Did he love me? Did he love Megan?"

"Your father thought you could do no wrong," Stephen said.

"What does that mean? He thought I could do no wrong?"

"Allie, you're trembling." He slid his hands along her forearms and onto her upper arms, holding her steady. "Come inside."

"I'm sorry. I know I don't have any right to just show up here and start throwing questions at you."

"I told you I wanted to help you, and I meant it. Come on in," he said again. "You can ask whatever you want."

She found his house quite similar to hers, but lovingly maintained, furnished with a pleasing mix of well-preserved antiques and new pieces, a true showplace. He led her to the back of the house to a cozy-looking room filled with wicker furniture. Sunlight, warm and cheerful looking, streamed inside from windows that filled the back and the side walls. Stephen led her to a chaise lounge, and she sank back into the pillows.

It was nearly noon, and once he found out she hadn't eaten, he wouldn't let her say a word until he returned with hot coffee, sandwiches, and some fruit, courtesy of his parents' housekeeper.

She ate, finding that she was indeed hungry, and then she leaned back against the comfortable cushions and let the sun warm her right down to the bone. But she was still trembling from the ugly things she'd heard about her family.

"You look tired," Stephen said. "Are you sleeping all right over there by yourself?"

"No," she admitted.

He took her hand once again and held it. Allie closed her eyes and let herself feel the simple pleasure of his touch. After that scene in the lawyer's office, she couldn't help being reassured by the way she responded to him—easily, naturally. She didn't have any hang-ups about being touched, about sex. It wasn't something she'd done often or casually, but she'd had sex before. Perfectly normal sex. She didn't cringe at the idea of a man touching her. It didn't bring back any odd memories, because there were none. Her father never touched her that way.

Unnerved nonetheless, Allie pulled her hand from Stephen's and sat up. "I heard that after my mother and I disappeared, people thought my father had done something terrible with us."

Stephen frowned at her, but he wasn't surprised.

"You knew? You could have told me, Stephen."

"Why? What does that do for you, Allie? How does that help in the least? The way I see it, all it's done is hurt you."

"It's what happened," she cried. "Stephen, he was my father, and this is what happened to him after we left."

"Is that the kind of thing you came back here to

find out? Is that what you honestly want me to tell you?"

"I want the truth," she said, practically begging. "This is my life we're talking about, and I deserve to know the truth."

"I think you deserve something better than that, Allie," he said. "To not be hurt anymore. Have you thought about that?"

He'd told her that before, but this time it scared her into an uneasy silence. The scene this morning had tapped into her own private nightmares about what was waiting for her here. After all, her own mother couldn't bear to come back. Even after she was diagnosed with a potentially fatal disease, she hadn't been strong enough to be honest with Allie about the past. She hadn't cared enough to do something with this house, with all their things, leaving it instead for Allie to take care of on her own. It was one of the most selfish and most cowardly things her mother had ever done, but Allie couldn't deny that she'd been a coward herself.

"It scares me," she admitted. "But I've had years of living with it. I've imagined every rotten thing that could possibly have happened, and if I hadn't been such a coward, I would have been here years ago. I would have seen my father again."

It was her greatest regret, one she didn't think she'd ever get over.

"Just tell me what you know," she said. Watching him, she had to add, "Tell me why you look guilty every time I say my sister's name."

"I do feel guilty," he admitted finally. Looking grim, he sat down on the edge of the chaise lounge. "And sooner or later, you're going to hear this. It might as well come from me. There's a lot I don't know about Megan's disappearance, but this part . . . I know this because I was there. When Megan disappeared, I was doing my undergraduate work at Vanderbilt."

"In Nashville?"

He nodded. "I was heading back to school one weekend when Megan came and asked for a favor. She said she needed a ride, that she was going to stay for a while with an aunt who lived in Tennessee."

"I don't remember having an aunt in Tennessee."

"You don't," he said sadly. "She was running away."

"Oh." Allie could hardly breathe at first.

"I'm sorry," Stephen said. "I'm so sorry. I didn't know, Allie. I swear. She just asked me to give her a ride. I dropped her off in front of a house in a little town called Greenbriar, Tennessee, and nobody ever saw her again. The police were never able to trace her from that point."

Allie took the news like a blow.

He'd helped her?

Stephen had helped her sister run away?

Allie gasped. She looked down at her own hands, once again held tightly in his, and she pulled away from him, not wanting to touch him, not sure if she wanted to hear anymore, cowardly as that might be.

She was simply stunned. She'd known he was hiding something, but she never imagined anything like this.

"You?" she whispered.

He nodded, watching her and waiting.

Allie didn't know what to say, where to go from here.

"I'd like to tell you what happened," he said.

And she needed to hear it. She needed to weigh

his words carefully and decide whether his explanation was at all logical, whether she believed it. She needed to know if he was hiding anything else from her, and she needed to stop thinking that she'd come over here knowing it would be so easy to crawl into his arms once again.

Even now, the slightest move toward him, and he'd pull her to him. Just as he'd done for Megan? It seemed so ironic to her that when Megan was in trouble and needed help, she turned to Stephen, and that fifteen years later, Allie was doing the same. She wondered if either of them was right in doing so, if he was someone who'd hurt Megan or helped her? If he'd be good for Allie or very, very bad?

"Tell me," she said.

"I didn't see anything unusual in her asking me for a ride. I never imagined she was running away. If I had, I would have tried to stop her."

"Then why didn't you tell me this before?"

"Would you have believed me?" he said, turning the question right back on her. He had a habit of doing that, she noted.

"I'm not sure," she admitted. Surely she wouldn't have. Surely she wasn't already so blind to him that she believed everything he said.

Stephen frowned. "I guess I hoped we'd have a little time to get to know each other. That by the time you found out, you might believe me. But it's all right. You're not the only one who had doubts."

"People thought you'd done something to her?"

"Some people," he admitted. "It's not that surprising, I suppose. I was the last person we know of to see her alive."

Allie felt a chill run through her. The last person to see her sister alive?

"She must have planned it for a long time, Allie. Because she waited until late the night before to ask for a ride. I offered to pick her up at your house, but she was waiting by my car when I walked outside early that morning. I'd gone to bed late, hadn't seen anybody that night or that morning. No one knew she'd gone with me. It was weeks before I even talked to anybody from here on the phone. Rich was in some kind of trouble at UK, and Dad was trying to fix that. My mother was planning a charity ball. By the time I heard . . . it was too late."

Allie supposed that was entirely possible. On the surface she didn't see any reason to distrust what he'd said, except for the fact that he'd waited this long to tell her and maybe because people made a habit of keeping things from her. He'd touched a raw nerve.

Still, she thought about the haunted look she'd seen so many times in his beautiful eyes, and she had to ask, "Is this what you meant when you said you blame yourself for Megan's disappearance? For her death?"

He nodded.

Allie fought the urge to sympathize.

She felt guilty herself and knew how irrational an emotion it could be. Hers was classic survivor guilt she'd been told by people who were supposed to know. It didn't seem to help. Whether the guilt was rational or irrational, it was still there. It still hurt.

She looked at Stephen again, waiting, seemingly ready to accept whatever judgment she came to about his own guilt or innocence.

She was still angry, still distrustful of his motives and whether he'd told her everything this time. But the fairer part of her, the part that felt guilty herself, had to add, "Stephen, if she wanted to run away that badly, she would have found a way, with or without you."

He didn't look convinced. It made her want to believe him even more.

Allie tried to think selfishly—about what she wanted, why she was here. She tried to avoid making any snap judgments about whether or not she trusted him. She didn't have to trust him to try to find out what else he knew. She would simply judge his actions and his words more carefully now.

"My father felt guilty, too," she said. "He told people he deserved to lose us, to end up here all alone. Do you have any idea why he felt like that?"

"He and Megan always had their differences," Stephen said carefully. "They never seemed to be close in the way you and your father were."

"What do you mean."

"I mean you were always his favorite. He indulged you."

"In a way that he didn't indulge Megan?"

"Megan was your mother's favorite," he explained.

Allie knew in an instant it was true. Some part of her had always known. If her mother had a choice of which daughter to lose, it would have been Allie.

She turned and looked toward the back of the house where it all happened. The past was all around her now. Sometimes it seemed so close it might suffocate her. Sometimes she felt like she couldn't even breathe.

"The night we left, he begged her not to go, not to take me. She told him she'd lost one daughter, that she wasn't going to lose another, and after that he didn't try to stop us. He just stood there and watched us go. I think my mother took me away to punish him, because she blamed him for Megan's death," she said as evenly and emotionlessly as she could. "I wondered if you had any idea why."

"No, I don't. And I didn't know your parents well," Stephen said, drawing her back. "I never talked to your father about why you and your mother left. I don't know of anyone who did, but . . ." He paused, considered. "I don't understand, Allie. If your mother was angry and wanted to punish your father, I can see her taking you away for a few days. But your mother kept you away for fifteen years. And it didn't just punish your father. It punished you."

It had certainly felt like a punishment, except she couldn't ever figure out what she'd done to deserve it. In truth, it was a relief to think that it wasn't her fault, that it was her father's or her mother's.

"What did your mother say about your father?" Stephen asked. "About why you didn't see him anymore?"

"She didn't. We didn't talk about him."

"One of those little boxes you mentioned?" he said softly.

Allie closed her eyes and swore softly. God, was there no limit to what she'd tell this man?

Stephen took her hand and held it.

Allie told herself not to feel anything at that. Not the warmth. Not the reassurance. Not the simple comfort that came from not being alone at this moment. She thought of how hard it had been just to make it this far, about how much farther she had to go to find out what happened to her family. She thought about long, empty years with no one left for her, no one who meant anything to her. What in the world was she going to do? When she left here, where would she go?

All of a sudden she felt so empty, so heart-wrenchingly empty inside. Beneath all the anger, all the pain, there was nothing, no one who cared, no one who mattered.

There hadn't been for so long, and now Stephen was here. Stephen whom she wanted so badly to take the loneliness away.

But he hadn't been honest with her. It had nearly taken her breath away. How much it hurt. How it felt to think so briefly that she had someone on her side and then have that yanked away.

She remembered that feeling so well from when she was a little girl. Her sister gone. Her father. Her life turned upside down. It seemed smart to her, under those circumstances, to simply refuse to let herself depend on anyone after that. Therapists could call it anything they wanted. To her it seemed smart.

And she'd forgotten that lesson with him.

Allie got to her feet and said, "I really should go."

"Wait. I picked up a few things for you." He handed her two business cards and a zoning pamphlet. "I'm afraid it's what I expected. The whole area's zoned for single-family housing. Anything else requires a variance from the zoning board."

"I know. I stopped by town hall today," she said, handing the pamphlet back to him. "And the business cards?"

"Two house inspectors. If you're seriously thinking of renovating that house, you need to have someone go over it carefully. Both those men have done business with me before. They're good."

"You're going to let them talk me out of it for you?" she asked.

"I just want you to go into this with your eyes wide open, Allie. They'll give you an honest assessment of the house."

"You still think I'll give up, don't you? You think I'll change my mind."

"I think a reasonable person would come around to my way of thinking on this."

Allie just stood there gaping at him. Not sure whether to tell him that was one of the most arrogant things she'd ever heard or to thank him for reminding her why she didn't trust men or anyone else. He'd done it quickly after all. She should be grateful she hadn't fallen any further for him before she remembered why she shouldn't. And he'd reminded her of the shelter. The reason she was staying here. The reason she would go on.

At one time Megan must have felt just as lonely as Allie did. There had to be other kids who did, as well, and Allie was going to help. She should be good at it, she realized. She was an expert in loneliness.

"I need to go," she said again.

"One more thing." He stopped her in the foyer, picked up a FedEx envelope lying on the table by the door. "That came this morning, and the driver thought your house was still empty. He came over here and asked, and I signed for it."

She glanced at the address label. Greg Malone.

"Trouble?" Stephen asked casually.

She wasn't going to tell him, but then she wondered . . . What else did he know? What might she find out if she could catch him off balance in the least?

"Police reports," she said. "On Megan's disappearance."

He gave away nothing save for a slight tightening of his jaw. *Damn.*

"What are you doing, Allie?"

"Trying to find out what happened to her."

"The police never knew what happened to her," he pointed out.

"I'm looking for any information I can find."

"From someone in Atlanta?"

Allie nodded, liking being the one with information someone else wanted for a change. "I hired a private detective."

"Why? And why someone from Atlanta?"

She used his own technique on him, ignored his question, asking one of her own. "What do you know about the car accident that killed Megan?"

"What's to know?" he said, questioning her again. "She was in Georgia somewhere, and her car skidded off the road in the middle of a bad thunderstorm. She drowned in a flooded creek that ran along the side of the road."

"Did she?"

"That's the second time you've asked me about the car accident. What's going on, Allie? Why are you asking questions about that accident now?"

"Because someone else is."

"Who?"

"I don't know," she said, liking this even more. How many times had he told her he simply didn't know?

"Tell me," Stephen insisted. "Tell me everything."

She weighed the pros and cons of that, decided she wanted to know if he recognized the name Jason Getty, and told him a bit about the man's letter and his cryptic questions about the accident.

"So you have someone using a made-up name, a fake address, asking the vaguest of questions and offering you nothing in the way of new information?" Stephen said.

"At the moment," she bluffed. "But I just got here. Who's to say what I'm going to find out?"

"Allie, listen to me. I never heard anything to indicate it was anything but an accident," he said.

"Really?"

Stephen swore and turned his head away. "I know I haven't given you reason to trust me. Not now. But I'm telling the truth about this, and I'm worried now. I think you need to be very careful."

"Why? If there's nothing to this? If there's nothing to find out? What would I have to worry about?"

"Think about the alternatives," he insisted. "If there's any truth to that letter, either someone's trying to tell you there are things you don't know about Megan's accident or that it wasn't an accident at all. If it wasn't an accident, if it was deliberate, there may well be someone else who'll be very unhappy about you looking into it after all this time."

Allie shivered. Because it was true. Someone else was looking. And now she had something even more worrisome to think about. Someone looking and someone else trying to keep them both from finding out the truth.

"Why would anyone ever want to hurt my sister?" she whispered.

"I don't know," he said, the words carefully enunciated, one by one.

"Neither do I," she said. "But I'm going to find out."

* * *

Furious, Stephen went straight for the phone. "Want to tell me about the accident, Dad?" he growled.

"What accident?"

"The one that killed Megan Bennett?"

"What about it?" his father said.

"You tell me. If I'm going to take care of this little situation for you, what do I need to know?"

"She slid off the road and drowned," his father said. "What's to know?"

Stephen didn't find that reassuring at all, and he no longer believed it, either.

Chapter 7

When Allie got home, she had the oddest sensation that she wasn't alone. She put the FedEx envelope and her keys on the table in the hall and stood there for a long time, not moving a muscle, just staring around her at the house that was making her crazy.

Suddenly she could swear she heard footsteps moving quickly and quietly above her.

"What?" she demanded of what appeared to be an empty house. "Am I supposed to run screaming from my own house? Is that what you want?"

No one answered her. No one appeared. There were no voices. Just footsteps.

Someone *was* moving around up there.

Stephen's warning to be careful still echoed in Allie's mind, but this was different, as if someone was toying with her—the footsteps, the window left open, the little things that went bump in the night. It was like someone was playing a sick joke on her to drive her away.

"Do you want me to leave!" she yelled up the steps. "I'm not leaving!"

She still heard footsteps. She could call the police and get the hell out of the house until they came. But what if she was wrong? Half the town thought she was a ghost, thought her house was haunted and her father was a murderer. Now they'd think she was crazy, as well. She felt half-crazy since she came here. Little Allie Bennett, who didn't know why she left, didn't know what happened while she lived here, who needed to ask total strangers the most basic questions about her own life. It made her feel like a freak, and she hated it.

Allie dug in the hall closet, remembering the baseball bat she'd seen there the other day. She found it and rushed up the stairs before she could even think of how much she hated going up there. She glanced nervously at the bedroom doors, all closed. She heard nothing.

She paused, looking up. On the third floor was a big, open attic room. From the top-floor windows, she would be able to see forever, to the tops of trees, down the river, across the fields, all the way to town. She and Megan used to play there. Being able to see so much seemed like a good idea at the moment.

Allie went to the next set of stairs. Dust flew as she went, swirling around her and tickling her nose, the particles dancing on beams of light coming from the window at the end of the hall.

Then she saw the footprints.

Her heart lurched in her chest as she knelt down for a closer look. The stairs were thick with dust, the impression of footsteps clear. Someone had gone up those stairs. How recently? Mr. Webster said someone walked through the house once a month to make sure everything was in order. The footprints could have been made by that person.

Or they could have been made moments ago.

Allie put her foot on the step, shifted all her weight onto that spot, then stepped back and examined the impression her foot left in the dust. She couldn't tell anything for sure in the dim light, and all the noises had ceased.

She walked back to the top of the main staircase, took two steps down, then sat there, leaning against the wall, the position giving her a clear view of the main hallway and most of the upstairs. The house was making her crazy. Being in this town was making her crazy. And it had taken her being convinced there was an intruder in the house to get her up these stairs.

Her bedroom was fifteen feet away. For two nights now, she'd been a flight of stairs away. Yet she hadn't found the courage to take those final steps. She'd come here for answers, yet all she'd done was clean out the kitchen. How much more impersonal a spot could she have chosen to start?

She leaned her head against the wall and took deep breaths, trying to make them even and smooth and slow, and she was still trembling. A part of her, the braver part, wanted to say that was just too damned bad. Poor little Allie was afraid again. Time to run away and hide, until the scary parts were over.

God, she hated herself for the coward she'd always been.

She sat there thinking until the doorbell rang, scaring her all over again.

Opening the door, she found an overgrown boy. All arms and legs, he seemed to tower over her, although judging from his face, she suspected he was only sixteen or so. He was wearing oversize jeans, the kind that were so much in fashion, a baggy sweatshirt, hair that probably hadn't been combed in a week, and a wary smile. Oddly, there was something familiar about him, although there was no way she could have known him.

"Hi," she said, because he hadn't said a word.

"Hi. My name's Casey," he mumbled shyly, then nodded off to the right. "I live down the street. I heard you're doing some work on the house, and I was wondering if there was anything I could do. Work in the yard, maybe? Or haul boxes and stuff? I'm really strong."

He was tall, but she wasn't sure about the strong part. He looked like he needed a hot meal more than odd jobs, and he probably should have been in school. But Allie didn't make an issue of that.

"I could probably use some help," she said, because she couldn't bear to turn him away if he was hungry. "Casey, you said?"

"Yes, ma'am."

"How old are you?"

"Seventeen," he insisted.

She didn't think she believed that. On impulse, she said, "I was going to make some coffee, maybe have a sandwich. Why don't you come inside, and we could talk about the job."

"Great."

He stepped inside. Allie closed the door and headed for the kitchen. Oddly, her friend Casey didn't need her to point out the way. He walked straight down the hallway and into the room ahead of her. He must have been here before, she realized, wondering if he'd been a friend of her father's. She offered him a seat on a stool by the counter, poured him a tall glass of milk, which he accepted with a nod. She poured one for herself, ready to forego the coffee, and gathered bread, cheese, sliced turkey, and mustard.

"Can I interest you in a sandwich?" she asked, turning back to the gangly boy.

His glass of milk was empty, she noted. Without saying anything, she got the milk out again and refilled his glass. He wouldn't look at her as she did it, his face turning a ruddy pink. He didn't want her to know how hungry he was.

"Mustard or mayo?" she asked, because she didn't want him to have to ask for the sandwich he so obviously craved.

"Either one's fine," he said, sipping the second glass of milk carefully.

Intrigued, Allie turned back to her sandwich fixings. Keeping her back to him, she said casually, "What did you say your last name was?"

"Adams," he said hesitantly.

"And your parents' names?"

"My mom's name's Patricia," he said.

"And your father?"

He shrugged. "Don't have one."

Which meant what? That he was dead? Disinterested? That he'd disappeared? "Where did you say you lived?"

"Two streets back," he said. "Dogwood Lane."

She vaguely remembered Dogwood Lane. "Have you lived here long?"

"No, ma'am."

"I thought you might have known my father."

Casey gazed back at her, his shaggy hair falling over his forehead, his dark brown eyes intent on her. "You really used to live here?"

She nodded. "A long time ago."

"I heard that around town, but people say all kinds o'things. They even say this house is haunted."

"You want to know if my house is haunted, Casey?"

He shrugged. "Ever'body does."

Allie handed him a plate with two sandwiches. His eyes grew wide at the sight, and that painful knot in her stomach intensified. She'd seen too many kids hurt in too many ways and trying to hide it at the shelter in Connecticut. Casey eyed the food warily, as if it might come with some strings attached, the notion even more painful to her.

"Go ahead," she told him. "If you're going to work for me, you have to keep up your strength."

He took one of the sandwiches and woofed it down. Three bites. It was gone. The second, he chewed deliberately slowly. She would feed him again, Allie decided, before she sent him home for the day. If he had a home to go to. She sat down on a stool beside him and sipped her glass of milk, thinking that he was the reason she wanted to turn this house into a runaway shelter. Not just for herself or for Megan, but for all the kids like him.

It felt good just to be able to provide him with a meal. This was the kind of feeling that could keep her going for a long time. She'd remember it when she got discouraged thinking about silly little things like zoning laws and disgruntled neighbors and a lack of funds. Or about men she shouldn't trust.

What she wanted to do was important. She couldn't forget that. If she did get discouraged, she'd think of this lost, hungry boy, and she wouldn't give up. Not until she'd done what she set out to do.

Allie felt so much better. Committed. Determined. Powerful, even. She'd never felt powerful in her entire life. But she could do this. She could help this boy and others like him.

"So," he said, when he finished eating, "you lived here when you were little?"

"Yes. The house belonged to my parents."

"Why'd you leave?"

"I don't know," she said softly. "Tell me something, Casey. It hasn't been that long ago since you were nine. What do you remember about being that age?"

"I dunno."

"Help me out. My memories are so vague. I wonder sometimes if that's normal. What do you remember?"

He looked uneasy, but started to talk. "We lived in Mobile. I played basketball. Got into trouble at school for talkin' too much and not payin' attention. Stuff like that. Why? What do you remember?"

"This house. My parents. My sister—"

"You had a sister?"

She nodded. "Her name was Megan."

"Did you guys . . . get along? Or fight? Or what?"

Allie thought about it. "I suppose we got along all right. She was seven years older than I was, so she probably thought I was an awful pest, tagging along behind her, wanting to do everything she did. Do you have any brothers or sisters?"

He shook his head back and forth, looking wary again.

Tomorrow she was going to find out where her friend Casey lived and why no one had bothered to feed him today. For now, she wanted to keep him here, to see what else she could find out about him, and having him help her around the house seemed like the best way to do that.

"Okay," she said, "if you still want to work for me, let's talk terms."

Allie decided to work on some much-needed maintenance in the yard while she had Casey's help. They put in six grueling hours, hardly making a dent in the job. Casey was indeed strong and a good worker. Allie paid him five dollars an hour, fed him once again, and then reluctantly let him go. She wanted to give him more than thirty dollars, but he argued that was a fair wage, and he promised to come back the next morning. She watched him cut through a neighbor's yard and disappear, wished she had the shelter up and running, so she could offer him a place to stay and so much more. For now, she had to be content with some food and a bit of money.

When she came inside, hot and achy, she spotted the FedEx letter on the table where she'd left it earlier. Opening it, she flipped through the police reports, then found a letter from Greg.

He said the records hadn't provided much new information, except for the name of the highway patrolman who investigated Megan's accident. That would be Greg's starting point. He was going to find the trooper, ask if he remembered anything that didn't make it into the written report, if he knew of anything suspicious about the accident.

Allie glanced through the reports, finding them frustratingly brief and vague. Curiously, she found no mention of Stephen's role in her sister's disappearance, no mention of him being under suspicion in connection with her disappearance. She wondered if that was courtesy of his family name alone. Allie didn't think Stephen actually hurt her sister. But the omission made her wonder what else had been left out of the official report.

Allie called Greg in Macon and told him what she'd found out from Stephen.

"Whittaker?" Greg said.

"Yes. His family lived next door to us. They still do, in fact."

"What does he do?"

"He owns a construction and real estate management company. His family's lived here forever. His father's a judge."

"Any relation to Richard Whittaker IV?"

"He has a brother named Rich who's in his late thirties. Why?"

"Richard Whittaker IV is the current governor of Kentucky, Allie. If this is the family I'm thinking of, one of his uncles is a U.S. Senator."

"Oh," she said. Stephen owned a sleek, fast Thoroughbred and his brother, whom she barely remembered, was the governor.

Greg laughed. "They lived right next door to you?"

"Yes."

"You grew up around money. Do you want me to check this guy out? Do you think he had something to do with your sister's disappearance?"

Allie thought about it. Did she trust Stephen Whittaker? Did she want someone digging through his past with her sister?

"I can do it," Greg said. "If that's what you want. . . ."

"No," she decided. "You're already in Macon. If you don't find out anything there, you could come here then."

And start asking questions about Stephen? Allie didn't know. She'd worry about that later, she decided, if they hit a dead-end in Georgia.

"Okay," Greg agreed. "Let's talk about what I found. I talked to the trooper this morning. He remembered the accident. He said when kids die, he always remembers. It's pretty much what the paper said—a bad thunderstorm. The creek wasn't normally that deep, but it was flooded that day and the current was strong. Your sister was driving what turned out to be a stolen car without a license. He assumed she was driving too fast on a slick, winding road—not unusual for kids. They're inexperienced drivers. They don't make allowances for things like slippery roads. They don't know how easily things can go wrong. It happens, Allie."

"Megan was a good swimmer," she remembered. "It seems like she would have been able to get out."

"You don't know what kind of shape she was in when the car hit the water. She may have been dazed, confused. She may have panicked. She may have had trouble getting the door open or the window. The water would have been cold. She would have had all that fighting against her."

"Oh. Okay." She sighed heavily. "So that's it?"

"Maybe. Maybe not. I'm here. I thought I might as well keep at it. They had a lot of accidents and downed trees that day. It took awhile before the trooper got there, but he remembers that one of the first people on the scene that night was a doctor who lived here in town. I talked to him a few minutes ago."

"And?"

"I didn't get anything concrete, and honestly, I don't know where to go with it from here. But I'd swear the man had something to hide."

"A doctor? Why?"

"I don't know. I asked a couple of people around town about him, and they all say the man's practically a saint. Does a lot of volunteer work at a clinic here in town, does a lot with his church. I didn't find anybody who had anything bad to say about him. Yet."

"So why would he lie to you about Megan's accident?"

"It's a good question, isn't it?" Greg said. "The trooper said there were three other people on the scene that night, two young men and a girl. He didn't remember their names. Not surprising—it's been fifteen years. He's not sure if he can find any paperwork on it or not, but he's going to check. If the doctor knew the other three, he didn't tell me their names."

"Three people?" she said. "Surely we can find at least one of them. One who can tell us something."

"I'll do my best, Allie. In the meantime, be careful. I don't like the way this feels."

"What do you think happened?" she asked.

"I don't know. I'm a suspicious man. That's just how I think. That's how people pay me to think. You be careful, and I'll call you tomorrow."

Allie put down the phone and shivered, thinking it was just her luck—to find another person who knew something about what happened to her sister who didn't want to talk about it.

She thought about Greg's warning, about Stephen's.

Feeling listless and out of sorts, she let herself gaze longingly at Stephen's house. She remembered how angry she'd been at him earlier, how betrayed she'd felt. Even so, she still wondered what he was doing. If he'd never told her about him and Megan today, it would have been so easy to slip through the back-yards and onto his back porch. He'd smile and open the door and invite her in, keep her company, maybe take her in his arms. The night noises would lose their power to frighten her. Everything would. But she couldn't go there. She couldn't. And she could handle this on her own. She'd handled everything her whole life on her own.

Instead Allie wandered outside into her backyard. It was nice out here, she realized. It was incredibly quiet, and if she wasn't so uneasy about simply being here, it might even be peaceful.

Then she heard a rustling sound from a clump of bushes at the right side of the yard and froze. Gathering her courage, she went to the edge of the bushes and started pulling them apart, to find nothing but one, scrawny-looking, scared kitten, its back arched menacingly, its tail sticking up in the air.

Allie laughed. At herself and the outraged look of the kitten. It didn't look very old.

"Poor baby," she crooned.

She hurried inside, dug through the cabinets, and found a dusty can of tuna. The kitten had come to the middle of the yard by the time she returned. Allie set the bowl in the grass. The kitten ate hungrily, then eyed her with a tad less suspicion.

"Still hungry?" Allie was happy to be able to feed another hungry mouth. Or maybe she'd just do anything for some company right now. "You have to come inside if you want more."

She took the empty bowl inside, the kitten on her heels. She made makeshift arrangements for the cat that night, promising to do better tomorrow.

In the family room, curled up on the sofa with the kitten, the radio playing softly in the background, the afghan wrapped around her, she felt almost comfortable and not quite so alone as she finally drifted off to sleep.

Chapter 8

Allie slept fairly well that night with the kitten curled up beside her. She got up early, drove into town, and rushed through the grocery store, stocking up on supplies. She had a cat to feed, and, she hoped, a teenage boy. Pulling into her driveway fifteen minutes later, she found Casey sitting on the front step, the kitten batting at his untied shoelaces.

He smiled shyly.

She beamed at him, happy for his company. "Hi. Ready to go to work?"

"Sure." He shrugged.

"I see you met my kitten," Allie said.

"It's yours?"

"We kind of claimed each other. If she's willing to stay, I'm going to keep her."

"Cool," he said.

"Help me carry in the groceries?" she said, putting a box of lunch meat, milk, soft drinks, and chips into his arms. "I got some empty boxes, too. I think I'm too sore to work in the yard today, so we can get started inside."

They hauled everything in. Allie claimed she was starving and fixed scrambled eggs and bacon, enough for four people, she thought, until she watched Casey eat with unabashed gusto. He caught her staring at him, flushed, and pushed his plate away.

"Sorry," he said.

"Why?"

He shrugged, looking bewildered and very young. "Did I do something wrong?"

"No. I'm just not used to feeding a teenage boy. I'm amazed at how much one can eat."

"I'm sorry," he said, looking guilty. "I—"

"It's okay, Casey. Eat as much as you like. I don't mind. In fact, I like having the company. I don't usually bother to cook if it's just me."

"You don't have to feed me," he said defensively.

"I told you, I like the company, and I figure if I feed you, I get to work it off you later."

He was sitting beside her at the breakfast bar, his face in three-quarter profile as he stared at her, all defiance and youthful pride. Once again, something about him seemed so familiar. He had sandy-colored hair, beautiful brown eyes, elaborately thick, full lashes—the kind a girl would kill for. An image teased at her brain, like a flash from a camera—blindingly evident one minute, gone the next.

What was it about him? He didn't seem like a runaway. Not like a kid who'd been on the streets for any length of time. Allie knew what they looked like. There was a hardness in their eyes, and they seldom offered their trust to anyone who wasn't another teenager on the run, too.

"Where did you say you lived?"

"A couple blocks over." He cocked his head to the left, the opposite of the direction he'd indicated the day before. "Why?"

"No reason."

She thought of what he'd told her about where he

lived and his mother. *Patricia Adams.* Allie wondered if there was such a woman. Her gut instinct said he was all alone, and for that reason, she felt a kinship with him. This time fifteen years ago, her own sister had been on the run somewhere, cold maybe, hungry, alone. She wondered if anyone had fed Megan. If anyone had taken care of her.

"So," he said. "Where do you want to start?"

"I thought we'd sort through the attic," she said, thinking of the advantage of his muscles again and his tireless energy. He could haul boxes down the two flights of stairs much easier than she could. And she wouldn't have to be up there alone. She could work from the top and the bottom of the house toward the middle.

"Attic?" He looked wary.

"You don't want to?"

"No. I just . . . It looks like it's going to be a nice day and all."

"Tomorrow," Allie said. "When I'm not so sore. I can't rake leaves and haul limbs today."

It was stuffy, dusty, and full to the brim. Allie's mother never threw anything away, it seemed. Neither had her father. Allie and Casey opened three windows, one of which Allie found unlatched, something that left her even more uneasy. The light wasn't that good, but she saw footprints. Still she and Casey had been walking around for a while by the time she thought to check.

She shoved that thought aside and decided to pitch her idea for the shelter to Casey, thinking he might open up to her about his own situation if she could turn the talk to runaways. She waited until he was sitting on the floor sorting through a box that so far had yielded nothing but old clothes, when she didn't think he was going anywhere fast, to say, "I was wondering if you could give me some advice?"

He shrugged, hardly looking up from his task. "Sure."

"I was thinking of what I could do with this house. It's too big for just me, and I was thinking about turning it into a shelter."

"Shelter?" He gave her a blank look.

"For teenagers. Runaways."

Still nothing. Allie tried again.

"It seems fitting," she said. "My sister ran away. I was thinking that maybe if she'd had someplace to go, someplace where she was safe, she might still be alive today."

"She's really dead?" he said, the first spark of interest she'd seen.

Allie nodded.

"I heard that. Around town . . ."

And the tale hadn't moved him in the least?

"You don't worry about that, Casey?"

"Huh?"

"That she died. She ran away from home and died."

Casey didn't say a thing, just looked at her as if he couldn't imagine what she was getting at. Could he be that oblivious to the danger he faced?

"Would you come to a place like this?" she tried. "If you could get a hot meal and a shower and a bed to sleep in?"

He laughed then. "Allie, I have a place to go."

"You do?"

"I'm not a runaway," he claimed, then shrugged easily. "Not really."

How could one "not really" be a runaway, she wondered? "You're just . . . what? Sight-seeing?"

"Something like that," he claimed, seeming amused.

She was seriously annoyed, honestly worried about him and trying to help him. If anything happened to him, she'd never forgive herself. She'd just have to find another way to reach him. Maybe she would take a few psychology courses. It had to be so much more interesting than accounting and so much more useful to her once she got the shelter up and running.

She gave up for the moment on getting Casey to talk to her. They'd filled six boxes with trash, four with items to donate to Goodwill, when the phone rang. Allie ran downstairs to answer it.

"Hi," Stephen said. "I wanted to see you last night, but it was late before I finished work and I didn't see any lights on your house."

"I went to bed early," she said, then sighed.

She was ridiculously happy just to hear his voice, and yet not a day ago, she'd been so angry with him, so hurt. But she still wasn't sure if she trusted him, either, and she didn't know how to reconcile that with the warmth flooding through her at the moment.

Oh, hell. Who was she kidding? There was no way to reconcile the two. It made no sense at all to like him so much, yet not trust him.

"I like you, Stephen," she blurted out, thinking she might as well lay it out there on the table for them to deal with. "I want to run to you with every little piece of information I find, every time anything at all upsets me—"

"You don't think I'd object to any of that, do you?"

"No. It's not that . . ." She struggled to explain. "It's just too easy. You know that, don't you?"

"What's too easy?"

"Being with you," she admitted. That was the problem. She was trying to be cautious and careful, and it was simply too easy, felt too good, to be with him.

That obviously pleased him because he laughed, the warm, rich sound already imprinted in her memory. She loved hearing him laugh.

"You're supposed to let me help you, Allie, remember?"

"Because of a promise you made Megan years ago?"

"There's more to it than that, and you know it."

Allie turned around and looked out the window, toward his house, wondering if he was standing there watching her, wondering just how dangerous this man could be to her.

"I told myself this is too complicated, that I should back off," he said in that deep, slow, sexy voice of his. "It doesn't seem to matter. And you feel the same way. You just told me so."

She closed her eyes, squeezing them shut, ran a hand through her hair. If this was an act, the man was good. So good.

Please, she thought, *let this be real.*

"Allie . . ." He said it like he ached. *For her.*

Of course, she could be wrong about that. He could feel sorry for her. He could feel guilty and be thinking he had a lot to make up to her sister. Or he could feel a genuine desire to try to make things better for her, because he truly cared about her. She had no way of knowing.

"I'm coming over there," he said.

"Don't, Stephen. Please," she begged, all her instincts telling her she was going to get hurt again, and she really didn't need that. "I'm confused enough as it is."

"Is that all it is? Because you sound . . . I don't know. Is anything wrong?"

"No more than usual," she said, managing a bit of laughter to soften the words. "And that reminds me . . . Is your brother the governor?"

"Yes."

"You didn't tell me that."

"Does it matter?"

"Stephen, he's your brother."

"I took you to meet my horse. That should tell you where Rich ranks with me."

Allie laughed. "You like your horse more than your brother?"

"I enjoy my horse much more than my brother, although if you ever repeated that to any member of the local media, my father would kill me."

"Oh?"

"Rich is running for reelection."

"Oh." That explained it, she supposed.

"Do you really care that my brother's the governor?"

"No, I was just surprised."

"One of my uncles is a U.S. Senator, if that matters. Anything else you want to know?"

"Not at the moment."

"Good. Now I have something I want to tell you. You don't have to go through this alone, Allie. You know that, right?"

Her heart gave a little lurch. It said, *What's so great about going slowly anyway?* The idea that she wasn't in this all by herself. That there was someone else who cared. She couldn't have done this without him. She'd probably have fled that first night when the electricity went out and darkness settled in around her. As she saw it, it had never been a good thing to need anyone too much. It set up expectations in her mind that so far no one had been able to meet.

They'd all disappointed her in some way. Stephen might well disappoint her more than anyone if the way she responded to him already was any indication.

God, what was she going to do now?

"Can I come over now?" he asked.

She laughed, because he was persistent, but he managed to do it in a way that didn't leave her feeling like he was walking all over her, like her mother had.

"Don't you have a job to do?" she said instead. "Things to buy and sell today?"

"I've been here since seven and spent all morning buying something."

"Oh. Well, buy something else. I'm busy."

"Doing what?"

"Cleaning out the attic. You wouldn't believe how much stuff is up there."

"I'll help you with it this evening," he offered.

"I found help," she said. "Someone with a nice, strong back."

His voice was a bit rougher, a tad impatient. "Anybody I know?"

"I don't know. His name is Casey Adams."

"I don't think I know anyone named Adams."

"What about Patricia Adams? On Dogwood Lane?"

"That would be his . . . wife?"

"No." She laughed and told him what she knew about Casey, what she suspected.

"Wait a minute. You're in the house with this kid, and you don't have any idea who he is?" he asked, sounding exasperated. "And you don't believe anything he's told you about himself?"

"He's a kid, Stephen. A hungry, scared kid."

"And he's probably six inches taller than you and outweighs you by at least fifty pounds. Come on, Allie. You know better than this, don't you?"

"I like him. He's just a kid, and I want to help him."

Stephen swore. "I don't know of anybody in the neighborhood named Adams. Did you at least look in the phone book?"

"I will," she assured him.

"Do it now," he insisted, then called out something to the woman she thought must be his secretary.

Allie dutifully searched until she found the book. "There's no listing."

"My secretary checked with the phone company. I have a friend there. There's no Patricia Adams in this town."

"They might not have a phone."

"Maybe. Or maybe nothing the kid told you is true," Stephen said. "You think he's a runaway?"

"If he is, I don't think he's been on the streets long. He's doesn't seem tough enough to have been on his own for long."

"Allie, if he's a runaway, it's no telling what he might do to you."

"He's just a lost kid," she insisted. "Megan was like that once, Stephen. How can I not help this boy when at one time Megan was just like him."

Silence greeted her. She thought she could feel him glaring at her through the phone lines, but it wasn't entirely unpleasant to think about him worrying over her this way.

"He's not your sister," Stephen said.

"No, but I like having him here. I like that he showed up here now, when I'm making plans for a shelter. I think it's fitting. If I can help him, maybe I can help other kids, too. Maybe he can help me understand what kids like him need."

Again, Stephen said nothing. Allie remembered how opposed he was to her plans, and she found that odd. She didn't see him as an uncaring man. She would have sworn he had compassion for people less fortunate than he was. So it didn't fit—his being so skeptical of her plan for the shelter.

"I'm going to do some checking," he said finally. "Describe the kid to me."

She did.

"Could you at least try to be careful while he's around?" Stephen suggested. "Do you have a cordless phone?"

"Yes."

"Keep it with you. All the time. If anything out of the ordinary happens, call me. Or call 911."

"Stephen, this is ridiculous."

"You're the most trusting woman on earth," he complained. "You let me into your house that first night, even though you live in the middle of nowhere, all alone. I could have been an ax murderer."

"You're the boy who lived next door to my family for the first nine years of my life."

"I could have grown up to be an ax murderer," he argued.

"You really are worried about me?"

"Of course I am."

She closed her eyes and thought, *Stop it. Just stop it.* He might as well have a direct line to her soul. He knew just how to get to her, right there.

No one had worried about her in the longest time, and she wanted to believe the kindness and concern were genuine. That he was a strong, determined man, and that he would know very well how to take care of a woman.

"You know, you don't have to stay there all by yourself. You could stay here," he offered.

"No." She knew better than that.

"I'm offering you a room, Allie. Nothing else."

She was tempted, but she knew better. She was going to prove she was capable of resisting him. "I'll be fine here."

"I'd feel better if you weren't there all alone."

"*You* would feel better?"

"Yes."

"And the world usually does what Stephen Whittaker wants?"

"Quite often, it does."

"Because you're always right?"

"I'm not sure if I should answer that," he said. "I'm pushing too fast?"

"Yes."

"One of my many faults."

"You have faults?"

"Don't think I'm going to list them for you. I'm trying to get you to like me, remember?"

"I do like you," she said softly. "Too much."

"Okay, that's better. Maybe my ego hasn't sustained a mortal wound."

"Your ego is quite healthy."

"Hey, it's taking a beating with you."

"I'm sure it will survive."

"I'm not," he claimed.

"And I don't know what to do with you," she confessed, then had to take a breath. "Not at all."

"You don't have to decide right this minute. Take some time. Think about it. I'm not going anywhere."

"All right," she said. "I will."

"I'll call you as soon as I find out anything about the boy," Stephen said. "Be careful."

"I will." Allie put the phone down, dutifully found the cordless phone, and kept it with her. Not because she was afraid of Casey. Because she promised Stephen she would. Because she liked the idea of him worrying over her a little. It made her feel warm inside. She could tell herself to be careful, to be smart, to put on the brakes. Now.

But she couldn't stop that little warm glow.

She and Casey were upstairs a few hours when she heard a vehicle pull into her driveway. She watched from the attic window as a man she didn't recognize climbed out of a beat-up pickup and walked toward the front door.

"We've got company," she said to Casey.

"Who?" He looked worried.

"Maybe the house inspector."

"House inspector?"

"I hired someone to come look over the house. He's going to give me an idea of what needs to be done to the house, to fix it up. You know, for the shelter we talked about," she reminded him. "Grab a box, okay? We might as well start hauling some of this stuff down."

Allie set her box down in the entranceway as the doorbell rang. She opened the front door and found a man who looked to be in his fifties standing there. He wore coveralls stained with paint, a T-shirt, and work boots, and he looked taken aback. In fact, he looked a little like Stephen had that first night.

"Hi, I'm Alicia Bennett," she said. "Are you Mr. Reynolds?"

The man shook his head, looking bewildered, then whispered, "You sure do look like your mother."

Allie smiled gently, because the man had a kind face, weathered and worn, but kind. "Did you know her well?"

"Oh, Lord," he said, sounding shaken. "We went through school together. You've got her smile. I hope you don't mind my saying so. Somebody told me she passed away not long ago."

"Two months ago," Allie said.

"I'm awful sorry to hear that, little lady. I thought the world o' your mother."

She held out her hand to him. "Please, call me Allie."

He took off his cap and shook her hand. "I'm Tucker Barnes. Sorry I didn't introduce myself right off."

"It's all right," Allie assured him, wondering where she'd heard the name before. From her mother, she supposed.

She turned to Casey and introduced him to Mr. Barnes. Tucker stared at Casey. Casey backed away and said, "I'm going to finish bringing those boxes downstairs, Allie."

"Thanks." When he was out of earshot, she turned back to Tucker. "Do you recognize him?"

"Can't say for sure." Tucker sighed. "You say he lives around here?"

"That's what he told me.

The old man stood there in the doorway, not taking his eyes off Casey, who brought two more boxes downstairs, then disappeared again.

"Adams, you said?"

"Yes."

"I don't know anybody named Adams," he said finally.

Odd, Allie thought. This was so odd. "Mr. Barnes?—"

"Tucker," he said. "Everybody calls me Tucker."

"What can I do for you?"

"I just wanted to come by and tell you how sorry I was to hear about your mother, and tell you if there's anything I can do to help you close up the house or fix it up—whatever—you just call me." He handed her a slightly creased business card from his shirt pocket. "I paint. I hang Sheetrock. Do a little electrical work. Whatever. Won't charge you nothing but the paint or the materials, either. I figure I owe it to your mother. So you just give me a call. I'd be happy to help."

Allie took the card. "Thank you."

And with that, the man was gone.

She stood at the front door watching him leave. She wasn't afraid of him, just confused, intrigued. That had to be one of the oddest conversations she'd had since coming back to Dublin, and that was saying a lot.

Martha got home late, finding Tucker at her kitchen table. More often than not, he was there when she came home, although he didn't officially live with her. They didn't have that kind of relationship, probably never would. But it was more than Martha ever had with any other man. Maybe one day, she would convince herself it was enough.

Tucker kept a room in a house across town, although he didn't spend much time in it. He was usually keeping Martha's bed warm, eating her food, taking care of her. He wasn't a moocher, looking for a willing woman and a cook and a housekeeper and a free place to stay. He paid her money toward the rent and bought the groceries and took her out every now and then. He was better to her than any man she ever had, but he didn't love her.

He'd never made any promises to her, except that he would never love her and never lie to her, and Martha didn't think he'd ever broken either promise.

He didn't drink much, either. A cold beer or two after work, but Martha didn't consider that "drinkin'." Drinkin' involved downing too much, too fast, getting mean and smartin' off, saying things to hurt people, or maybe taking a hand to someone.

Tucker didn't do any of that.

So for him to be sitting at the table with a bottle of Jack Daniel's in front of him, something had to be wrong. He eyed her as warily as the half-empty glass in his hand when she walked in and sat down at the table without saying a word. Asking wouldn't do any good, she'd found. Tucker would tell her when he was good and ready. To push him only made him mad, and she'd always worried that if she ever made him mad enough, he'd take off and never come back. So she'd learned to stay quiet when something was troubling him.

Finally Tucker emptied the glass and said, "I went to see her."

Martha didn't have to ask who he meant. "Did you tell her who you were?"

"Just that I was a friend of her mother's since we were little kids. I offered to help her, if she needed anything done to the house."

Martha waited. None of that sounded *so* bad. And what did she have to be worrying about anyway? Janet Bennett was dead and buried. She couldn't take

Tucker away from Martha, although Janet's memory was what kept him from loving Martha. And that hurt. It made her angry, but she tried not to get all bent out of shape about it, because Janet was gone. Martha wasn't going to waste her time being jealous of a memory.

"Have you seen the boy?" Tucker said.

"What boy?" Martha asked.

"There was this boy at the house with her. A scruffy-looking teenager. You know, with those stupid lookin' pants that are too big, the kind you can't even walk in without steppin' on 'em, and a ratty T-shirt and funny hair."

"All the kids look like that now, Tuck."

"But you don't know this boy, do you? When she was in town, did she have this boy with her?"

"I didn't see her with anybody," Martha said. "Why? What's so special about this boy?"

"She said he was some neighborhood kid helping her around the house, acted like she didn't even know who he is, but that can't be right. I don't know why she'd try to hide it, but . . ." Tucker poured himself another drink and took a swallow. "He looks just like . . . like . . ."

He couldn't say her name. Well, maybe he could, but he didn't. Not if he could help it. It hurt Martha's feelings all over again. "Janet?" she asked. "This boy looks like Janet?"

Tucker nodded. "I thought she might have had a son. After she left here."

Martha nodded, understanding. That would upset Tucker, if his precious, long-lost love found someone else, if another man had fathered another child with her.

Feeling uncharacteristically old and bitter, Martha

wondered once again why Tucker hadn't taken off to find Janet years ago, when Janet had taken her daughter and left her husband and gone away. If he loved the woman so damned much, why hadn't he gone and found her then? Why had he stayed here waiting for her to come back?

Martha had watched him and wanted him for years, had waited patiently for him to get over the woman who'd broken his heart, the woman who made it impossible for him to ever love Martha.

So why hadn't he gone to find her? Martha almost asked him. She almost shouted it at him and ruined everything.

And then she got all sad and hurt and wisely kept quiet. She supposed it wasn't so hard to figure out why Tucker stayed where he was, waiting and hoping and making the best of things with Martha. After all, Martha did the same thing herself. She stayed right here with him, hoping all the time that he would come to love her someday. Maybe just a fraction as much as he'd loved Janet Bennett.

Allie and Casey gave up on the attic around six, and she offered to cook dinner for him, but he declined. Not wanting to let him go without some food, she professed a great desire for a foot-long chili dog and soft-serve ice cream, desires that could only be satisfied at a tiny Dairy Queen on the edge of town. She'd passed it the day before and remembered going there as a child. Finally, after she raved and raved about the food there, Casey agreed to go with her.

"You got to be kidding," he said as they pulled into the miniscule parking lot of the whitewashed, cinder-block building.

"No. The food's great."

"But . . ."

"It's always looked like this. It's always crowded. There's never enough room to park or hardly any place to sit down, but nobody cares. Because the chili dogs are fabulous. We're lucky they finally added a furnace to heat the place. It used to only open for a couple of months in the summer."

Casey still looked skeptical.

"Just wait," she said, standing in line at the window at the front of the building.

Allie had also wanted to come here because it used to be a teen hangout. She'd wondered if there were more kids like Casey in town and where they would be. And she was still certain Casey was a runaway, no matter what he said.

She ordered for him and for her, paid for their meal, and then slid to the right of the window to wait until the food was ready. There were groups of kids clustered around two of the picnic tables set up in the grass at the back of the parking lot and a few more clustered around various cars. Laughing, seemingly happy kids.

She searched their faces, finding herself reassured. They were okay. And then her gaze caught on a teenage girl, standing all alone near the back corner of the building. A girl with stringy hair that looked like it hadn't been washed in days and wrinkly, dingy-looking clothes. One with a hollow look in her eyes and a bit of a snarl on her face that seemed to dare anyone to try to get near her.

Allie must have been lost in thought, looking at the girl, because the next thing she knew, Casey put a bag of food and a drink in her hand. She led him back to the car, since there was no place else to eat.

They set their drinks on the hood and carefully dug into the chili dogs, which were indeed a foot long and not the easiest food in the world to eat.

"Not bad," he said after he swallowed the first mouthful.

"Told you." They were every bit as good as she remembered.

Allie let him plow through two of them, in what took maybe two minutes, before she pointed out the girl. "Do you know her?"

Casey shook his head back and forth.

"You haven't seen her around?"

"No."

"She just looks . . . lost. I wondered if she had a place to go."

"You're not gonna ask her, are you?"

"I don't know. I just . . . I wondered how she ended up here. All alone. I wondered what might have happened to make her think she was better off on her own, on the streets, instead of with her family. . . ."

She looked up at Casey, who seemed to be fighting a grin.

"You just don't give up, do you?"

"Actually, most of the time I do. I always have," she said with painful honesty. "It's one of the biggest regrets of my life."

"Well, you don't give up on this," he said. "And if this is about me, Allie, I swear, I'm fine. I've got a home. I've got a mother. She loves me a lot."

"But you're here. You're all alone, aren't you? You don't live two blocks away from my house."

He shrugged easily. "My mom and I had a fight. That's all."

"Must have been some fight."

"Yeah. It was. I wouldn't have taken off over just anything. I'm a good kid. But this was somethin' big. Somethin' important. I did what I had to do."

"Running isn't going to solve anything," Allie insisted.

"Sure it is. Anyway, I'm not running away from anything. I'm running to somethin'. There's somethin' I have to find out, and I couldn't do it at home."

"Something worth risking your life?"

"Allie—"

"I know. You think you're indestructible. All kids do. And it just isn't true. Believe it or not, your mother does know some things, and you should listen to her."

"I do," he insisted. "Most all the time, I do."

"I think you made a mistake," she said, even though she risked alienating him all together.

Maddeningly calm, he shrugged again. "I don't."

"And I think you should go home."

"I will. When I've found out what I need to know."

"Have you called your mother, at least?"

"Nope."

"Casey, she has to be worried half to death."

"She doesn't even know I'm gone."

Allie gaped at him. "You're kidding?"

He shook his head back and forth, the amusement returning.

"How can she not know? You said she's a good mother. You said she loves you. . . ."

"She does."

"You're not making any sense at all," Allie argued.

"It's complicated. But I've got it under control. Really."

Allie wanted to tear his hair out. Or maybe hers.

He seemed absolutely oblivious to the danger he was in—a kid on his own, who claimed to have a perfectly good home to go to. She wondered about that part. He didn't seem like a hotheaded kid. He'd been polite and well mannered, a hard worker, no trouble at all except for his stubborn insistence that he was perfectly safe by himself on the streets. So why had he left?

"Your mom . . ." she began. "She really treats you well?"

"Yes."

"She doesn't drink?"

"No."

"Do drugs?"

"No, Allie."

"She doesn't . . . hurt you?"

"No." He did laugh then. "We're not exactly the Brady Bunch. It's just me and my mom, but that's okay. We're tight, you know?"

Allie shook her head sadly. She didn't know.

"I've always known she'd be there for me. No matter what. If I get into trouble here, I could call her today, and she'd be here tomorrow—"

"Assuming you had a chance to make that call. That she could get here fast enough to save you," Allie pointed out.

"She'd get here. She'd do whatever it took. She'd yell and stuff about me taking off, but she'd get over it. Because she loves me. We do that me-and-her-against-the-world stuff." He frowned. "That used to be a song, right?"

"I think so," Allie said.

"She used to sing that to me when I was little," he admitted, blushing a bit. "And it's pretty corny, but . . . that's the way it is with us. She'll never let me down, you know?"

"No," Allie said. "I don't know."

"Really? You and your mom?" He fumbled with the words. "You didn't—"

"No." Allie cut him off.

"Your dad?"

"Never saw him again after my mother and I left when I was nine."

"He just didn't want to see you?"

"That's what my mother said."

"You never asked him?"

"No," she admitted.

"So, when you were talking about giving up . . . You were talking about that?"

"Among other things, yes." Allie frowned. "But we weren't talking about my problems. We were talking about yours."

Casey just grinned at her. Allie wanted to hug him, but fought the urge. She didn't think teenage boys appreciated those kinds of things.

"You think you don't have a problem, do you?"

"Nope."

"Casey—"

"Allie, if you need to take care of someone else today, why don't you go buy that girl some food," he suggested. "I know you won't leave until you do."

Allie frowned. He was right. She was going to buy this girl dinner. But she wanted more than that.

"Casey, I want you to help me with the shelter. I need to talk to someone who knows kids, someone who can help me understand them, can help me plan a place where they'd feel comfortable. A shelter they'd use."

"I've never stayed in a runaway shelter, Allie. I've

never needed to. I don't know what I can say to make you believe me about that, but it's the truth."

Allie didn't know what to say, either. He seemed absolutely sincere and completely unmovable. She supposed it was possible this was a complete anomaly to him—to be here on his own like this. But why?

"I want to understand," she began. "Help me make sense of this—"

"Let's make a deal," he interrupted. "When you're ready to come clean with me about some stuff, I'll tell you all about me."

"Me? Come clean about what?"

"Everything."

"I don't know what you're talking about," she said.

He shrugged again, maddeningly nonchalant. "Then, neither do I."

"Casey?"

"I've had enough of this for today, Allie. I'm done."

And then he turned and walked away. Allie called out his name, fought the urge to run after him and grab him and make him explain. What in the world did he think she was keeping from him? She didn't have anything at all to hide, and the whole damned town seemed to know all of her business. He must; he'd certainly heard enough gossip based on the questions he'd asked her.

Feeling very sad and frustrated and at a total loss to understand the boy or what she'd done wrong, Allie stood there for a long time watching people come and go in the Dairy Queen parking lot.

There were lots of kids here, a few who seemed a bit lost, a bit wary, but only one—the girl she'd spotted in the beginning—who appeared to be in a truly troubling predicament. Casey was right about one thing—there was no way Allie could leave without making sure the girl had something to eat.

She walked back to the window at the front of the restaurant and ordered yet again, walked up to the girl, who glared at Allie with each step she took, and then handed the girl the bag of food.

In the end Allie didn't try to ask her anything at all. She realized she wasn't ready. She didn't know how to deal with teenagers like Casey or this girl yet. She had a lot to learn.

Night classes, she thought. UK wasn't that far away. Neither was Eastern in Richmond. She'd take some classes at night—adolescent psychology and things like that—and worry about zoning issues and fund-raising and renovations to her house during the day.

It seemed more daunting than ever before. She was finding out how little she actually knew about all the things she would have to do to make this project work. But she was every bit as determined as before. More determined, even.

She was worried about Casey and this girl and all of the others she hadn't even found yet, and she felt a sense of urgency. The kids were out here, and she had to help them. Before anyone else died like her sister had.

Allie was curled up on her sofa that night making yet another list of things she needed to do. She supposed that was progress. Figuring out all the things she didn't know about starting and running a shelter. It gave her a starting point, at least. A course of action.

She'd called and requested course listings for the

upcoming terms at the University of Kentucky and Eastern Kentucky University. She'd talked to Holly again about the academic qualifications and work experience of the people who worked at the shelter in Connecticut and the kinds of courses Holly felt had helped her most of all in dealing with the kids there.

Holly suggested Allie talk to local social workers, police officers, and even judges to find out more about how many runaways were in the area. What the social services system had to offer them. What the kids needed most. What would be most helpful to them.

Allie dutifully added that to her growing list. She'd start with Mr. Webster, she decided. He would likely have names. She'd start there.

She was prioritizing items on her list when shortly after eight, the phone rang. It was Greg.

"I think we're getting somewhere," he said. "I went back to the trooper. He told me they had a group of runaways in town that winter, living in an old barn east of town—"

"A barn?"

"Yeah." Greg sighed. "I know."

"It was February," she said. "It's cold in Georgia in February."

"They had a roof over their heads, Allie. A lot of runaways don't."

"Okay. I'm sorry, I just never imagined my sister living in a barn." God, Allie hated the thought.

"It turns out one of the boys in the group staying at the barn that winter ended up living in town for a while after the others left. A guy named Mitch Wilson. Seemed like a pretty responsible kid, from what I've heard. I was thinking he might be able to tell us what was going on with Megan back then."

"Great. Is he still there?"

"No. He's in Kentucky. Odd coincidence, isn't it? Did Megan know anyone named Mitch Wilson?"

"I don't think so. I don't remember the name."

"From what I've found out so far, he was born and raised in Michigan, but, as I said, it's odd that he'd meet Megan in Georgia as a teenage runaway and end up living so close to her hometown."

"He's in Dublin?"

"Lexington. If it's the same Mitch Wilson, he owns a restaurant and bar just off Vine Street in downtown."

"Have you talked to him?"

"Not yet. I will, if you want me to. I'll come up there and do it in person, when I'm done here."

"No, I'll do it," she said. She wanted to look the man in the face when she asked him about Megan.

"Okay." He gave her the address and phone number. "I'll stay here. I want to talk to my doctor friend. Allie, if it's all right with you, I'd like to tell the doctor I'm working on behalf of Megan's sister. Maybe he'll open up to me, if he knows you're the one looking for information."

"All right. Do it," Allie said.

"I'll call you, as soon as I know anything else."

She thanked him and hung up the phone, thinking of a man named Mitch Wilson and what he might be able to tell her about her sister's last days. She thought about the fact that she'd always had a roof over her head and enough to eat, while her sister, at one time, had lived in a barn in February, and there were certainly runaways living in worse conditions.

Not here, Allie decided. It wouldn't happen in this town. Not anymore.

Chapter 9

Stephen called her at the crack of dawn the next morning. Five minutes after she turned on the light in the family room, to be exact. She asked if he was spying on her, and he claimed it took no effort at all. All he had to do was look out his bedroom window. Allie fought off a hint of unease. If he wanted to spy on her, he was in a perfect position to do so. She was getting more paranoid with each passing day.

He claimed he wanted her to spend the morning with him, that he had something else he wanted to show her, something he hinted was connected to the shelter.

Allie sighed. She'd lasted an entire day and a half in her resolve to keep some distance between them, and she'd missed him terribly. Which should have told her how much trouble she was in where he was concerned.

But if he wanted to, he could help her so much with the shelter. She believed she could win him over to her side. Maybe she'd already done so. After all, he had something to show her. For the sake of the shelter, she absolved herself of her vow to stay away from him and agreed to go with him, felt not quite so guilty when she realized they were heading for

Lexington once again. Mitch Wilson's restaurant was in downtown Lexington. Maybe Stephen would help her find it. Maybe he'd go with her to talk to the man.

Allie was surprised when Stephen drove her to an old brick building. It wasn't the best of neighborhoods, but not the worst, either. He led her to the front door and produced a key.

The building was vacant, and once she was inside, she could tell by the setup that it had once been a school. A former school for the blind, he said, housing thirty-five students and several staff members.

"It has an industrial-sized kitchen," he said. "Enough exits to meet the fire codes, a nice-sized courtyard in the back, and I don't think anyone would give you much trouble over the zoning."

"You want me to put the runaway shelter here?"

He nodded.

Allie looked around the building once again, seeing something that reeked of the word "institution." She hated it. It was absolutely wrong, absolutely the opposite of what she envisioned.

"This isn't right, Stephen."

He ignored that and went right on. "The guy bought it four years ago for a song, probably betting the neighborhood was going to get a lot better than it has. Right now he has a fortune sunk into a condominium project off Tates Creek Road and a permit to develop this that's expiring within the next six months. I think if you give it some time, maybe a few months, you could pick this up for next to nothing."

"It's not a house. It's not Megan's house," she explained. Surely he could see her point. Aside from her sentimental attachment to the house in which she grew up, he had to see that no one would ever feel at home here. Allie knew what it meant to long for a place to belong, for a home, and maybe her judgment wasn't what it should be on this subject. But she knew what she'd wanted all her life, and she imagined she knew what kids desperate enough to run away wanted, too. They wanted a home.

"Let's look at some other variables. To staff a runaway shelter, you need a volunteer base and a lot of money, a community big enough to support it. Dublin can't do that."

"You think the only people who'd support a runaway shelter in Dublin are the people who live there?"

"For the most part, yes," he said, sounding maddeningly sure of himself. "People take care of their own. Their town, their backyard, their neighbors' needs."

"True, but—"

"Dublin has a population of less than ten thousand," he said. "Have you made an operating budget yet?"

"No," she said, although she had talked to the shelter director in Connecticut again and knew the financial commitment was staggering. She'd known Dublin was small, but less than ten thousand residents? Only a fraction of those would contribute to charity in any significant amounts, and she hadn't gotten as far as thinking of volunteer staff, either. Mostly she hated that he was coming at her with calm, cool logic. She'd been utterly logical her entire life.

"I know it's not what you envisioned." Stephen came to stand right in front of her and took her by the arms. "But I think you could make this work."

"I'm not ready to give up on the house. Not yet."

"You want to make the project work?"

"Of course I do."

"Okay. This is my job, Allie. I know what I'm talking about. You have to be careful with any big project. You want to think it through, anticipate objections, find ways to overcome them, before you ever go public with your plans."

Allie stared at him, not sure if he was right or if she was just very, very wrong. "I get the feeling you're taking over—"

"Sorry." He grinned a bit. "It's in my genes, I'm afraid."

"Whittakers tend to take over, too?"

"Goes along with thinking we're always right."

"You mean you *have* to be right. That you don't enjoy losing."

"Who could possibly *enjoy* losing?" he said in all seriousness.

Allie frowned, thinking it was a quality that could be admirable, but also seriously annoying when she happened to disagree with him. And she had a funny feeling about this. That there was more going on than he'd admitted.

"I'm sorry," he said, backing down. "I came on too strong. It's an instinct I try to curb outside of business. This just feels like business to me. It's what I do. I know what I'm talking about when it comes to planning a project, to siting it, to getting all the approvals, to finding the money."

"I know, and I appreciate what you're trying to do, Stephen. Maybe the whole project is just too personal to me—"

"It is."

"And I can't be as objective as I should be. I admit that."

He nodded.

"You're starting to really annoy me," she warned.

He just grinned.

"This just isn't what I want for the shelter," she said. "It practically screams institution."

"Okay. I understand. But will you do one thing for me? Before you go announcing any kind of plans about turning your old house into a shelter—"

"I haven't made any announcement."

"You don't have to. Not in a town the size of Dublin. Walking into the zoning commission's office was probably enough to get news out. But just in case the whole town isn't talking about it yet, will you just take some time? Think about some of the things I've said? You might not agree with me now, but in time, I think you'll see . . ."

"That you're right?"

He nodded.

"Stephen, we talked about this. You don't enjoy it, but sometimes even you have to admit that you might be wrong."

"I'm not wrong about this," he insisted.

"I don't think I like you like this," she complained.

"The whole idea was to make you like me before you saw this side of me," he claimed. "And I'm giving you good advice, Allie."

"Maybe," she conceded, growing more uneasy by the minute. "But why are you so insistent about this? You don't even want me to *talk* about the shelter with anyone yet?"

"I think it would be better if you didn't."

"Why? What do you think's going to happen?"

"I'm nervous about the letter you got," he admitted. "I think it would be best if you kept quiet about everything for a while."

"That's it?"

He looked decidedly uneasy. She felt like the whole situation was about to take a bizarre turn, one she wouldn't like.

"What's going on here?" she asked softly.

"I don't know. That's why I want you to be careful."

"Why do I think you do know, Stephen? Why do I think there's so much more to this than you're telling me?"

She thought about it, how he just wouldn't let go of this, how he kept pushing when it came to the shelter. Everything came back to her sister. It always had. Why Megan left, why she stayed away. Stephen didn't want Allie telling people about the shelter, didn't want people talking about it. What did he think she'd hear? What did he know?

"Have you told me everything you know about Megan's disappearance?"

One look into his eyes, and she knew. Dammit, she knew.

"God," she said. "I don't believe you."

She shoved past him and headed down the hall. He followed her, stopping her at the front door, his arm extended, palm flat against the door, effectively trapping her between his body and the door.

"Just listen to me, Allie."

"I have listened to you, and what have you told me? You told me about all these things you just don't know—"

"I don't."

She felt so stupid, so very stupid. "And now you want me to listen while you spin some more lies for me?"

"I haven't lied to you." He slipped an arm around

her from behind, drawing her gently against him and wrapping his arms around her waist, the back of her body flush against the front of his. He was a tall man, broad through the shoulder, his arms strong and powerful, his touch ever so gentle.

"You drove my sister out of town the day she disappeared, and you didn't tell me. People suspected you'd done away with her, and you didn't tell me that, either."

"I didn't tell you everything I knew, but I didn't lie to you. I won't."

"And you think there's a difference?" She shoved back against him, to dislodge him, so she could open the door, but he held her fast.

"Listen to me," he whispered, his lips against her ear. "I can help you. I can figure this thing out, if you'll just give me a little time. I want the answers, too, Allie."

"You?"

"Yes, me. I cared about your sister." He turned her to face him. "Not like *that*. I never saw her as anything but a girl who'd always lived next door to me. That's it. And I've felt guilty about her death for years. So if there's anything to find out, I want to do it."

"And what am I supposed to do?" she said. "Wait for you to take care of everything?"

"I'd feel better if you did."

"It so happens I don't give a damn how you feel."

"You'd be safer that way, Allie."

"And your big concern here is my safety?"

"Yes."

"No. You just want me to be quiet and not ask any questions that make you uncomfortable."

"I'm not the one you have to worry about," he insisted.

"Then who? If I'm in such danger, tell me who I'm supposed to be so afraid of?"

"I don't know," he said.

"Of course." Allie laughed. "How did I know you were going to say that? You know I'm in danger, so much so that I shouldn't even ask any questions about anything to do with my sister, but you don't know who's out to get me."

"I don't. If I did, I could deal with it. But right now, I don't know, and I'm worried about you. Could we leave it at that, please?"

"No, *we* couldn't," she shot back.

"Allie—"

"Tell me," she said.

"I won't."

"What?"

"I won't. I can't."

Allie gaped at him, fury rushing through her. The next second her palm connected solidly with the side of his face, the sound echoing through the corridor. The blow turned his head to the left. Her handprint came up red on his cheek, and for another long minute, they just stared at each other.

She couldn't believe what she'd done. She didn't think she'd ever struck another human being in her entire life, and yet she was still furious enough to want to do it again. She'd believed him! About everything!

"Tell me," she said. "Dammit, just tell me!"

Her hand came up again, and he caught her by the wrist to keep her from landing another blow. She struggled against him for a minute, frustrated beyond belief and started yelling.

"Stop it! Allie, stop it!"

He was much stronger than she was. There was no way to fight him and win, though she kept struggling against him, pointless as it was. To her horror, it wasn't long before she felt hot, angry tears running down her cheeks. When she was too weak to fight him any longer, he pulled her into his arms.

"Oh, God," she said, trembling, her knees going weak. "I can't believe I did that."

"It's all right. I deserved it."

Stephen's lips found the side of her face, stringing soft kisses along her cheekbone and her brow. Despite all her resolve, Allie sagged against him, exhausted and spent.

"I'm sorry," he said.

Was he? Too stunned at the moment, she couldn't begin to judge. She'd never lost control like that, never been quite that mad. Because she'd trusted him. She'd told him things she'd never told anyone else, believed in him, and now she felt like she didn't even know him. He didn't understand her at all. Not if he could do this.

"You just don't know . . ." she said.

"What? What don't I know?"

"How awful it is for me to be here. To remember all these things. I've been running from the truth my whole life, Stephen. You're right. I'm scared of it, too. And being here is tearing me apart."

"Okay," he soothed. "I'm sorry."

Allie lifted her head from his shoulder, and a moment later his mouth was on hers. She couldn't have been more surprised, couldn't deny him anything, it seemed. She opened herself up to him so easily, gave herself over to the smooth, slow-building heat between them. He kissed her as if they had all the time in the world, as if he knew just what he was doing, just where he wanted to take her. Maybe he did, she thought. Maybe this was all part of his plan to keep from telling her anything just yet. Maybe he knew how easily he could distract her with his touch.

Poor, little Allie, all alone in the world and scared. Starved for another human being's touch. For a bit of gentle concern. For strong arms around her, so she wouldn't be so afraid. Every bit of that was true, she acknowledged bitterly, pulling away from him. She saw dark, compelling eyes looking down at her, little lines of tension at the corners of his eyes and his mouth, a grim set to his jaw.

"I'm sorry," he said bleakly. "And I truly don't want you to get hurt."

"Stephen, I've lived my whole life with someone who wouldn't tell me anything, all in the name of protecting me."

"Allie." He reached for her again.

"Don't." She held up both hands to ward him off. "Not anymore. Not today."

"If you could just trust me a little bit, I could find the truth for you."

"That would be a first," she said wearily, bitterly. "No one else has ever told me the truth."

He reached for her one last time, but Allie slipped out the door and ran into the street. She got lucky. There was a cab, and she slid into it. It pulled away from the curb just as he came outside, and she couldn't help but watch him, standing there watching her, until the cab turned a corner and he disappeared from her sight.

God, help me, she prayed. There was still a part of her that wanted to believe every word that came out of his beautiful mouth. Another part just as determined not to let go of any of this. Not her need to find out what happened to her sister, not her determination to make the shelter work.

She just didn't know how she was going to come out of it with a whole heart.

Stephen stood at the curb, swearing as he watched the cab pull away and disappear from sight. He couldn't believe he'd so thoroughly lost control of the situation.

The woman was giving him fits, nearly as much as the situation. The private investigator digging into her sister's so-called accident, the mysterious letter writer, the fact that she was in that house. It was no telling what she might find there. And she was remembering. He hadn't been able to get his father to say exactly what might be inside Allie's head for her to recall. She would not let go of the idea of turning her house into a runaway shelter, and now there was the mysterious boy who showed up at her house.

Casey Adams didn't exist, as far as Stephen could determine. So who the hell was he? Stephen tried to reassure himself that his father wouldn't have sent a kid to deal with Allie. Still, the whole thing made him uneasy as hell.

And now Allie didn't trust Stephen at all.

He swore yet again. He'd just wanted to stop this shelter idea before it got out. Before his father heard about it. That's all he meant to do today.

And he'd blown it.

He raked a hand through his hair and wondered how one woman could so thoroughly throw him off balance. Could make him feel so guilty and at the same time . . . he liked her. He genuinely liked her.

He'd told her things he'd never told anyone. About being lonely. About knowing he'd been a grave disappointment to his father his entire life.

Which made it even worse that he couldn't tell her the things that truly mattered here: that his father was under the distinct impression that Stephen was working for him right now, that Allie was a little problem Stephen was *handling*. That Stephen was starting to fear that if someone was responsible for her sister's death, it was someone named Whittaker.

Allie sat in the cab with tears streaming down her face. Thankfully the driver pretended not to notice. He kept his gaze firmly on the road ahead and inquired politely about where she'd like to be taken. She looked around and realized they were near downtown. Mitch Wilson's restaurant and bar were near downtown.

"Vine Street?" she said. "I'm not sure of the street number, but the restaurant is called Mitch's on Vine."

"Sure thing, miss."

Glancing at her watch, she saw that it wasn't quite seven and doubted they'd be open, unless they catered to the fancy coffee and bagel crowd. Allie decided to try it anyway.

His restaurant was pretty, full of polished wood and all sorts of greenery. It wasn't open, but she caught an employee going inside, and the man let Allie in and offered to find Mitch for her.

Allie was standing by the front window, staring out into the street, when she heard footsteps coming up behind her and a man said, "Can I help you?"

She turned around and said, "Mitch Wilson?"

"Yeah. What can I . . ." All the color drained from his handsome face. He went stark still and closed his eyes for a moment. With equal parts of disbelief and hope, he looked at her again and said one word. "Megan?"

Allie shook her head back and forth and took a step closer to him, so he could see her more clearly. "I'm her sister. Allie."

He gaped at her, leaning back against the bar, as if he were too weak to stand. He was a tall man, handsome, broad-shouldered, dark-haired, dark-eyed, and at the moment she guessed, unusually pale.

"You knew her in Georgia, fifteen years ago, didn't you?"

He didn't say a word, just struggled to breathe.

"I need to know what happened to her there," Allie said. "And what happened to her here, too. If you know anything about that."

"You're telling me you don't know?"

"No." Allie shook her head. "We never knew much about the car accident. Or if my parents knew, they didn't tell me, and they're both dead now. And I was so young when she ran away from here."

"She didn't say much about this place," he said. "And I learned to stop asking questions about her a long time ago."

"What do you mean you learned to stop asking questions about her?"

He turned his head to the right and fingered the long, faint scar running down the side of his jaw. "I learned my lesson."

"Someone did that to you?" Allie couldn't believe it.

The man nodded.

"When?"

"A few months after she died."

"Because you were asking questions about Megan?"

He nodded.

"Oh, my God. Who?"

"He didn't give his name, just sent a couple of his friends to deliver his message. Megan was dead and buried. End of story."

"I don't understand."

"Neither did I," he said, his face impassive.

"So, you just let it go? Just like that?"

"Those men put me in the hospital," he said. "They said the next time, they'd put me in the morgue, and I tended to believe them."

"But—"

"Like they said, Megan was dead. I decided to let her go."

"You thought they were going to kill you?" Allie thought that was what he meant, but she had to hear it for herself in order to believe it.

"Yes," he said.

"Oh, my God," she whispered. Despite all the odd things—the mysterious letter, the fact that someone else was looking through the records and the doctor who seemed to be lying—it was hard to believe anyone would threaten to kill someone because he was asking questions about her sister's death.

Allie watched with wide eyes as Mitch came closer. He put his hand to her face. She trembled, but stood her ground.

"Judging by the resemblance, I don't think there's anyone you could be but Megan's sister. And I'd like to help you, but I've got to wonder if this is a test?"

"Test?"

"To see if I forgot that I'm not supposed to talk about Megan," he said. "People are asking questions about me in Macon after all this time, and I don't like it."

"I hired a private detective," she said. "He's there. Someone wrote my mother a letter. I guess they didn't know she was dead. They said they had questions about Megan's accident and information they were willing to share."

"What kind of information?"

"I don't know. I traced the letter back to a man in Georgia who claimed to know nothing at all about it."

"What man? What was his name?"

Allie took a breath and said, "I don't think I'm going to tell you. Not if you don't have anything you can tell me. But . . . you don't have to worry about the man in Macon asking questions. He's working for me, and we don't have people beaten up for refusing to talk to us."

"I'm sure I'll sleep better at night knowing that."

"I'm her sister," Allie said, ready to beg. "I just want to know what happened to her, that she was okay those last few months. Anything . . ."

"She was scared," he said.

"Of what?"

"You tell me. You were here."

"I don't know," she cried. "I don't."

His gaze narrowed on her. He hesitated, then said, "If you're asking questions about her, you should watch your back, even if it has been fifteen years. She was terrified of someone back here. She thought he followed her all the way to Macon. She thought she saw him the day before she died."

"You think someone murdered my sister? Someone from here?"

"Watch your back," he said, and left her standing there, dizzy and hot all over and more scared than she'd ever been in her life.

Chapter 10

In a daze she caught another cab. Shivering, she sat there trying to imagine why anyone in the world would want to kill her sister. What kind of secrets could exist to push someone into making death threats against a man merely asking questions about Megan? It sounded like something out of a bad TV movie. She simply couldn't fathom it.

She also didn't want to consider that Stephen warned her of nearly the same thing Mitch Wilson had. She'd slapped Stephen's face for it, and had believed Mitch Wilson, a man she'd never even seen before. The scar had been convincing, along with the absolutely stunned look on his face when he first saw her. Maybe the way his hand had trembled when he'd touched her face, as if he couldn't quite believe she was real. Maybe the certainty with which she believed that at one time Mitch Wilson had been in love with her sister, that he might still be today. Had he come here seeking revenge on someone for her death? And he was leery even now, fifteen years later, simply talking about Megan and her so-called accident.

Who could have done it? Who could have hurt her sister? Who could have wanted her dead?

All too soon, the cab pulled to a stop in front of

the house. Allie didn't want to get out. She was starting to dread walking across the threshold. What in
the world happened inside that house? Steeling herself, she paid the driver and sent him away with her
thanks. She was relieved to see Casey on the porch,
her kitten in his arms.

"Hi," he said cautiously. "You okay?"

"I will be." Allie gave him a smile she felt must
have wavered badly. "And I'm so glad you're here."

She looked at the boy and the kitten, so grateful
not to be alone now and wondering why she hadn't
started taking in strays years ago. It was certainly
one way to keep from being alone. She could gather
people around her, rather than simply mourning the
loss of her family. She could build something here,
something lasting. Maybe she could help herself as
much as she could help Casey and other kids like
him.

One step at a time, she told herself. It might not
seem like it, but she was making progress. She would
let this thing with Megan play out. Sooner or later
the answers would come. She would make her plans
for the shelter, move on, build a life. Maybe, she'd
finally be happy.

For the moment she'd deal with what was at hand.
She fed Casey and the kitten, put him to work in the
attic so she could call Greg without Casey hearing
her end of the conversation. She passed along the
cryptic warning from Mitch Wilson. Greg promised
to dig a little deeper and again warned Allie to be
careful.

Waiting for her on the desk in the hallway was the
preliminary report from the home inspector who'd
come the day before. Glancing at it, she decided the
news was grim indeed. Outdated plumbing and elec-

trical systems, inadequate heating and air-condition-
ing, a roof that needed to be replaced, not counting
cosmetic work needed throughout. The rough esti-
mate was staggering.

She would deal with it, she vowed. There had to
be a way. If it simply took more money, she'd find
a way to raise it. Which reminded her—somewhere
in the middle of her argument with Stephen, he mentioned population figures. The library would have
statistics on population and personal income, as well
as information on past fund-raising events and how
successful they had been, even who had raised the
money and for what causes. She needed to know
who those people were, needed to try to win them
over to her side, so she could make this work.

Allie called the librarian, who remembered her,
and told her what she needed. The population and
income statistics were there and easily located. The
librarian also offered enough information on three
past fund-raisers—one for the town library itself and
two for the hospital—that Allie could pull newspaper
articles on those herself next time she was in town.

She hung up the phone feeling marginally better.
No matter how upsetting the morning had been,
she'd managed to take one more small step forward.
That was all she had to do. Just find the next step
and keep going.

She was mulling over her next move when a car
pulled into her driveway. Her heart kicked into high
gear, remembering that she was in an isolated spot
with nothing but an overgrown boy and a baseball
bat for protection, and now she was seriously afraid
to be here.

But the would-be intruder turned out to be a floral
delivery boy. He had an extravagant, but delicately

beautiful arrangement of cut flowers in pretty blues, pinks, and purples. She took the heavy crystal vase in one hand, tipped him, and locked the door behind him.

The scent of fresh flowers filled the entire foyer. Allie set them down on a small table in the family room and looked at the card. It said simply:

I'm sorry.
Stephen

Allie sighed, the hand that held the card still trembling. She didn't want to like him anymore. She didn't want her sense of fairness arguing on his behalf.

He'd told her he was almost always right, and it seemed he was. He'd scared her a bit this morning, his intensity, his determination. He'd scared her by making her wonder what in the world he knew that he didn't think he could tell her, and that still made her so angry. Who was he to keep things from her? Things about her own family?

Why would he do that? If he truly didn't have anything to do with Megan's disappearance . . . If he truly cared about her sister, but only as a friend . . . Could he want the answers as badly as Allie did? He said he did, and her gut instinct was to believe him on that point.

Still, he was keeping things from her. Why? The only reason she could think of was that he was protecting someone else. If not himself, then who? She'd seen evidence of that protective streak inside of him. She'd felt it directed at her and found it practically irresistible. To have such a strong, determined, capable man watching out for her, fighting for her, protecting her. She'd needed someone like that her whole life. She'd never known how much until she met him.

And it seemed Stephen was right once again—annoyingly right—when he said there truly was danger here. She didn't understand why he would be so dead-set against her plans for the shelter, but the hard truth was she couldn't refute any of his impossibly logical objections. Every one she'd checked out so far had proven true.

Allie swore softly and picked up a small, framed photo of her sister she'd placed on the table in the front hall. She might never understand Stephen Whittaker. She was tired and more confused than ever.

But she wanted so much to make the shelter work. She hadn't been able to help her sister years ago, but Allie was here now, a grown woman with a big old house and a big dream.

"Help me, Megan," she said. "Show me the way."

Her sister didn't magically appear. No more memories flooded her mind.

"Allie?" She jumped at the sound so close behind her, even though it was just Casey.

"Sorry," he said, looking at the photograph. "Is that your sister?"

Allie nodded.

"I know you said she ran away. . . ." He hesitated. "But some people . . ."

Allie groaned. "What did people tell you?"

"That real bad things must have happened to her here for her to take off like that and never come back."

"What bad things?" Obviously, she and her family were the highlights of the gossipmongers once again. Maybe all she had to do was send Casey to town to gather information for her. Maybe they would tell him more than they'd ever tell Allie to her face.

"I don't know." Casey shrugged and looked down at his big wide feet. "A couple of guys over at the pizza place told me your father must have . . . you know . . . gotten rid of her."

"Really?"

"Yeah. They said he strangled her and buried her body in the basement, and that's why the house's haunted."

It was so sad and so outrageous, she just stared at him for a moment. Then she started to laugh. The sound tumbled out of her with a momentum all its own, an odd, uncontrollable, woman-losing-it laugh, and she couldn't stop. People were saying her father killed her sister and hid her body in the basement?

"Sorry." Casey sat down beside her and awkwardly touched her arm. "I didn't mean to upset you."

She clamped a hand over her mouth and worked hard to slow her breathing, to get herself under control. When she could, she told him, "My father didn't murder my sister. She died in a car accident in Georgia."

Casey looked as if he didn't believe her.

"Look." She grabbed the newspaper articles from the desk. "Photocopies of stories about my sister and the accident."

Casey glanced at them, still looking skeptical.

"You still don't believe me?" Allie asked.

"No, it's just . . ."

"The gossip's much more entertaining?"

Casey sighed, looking old beyond his years and still confused. "Are you sure it was her? In that accident?"

"I didn't want to believe it could be her, Casey. None of us did."

"But you're sure? I mean . . . how could you be sure?"

"I'm sure someone identified her body before we brought her back here and buried her," she said. "Casey, I really want to help you. I'm sorry for whatever I said that upset you yesterday. But I'm really worried about you. Please let me help."

He looked wary once again. "I didn't want to come back here."

"I'm glad you did."

"I didn't know where else to go," he admitted. All of a sudden, his breathing was hard, shoulders heaving, and he looked heartbroken. "I get so sick of all the games, but I didn't know where else I could go, and I just wish somebody could be straight with me. Just once."

"I have been, Casey. What makes you think I haven't?"

He gave her a sullen stare, spoiled somewhat by the tears gathering in his eyes.

"Do you know something about what happened here?" she asked. "Did you hear something around town you haven't told me?"

"No," he cried.

He looked absolutely heartbroken. Then he turned around and kicked his foot against the wall, hard enough to make Allie wince. Why would he think she was lying to him? And what could she have said to hurt him like this?

"Casey, whatever it is, just tell me. We'll figure it out. I promise. I want to help you."

"My mother always said that to me. *Trust me, Casey. I'm doing what's best for you. I don't want to hurt you.* I've heard it all my life, and it's a load of shit, Allie. Pure shit, and I don't want to hear it anymore. Especially not from you.''

"I wouldn't do that to you," she tried to explain. Never. After all, she'd been raised by a mother who'd done exactly the same thing. But Casey wasn't listening. He turned around and stormed out the door. She went after him. "Casey, please don't go like this."

He kept right on walking, cutting through the backyard, crossing the creek and disappearing.

"Oh, Casey," she whispered, wishing she'd insisted on knowing more about him. If he didn't come back, she didn't have any way to find him.

She wondered where he would sleep tonight, wondered what he'd eat and whether he would be warm enough, even as she prayed he'd come back.

Allie stood there for a long time worrying about Casey. Then she came inside and stared at the photograph of her sister, then the flowers from Stephen. She was tired and restless and feeling antsy, like something was about to happen, something she wouldn't like.

She wandered through the downstairs, trying not to think of the things that awaited her on the second floor, in the bedrooms she'd been too cowardly to enter at this point. It had to stop. She knew that. But they hadn't made a dent in the yard or the attic. It wasn't as if she was sitting here doing nothing but being scared of what was in the bedrooms. And there was certainly enough work to be done on the first floor to keep her busy for at least a week.

She walked through the first-floor rooms one by one, just needing to move. There were furnishings here she would likely donate to charity, other pieces that were probably antiques. Which meant she needed someone to tell her what was valuable and what was not. She made a mental list. Antique dealer. Charitable organization. A truck to haul everything away. She was good with lists.

Still feeling oddly out of sorts, Allie peeked into the formal living room, her gaze caught on the delicate, cream-colored chair in the corner.

She stared at it for the longest time, and her vision blurred. She blinked to clear it, finding her eyes oddly drawn to that spot. And then she remembered her mother sitting there, weeping, the night they found out Megan was dead.

Allie shuddered. She remembered hiding on the stairs, the stairs she absolutely hated climbing, and listening to her mother cry. It was the worst sound Allie had ever heard, nothing like the halfhearted, manipulative noises her mother made in the years that followed.

She could hear it so clearly now, see it. Bright, late-afternoon sunlight streamed in the windows. Her mother sat in the shadows in the deepest corner of the room weeping, her face lined with pain, her arms wrapped tightly around her middle, her body curled inward, as if she'd been struck a mighty blow.

"Janet . . ." Her father said. *"Oh, God, Janet."*

Allie eased forward, so she could see more of the room, just as she'd done that night.

She saw her father's hand reach out for her mother, saw her mother slap his hand away.

"Are you happy now?" her mother said.

"Happy?" he gasped. *"She's dead, Janet. You think anybody could be happy about that?"*

"*It's what you wanted,*" her mother sobbed. "*You wanted her gone. Now she's gone forever.*"

Allie gaped at the empty room, the image and the voices gone as abruptly as they'd come. She couldn't believe that of her father. She wouldn't.

She ran down the hall, out the front door, down the front steps, and into the yard, until she couldn't hear her parents' voices or see her mother's face in her mind. She collapsed on the ground at the base of a massive willow tree. In spots, its heavy branches nearly dragged the ground, shielding her from sight, protecting her. Megan had liked to hide here, she remembered. She had hidden among the willows, and now Allie did, too. She didn't ever remember hearing this conversation on the day Megan died, but maybe she'd blocked it out of her mind. It had been too painful to remember, to even consider. It still was.

You wanted her gone.

Allie hugged her knees to her chest. There was no way on earth she'd ever believe he wanted Megan dead. Or that he had anything to do with her sister's death.

Mitch Wilson's words came back to her. *She was terrified of someone back here. She thought he followed her all the way to Macon. She thought she saw him the day before she died.*

It was crazy. Her own father hunting down her sister? No way. It had to be a mistake. Mitch Wilson could be lying through his teeth, for all she knew.

She thought about the letter. Who had sent it? Why were they playing these games with her? If someone knew something, why not just tell her? Why couldn't anyone just tell her what was going on?

Allie sat there huddled against the base of the tree,

staring at the house, not wanting to go back inside, feeling more alone than she ever had in her entire life. Maybe Stephen had been right all along. The truth might well be too painful, and nothing she was going to find out would change anything. Her entire family would still be gone. She'd still be all alone.

Oh, Daddy, she sobbed. She had loved him. All her life, she'd loved him, despite everything. She'd always thought things would have been so different, so much better, if only she could be here with him. And he was gone now. Her mother was gone. Her sister was gone. Absolutely everyone was gone.

"God," she said, absolutely aching. Every pore in her body ached. Everything inside. Every thought running through her head.

She didn't want to be here, and yet she had no place to go. Even if she left now, she'd never escape what she'd seen and heard here, never forget. There would be no peace for her. She was trapped.

Gazing at the house, Allie shuddered. It would be dark before long, and she didn't want to be inside that house. She was so sick of being alone. Even when her mother was alive, Allie had felt so lonely.

Her gaze went unerringly to Stephen's house. Stephen, who might be lying to her, who was at the very least keeping things from her. Stephen, who it seemed might have been right about everything.

She wanted him now, despite everything else. The mere idea of his presence seemed an incredibe luxury to her. She wasn't afraid when he was nearby. Angry, perhaps, confused, but not afraid.

She closed her eyes and sank back against the trunk of the big tree. He said he'd mourned her sister over the years, that he felt guilty for not doing more to save her, and Allie believed that.

He was a complicated man. Strong, solid, so sure of himself, so determined. Sometimes frustrating, sometimes annoying, quite often incredibly kind, caring, gentle, sympathetic, protective, and very, very sexy. The kind of man a woman could count on? That was the question at the forefront at the moment. She was truly frightened now, so upset, feeling so horribly lost. It was crunch time. The time when she had to consider everything he'd told her, everything he'd shown her about himself and everything she believed about him.

When it came right down to it, she knew if she called him, he would come to her. She had absolutely no doubts about that. She trusted him to make whatever was wrong better. Allie closed her eyes and felt her sense of panic receding. Just knowing she could call and he would come, made her feel so much better. She could only imagine having a man like that standing beside her all the days of her life. She would never be afraid of anything.

He was a man capable of chasing away the darkness and all of her fears. With him, her loneliness dissolved away. He'd told her he knew all about being alone, and she believed he did. In the beginning, she'd judged him as he said so many women had—by appearance and family name alone. But just because his family appeared to be so much more stable than hers didn't mean it was.

She was also starting to believe he might well want the same thing she did. A place to belong. A haven. Just one person she could count on.

Allie sighed and pulled out the cordless phone he'd insisted she tuck into her back pocket, when he'd been worried about Casey being here with her. He'd lectured her, sounding like a man who cared deeply about her safety, and it had brought on an odd tugging sensation in the region of her heart. She wanted him to care, she realized. She'd be happy to have anyone in the world to care about her, but most of all, she wanted it to be him.

The shadows were deepening around her, her tears finally dried, when she picked up the phone and called. He answered right away, speaking curtly, practically barking his last name into her ear. She'd never heard him like that.

"Am I catching you at a bad time," she asked.

"Allie? What's wrong? Did something happen with that boy?"

"No. He hasn't done anything, except work hard and eat enough for three grown men."

"You're sure? When I heard your voice like that, I was worried."

"I'm okay," she insisted.

"Allie? About this morning . . . I'm sorry."

"I know."

"You got the flowers?"

"Yes. They're beautiful. Thank you," she said. "I'm sorry, too. I hit you—"

"It's all right."

Allie wasn't sure it was. But she didn't want to argue, didn't want to run through the whole thing again. She wasn't sure what she wanted, except to hear his voice.

"Is everything okay there?" she said. "You don't sound like yourself, either."

"Okay, I'm busted. This is the work *me*. The bad-tempered businessman *me*."

"Oh. I'm interrupting, aren't I?"

"Everyone else has been interrupting me today,

but not you. I'm really sorry about this morning, Allie. I'm sorry about everything."

"Me, too."

"Now . . . what can I do for you?"

He said it like an invitation, like she could ask him for anything, and he would give it to her. That was what she wanted; it was why she'd called. She'd had an awful day. She was scared, tired, confused and so very alone, and she just wanted to put it behind her for a little while. She wanted him to make it all go away, had no doubt that he could.

"I don't want to be alone tonight," she said.

"Allie, what happened?"

"Nothing. I just don't want to think about my sister or anything to do with her disappearance or the shelter. I want to forget all of it tonight."

"With me," he suggested.

"Yes," she admitted. No one but him would do.

"Done," he said.

"Just like that?"

"Just like that. What would you like to do?"

"I was wondering if you were free for dinner?"

"That sounds promising," he said.

"You don't know what kind of cook I am," she warned.

"Food isn't the attraction, as far as I'm concerned."

"Oh."

He could be so smooth. Stephen the ladies' man. She'd never been the focus of the attentions of a man like him before. Not that there had been a lot of men in her life; there simply hadn't been time. It seemed she'd never truly been young and carefree and in love—that giddy, the-whole-world-is-beautiful kind of love that comes with youth and optimism and a reckless notion that nothing really bad will ever happen. She hadn't missed it until now.

"Hey?" Stephen teased easily. "Don't get scared on me now. We're just talking about dinner."

"Okay."

"You and me," he said. "Here and now. No past. Just us. Just for tonight."

"Yes." That was what she wanted.

"Let's go out," he suggested.

"If you'd rather."

"I would. I know just the place. I'll pick you up at eight."

Chapter 11

He rang the bell at eight on the dot. Allie was in the kitchen, sipping nervously from a glass of sherry. She'd made a frantic run through town to buy a dress and shoes and perfume, her nerves and doubts warring with an undeniable sense of excitement. She was going on a date. With Stephen.

She opened the front door, and her kitten promptly tried to escape.

Stephen snatched it before it got too far. "Hey, who's this?"

"We found each other one night. She doesn't have a name yet," Allie said, and it did something funny to her insides to see her kitten cradled so gently against his chest, to see him stroking it with his big, gentle hands.

"You make a habit of taking in strays?"

"Not until now, but I think I will." It was one way to keep from being alone.

Stephen put the kitten down on the floor. He straightened, and she got her first good look at him, wearing a beautifully tailored navy suit that made his eyes look more blue than green and a white shirt that contrasted with his sun-browned skin. He looked impossibly tall and lean and polished, the man she'd come to know, but more imposing, more powerful, even more overwhelming.

Her heart started to thud inside her chest. Little shivers of sheer pleasure ran through her. She wanted him, for reasons that had nothing to do with needing to forget her troubles. It seemed she'd traded one dangerous situation for another.

"You look beautiful," he said with just the right touch of sincerity that she believed every word. He really was good at this.

"Thank you," she said.

"Ready to go?"

She nodded. They walked outside, and she found a tiny convertible in a deep, dark green with caramel-colored leather interior parked in her driveway.

"It looks like a toy."

"It is," he said unapologetically, holding open her door and stepping back so she could sink into the buttery soft seat.

They headed away from town, down a twisting, turning road that followed the river, slipping through a cascade made by the broad, full trees lining the water. The road wound down, closer to the water, the night pleasantly warm, the stars shining brightly overhead. He'd turned on the music, something with a thrumming guitar playing a cross between the blues, rock and roll, and country, the male vocalist crooning in a deep, husky baritone.

She leaned back, her head against the headrest, watching the stars as they raced through the night. The little car was low to the ground, hugging the road as Stephen accelerated into the curves. Obviously, he knew the road well, and she didn't even care that it seemed as if they were going even deeper into the middle of nowhere. Because it also seemed he was taking her far away from everything that frightened her, scared her, and puzzled her. It was like slipping into another world, that marvelous man-to-woman world, where nothing mattered but being with him.

"Cold?" he asked a few minutes later, taking her hand.

"No. I'm fine. It's wonderful out here tonight."

"I thought you'd like it."

"You don't even have to feed me," she said, feeling relaxed for the first time in weeks from the music, the night air, the feel of his warm hand in hers. "Just drive me around and let me look at the stars."

"I hoped you'd like this. Taking this road at night is one of my favorite ways to unwind."

He pulled to a stop in the restaurant parking lot ten minutes later, cut the engine, and killed the lights. She found him leaning toward her in the darkness, taking her chin in his hand, turning her face to his, and pausing there. She sensed his reluctance, sensed that he was somehow at war with himself. The atmosphere between them had changed somehow. Foolishly perhaps, she hadn't been able to forget the times his mouth had settled over hers. She sat, not moving, barely breathing, stunned by how very much she wanted him to kiss her again.

Stephen exhaled raggedly. His hand cupped the side of her face, his thumb brushing gently across her cheek and studying her face.

"You're tired," he said. "I'll take you back, if you want."

"No," she insisted, because she wanted to be with him. Even if she hadn't been afraid, even if the house hadn't been making her crazy, she'd still want to be with him.

occupations for a Whittaker," she said. "Do women really want to be with you because of who you are and who your family is. Because of your money?"

"Yes," he insisted.

"Not that you're without your charms. . . ."

He frowned at her. "I hope there's a little more to me than a name and a stock portfolio. I'm not interested in making a political or a financial alliance out of a marriage."

"Which is what some people would like you to do?"

"The subject's come up. How well suited a particular woman and I might be. How much we might have in common. How much sense a particular alliance might make."

"It sounds positively medieval."

"Well, we're not big on emotions in the Whittaker family."

Maybe not the family, but she thought he was. He certainly brought out a host of emotions in her. "You've never been married?"

"No."

"Ever come close?"

He nodded. "Close."

"What happened?"

"I discovered she really didn't know me. I don't think she was all that interested in knowing me, and once I thought about it long and hard, I really didn't like what I knew about her."

He was saying he felt lonely with that woman, she realized. Lonely even when he was with her. Maybe he did understand Allie better than she realized.

Stephen took her hand, and she sat there imagining him all alone, imagining him taking away the loneliness that ate at her.

"You make me want things I'm afraid I'll never have," she said later when she was tucked away in his arms. After they'd eaten a very good dinner, he'd taken her into the bar, which had a small dance floor, one man singing and playing his guitar. As they danced, close and slow, to sad, hauntingly beautiful songs, Allie nestled against him, her body seemingly so in tune with his.

"What things, Allie?"

She closed her eyes and thought, *Someone who loves me. Truly loves me.* There was no way she was going to say that to him. Even if every time she was around him she felt the ridiculous urge to pour out her heart to him. She wanted a man who could make a place in the world where she would feel utterly safe and secure. A place by his side where she would always belong, a place that could never be taken away from her.

It simply didn't exist, of course. She was foolish to want it. From everything she'd ever seen of love, it didn't last. She'd been hurt and controlled and deserted, all by the people who were supposed to love her. She didn't expect to find a man to make all that better.

"I want the impossible," she told him.

"I don't believe anything's impossible," he insisted.

Allie laughed. It was so like him, confident to the point of arrogance. She couldn't help but think what it would be like if he could love a woman with the intensity and the determination he did everything else. What would it be like to be the woman Stephen Whittaker loved?

"Tell me what you want. Right now," he said.

"Just this," she said. "This is enough."

He seemed willing to oblige, because he didn't say

anything else, just held her close. She could have stayed in his arms on the dance floor forever, swaying gently in time to the music. Feeling the brush of his flat stomach, the hard muscles of his thighs, his . . .

Allie swallowed hard. He was aroused. He wasn't holding her close enough that she could be certain, but every now and then, her breath caught in her throat as some intriguing part of his body, hard and heavy, brushed against hers. She had to fight against the impulse to blatantly press herself to him and feel just how aroused he was. Allie gave herself up to the sheer pleasure of the music, the little buzz she had from the wine, the clean, fresh smell of him, the heat, the possibilities.

She was in a daze, utterly content, when he stopped dancing abruptly, threw some bills on their table, and led her outside, to the side of the restaurant, night noises of birds and crickets and a distant sound of rolling water closing in around them. They turned one more corner, and Stephen pushed her up against the wall, his body holding her there, keeping her there, as his mouth came down on hers in a hard, devastatingly tempting kiss.

He drank deeply from her mouth, obliterating everything else from her mind. He was definitely very aroused. Allie didn't try to hold anything back. She opened herself up to him, didn't try to stop the helpless little sounds she made deep in her throat. She hadn't planned on this, hadn't planned on things moving forward so quickly it made her dizzy, hadn't counted on just how powerful the heat he generated could be. It was so powerful it could indeed wipe every thought from her head.

But she wanted all of him, all he had to give. Her

legs were trembling so badly she could hardly stand. She kissed him until she simply couldn't breathe anymore, until her body was weak and utterly empty without him. His big hands palmed her hips, lifting her to him. She spread her thighs willingly, letting him in, wanting him to ease the ache inside of her, to fill her.

"Dammit," he said, pulling back a fraction. "We are not going to do this standing up against the side of a building."

Dazed, she asked, "We're not?"

He swore, kissed her again, then pulled her to him as he led her to the car and put her inside it. He shrugged out of his suit jacket and covered her with it. The scent of his body clung to the cloth, the warmth as well. Stephen slid behind the wheel and revved the engine. The car was a five-speed, with the gearshift between their seats. He waited until he had the car on the road, tearing along at an exhilarating pace, before he pulled her to him. She snuggled into the awkward position, her head against his side. Her palm landed on his right thigh, his muscles clenching beneath her touch as the car shot forward.

He flipped a few switches on the dashboard, and she felt heat come billowing out. Before long, she slid down until her head was in his lap, her cheek pressed against his thigh. His hand tangled in her hair, letting her know it was fine to rest there. But a part of her felt like exploring. She still had her hand on his thigh, liked the way he felt, all solid and hard beneath her palm. She liked being surrounded by his smell, the heat of his body, the cold night air. She liked the way he stroked her hair with his fingers, and she thought of turning her head toward him, nuzzling her face in his lap, maybe even undoing his slacks and taking him into her mouth.

Allie had never done anything so wicked. She'd never wanted to. But it was dark now. The road was all but deserted. No one would see them, and she wanted to know how it would feel, to be so shockingly sinful and so free. She wondered about the taste of his skin. She wondered if she could make him every bit as crazy for her as she was for him, wanted him to wipe every thought from her head, until there was nothing but him.

Absently, she stroked his hard thigh, liking the way it made him catch his breath.

His hand tightened in her hair. "Allie, you're playing with fire."

She shivered, with pleasure and a bit of nerves. When they got to her house, he wouldn't be leaving. She didn't want him to leave.

"Just let me get us home in one piece, and we'll talk about this, Allie."

She didn't want to talk. She wanted him to take her, quickly and urgently, then sleep beside her all night. She wanted the oblivion and heat and need that only he could give her.

He slid a hand beneath her dress, along her thigh, her hip, across the tender skin of her belly. He pushed aside the flimsy fabric of her bra, until he held her breast in his hand, his thumb finding and teasing at her nipple until it jutted out against his hand.

His hand was everywhere, moving leisurely, lazily, exploring, arousing. She moaned happily, finding this slow, sweet seduction to her liking. The car zipped along, swaying this way and that with the curves of the road. Allie was warm and tired and pleasantly aroused. At some point she must have drifted off. When she woke, her body was filled with a pleasant aching need, and she thought she remembered the feel of his hands on her—everywhere—but she couldn't be sure. They were at her house, she noted. Stephen lifted her out of the car and into his arms. He carried her to the door, somehow managed to unlock it, then headed for the stairs.

The stairs . . .

Her room . . .

"Stephen," she said, too loudly, too urgently. "Wait."

"I was just taking you to bed, Allie," he said quietly. "You're beat."

"I . . . I've been sleeping in the family room. On the sofa."

He paused, considered, then turned and headed for the family room. He laid her down on the sofa, then sat down on the edge of the cushion facing her. His hand tilted her face up to his, and she reached for him, pulling him to her and kissing him hungrily, wanting to be lost in him once again. She'd liked it in the car. There'd been something so wanton about snuggling against him with her head in his lap while they raced through the night. But this was better. She was lying down on the sofa, her back and her head propped against the pillows, and he was on top of her. Which left her free to enjoy the feel of his chest and his shoulders on top of her, his weight pressing down on her.

She kissed him with no thought of restraint or pride or even caution. It was dark, and they were alone in a house that frightened her, and it was heavenly to touch him this way, to taste him, to have him chase away all her demons.

"Stephen," she said, her voice full of hunger and need.

"Wait a minute." He dragged himself off of her with a ragged sigh. "You had something to drink before we went to dinner?"

"What?"

"To drink, Allie. When I came in you were drinking."

"A glass of sherry."

He hadn't bothered to turn on the lights, so they had nothing but the faint light from the hallway, but she could see the concern in his expression.

"And you had two and a half glasses of wine with dinner."

Had she? She hadn't kept track, was surprised to find that he had. "I'm not drunk, Stephen."

His thumb brushed the darkened skin below her eyes. "You're tired."

She nodded. Tired, deliciously warm and aroused, her head spinning just a bit, but that was more from him than the wine.

"I'm not drunk," she said again, lifting her hand to his face and pulling him to her. He kissed her again, those sweet, deep, drugging kisses that had her tingling all over and deliciously warm once again. "Stay with me tonight, Stephen."

He groaned.

"Would that be so wrong?" she asked. "I have to admit, I'm not very good at this. I'm not sure of the proper procedures here . . ."

"Procedures?"

"Of two people who don't know each other that well going to bed together."

"There's no reason you should be," he said, sounding thoroughly irritated. "And it's certainly not something I'm going to explain to you."

"You want me," she said, but somehow it came out like a question.

"God, yes," he said. "But I'm not going to take you to bed with me tonight."

Still, he leaned over her and kissed her slowly, soothingly. His hand skimmed down her throat. He palmed her breast for a moment, his fingers spread wide, his touch as gentle as it was arousing. She put her hand over his, to keep it there, to keep him close.

"Allie," he said raggedly. "It's going to be hard enough to walk away from you, as is."

"Then don't," she urged, ready to plead with him if that's what it took.

"You need to think about what you want."

"I've done nothing but think and worry since I got here," she said. "I don't want to do that anymore."

"This morning you hated me, and God knows, you had the right."

"I don't hate you," she said. "I can't."

"But you don't know me. Not well enough for this."

Her face burned at that. She couldn't quite believe he was calling a halt to this. In her admittedly meager experience with men, they took what was offered, took it eagerly and without any twinge of conscience.

"I'll still be here tomorrow and the day after. I'm not going anywhere," he said. "I want you to be sure, Allie."

She groaned and turned her face away, humiliation soaking through her.

He sat there beside her for a long time. She hoped he'd change his mind, that he'd stay, but all he said was, "Will you be all right here?"

"Of course I will," she lied.

He stood up, looked around the darkened room, then back to her. "Allie, why are you sleeping down here?"

Damn. He saw too much.

"It's comfortable," she lied.

"There are five bedrooms in this house, and I assume five beds. Are you telling me there isn't a comfortable one in the bunch?"

She waited there in the darkness, not wanting to admit how foolish she'd been, coming here for answers and then finding herself afraid to look for them.

"Why do you want me to stay so badly?" he asked.

"I thought it was obvious. . . ."

She wanted to die. Her pleasantly warm buzz from the wine was gone, and she wasn't so sleepy anymore, just mortified. He'd come frighteningly close to figuring out her motivations in calling him this afternoon and asking him to spend the evening with her. But somewhere along the way this evening, she'd known she didn't simply want to lose herself in a man. She wanted to lose herself in *him.* Allie wasn't the kind of woman to go to bed with a man just because she was feeling lonely and afraid. She was too reserved to use sex as a substitute for companionship.

"Don't lie to me. Not about this." He turned back to her, pinning to the spot with the look in his eyes. "Has something else happened here? In this house? Something that frightened you?"

"No."

"You're afraid to be here. God, I didn't know it was that bad."

"It isn't. I'm being silly," she lied. *Damn.*

"Why did you want me to stay?"

"I thought it's what you wanted," she said because she needed to hear him say it so she could believe it herself.

"It is, but this isn't just about me and what I want. This is about you, too, and I think you really don't want to be here by yourself. Enough that you'd go to bed with me?" He looked pained by the idea. "So you wouldn't have to be alone?"

"I don't sleep in the bed, remember?" she said bitterly, humiliated beyond belief, then forced herself to go on. "And you're right. I didn't want to be alone tonight. But I haven't been with anyone in a long time. It's not something I take lightly."

"I didn't think you did," he said.

"And I would never . . ." She broke off, heat infusing her cheeks at the mere suggestion that she'd have sex with a man so casually. Intimacy was right up there on the same plane with trust in her book, and he knew all about her trust issues. Which should have told him everything he needed to know. Just in case it didn't, she forced herself to say the words. "I wanted you."

"Oh, Allie." He could make her name sound like a painful thing, as if he hurt for her. He made it sound as if he would take her pain and make it his to bear if he could. "I'm sorry. You tried to tell me this morning, and I just didn't realize. If I had known it was this hard for you to be here, I never would have left you here by yourself for the last five days."

"I can handle it," she said. "I just don't like the stairs. Or the bedrooms."

He turned away and swore softly again and again, shaking his head.

She reached for him, pressing her palms against his chest, feeling the heat and the reassuring beat of his heart. "Stephen, it's okay. I'm dealing with it. Maybe not well, but . . ."

"No. It's my fault. I'm rushing you. I know everything's a little crazy for you right now. I shouldn't push."

"You're not. Tonight . . . it just happened, and it was what I wanted, too."

"Too soon," he insisted. "But it won't always be like this, Allie. Things will calm down, and I'll be right here. We'll figure all of this out. Everything that's between us. I promise."

She felt hot tears pooling in her eyes and rushing down her cheeks. He had no idea how much she wanted to believe him. He sat down beside her and hauled her into his arms, holding her gently and stroking her hair, warming her with his body, reassuring her with his presence.

A long moment later he took her face in his hands, and said, "This is silly. You don't have to be here. Come home with me. I have five bedrooms, too. You can take your pick. Or you can sleep with me if you want. I won't touch you. Or, I will, but I won't do anything else. I can handle that, I think."

"Stephen . . . No."

"This place frightens you, and I'm not leaving you here."

"If I leave now, I may never come back."

"You can come back tomorrow, in the daylight," he said.

"Like a little girl? Afraid of the dark?" Allie thought of the loathsome, spineless creature she'd always been, the one who went along with everything, who always took the easy way out. She never wanted anyone to see her that way again, especially not Stephen.

"You're one of the most determined women I've ever met," he said.

"No, I'm not."

"You are. This place scares you to death, but you're still here. You're still fighting it, and I admire that about you, Allie."

"Stephen, I'm a coward. I've been one my whole life."

"A coward wouldn't have come here. She wouldn't have stayed," he said. "And you've got to stop beating yourself up over what you've done in the past. You did the best you could. And you're not the only one who's ever made a mistake. God knows I've made my share of them."

"You? You're perfect. And you're always right."

"No, I'm not."

"I think you're one of the best people I've ever known," she whispered.

"You don't know me that well, remember?"

"So tell me. Tell me all about the Stephen Whittaker I don't know."

"Tomorrow, all right?" He sighed. "I'm tired. You're tired. Come with me. Come to my house."

"I can't."

"Of course you can. It's a hundred yards away. We'll be there in two minutes. I'll carry you to the bed of your choice."

"I'm staying here, Stephen. I have to."

"Okay. I'll stay here with you. Invite me to stay."

"I feel so foolish."

"What if I want to stay? What if I want you curled up beside me, your body touching mine all over? What if I want to wake up here with you?"

"Well, when you put it that way . . ."

He was already loosening his tie, pulling off his belt, then his shoes.

It was a tight fit, the two of them curled onto the sofa this way. He shifted her around until she was practically lying on top of him, his body all hard muscles and heat, and the kind of strength she'd never known. She felt absolutely safe here with him and still terribly aware of him, of every rise and fall of his chest, every stroke of his hands along her back.

She knew he was still keeping something from her. But she needed him, and this felt so right. She'd taken so little on faith in her life, had missed out on so much. She didn't want to miss this, didn't want to miss him.

He shifted once again, and one of her legs fell between his, his thighs warm and hard. Her left leg shifted higher into the notch made by his thighs. He sucked in a breath when she realized he was still fully aroused, the hard length of him now nestled against her thigh. She was just as aroused, she realized. That quickly, that unmistakably.

Stephen groaned and pressed her head against his chest. "You're not an easy woman to resist."

She thought he'd done an admirable job of it so far, but if she told him that, they'd argue again, and she liked this spot too much to surrender it to an argument she wouldn't win anyway. So she stayed where she was and didn't contradict him.

"This is nice," she said instead, feeling sleepy and strangely content, just to know he wanted her, too, just to have him here.

"Go to sleep, Allie. I'll be right here."

And she drifted off in his arms.

Chapter 12

Allie woke in the wonderfully warm cocoon made by his body and hers. There was an afghan pulled over them both. She was sprawled on top of him, had hardly moved all night, and she hadn't been afraid. If this was what two glasses of wine, a bit of sherry, and a man could do for her, she'd keep him and a bottle on hand for the duration of her stay.

Lifting her head off his chest, she saw the shadow of morning whiskers covering his jaw, saw his dark hair tousled in sleep, his eyes still closed. She nuzzled her cheek against his, liking the unfamiliar, rough sensations, wondering what it would be like to kiss him this way, wondering if he'd turn her away this morning as easily as he turned her away last night.

She went to lift herself off of him, but his arms tightened around her in what seemed a reflexive action.

"Don't," he whispered.

One hand pressed her hips to his, the other pulled her mouth to his mouth. Her lips parted automatically, fitting themselves to his. His jaw was indeed rough, the feel unexpected and erotic as well. She could just imagine him kissing her all over, his rough jaw tickling her skin, his lips soothing.

Allie opened herself up to the kiss, to the magic that was Stephen. Their legs were scissored together, his, hers, his, hers, in an erotic combination of hardness and softness, insistent pressure and aching emptiness. Just like that, she thought. A kiss, the brush of his hand, the feel of his lips, and she was right there, right back on the edge, as she had been last night when he pressed her up against the wall outside the restaurant.

He kissed her hungrily, greedily, his erection throbbing between them. He was so close to being inside of her, where she wanted him, needed him. His hands expertly brushed her clothes aside, finding her breasts, taking them into his hands, his mouth. The way he was kissing her breasts and sucking on them created a hard tugging sensation between her legs, as if there were a direct line running between the two. Her whole body started to tremble, to soften, to open to his. Her hands clutched at his shoulders. She took in great gulps of air between wicked, greedy kisses, as he stripped her of her panties and rolled her to her side. His hand slid between her legs, his fingers slipped inside of her, and she gasped.

His eyes shot open. Sleepy-eyed, he looked at her—truly saw her—then groaned, his forehead coming down against hers. "Dammit, Allie."

But he kissed her again. The urgency of her need sneaked up on her. She felt herself suspended in midair, thinking she might come crashing down or she might go soaring instead. It was a heady kind of heat, the kind that came with being so high and so free. She arched into his touch, his fingers moving inside her, sending her splintering over the edge. She cried out his name, felt as if she did indeed go soaring up and over.

He caught her hard against him, his breathing as unsteady as hers, his heart pounding, too. She felt her body quiver, convulsing around his fingers, which were still teasing and tormenting her, and she wanted him desperately.

"Please." She reached for him. "I'm not drunk. I'm not confused. I'm not scared. I'm a grown woman, and I know what I want."

Her hand slid down his chest, down the front of his pants, and through the material she rubbed her hand against his rigid flesh. He shuddered once again, the look in his eyes telling her clearly exactly what she was doing to him.

"You'll regret this," he warned.

"You don't know that."

"Yes, I do."

She answered him with a kiss, a quick, hard kiss on his mouth, and she found herself wondering how his skin would taste as well. She wanted to feel bare skin beneath her hands, to see him, as she took him inside of her. There was a greediness within her that she'd never felt before. She wanted all of this, all of him. Every touch. Every taste. Every sensation. Now.

In the end she settled for pushing his shirt out of the way, so she could at least feel her breasts against his bare skin. He loosened his pants and shoved them down, grabbed his wallet, and quickly sheathed himself in a condom, then he took her by the waist and pulled her down on top of him. Her thighs parted easily. He slid his hands under her dress, took her hips in his hands, guiding her to him, sliding inside of her in one long, sure stroke.

She gasped and shuddered, her body slick and ready, yet still having to stretch and strain to accommodate the full length and width of him.

It had been so long, after all, and she'd never done it like this, with her on top. For a moment she couldn't do anything at all, just leaned forward, bringing the top of her body down to his, letting her head fall to his shoulder. His hands were still under her dress, guiding her back and forth in a rocking motion that had him withdrawing, almost all the way, then pushing inside of her again. She marveled at the feel of him each time he did it, then cried out from the sheer pleasure of it. Already, she could hardly stand it. He soothed her with his hands and his mouth, gently rocking his hips up to meet her shallow thrusts. He slid in and out of her easily, filling her to the brim, and she found she simply loved the sensation of having him inside of her.

He teased her, as if he had all the time in the world, as if he lived to make her come apart in his arms. No man had ever played her body with such skill or such patience. She couldn't understand how he could be so in control when an urgency was building inside of her that would not be denied.

Then he pushed her up, into a sitting position, which brought her full weight down upon him, burying him deep inside of her.

"It's too much," she said, pulling back. "I can't. I can't take it."

"You can," he whispered. "I'll show you."

He pushed up into a sitting position himself and held her. He swung his body and hers around, until he had his feet on the floor, was sitting on the sofa with her straddling him, him still so deeply inside of her.

"Stephen," she said, because she simply couldn't say anything else.

It felt so good, and it most definitely chased all the

loneliness away. Eradicated it. Seared it. Vaporized it. He was inside of her, so deeply she'd never forget it.

He arched against her, showed her the rhythm he wanted with his hands on her hips. When she begged, when she pleaded, when she told him she absolutely couldn't stand it any longer, when she screamed, he kept right on going until her body shuddered around him, until he exploded inside of her.

His arms tightened around her. He'd been teasing at the sensitive skin at the side of her neck, but now he bit down gently, sending another wave of pleasure through her until she thought she could die happily in that moment, that there was nothing else in life she needed or could possibly want. This was sheer bliss, unadulterated happiness.

Slowly she became aware of the world around her. His chest was heaving as he strained for breath, his skin damp with a fine sheen of perspiration. She nuzzled her nose against his neck, was happy to feel him shudder in response. He still held her hips in the palms of his hands, still held her tightly against him. She still felt him throbbing inside of her.

She let her head fall to his shoulder, thought life would be just about perfect if they could stay this way for a while longer. She wanted to sleep sprawled all over him again, wanted to have his arms around her and wake up with him again. She wanted to do this all over again, already.

He made her greedy for the feel and touch and taste of him, made her wonder already how she was ever going to do without the sensation of him inside of her.

Was it always like that with him, she wondered? Had she simply been doing it wrong? Or with the wrong man? Maybe it was the fact that Stephen was so very much a man, when the others seemed terribly immature in comparison. Or maybe it was just that this was Stephen. Maybe foolishly, naively, she'd fallen for him completely, and she would simply have to live with the consequences. From the look on his face, he seemed to be considering consequences himself.

"Don't," she whispered. "Don't you regret it, either."

She also didn't want him to forget. She wouldn't. Not if she lived to be a hundred years old and took a dozen lovers to her bed. She didn't think it would ever be like this.

Stephen took her in his arms and shifted them both again until he was lying down and she was draped over top of him once again. She nestled against his chest, finding a spot that felt absolutely perfect.

"I slept just like this," she said.

He nudged his hips against hers. He was still inside of her. "Not exactly."

Allie laughed, then lifted her head to smile down at him. "You do regret it. I can tell. Stephen—"

"Right now, I'd like to enjoy it just a little bit more," he said, pulling her mouth down to his once again, kissing her deeply, smoothly, soothingly, until it was all they could do to breathe.

She woke the next time to the familiar sound of footsteps overhead. Stephen's arms tightened around her, and she felt him slowly coming awake. Opening her eyes, she found morning sunshine streaming in through the sheer curtains at the back of the family room.

The sound of the footsteps came to her again.

"What the hell was that?" Stephen said, looking incredulous. "Allie, is someone in this house?"

She went cold all over, despite having his warm body pressed against hers. "You hear it, too?"

"What do you mean *Do I hear it, too*?"

"I thought it was just me," she stammered. "I thought I was hearing things. I didn't think it was real."

His eyes narrowed down to hard, dangerous slits. "You mean someone's been here before? And you didn't tell me? You didn't do anything about it?"

He levered himself up and off of the sofa. She had only a second to admire the clean, smooth lines of his body before he pulled on his pants and his shirt, not taking the time to button it.

He shoved his cell phone at her and said, "Call 911 and tell them someone's in the house. And stay down here."

Then he took off up the steps.

Her hands trembled as she punched in the number and gave the dispatcher her address and an only semi-coherent explanation of what the problem was. He wanted her to stay on the line, kept asking her all sorts of questions, few of which she could answer. Against his advice, she broke the connection, straightened her clothes, and headed up the stairs.

There was no one, real or imagined, on the stairs or on what she could see of the second floor. But all the doors to all those rooms were open. She slowly made her way up, closing all the bedroom doors on the second floor. At the bottom of the stairs to the attic, she called out, "Stephen?"

He didn't answer.

She nearly choked. She'd been warned. By Stephen. By Greg Malone. By Mitch Wilson, that she might be in danger here.

Slowly she climbed the last flight of steps and stepped onto the attic floor. Someone grabbed her from behind, and she screamed before realizing it was Stephen.

"I told you to stay downstairs," he said, hauling her into his arms. "Couldn't you do as I asked? Just once?"

"I . . . I wanted to be where you were."

Because he had his lips pressed against her forehead, she felt rather than saw his exasperated smile.

"Under any other circumstances, I'd agree with you. But not now." Still, his hand was at the back of her head, tucking her face against his chest. "You scared me."

"You scared me, too."

"Did you call 911?"

"Yes. The sheriff's department is sending someone."

"Good." He looked even more stern and more worried than before. "Now, why don't you tell me what's been happening over here?"

His voice rose on every word, anger creeping in. But his arms tightened around her at the same time. He'd been worried about her. Allie took a breath and snuggled closer to him.

"I'm not sure," she said.

"You haven't been camping out in this attic, have you?"

"No. Why?"

"There's a sleeping bag in the back corner, tucked into a dusty, old box. A bit of food and a few clothes. And a laptop computer."

"A laptop?"

Stephen nodded. "Someone's been staying here."

"Casey?"

"That would be my guess. I saw a tall, skinny boy in a pair of ratty jeans and a black T-shirt take off through the backyard." Stephen pointed to the window in the corner. "That opens onto the roof, and there's a trellis leading to the ground. The window was unlocked. That's how he gets in and out."

Allie was so glad he was safe, that he'd found a place that was warm and dry. She wished he'd trusted her with the truth, too, but they could work on that when he came back. Surely he'd come back. Surely she'd have a chance to help him.

"Did you know he was here?" Stephen asked.

"I heard footsteps a few times. At least, I thought I did. I couldn't be sure. But I never saw him. I just thought I was hearing things."

"Is that all, Allie? Footsteps?"

"It's noisy here," she said. "The wind. Tree branches. Drafts coming down the chimneys. Everything creaks and moans. I'm not used to that. The house my mother and I had in Connecticut wasn't this old."

"That's all?" he said. "A few creaks and moans?"

"What else would there be?" she said nervously.

"You tell me." His hands settled on top of her shoulders. He kneaded the muscles there, his touch inviting her to lean against him, to rest there in his arms. "Allie, please? I'm worried about you."

"You'll think I'm crazy," she said. "*I* think I'm crazy."

"Tell me."

"I'm remembering things. I told you that."

"That's it? Memories?"

"They're so vivid sometimes. It's like I can hear their voices," she admitted. "My mother's. Mine.

224

Megan's. I could swear I heard her playing the piano the day I saw the bruises on her arms. Sometimes I feel like I could reach out and touch them."

Stephen frowned. "I know it's been difficult for you to be back here. I know you haven't been sleeping well. I know you're under a lot of stress."

Allie leaned against him, let him wrap his arms around her waist. "You think I'm losing it."

"No," he insisted, his arms tightening around her. "Is that all?"

Allie sighed. Was she truly going to trust him? She'd spent the night sleeping in his arms. She'd made love to him, and a part of her was ready to topple right over the edge into love with him. How could she not trust him with the rest of it?

"Tell me," he urged.

"The private detective I hired says he's not the only one looking into Megan's accident. Someone else is asking questions . . ."

"Allie, I hired someone the other day to do the same thing. I didn't know anything about this man you hired, and I didn't want to take any chances. I have a man I've known for years, someone I trust. He's been in Macon since yesterday."

"Why?"

"I told you I wanted the truth. I told you I was going to find it for you. I meant that." He frowned. "So we've got two private investigators chasing each other through Macon, Georgia. What else?"

"Greg found a man in Lexington named Mitch Wilson, who knew Megan when she was in Macon."

Allie told him all about Mitch Wilson, including the fact that someone supposedly tried to kill him simply for asking questions about Megan and that Megan was desperately afraid of a man from Dublin, that she thought she saw him in Macon the day before she died.

Stephen paled at that. Every ounce of color drained from his face. "Shit."

"You didn't know any of this?"

"No." He swore again. "Anything else?"

"Yesterday I remembered my mother and my father talking the day we found out Megan was dead. And my mother said my father should be happy that Megan was gone, because that was what he wanted."

"Why in the world would your father want her gone?"

"I don't know. I don't know anything else at all. Except that I'm scared. Right now, I'm really scared."

"You're not in this alone anymore. Remember that." She thought he was going to kiss her again when they heard the sirens down the road, coming closer. "And you and I need to talk."

"I know." She cautioned herself against presuming too much. Just because he'd spent the night. . . . But she didn't have time to ask. The sirens came closer.

"Come on," Stephen said. "Let's see if we can explain this to the deputy."

"Wait a minute. Just about Casey, right? We don't need to tell the deputy anything about Megan or Mitch Wilson or anything like that, do we?"

"I'd rather handle that ourselves. But I want to know why this kid is camping out in your attic."

"He must have thought the place was empty. It has been for years."

"He has a laptop. What's a runaway kid doing with a laptop?"

"I don't know, but I don't want the sheriff chasing after him like he's a criminal."

"He is a criminal. He broke into your house, and

he scared you," Stephen growled. "He's a lot bigger than you. He could have hurt you, Allie. He could have done anything he wanted to you."

"He didn't. He wouldn't," she claimed.

"You don't know that. You don't know him. I bet nothing he told you is true. I know his name isn't Casey Adams."

"I can't believe you're this hard-hearted, that you'd be this tough on a kid in trouble."

"He scared you," Stephen repeated, sounding like the growling businessman she'd spoken to on the phone the day before.

"And that's an unforgivable sin?" she asked, fighting a grin.

"It's no way to get on my good side." He frowned. "And what's so funny?"

"You," she teased. "Growling at me like this. It's not like you."

"I'm worried about you, all right?"

"This is how you sound when you're worried?"

"No, this is how I sound when I'm *irritated* and worried."

"I know why you're worried. Tell me why you're irritated."

They'd reached the first floor and stood in the foyer near the front door. He was leaning against the wall, his hands shoved into his pockets. His shirt was unbuttoned all the way, his feet bare, his hair a bit of a mess, and he looked wonderful, even if he was cross as a bear.

Allie dared to reach out and touch him. She tried to smooth his hair back into place, and then started buttoning his shirt. This close, she could smell him, something warm and dark and distinctly him, a scent that had clung to his skin every time she'd been near him. Her fingers were clumsy and felt too big for the task she'd given herself. She could barely work the buttons through the little hoops, and she kept getting distracted by the sight of the chest she was covering up with every button she fastened.

"Why are you irritated, Stephen?" she asked.

"Oh, hell, I deserve it. I know that. I've kept things from you, too. But you were over here all alone at night, hearing footsteps in this damned house and God only knows what else, and you didn't tell me." He took her by the arms, holding her a few inches from his chest, his eyes blazing. "Dammit, Allie, I told you I was right over there. I told you if you needed anything, to come to me, and you didn't."

"I guess I'm not used to having anyone look out for me."

"Get used to it," he said.

She felt a quick, hot rush of warmth shoot all the way through her at the thought. "I might be able to get used to something like that."

"Listen to me." He took her chin in his hand, his voice soft and seductive and full of promise. "You can count on me. If I say I'll be here for you, I will, Allie. Anytime, anywhere."

Her eyes swam in a thick flood of tears. Of all the things he could have promised her, there was nothing she wanted or needed more. Nothing in the world.

"Don't say it unless you mean it," she whispered.

Leaning down, he fitted his lips to hers. She wound her arms around his neck, kissed him with all the urgency of the night before. When he lifted his head, he looked down into her eyes and said, "I mean it."

She nodded, no words getting through her too-tight throat.

"Hey?" He smiled as he wiped away one of her tears. "There's a flip side to this. That if you need me, you come to me. If you're scared. If something happens that just doesn't feel right in the least, little way, you tell me."

"All right."

She thought she'd have to let him go then, but he lingered there beside her, still holding her loosely, close enough to nuzzle his cheek against hers. She breathed in that wonderful scent that was uniquely his, shivered a bit thinking about the pleasure he'd brought her this morning and hopefully of all the pleasures to come.

"I know we've left a lot of things unsaid," he offered.

Allie nodded. They'd made love, and it meant a great deal to her. But she had no idea what it meant to him.

"I don't want to let you go right now," he said, and only then, with the sirens stopping in front of her house, did she become aware of the tension invading his body. He gently separated himself from her, holding her at arm's length, waiting until her gaze met his.

Oh, no, she thought, too late to ever be prepared for being blindsided one more time. Oh, no.

"Allie, I've handled this whole thing badly," he began, his eyes dark and troubled, his expression grim. "And I'm sorry. This morning . . . I didn't mean for it to happen. Not so soon. Not before you knew . . . *God,* Allie, there's so much you don't know."

"What?" she whispered as her pulse started thundering. He knew things? Serious things. She could tell by the anguished expression on his face, and she couldn't believe this was happening to her again. That he'd done it to her again. "You said *you* didn't know what happened to Megan."

"I don't. But I have my suspicions—"

An involuntary, pathetic-sounding groan escaped her. He took a breath and looked away, guilt written all over him. She felt like she'd been kicked in the stomach and started backing away from him.

"I don't believe this," she said.

"If what I suspect is true, neither one of us is going to like it," he went on. "And dammit, I can't explain it right now. The deputy's right outside."

He was. She heard a car door slamming, heard the crackle of what she thought was a police radio. But she had trouble switching from one subject to the next. She wanted an explanation from Stephen. Right now. And yet, she was afraid of what he was going to say.

"Allie, this is between you and me. Not for the whole town, all right? But the deputy's coming, and we have to tell him something."

She supposed after calling so frantically, she couldn't just say it was all a mistake and ask the deputy to please go away. Which meant she didn't have time to fall apart. Later. Not now . . . She laughed a bit, edgily, right on the brink of losing control.

Stephen looked grim as ever. "Let's deal with the deputy. Just that. For now."

Chapter 13

The deputy looked excited by the prospect of trouble at the supposedly haunted Bennett house. They told him about Casey. A quick computer check showed no Patricia or Casey Adams within the county. The deputy, a lifelong resident, had never heard of them. He took a description and promised to check reports of missing teenagers, and then he was gone.

She was alone again with a man she definitely did not know. How many times had she told herself that? She did not know him.

Allie stood with her back against the front door, her arms crossed, hands buried in the crook of her elbows to hide the fact that they were shaking and maybe to keep herself from slapping Stephen's handsome face once again.

He'd made a call on his cell phone as she showed the deputy out, and now he slid the phone into one of his pockets and turned to face her.

"I've been in touch with a security firm I use from time to time on job sites. They're sending a team over. I want someone watching the house and you when I can't be here."

"You're going to watch over me?"

"Yes."

"Just like that?" She laughed bitterly. "*You've* decided?"

He stood there, unmoving, giving her a look that said he certainly had decided and that somehow, he expected to convince her to go along with his wishes. Obviously slapping him wouldn't be enough. Allie thought about strangling him instead.

"I know you're angry. I know I hurt you, and I'm sorry." He ran a hand through his hair. "I know I owe you an explanation, but I don't have time to give you one right now. I have an appointment I have to keep—"

"An appointment?" she growled.

"I want to know about this kid hiding in your attic and have a talk with Mitch Wilson. I'd like for you to stay here until I get back."

"And you think I give a shit what you want right now?"

"No, I don't." He looked so calm, sounded so reasonable. It made her want to strangle him all the more. "But somebody invaded your house, Allie. Your house. He was here, probably watching every move you made. Have you thought of that? Have you thought about the kind of danger you've been in?"

"You can't possibly think Casey's part of . . . What? Some grand scheme to make sure I never find out the truth about what happened to my sister?"

"Mitch Wilson told you your sister was scared to death of someone here. She thought she saw him in Macon the day before she died, and then someone threatened to kill Wilson just for asking questions. Dammit, Allie. What does it all add up to? The fact that you're not safe."

God, he was unbelievable. He thought she was

going to ignore all he'd done to her? The fact that she was furious with him?

"You think *you're* going to keep me safe?" she repeated.

"I am."

"And you expect me to just sit back and let you? Let you lie to me and then walk away from me? You think I'll be waiting right here when you come back to lie to me some more?"

"The security guards will be here," he said. "They'll stop anyone from coming into the house without your okay. Please be careful about who you let inside. And if you're too damned stubborn to stay here, they'll follow you. I hope you won't try to ditch them. Hate me for all of this if you want. I wouldn't be surprised if you refused to see me or talk to me when I come back. But I will be back, and until then I'm going to do everything within my power to see that you're safe."

"You're forgetting," she said, laughing bitterly, a world of hurt in the sound. "The thing I really need is for someone to protect me from you. Who's going to do that, Stephen? Who's going to keep me safe from you?"

She was rewarded with a flinch and a distinct tightening of his jaw, but it was little satisfaction given the pain of betrayal rushing through her.

He reached out—for her, she thought—and she skittered out of the way. There was no way she could let him touch her right now.

But it seemed he was reaching for the doorknob instead. He opened the door and picked up Casey's laptop from the table in the entryway.

"I think I'll wait outside. I hope to be back in a

few hours, and I'll do the best I can to explain, if you'll listen," he said. "I'm sorry, Allie."

Twenty minutes later, Stephen stood on the back porch of his parents' home and lit a cigarette, his fifth of the day, thinking if Allie stayed here much longer he'd be smoking a pack a day, something he hadn't done in more than five years.

The first team of security people had arrived. He'd just finished briefing the man he was leaving in charge, telling him next to nothing, except that he didn't want anyone getting near Allie and that he wasn't sure she was going to cooperate in their efforts to protect her.

In the time he'd been waiting, he'd talked again to his man in Macon. He'd heard about the doctor who seemed to be holding out on them and asked for a background check on Mitch Wilson. He'd also fired up the laptop he'd found in the attic and discovered he couldn't make it past the password protection software installed on it. He knew a lot about computers, and most people's security systems sucked. The teenager spying on Allie had one of the best he'd ever seen. Which really worried him.

Hell, everything about this worried him, and he had to go in just a minute to that appointment he had to keep.

But for the moment he was smoking another cigarette and staring at Allie's house. He didn't want to leave her this morning, but if he'd stayed another minute, he was afraid he would have told her everything, absolutely everything. Which had to be the worst thing he could do at this moment. He saw that so clearly, just from the hint he'd given her that he was still keeping things from her. In attempting to ease his guilty conscience, he'd almost ruined everything.

If he told her everything, she would absolutely hate him, and she wouldn't trust him at all. He couldn't afford to have her completely distrust him now, not when he honestly feared she was in more danger than ever before.

He still couldn't forgive himself for the kid being in the house with her. Maybe he was nothing but a runaway teenage boy, and maybe he wasn't. But the whole time Stephen had been right here, so arrogantly thinking he could handle this situation all by himself, that he could keep her safe. While the kid could have done anything he wanted to Allie. He felt sick just thinking about it.

And that was just the beginning. Stephen's father was nervous as hell and likely on his way back from the Mediterranean at this moment. His brother had been dodging his calls for three days now, and as Stephen saw it, anything could happen in the next twenty-four hours. He was afraid it was all going to explode around them, and as soon as he kept his appointment this morning, he wasn't going to let Allie out of his sight.

When this was all over, when Stephen was convinced she was safe, he'd tell her. Maybe he'd say everything else he wanted to say to her first—like *Stay with me.* Like *You belong with me.*

But he couldn't tell her now that he'd been spying on her for his father ever since she came back here. Because he'd gone into this with one goal in mind— to make sure no one from his family hurt her, the way he feared they'd hurt her sister. He was going to protect her to the end. Even if it meant she never forgave him.

Stephen's mouth settled into a tight line. She might have forgiven him. He might have had a fighting chance if he hadn't made love to her this morning.

He closed his eyes and looked toward her house yet again, remembering that she was okay right now. He had round-the-clock security on her house, something he should have done the minute she showed up there.

Oh, hell. Who was he kidding? He should have done a better job of looking out for her sister fifteen years ago, and he should have insisted on knowing exactly what his brother and his father had done to her.

He should have called them on that or a dozen other suspicious things over the years instead of looking the other way and keeping his distance from them and wishing they were anything except what they were—his family. He'd never quite figured out how to sever those ties. He'd made himself be content with compromise after compromise where they were concerned, all in the name of preserving the illusion that the Whittakers were one, big, happy family, or at least a family who could tolerate each other.

He should have stopped trying to cover for them and trying to shield his mother from the things they did. His mother made her choice years ago, and he honestly didn't think his sister-in-law Renee had any illusions left about Rich at all. He'd always lived right on the edge, somehow had always gotten away with things. His drinking had gotten worse recently, Stephen had heard, and the reckless streak had always been there. But even it was more pronounced of late. Still, Rich also had two beautiful, innocent little girls, and Stephen would hate to see them hurt.

The girls and his mother and his brother's wife. He had hoped to shield them from some of this. He'd hoped there was nothing to his suspicions, that all Allie would find while she was here were a lot of ugly rumors. If that's all it had been, he would have tried to keep the whole thing quiet for the sake of the women in his family.

But it wasn't just rumors. He was convinced of that now. And now he was going to pay for all the little compromises he'd made his whole life.

To have preserved any chance at forgiveness, he should have told Allie everything this morning, or last night when he'd brought her back here and wanted her so badly he ached with it.

He might have another twenty-four hours with her, and he wasn't above using what little time he had to try to bind her to him even more completely, to say to her all the things she wouldn't listen to later, when she knew everything.

But even now he doubted it would be enough.

And with that, he snuffed out his cigarette and went to ambush the one man, aside from his father, that Stephen thought could tell him what happened to Megan fifteen years ago. His brother.

Allie had to do something. She couldn't just sit here and think about Megan and her so-called accident, Stephen and all his secrets, Casey and all of his. And of all the thoughts racing through her head, it was Casey she was most worried about at the moment.

Megan, she couldn't help anymore. Stephen was a grown man and no doubt could take care of himself, but Casey was just a boy, forced by circumstances unknown to her to seek shelter in her attic. He must have been so desperate to break in and stay here, even though Allie was living here. And she hated that he hadn't trusted her enough to tell her what was wrong.

She wanted to go out and look for him, but she didn't have a clue where to start, and she still hoped he might come back. Allie worried, too, that once again in her life, she might have come to a decision too late. This time about the shelter.

It was a good idea. She knew it deep in her heart, and if she'd had any doubts, Casey had convinced her. He needed the shelter now. She had to hope that if the shelter was here, he'd be here, too, safe and sound. She truly thought she could make a difference with him.

But she wasn't ready. She didn't think she could push forward fast enough with her plans now. No matter what she found out about Megan or what happened between her and Stephen, she had to get to work on the shelter. She never wanted another runaway living in a barn or an attic in Dublin, Kentucky.

Determined to stay too busy to think, Allie looked for her next move. She had to start talking to people, to understand this neighborhood. Could they be as opposed to the shelter as she'd been led to believe? And who would know?

Allie finally decided Carolyn Simms was her most obvious choice. She called and invited her over for coffee.

While she waited for Carolyn to arrive, nervous energy propelled her up the stairs toward the bedrooms. She'd hated admitting to Stephen that she hadn't even set foot inside any of the bedrooms.

She found that even in the bright light of day she

was still apprehensive, but she charged up the stairs, anyway, and pushed open the door of her own room. Allie found it just as she remembered, as if all her things were waiting eerily for the day she finally came home.

Somehow she'd known it would look just like this. She could imagine her father keeping the door firmly closed, trying not to even look at it as he walked past. She could imagine every now and then his resolve slipping, and that he made his way inside, sitting on her bed surrounded by all her things, feeling every bit as miserable as she did when she'd done the exact same thing after Megan left.

And she simply couldn't believe the things she heard her mother say to her father had been true. He hadn't wanted Megan gone.

Allie carefully explored the room. There were no hints of misery to come, no hints of impending disaster. It was just a room—a little girl's room, and that little girl was gone. Allie couldn't bring her back, couldn't get back the years she'd lost. All she could do was go forward from here.

She did, moving ruthlessly through her old room, stripping it of nearly all her possessions. She didn't ever want to walk back in here and find it the way she'd left it the night she and her mother ran away. She sorted things into piles the kitten explored with glee, finding a very few things she wanted to keep. There were hair ribbons and bows, books she'd treasured as a child, dolls, old clothes, a half-finished math assignment she'd never turned in, and a photograph of a boy she had a crush on in third grade.

Allie wasn't nearly done when she heard a knock at the front door. Carolyn and her daughter, Missy, had arrived, bringing her Carolyn's mother's best wishes along with a chicken casserole.

Allie put the casserole away and served drinks. They all went upstairs to Allie's old room, and Missy was content to fuss over the kitten, the old dolls, and the pile of hair ribbons and bows.

"Do you remember when all it took to make you that happy was a few hair ribbons?" Carolyn said.

"No. I don't." Allie forced a smile.

"I'm sorry, Allie. I knew this would be difficult for you."

"It is, but I'm dealing with it."

"And I don't want to add to your troubles, but I thought I should warn you . . . One of my parents' neighbors works at town hall. She told my parents you're thinking of turning the house into a runaway shelter?"

"Yes."

"Oh, Allie. They're not happy at all."

"That bad?" Allie said.

Carolyn nodded. "Don't get me wrong. I think a shelter's a wonderful idea. I'm sure most of these people would agree. But not here."

"Stephen said the same thing."

"I heard he's staying at his parents' house while they're away." Carolyn wandered over to the window and looked out.

"Yes."

"I also heard you've been seeing him."

Allie fought the rush of hot color into her cheeks. She'd certainly done more than see him, and she didn't want to talk about him. Not now. She settled for adding a vague, "He's been . . . helpful."

"And still as gorgeous as ever, I assume."

Hating herself for it, but curious all the same, Allie

realized she knew next to nothing about Stephen's social life. She'd assumed there wasn't a woman in his life at the moment, no one important at least. But suddenly, it seemed a big assumption to make. Could this possibly get any worse, she wondered?

"Do you know if Stephen's . . . seeing anyone?"

"Not that I've heard. Of course, he spends most of his time in Lexington. I'm not sure if I'd know if he was seeing someone." Carolyn stared at her, then said, "I always thought he was a nice man. Amazing, coming from that family."

"Really? I don't remember that much about the others."

"His mother's very nice, although I can't understand how she puts up with Stephen's brother or his father. The judge, as he likes everyone to call him, always acted like he was so superior to everyone else, and Rich . . ."

"What about Rich?"

"He can be such a jerk. Like the state is a monarchy, and he's king."

"Oh?"

Carolyn nodded. "It's bound to catch up to him someday. Politicians are getting caught in all sorts of things these days. I'm sure he'll get his soon enough."

"What's Rich done?"

"Oh, I don't know anything specific. Not lately. We used to end up at the same parties when I was at UK. He always liked to drink a bit too much, and he tends to get nasty when he does," Carolyn said. "But enough about Rich. We were talking about Stephen, and I've always liked him."

Allie held her tongue.

Carolyn had a speculative look in her eyes. "Someone I know swears she saw Stephen last night dancing very slowly and very close to a woman who sounded a lot like you."

Heat burned through Allie's cheeks yet again.

"Wow," Carolyn said, looking genuinely pleased and much too interested.

So much for denying it all. Still, Allie tried.

"It's nothing, really. He's been . . . Well, it's been difficult to be here, and he's been . . . kind," she settled for saying. At many points along the way, he had been kind, and she'd been a fool. She'd fallen for his whole let-me-help-you act.

"I can understand how being here would throw you. It's so odd for me to walk inside after all these years." Carolyn took one last look around the room. "It brings back so many memories of Megan. She was like the big sister I never had."

"To me, too," Allie said. "She's like a phantom. My sister, and yet I hardly remember the time when she was actually with me."

"I forgot how little you were when all of this happened." Carolyn sighed. "I wish things had turned out differently."

"Me, too," Allie said. "That's what gave me the idea for the shelter. Maybe if there'd been something like that where Megan was, someone might have helped her. I keep thinking that she shouldn't have died. No one her age should die."

"No," Carolyn agreed. "They shouldn't."

"Your parents are really upset?"

"Everyone in the neighborhood, I'm afraid." Carolyn frowned. "It's all people are talking about. And I've heard the wildest stories—about vandalism, robberies, assaults—that we'd be just asking for trouble having those kids living here."

"But . . . they're just kids."

"Troubled kids."

"Which means they need help even more," Allie insisted.

"I know, and I admire you for what you want to do."

"It's more than that. I think it's what I was meant to do," Allie explained, thinking that Carolyn Simms couldn't possibly understand this part. "You have a husband and your children, your family. All of those people in your life, and I . . . I've just been drifting along, never really sure about anything in my life. And nothing felt right except this. There are kids who need this."

"I know, Allie."

"And I can help them. I think I can identify with them."

Even if the only time she'd ever run away from home, she'd done so with her mother and not by her own choice, Allie knew about feeling isolated and powerless, thinking nothing was ever going to get better and not being able to trust anyone. She'd been there, in that awful state, and so many times she'd wished she could just walk away and leave everything her life had become behind her. Start over. Make everything right.

Surely that was what the urge to run away was all about. Leaving all the problems behind.

Allie knew it didn't work that way. She knew you couldn't outrun your problems. She would be speaking from experience.

"I have to do this," she said.

"Allie, I want to believe that. I do. And maybe it will work. But not here. I can't see you ever getting permission to turn this house into a shelter," Carolyn said. "In fact, I don't know if you realize it or not, but two of the town zoning board members live right down the road from you. They've been telling everyone in the neighborhood not to worry. That they will never vote to allow anything like a shelter here, and they can't imagine the other board members ever being willing to, either. In fact, they're sure it's not even needed here. That it's much more suited to a big town, like Lexington."

Allie closed her eyes and felt like she'd just had the wind knocked out of her.

"I'm sorry," Carolyn said. "Obviously, it means a lot to you."

"I didn't know I had zoning board members for neighbors." She fought off a sense of despair. It was one thing to try to sway people to your point of view. Another to hit people where they lived. They'd already decided against it, and she hadn't so much as filed an application yet.

Maybe the situation was every bit as bleak as Stephen had painted it. Maybe he was right once again. Allie groaned at the thought. Eventually he had to be wrong about something, and she'd counted on it being the shelter. That in the end, she could make it work.

"If you think of some other way, I'd like to help," Carolyn suggested. "I'd love to do something in Megan's memory. I've really missed her. I'd do anything I could to help you, Allie."

"Thank you. I appreciate it."

Carolyn said she had to be going. She rounded up Missy, who was thrilled to be taking home three new hair ribbons and a bright pink bow, and they headed for the door.

"You know, there is one more thing . . ." Allie began, stopping them on the porch. "About Megan."

"Anything."

She took a breath and said, "I was wondering if you knew. . . . Why did she run away?"

"Oh, Allie." Carolyn looked devastated. "I'm sorry, I don't know. There were rumors, of course. All sorts of rumors. But I never knew anything for sure. I don't think anyone did, except for your mother and father and Megan, maybe Stephen."

Stephen? "Because he drove her out of town that day?"

"Well, there's that, of course." Carolyn nodded. "But I was thinking of the baby."

"The baby?" Allie said blankly.

"I wasn't sure if you knew." Carolyn hesitated. "Or if I should even bring it up, because it sounds like you and Stephen are . . . interested in each other, and I'd hate for old gossip to mess that up. I want you to know, I never believed it was Stephen's baby she was carrying."

Stephen's baby? Allie couldn't say a word.

"Oh, Lord, I'm sorry," Carolyn said. "I can tell I've upset you, and honestly, that's the last thing I wanted to do. Megan always had a terrible crush on Stephen, and a lot of people swore it was his baby she was carrying when she left. But I always thought the two of them were just good friends."

Allie felt sick.

"She was pregnant?" Allie asked. "You're sure?"

Carolyn looked stricken. "I'm sorry. I just thought your mother would have told you or maybe that Megan did. I don't even know if that part was true. She looked different that summer. Quiet. Worried. Pale. I think she threw up at school one morning, but honestly that was probably all it took to start the rumor that she was pregnant."

"And people thought it was Stephen's baby."

Carolyn nodded. "Especially after he helped her get away. There was even some wild talk about him taking her off somewhere and getting rid of her. But all of that was nonsense. I could never believe Stephen would hurt her. They were friends. In fact, I think the only reason people speculated that the baby was his was because they never saw Megan with anyone else."

"Nobody?"

"Not that I remember," Carolyn said. "I'm sorry. Stephen didn't tell you any of this?"

"No."

Allie closed her eyes, her stomach churning. She'd slept with him. He'd been charming and kind and supportive, and she'd fallen for him, even though she'd known better. All along, she'd known. And he hadn't said a word about her sister carrying his baby.

"I can't believe this." Allie had to stop to breathe. "I can't believe he'd take Megan to Tennessee and just leave her there when she was carrying his child."

"Allie, this is just old gossip. Megan never said a word to me."

"I have to find out," Allie said, turning to look through the trees to the roof of Stephen's house.

"Ask him," Carolyn said. "If there's anyone left in town who should know, it's him."

Allie nodded. "I will."

She doubted she'd believe anything he had to say, but she would ask.

Chapter 14

She refused to think about Stephen at all. She couldn't. For now, she was thinking of this as simply one more clue about what might have happened to her sister. So, if Megan had been pregnant, it could explain the tension between Megan and their parents. It could explain her running away. But it didn't explain her *staying* away when she was pregnant and all alone.

Allie ran the numbers in her head. Megan ran away in September. If she ran away because she already knew she was pregnant and their parents reacted badly, she must have been two or three months along, couldn't have been more than four, maybe five. Because no one seemed sure she was pregnant, so she must not have been far enough along that it was obvious. She died in February, which meant she had to be close to giving birth, if she hadn't already at the time of her death.

Allie called Greg Malone first, to ask him to find out if Megan had been pregnant when she died.

"There's no mention of it in the autopsy report, Allie."

"You checked? Did you hear something about her being pregnant?"

"The questions came up after I got here. You

hadn't said anything about the possibility of your sister being pregnant, but I found out there were two runaway girls in Macon that winter. One of them was pregnant. I'd ask around town if anyone remembered a runaway, and people would ask if I meant the pregnant one, or the other one. So I checked," he explained. "I would have said something to you, but I assumed that if you'd known, you would have told me. Besides, I had the autopsy report in front of me. It was simple enough to check. She wasn't pregnant."

"Oh." Allie had felt a reckless, irrational surge of hope when she'd first hit on the idea. Megan was pregnant, and apparently the girl who died wasn't. She would have loved to believe someone had made a terrible mistake all those years ago, that somehow her sister hadn't died.

Then she thought of one more possibility. "What if Megan had the baby already?"

"If she'd given birth recently, it would have shown up on the autopsy, Allie. I know," Greg said. "It was an issue in a case I had last year. I ran through a similar scenario with a coroner in Atlanta, and she explained that it takes a while for the internal organs to return to their normal size after pregnancy. If Megan had given birth before she died, it would have shown up on the autopsy and been noted in the written report. Sorry."

Allie said nothing. She couldn't.

"You're grasping at straws, right?" Greg asked. "You don't have any proof that she was ever pregnant?"

"No," Allie admitted. "Just old gossip."

"Don't do that to yourself, Allie. They found her body. Your father made the ID himself. She's gone.

Let's just concentrate on finding out how and why it happened."

"Okay. I just . . ." She had other reasons for wanting to know if Megan was pregnant. She wanted to know if it was Stephen's baby. And if it wasn't Stephen's, whose was it? "It might play into what happened to her. It might lead us to someone who could tell us something. . . ."

"You're reaching," Greg warned. "But let's run through the possibilities. She wasn't pregnant when she died. She hadn't given birth recently. I suppose it's possible she had an abortion or a miscarriage months before. You could try talking to your family doctor. Or school friends of hers. You could see if there's anything in the house. A diary. A doctor bill or an appointment card, anything like that."

Allie thanked him and tracked down the family doctor through Mr. Webster, who'd paid her father's final medical bills. The family practitioner who'd once treated her entire family said he knew nothing about her sister being pregnant. He also said for problems like that—an unmarried pregnant teenager—people in small towns didn't normally see their family doctor. A girl would likely go to one of the clinics in Lexington, where no one knew her. Which meant Allie hadn't really learned anything.

As she saw it, she could either call Mitch Wilson, if he'd talk to her, search her sister's room, or ask Stephen. What a choice. Walking into her sister's room for the first time in fifteen years. Talking to a man who thought her sister had been murdered. Or asking Stephen if her sister was carrying his baby when she left.

* * *

Stephen struck out with his brother. Rich had managed to dodge him once again. But he had found Mitch Wilson, who hadn't told him anything new. But just the man's reaction to the questions Stephen asked was enough to make Stephen even more concerned.

He was on his way back to Allie's when he spotted a boy walking down one of the side roads near her house. Allie's lost boy, he thought. A computer check of reports of missing children told them he was apparently only thirteen and from Birmingham, Alabama. A runaway, the deputy told him when he checked in a few minutes ago.

Stephen pulled off to the side of the road a few feet in front of the boy and got out of the vehicle.

Taking in the kid's ragged appearance, his expression a cross between sullen disinterest and out-and-out panic, Stephen said, "Don't you run away from me."

He was in no mood to chase the kid.

"What would you care if I did?" the kid mouthed off.

"I never said I would, but Allie does. She'd never forgive me if I got this close to you and lost you."

The kid looked unconvinced, but he didn't run. "You're a friend of Allie's?"

"You know who I am. You've been staying at her house, scaring her half to death by sneaking around in the attic. I'll tell you right now, I don't appreciate that one damned bit."

"What? Me bein' in her house?"

"I don't appreciate you frightening her," Stephen growled. "Did you think of that?"

"That's all we're going to talk about? Me bein' in her house?"

"To start with. Let's get that straight right now, okay?" Stephen grabbed the kid by the arms and pushed him up against the nearest tree. "You're not going to hurt her. You're not going to scare her. Not ever again. If you try, you'll answer to me."

"You think you own her or somethin'? Just because you spent the night with her?"

"I think it's none of your business what Allie and I do together, except that you understand I won't let you hurt her." Stephen glared at him, wondering if it was possible to intimidate a thirteen-year-old who thought he knew everything. "I'm bigger than you are. I'm stronger. I'm faster. And I know all three of the local judges. If I wanted to, I could have you locked up on a breaking-and-entering charge. Or I could have you on a plane on your way back to Birmingham. Tonight."

The bravado drained right out of the kid at that.

"Yeah." Stephen backed off and let the kid go. "We know who you are. The sheriff's trying to find you right now to send you back."

"So you want me gone, too?"

"All I'm saying is that I could get you out of this town tonight, if I wanted to," Stephen said. "But I may not do that. Allie wouldn't like it, and unlike some people, I happen to care about her. I don't want to do anything to upset her."

The kid finally lost a bit of his cockiness. "I like Allie. She's been okay to me. And I wasn't gonna hurt her."

"No, you're not. I'm going to make sure of that, and much as I hate to do it, I'm going to make you a deal. I can take you back to Allie's house or I can call the sheriff. You know what the sheriff's going to do with you. Allie will probably offer you a shower and a meal and a whole lot of sympathy. If you're straight with me and her about what's going on with you in Birmingham, she may not call the sheriff. She may try to help you herself instead."

"That's it? That's your deal?" Casey gaped at him. "I piss you off, I get shipped back to Birmingham."

"You were expecting a better offer?"

"Man, I don't believe you." Casey was so agitated he couldn't stand still. His chest was heaving, his weight shifting back and forth from one foot to the other. He practically danced with nervous energy. "You don't have anything else to say to me?"

Stephen had the feeling he'd walked in on a movie and missed the entire opening sequence. He didn't have a clue what was going on, but he was starting to get a really funny feeling about this.

"Why don't you tell me what's going on here, Casey?"

"Why don't you tell me. Because I know who you are. You're Stephen Whittaker."

Stephen looked more closely at the mouthy kid. "Am I supposed to know you?"

"Hey, why would you?" Casey was nearly in tears. "If you don't want me here, at least have the guts to say so."

"If *I* don't want you here?"

"Yeah. Just say the word."

"Casey—"

"You really don't know?" the boy said.

"Know what?"

"I asked around about you today, after I heard your name. Everybody knows, so I don't see how you could not know."

"Know what?"

"Who I am."

Stephen looked the boy over carefully, head to toe. He needed a haircut. He was too skinny, his feet and his hands and his ears looked a mile too big for the rest of his body, but Stephen supposed that would all change in the next few years. The kid had blondish-brown hair and dark eyes, and there was something about that surly expression on his face that seemed familiar. Something cold and hard settled in the pit of Stephen's stomach.

"I don't want your money." Casey managed to look furious and hurt and terribly proud. "I don't want to stay at your house. Don't want to embarrass you or anything. You don't ever have to see me again. I just want one thing from you."

Stephen didn't so much as blink. "What's that?"

"I want to know if you're my father."

"What?" Stephen whispered. He would have laughed if he hadn't seen how stricken the kid looked, how deadly serious, too.

"No more games, all right? No more lies. Just tell me."

Of all the things that could have come out of the kid's mouth, that was the last one Stephen expected. Still, there was something familiar about the boy.

"I don't have any children. I'm careful about things like that, and I don't walk away from my responsibilities," Stephen said, looking at the kid more closely, wondering if Casey had confused him with his brother. It wouldn't surprise Stephen at all to find out his brother had an illegitimate child running around somewhere. "Why don't you tell me why you think I'm your father?"

"People around town say you're the only one they ever saw my mother with that summer. So you must be the one."

Stephen braced himself, sure he wasn't going to like the answer. "Who's your mother, Casey?"

"I think, a long time ago, her name was Megan Lynn Bennett."

Stephen let out a breath in a dizzying rush, thinking it couldn't possibly be true. Megan was dead. She'd been dead for a very long time. He'd heard that she was pregnant when she left town, but then there had been all sorts of rumors. He hadn't heard anything about her being pregnant when she'd been found dead, so he'd assumed that she wasn't, although she'd been gone a long time before she died. He supposed it was possible she'd given birth before she died.

"When's your birthday?" Stephen said.

"March 6, 1986."

"Megan Bennett died February 15, 1986."

"Did she? Or did she just want everybody to think she died?"

Stephen took a step back, shaking his head, thinking it was something to be bested by a thirteen-year-old in verbal combat twice in one day. He was simply stunned. For a second, he couldn't think. Of all the ways to explain that little discrepancy . . .

He couldn't help but think of Allie's mysterious letter, of Mitch Wilson who claimed someone had threatened to kill him if he asked any more questions about Megan.

After talking to him, Stephen spent the morning having the man checked out as best he could. He found nothing to indicate Mitch Wilson was anything but what he seemed—a man who ran a successful restaurant and bar in Lexington after moving here years ago to work his way through school at UK. He hadn't been in any trouble since he was a juvenile, and even then it had been nothing serious. Stephen hadn't found any previous ties to Megan or Kentucky. Which had him wondering what in the world Mitch Wilson was doing here. Now he wondered . . . had the man come here asking questions about Megan's death or looking for her? Because he had reason to believe she wasn't dead?

Of course, that was a question for another moment. Right now he had one very upset teenage boy to deal with.

"Why would Megan want everyone to believe that?"

"You tell me," Casey said, as changeable as the wind and once again the fragile-looking teenager. "Why'd she leave in the first place?"

"She didn't tell you?"

"She didn't tell me much of anything."

"Wait a minute," Stephen said. "Let's back up here. What's your mother's name?"

"Margaret Addison," he said. "But everybody calls her Meggie."

Stephen nodded, feeling worse by the minute. *Meggie.* He'd heard people call Megan that. "How old is she?"

"Old," Casey insisted. "Thirtysomething?"

"That old, huh?" Stephen thought of one more possibility. "Casey, are you adopted?"

The boy paled. "What?"

"The woman who raised you. The woman you think of as your mother. Could she be your adoptive mother? Could Megan Bennett have been your birth mother?"

The boy turned the color of chalk. For a minute he looked like he was going to be sick. "I don't know."

"Okay." Stephen put his hand on the kid's shoulder, to steady him, to try to apologize for springing that question on him so abruptly. "It was just an idea. Don't worry about that part of it right now."

Still, Casey looked positively ill.

"Let's go back to what you do know, okay?" Stephen tried. "Your mother, Margaret Addison, one day she . . . What? Told you her real name was Megan Lynn Bennett?"

"She was dying," Casey blurted out. "She hadn't told me much of anything until then. She said we didn't have any family. But . . . she was dying, and I guess she wanted to clear her conscience first. People do that, right? When they're dying?"

"I suppose," Stephen conceded. But he didn't think this was the truth. He thought the kid was lying through his teeth now, and he wished he'd gotten some more information out of the deputy, who called to tell Stephen he might have ID'd the runaway boy. A kid named Casey Addison had been reported missing from Birmingham, Alabama, and matched the description they had of Allie's runaway boy.

"So," Stephen continued, "on her deathbed, this woman who'd raised you said her real name was Megan Bennett, and that she was from Dublin, Kentucky."

Casey nodded, unconvincingly.

"What else?"

"Not much. She was pretty messed up. She got shot." He shrugged again, as if to say it was just one of those things. "We didn't have much time to talk. She said if anything happened to her, I should come here."

"Here? To this town?"

"Dublin, Kentucky, 307 Willow Lane. She said I should find Janet Bennett, that she was my grandmother. I couldn't believe it. All this time I had a grandmother, and she didn't even tell me."

"And then what happened."

"She died. I got sent to a foster home, but I didn't like it there. I didn't see why I should stay there if I had a grandmother. So I took off to find her." The kid kicked at the dirt with his oversize shoes. "So . . . if that lady was my grandmother, that means Allie's my aunt, right?"

"She would be," Stephen conceded, even as he dismissed nearly everything the kid said. It had the feel of a lie that got bigger with every question Stephen asked him. Except for the part about the adoption. The kid's reaction had been frighteningly genuine on that question. He'd been so scared, it had nearly made him sick.

Could some part of his story be true? Could this boy be Megan's son? One born right before she died and adopted by a woman named Margaret Addison from Birmingham, Alabama?

Stephen would love to believe that—complicated as it would be. He would love to find out that Megan had a child who was standing here in front of him. Because he cared about Megan, and he felt something even bigger and stronger for Allie. He knew what it would mean to her to have part of her family back. Allie, who ran on emotion alone and would want to believe everything Casey had to say, without a shred of proof.

"So," Casey said. "What did they do to my mother? To make her run away, I mean. Was it 'cause of me? 'Cause she was pregnant?"

"I don't know," Stephen said.

Casey rolled his eyes. "Yeah, right."

"She didn't tell me, okay? I don't think she told anybody."

Casey glared at him.

"I'm not lying to you," Stephen said. "I don't know.

The boy looked mad as hell. God, did he look a little bit like Megan, as well? Stephen ran a hand through his hair and tried to think. It was just as hard as it had been a minute ago when Casey dropped his bomb.

"You helped her get out of town," Casey argued. "And nobody saw her with anyone else that summer. I know because Allie's friend said so."

"What?" Stephen asked, thinking the situation couldn't possibly get any more complicated.

"I was at the house today. Allie's house . . . I went back to get my laptop. You found my laptop, right?"

"I found it. Tell me about Allie's friend."

"Carolyn. I heard her and Allie talking on the porch. Carolyn said everybody was sure Megan was carrying your baby, 'cause you're the only one anybody saw her with that summer."

"Carolyn Simms told Allie that Megan was pregnant with my baby?"

"Yeah. Explain that."

"Shit." That was it. Things couldn't get much worse than that. He should have told Allie this morning, but it wasn't something a man said to a woman after he'd just made love to her for the first time. *By the way, half the town thinks I got your sister pregnant fifteen years ago.*

"Shit," he said again.

"Yeah," Casey said. "She's probably dying to see you right now."

Stephen shook his head back and forth again. He

had thought he could control this situation, like he controlled everything else. He had thought he could dish out the information a little at a time, all the while winning her friendship, her trust, and keeping his father and his brother the hell away from her.

He'd blown it all to hell instead.

"So," Casey said. "What do we do now, *Dad?*"

Stephen looked up and saw one angry, confused teenager standing in front of him, one who was obviously in dire need of a little male guidance and some manners.

"You and I are going to have to cut a deal," he said.

Allie sat on the floor of her parents' bedroom, stuff strewn all around her, when she heard the car pull into the driveway.

Anybody but him, she prayed. Anybody but Stephen.

He rang the doorbell, called out her name. She thought childishly of hiding in the house, hoping he'd go away, but she knew he wouldn't. Her rental car was in the driveway. If she didn't let him in, he'd come inside himself and start looking for her. Which meant she had to deal with him. She had to calmly, firmly send him away.

Allie shoved open the window and called out, "I'm up here." She took her key ring from her pocket and threw it down to him, thinking she'd stay right here, keep the length of the room and all of this stuff between them. "Come on in. I couldn't get to the door right now if I had to."

She sat back down, all sorts of papers and clothes and jewelry in piles all around her, thinking she'd simply sit here and work like a woman possessed while he said whatever he wanted to say. She would be calm and cool and rational, when a part of her wanted to scream at him, wanted to drag him in here and make him look at this room, make him look at what it was doing to her to be here, to not know anything for sure. Let him watch her dig through her mother's papers like a madwoman, searching for some clue about her sister's life, when he probably knew everything and had simply chosen not to tell her.

Allie brushed an impatient hand across her cheeks, angrily swiping away tears. How dare he do this to her? How dare he make her care about a man she suspected must not even exist, a man he made up to put her at ease? To cast some sort of spell over her so he could control her, control what she found out about her own family and the things she believed and everything she felt.

Damn him.

"Allie?"

She looked up and found him standing in the doorway, trim and fit and so very handsome in a pair of tan slacks and a dark blue blazer. His gaze flickered from her to the destruction she'd wrought in the room, then came back to her again. He smiled, but she thought he looked a little sad, and she had the strangest feeling that he knew everything. Everything she'd heard that day, everything she felt about him. Somehow, he always knew.

"I brought you a surprise," he said quietly.

She frowned, wondering if he thought of her as a child he could win over with a trinket here and there. Then he stepped aside, and Casey filled the open doorway.

"Hi." Allie felt happy for the first time all day. She

fought the urge to get up and run to the boy, to wrap her arms around him and hold him tight, to make him promise never to scare her again by running off.

"Hi." Casey scuffed the toe of his sneakers across the hardwood floor and wouldn't look at her.

"I'm so glad you're back," she said, hating that she automatically looked to Stephen for help. It seemed an ingrained response, from the first time she saw him six days ago. She was scared, and he was here. She needed to cry, he held her. She needed to feel safe and loved, he'd make love to her, lying to her the whole time.

"Casey tells me his mother died a few weeks ago," Stephen said, carefully keeping the distance of the room between them.

"Died?" Allie looked to Casey, who immediately looked away. He'd told her emphatically that he had a home to go to and a mother who loved him very, very much.

"He was in a foster home in Birmingham," Stephen continued, "and he doesn't want to go back. He'd like to stay here for a few days and try to sort out his problems. If that's okay with you."

Allie held her tongue about the contradictions between what Casey had told Stephen and what he'd told Allie. They could sort it out later. For now, she wanted Casey here with her.

Of course, that meant she had to deal with Stephen, too. She had to wonder—was this his true talent? That he could be anything a woman wanted? He could somehow figure out what a woman needed and mold and shape himself to fit her needs? There was nothing he could have given her at the moment that she truly would have appreciated, except bringing Casey to her. Nothing that would have made her even want to talk to him, except to find out what he knew about Casey.

Allie tried to wipe the anger from her expression, and when that didn't work, she settled for looking at Casey instead, who seemed upset and in great need of reassurance. He was only thirteen, just an overgrown boy. She knew because the deputy had called her. From the sketchy, initial report he had, it didn't seem like anyone had even been looking for him until today. And as worried as Stephen had been, Casey hadn't done anything bad at all, except run away.

"I'd like for you to stay," she said.

"You won't call the sheriff?" he asked.

"I wouldn't have called before if I'd known it was you up there." Allie frowned. "You could have told me, you know. I would have helped you."

He said nothing. Stephen glared at the boy a minute longer, and finally Casey said, "I'm sorry I scared you. I didn't mean to. At least not once I got to know you."

Allie laughed at the confession. "You were here all along? From the first night?"

Casey nodded.

"That's all right," Allie said. "I'm guessing you could use some food, a shower, and some clean clothes right about now."

He frowned. "I smell pretty bad, huh?"

"Come on." Allie got to her feet. "My father's clothes are still in the closet. I'm sure we can find something for you to wear."

He looked like a little boy then, and she remembered that he was only thirteen and all alone in the world, just like she was. She wondered what he'd do if she tried to hug him. He looked as if he expected her to reject his apology and send him back out onto the streets.

"Everything's going to be all right," she promised.

Chapter 15

She gave him everything he needed to shower and dress, then went downstairs to face Stephen. The back door was open. He stood just outside the doorway, leaning against the side of the house and smoking.

"I've never seen you do that," she said, intrigued.

"I try not to make a habit of it," he said wryly, taking one more drag off the cigarette before putting it out and coming inside.

"Thank you for bringing Casey back," she said, because she was grateful and she'd been raised to be polite. "He told me he had a home to go to. A mother who loved him very much. He seemed absolutely sincere."

"He said a lot of things, Allie. So far none of them have been true."

Allie nodded. She didn't want to accuse Casey of lying, not now that she finally had him back. There would be time later for explanations, she hoped. And then she thought of something else.

"Stephen, you didn't call the sheriff did you?"

"No. I meant what I said to Casey. I think he should stay here for a few days while I try to find out what's going on in Birmingham."

"*You?*" she asked.

"Do you trust me to do that, Allie?" He gave her a bleak look, his eyes guarded, tiny lines of tension at the corners of his mouth. "To find out what I can about the boy and tell you?"

She looked at him for a moment, then looked away.

"Fine," he said. "A friend of mine from law school practices there in the family court system. He could probably help cut through some of the red tape for you. If that's what you want."

"*What I want?*" she said. "What does that mean? That you're suddenly so concerned about what *I* want?"

"I'm concerned about everything to do with you. Do you believe that at all? Do you believe anything I've said to you? Anything that happened between us last night and this morning? Or do you think the whole thing was a lie?"

Her face burned at the mention of this morning. It was too easy, now that he was here, to remember things she shouldn't about those stolen moments on the sofa, about waking up beside him, about the feel of his skin and the weight of his body on top of hers. It had felt so good, so right. Like coming home, the way she'd always wanted it to be and not the way it actually felt to be back in this lonely old house that was making her crazy.

Why did he have to do that to her? Why did he have to show her how good it could be, then yank it all away? It had been nothing but an illusion, after all. Some trick of smoke and mirrors and lies. And he was angry enough that he had to have heard she knew about him and Megan.

"You talked to Carolyn," she guessed.

Teresa Hill

"No, I talked to Casey. He was here. He overheard the two of you."

"Oh." The silence stretched out between her and Stephen, an awkward tension that built with every passing moment until it seemed insurmountable, until she wanted to scream.

"Are you even going to ask me?" he said finally, sounding angrier than she'd ever heard him. "Or have you already made up your mind? Are you really going to condemn me on the basis of fifteen-year-old gossip?"

Allie stayed quiet, because she hadn't decided how to handle this, because the situation seemed as if it might explode.

He came to stand in front of her. She backed away until she was trapped, the wall at her back, him in front of her. He stretched out his long arms, until his hands rested on the wall at either side of her head, his big, powerful body crowding hers until she shrank away from the man whose touch she welcomed hours before.

"Ask me, Allie," he demanded. "Was Megan pregnant with my baby when she left? Ask me."

She swallowed, seeing a whole different side of him. This was the ruthless businessman who intimidated people and knew exactly how to get his way. This was a man she didn't know, a man who didn't seem to have an ounce of tenderness or compassion in him. She couldn't believe she'd fallen for him so completely, that she'd given herself to him this morning. Not just given, her conscience taunted her. She'd thrown herself at him, had begged him to make love to her. *Damn him.*

"Ask me," he demanded.

"Why?" She'd been pushed to the point where she

266

didn't care if all her instincts screamed at her to be very, very careful with him right now. "What's the point in asking if I won't believe anything you say?"

Granite-hard eyes narrowed, his gaze fixed on her. She saw him fighting for control, saw his jaw tighten, the muscles in his arms tremble with tension. Slowly, carefully, he backed away from her, then turned his back to her.

"I have never lied to you," he said quietly.

"Of course not. You just never tell me anything. Is there really a difference, Stephen? Do you honestly believe they're not one and the same?"

"How would it have helped you to hear something like that?" He turned to face her. "All it would have done is hurt you and worry you and make it harder for you to trust me."

"And this helped?"

"You're saying if I had told you, you would have believed me?"

"I'm saying it makes me mad as hell to think that just about everybody in this town knows more than I do about my own family, and it's even worse when someone who professes to care about me chooses to keep something like this from me," she cried. "Do you have any idea how it felt to have Carolyn Simms tell me that my sister was pregnant when she left here—"

"Does she know that for certain, Allie? Did Megan tell her that? Or is she just repeating something she heard?"

"Is that your cryptic way of telling me my sister wasn't pregnant?'

"It's my way of saying I don't know."

"How did I know you were going to say that?" she asked bitterly. "It's just so convenient, isn't it?

Because if you don't know for certain, you don't have to tell me."

"It's damned inconvenient, believe me. I wish I knew, but Megan never told me. As far as I know, she never told anyone else, either."

"And if she was pregnant?" Allie asked, losing all shreds of control. "If she was, was it your baby? Could it have been?"

"No," he said tightly, unequivocally.

He held her gaze, never wavering, never hesitating. It was Allie who had to look away, Allie who was left wanting to believe him once again, despite all the reasons she shouldn't.

Silence descended again, a taut, suffocating silence.

"I guess you were right," Stephen said finally. "There was no point in denying it when there was no chance you'd believe me."

"Think about it, Stephen. People are saying you slept with my sister, that she was carrying your baby, and you didn't even tell me."

"Because it isn't true, Allie. I heard that your father, in an absolute rage one night, strangled you and your mother and hid your bodies in the basement, too. That's why your house is supposed to be haunted. But I didn't choose to tell you that, either. It wasn't true, and it would only hurt you to hear it. Are you going to condemn me for that, as well?"

"That must be one of the more popular pieces of gossip." She laughed bitterly. "Casey told me that."

Stephen swore, a tightly controlled string of curses in a deadly, even tone. Then he came across the room again in three strides, catching her by her arms and standing there, all heat and dangerous sexual pull, until she looked him in the eye.

"I care about you," he said. "I cared about Megan,

too. But in a totally different way, and the last thing I want to do is hurt you."

"If that were true," Allie said, "you'd tell me what happened here. That's what matters to me now."

"The only thing?"

"I can't deal with anything else right now, all right. I'm a mess, and being here is tearing me apart. Sitting in that room, going through all their things . . . It's tearing me apart. You can't even begin to understand what this is doing to me."

Her voice broke on the last few words. He went to take her into his arms, but she shoved him away.

"Don't," she said. "Not now."

"All right." Stephen took a deep, slow breath, then backed away. "I'll do what you want."

"You'll tell me what you know?"

"I'll take you with me while I try to find out what happened. I've been trying to get in touch with someone who keeps avoiding me. I'm not going to let him do that today." He looked over her outfit, the dusty shirt, the ragged jeans. "You're going to need to get dressed. Something nice, like the dress you wore to the restaurant last night."

"Now?" she said. "Where are we going?"

"To see my brother."

Allie gaped at him. "You think your brother had something to do with Megan's disappearance?"

"Yes," he said unequivocally.

Allie couldn't have been more surprised. Of all the things he might have said . . . His brother? She'd never known his brother well, although what she'd heard—his arrogance, his penchant for trouble, his drinking—might lead one to think it was possible such a person might have been capable of much worse things.

But he was Stephen's brother. Even when she'd doubted Stephen and been so angry with him for keeping things from her, she'd never quite been able to make herself believe he was capable of doing away with her sister. It was hard to think of someone as close to him as a brother being so evil. And it didn't fit. Not from what she knew of her sister.

"I don't think Megan even liked your brother."

"Then she was a smart girl," Stephen said.

"If she didn't like him, I can't imagine her becoming involved with him. Did you ever see them together?"

"I saw him slipping out of the house to meet someone a few times, and I can't imagine why he would have done that unless it was someone he shouldn't have been with. Maybe someone else's wife, some other guy's girl. Maybe someone whose parents would object to her seeing a boy his age. Or one with Rich's reputation."

"What kind of reputation did he have?"

"For getting whatever he wanted. For being arrogant enough and spoiled enough to think he deserved to have whatever he wanted," Stephen said. "And I hate the thought of you knowing him and my father, knowing what they're like, and thinking I must be just the same."

"What did they do, Stephen?"

"What haven't they done? They'll lie about anything. Steal, cheat, break a woman's heart without thinking twice about it. My father's latest mistress was making a scene around town this past summer. Things have been particularly ugly. That's why my parents are on this extended trip, to try to patch things up, while I guard the house."

"Guard the house?"

"My father's mistress came to visit one day and made a bit of a mess. My mother does love the house, and she was uneasy about leaving it empty."

"God, Stephen," Allie said.

"And Rich has been drinking again. So far, he's managed to hide it fairly well. But I don't know how long that can go on. I don't know what drives him to it; I'm afraid to know. But there's always been a recklessness to him. All those things you hear about rich kids—spoiled and arrogant and used to getting whatever they want? Rich could be the poster child for the lot of them."

And he and his brother were so different. That was her first thought. Stephen wasn't like that. Irritating, controlling, secretive when it suited him. But despite what he'd done to her, despite how angry she was at him, she didn't think he was reckless or evil. Still . . .

"You can't stand your own brother?" she asked. "And yet you've been protecting him all this time?"

"Not him. Not my father. But everyone else in my family. My mother's had a tough time of it lately, Allie. I was afraid Rich might have done something to Megan all those years ago, but I never had any proof and I didn't want to say anything unless I was certain," Stephen said. "He has a wife and two little girls, too. It's one thing to condemn a guilty man, but another to let innocent women and children suffer from nothing but old rumors. I never imagined he might have had her killed. I hope you can understand that. I hope . . ."

He reached for her.

Allie backed away from him one more time. The wound was still too raw. She was still shocked by what he'd told her, yet still thinking that every time she caught him keeping something from her, he managed to come up with what she thought was a perfectly reasonable excuse for what he'd done.

So . . . he'd been protecting the people he loved all this time? He'd been worried enough about them to hide so many things from her, to hurt her badly?

She looked up at him, trying to see him clearly, as if for the first time, and kept thinking, *his own brother? A killer?*

She didn't want to think about how she'd feel if that were true. She couldn't. And she had so little to judge his brother by. She knew he was a few years older than Stephen, not as handsome or as pleasant. She remembered him being dismissive of her and Megan, sometimes downright rude. Had Megan warned her away from Rich one time? Allie couldn't quite remember. She probably hadn't ever said five words to him in her whole life.

"You really think Rich did it," she said. "You think he was following her. That he might have killed her."

"Why would he?" Stephen asked. "Don't misunderstand me. I can accept the possibility that he might be capable of killing someone. I've seen him drunk and absolutely out of control before. In a rage, Allie. But when I think about it logically . . . Megan was already gone. It didn't look like she was coming back. What kind of a threat could she be to him from Macon, Georgia?"

"Maybe he wanted to make sure she never came back."

"I don't know, Allie. All this time . . . I guess I was afraid to find out."

"You knew all along he had something to do with her disappearance?"

"No. It wasn't until later, after she was gone . . . I overheard something that made me think he might have gotten her pregnant. I could imagine him suggesting she get out of town and never tell anyone the baby was his. But I never thought he'd do anything like kill her. I swear, I didn't."

Allie stared at him, wanting to believe that, trying not to think that he could have a brother who might have killed her sister, one who might have been responsible for her family falling apart. A man who'd taken everything from her.

Stephen must have seen it in her eyes, all the doubts, all the hurt.

"Let's go find my brother," he said in a tightly controlled voice.

Twenty minutes later Allie had changed her clothes, spoken with Casey, and climbed into the car with Stephen. She watched as he smoked another cigarette, which seemed to irritate him to no end. She was amazed at what seemed to be a blatant lack of control on his part.

She didn't ask where they were going, and he didn't say anything, except to pick up his cell phone, speaking quickly and with familiarity to a woman named Renee.

"My sister-in-law," he explained when he was finished.

"Oh?" she asked as casually as she could manage.

"Careful. I might think you'd care if there was another woman in my life."

"You'd be mistaken," she lied.

He never took his eyes off the road. The car shot forward as he said, "It meant something to me, too, Allie."

"What?"

"Last night. This morning. You can't be so inexperienced that you don't realize how special it was. How good we are together."

"We had sex," she insisted, needing to put it on that level. "And it was a mistake."

"Maybe. But not for the reason you're thinking. It was a mistake because it happened before you were ready. Before we knew each other well enough to trust each other, and I apologize for that. But not for the fact that we were together. It was bound to happen sooner or later. I think in your heart you know that."

"Stephen, don't.

"All right," he said. "I'm done for now."

They drove for another fifteen minutes before her need to talk things out overcame her reluctance to say anything at all to him.

"I still can't make sense of this. Even if Megan was pregnant, even if my parents reacted badly at first, they would have forgiven her and taken care of her. For the baby's sake, at least."

"You're sure about that?"

"They would have been disappointed, and my mother would have been embarrassed." Again, she thought of her mother's angry words to her father. *You wanted her gone.* Again, she dismissed them. "They wouldn't have turned their backs on her or her baby."

"Maybe. Maybe not. What do you remember about that summer?"

"That she was too thin, too pale. That she looked different, frightened maybe. What about you? What do you remember about her?"

"She had a way of pulling inside herself. Like she wanted to just disappear. She'd always been like that to some degree, but it was more pronounced that summer. I tried to talk to her about it one night, but she didn't give a lot away. She just seemed so sad."

"Did you ever see her with bruises?"

"No."

"Did you ever think my father had hurt her physically?"

"No. He seemed to be a very loving father to you. I saw the two of you together a lot, and I envied the relationship the two of you had."

"What do you mean?"

"You trailed after him like a shadow. He could be working in the yard or around the house, and you'd be right there with him. He always made time for you. He was patient and kind, and he wanted you with him."

Stephen said it matter-of-factly, but Allie suspected there were a lot of things he hadn't said about his relationship with his own father. "Your father didn't make time for you?"

"He was more interested in the idea of a son than the reality."

"And now?" she wondered.

"We have very little in common. He doesn't understand me, and I don't have any respect for him. I'm not my father, Allie. If you don't believe anything else I tell you, please believe that."

"I'm not going to judge you based on your father's actions, Stephen."

"Of course not." He laughed bitterly. "There's no need. Not when I've given you so much ammunition to hang me with."

"I don't know what I think of you," she said.

And to that, he said nothing.

A few moments later, Stephen zoomed through an intersection near the airport. He drove down a road amid tall trees and rows of parked cars, and pulled to a stop at the entrance to a massive stone structure, where a man in a green suit jacket hurried forward to take the car.

Allie got out and waited for Stephen to come around to her side of the car. He pressed the palm of his hand to the small of her back and led her inside a door marked "Clubhouse entrance."

"Where are we?" she said.

"Keeneland," he replied.

"Keeneland?"

"Allie, are you sure you were born and bred in Central Kentucky? It's a racetrack. A very famous racetrack. For Thoroughbreds."

She looked around, taking in the elegance and grace of the old stone building, the beautiful arching windows. "It looks like a castle."

"To the horse set, it is."

"Your brother's into horse racing, too?"

"In this state, in April and October, nearly everyone is. This is *the* Lexington social scene, but a lot of business is transacted here, too."

Stephen led her to an elevator marked "private" and had a few words with the attendant, who summoned the car and allowed them to enter. Allie found herself growing apprehensive about seeing Stephen's brother. She'd expected a private exchange between the three of them in an office in the governor's mansion. She now knew it would be anything but private. And she suspected it wouldn't be cordial, either.

"Does your brother know we're coming?" she said.

"No. He's been dodging my calls all week." Stephen looked at her. "I have been trying to find out for you, Allie. I didn't lie to you about that."

Allie said nothing. The elevator slid to a stop. They walked into a richly appointed clubhouse, elegant but obviously very expensive, then through a door also marked "private." The next room was even more richly appointed, all dark wood and a deep shade of green. There were perhaps two dozen people present, businessmen in suits and ties, a few well-dressed women, all clustered around the large windows in the front of the room or one of two TV screens mounted on the wall. A race was in progress, and Allie could hear people cheering, the roar of the crowd both outside and in.

Stephen slipped through the crowd, his hand in hers as he led her to his brother's side. "Rich? I've been trying to get a hold of you."

Richard Whittaker, taller and heavier than Allie remembered, his face a bit flushed and a woman in a low-cut dress hanging onto his arm, turned to face his brother. "I've been busy." He frowned. "I was going to call you tonight."

"I thought I'd save you the trouble," Stephen said. "And I wanted you to meet someone. An old friend, actually."

Stephen stepped back, leaving her face-to-face with his brother.

Richard Whittaker nearly choked on the whiskey he'd just put in his mouth, and he turned pale. Two men, security people Allie suspected, rushed to his side. Coughing, he brushed them off, then rudely got rid of the woman lingering by his side as well.

Furious, he turned back to Stephen. "Come with me."

Rich charged through the room, rudely dismissing all attempts at conversation, then stormed into an office and asked the startled man behind the desk to leave them alone.

The man closed the file on his desk and got up to leave, but not before looking over Allie and Stephen suspiciously. "Do you need anything else, Mr. Whittaker?" he said, obviously thinking of calling security himself.

"Just privacy," barked the man, obviously used to being obeyed.

"Nice touch, Rich." Stephen waited until the man was nearly out the door to say. "You really know how to handle the little people."

Rich glared at him, then turned his attention to Allie. She shivered as his gaze raked over her from head to toe.

"What's wrong?" Stephen taunted. "You look like you've seen a ghost."

"Megan Bennett," he said, shaking his head in disgust and downing what was left of the whiskey in his hand. "God, where did you dig her up?"

"Not from some creek in Georgia, that's for sure."

Rich moved more quickly than Allie would have thought a man of his size could. One minute he was two feet away, and the next he was right in her face. His breath reeked of alcohol, his grip hard and painful on her upper arms.

Allie knew instantly where the bruises on her sister's arms came from.

"What kind of lies have you been telling this time, Meggie?" he said menacingly.

Stephen didn't ask his brother to let her go. He shoved him out of the way, putting himself between Allie and Rich. Allie thought they were going to come to blows. She thought Stephen would have welcomed it.

"You'd better watch it, Rich. You'd have a hard time explaining a black eye on the campaign trail."

Rich blustered, his face flushed, a string of curses coming from his lips. "I don't know what kind of game you're playing, but if you're smart, you'll stop right now. And as for you?" He glared at Allie again. "I will destroy you. Nobody believed you fifteen years ago. What makes you think they will today?"

Allie drew herself up straighter, taller, hating this man on sight, ready to play along with the fact that she obviously looked enough like her sister to fool him. Maybe he had a guilty conscience, as well.

"It *was* your baby," she said.

Rich paled once again, and Allie knew it was true.

"You go through with this . . . you try to mess with me, and I will crush you," he threatened. "Remember what it felt like when nobody believed you, Meggie. Remember when your own father didn't even believe your little lies?"

The old Allie would have shrank away from him. She would have cried and run away, leaving all the secrets in the past, where everyone had always claimed they belonged. But not *this* Allie. She faced down Richard Whittaker as she imagined her sister would have liked to, if Megan were here today.

"I'm not a little girl anymore," Allie said. "I'm not scared of you, and I'm not going to keep quiet."

"You stupid little bitch—"

Stephen drew back his fist and slammed it into his brother's nose. Blood came gushing out, and Rich was swearing and gagging as he slumped against the desk, trying to stem the flow of blood from his nose.

"Shut up, Rich."

"She's nothing but a tramp," he yelled. "She came trotting after me that summer like a bitch in heat, all because you didn't know she was alive. All I did was give her what she was asking for."

"Of course. Can't stand to send them away disappointed, can you?"

"What the hell are you talking about?" Rich said.

"I think there was another girl, wasn't there? Who took exception to what you did to her. I think you were sure she wanted you, too. You have such a way with women, after all. I bet if I tried hard I could remember her name."

"You have no idea what you're getting into," Rich warned. "And you can't believe anything this woman says."

"Really?" Allie said. "You know, I saw you in Macon, and I'm going to tell everyone what you tried to do to me."

Richard Whittaker stared at her. He staggered backward a step. Then another. She'd never seen anyone go so pale so fast, and felt a small amount of satisfaction for being the one to scare the man so badly. Suddenly he looked about ten years older than he really was, and Allie knew. She knew he'd killed her sister.

"What do you think you're going to do?" Rich said menacingly, when he'd recovered a bit. "What the hell do you think you're going to do to me?"

"What you deserve," Stephen said. "What you've always deserved."

Stephen drove into an open field labeled OVERFLOW PARKING, still on the racetrack grounds, and cut the engine. Nervous energy pushed Allie out of the car, where she could pace back and forth. Stephen got out, too, and leaned against the side of the car.

"He raped her," Allie said finally. "Your brother raped my sister all those years ago. You knew that?"

"I thought it was a possibility. But no, I didn't know."

"God, Stephen? Is that your answer to everything? That you don't know for sure. So you just ignore things and look the other way. Is that what kind of man you are?"

"I'll tell you what I knew," he said, the barest hint of anger in his tone as he fought for control. "And then I'll tell you about me. After that, you can judge for yourself. All right?"

Sick, she nodded.

"I knew your sister was upset. I held her one night while she cried her eyes out, but I couldn't make her tell me what was wrong," he said. "Rich was always in trouble. From the time he was fifteen or so, my father was always getting him out of one kind of jam or another. He drank. He wrecked cars. He got into fights, acted like there were no rules that applied to him. He thought he had a license to do whatever he wanted, maybe because my father brought him up that way. Whatever Rich did, my father never thought it was that bad. He was always quick to cover things up, to make things right. Money could almost always fix whatever Rich had done. Then there was a girl I heard about. Rich supposedly slept with her, and she took exception to it afterward. I thought he must have gotten her pregnant. I never thought he was raping women. I wouldn't have kept quiet about that.

"I hardly ever saw him, Allie. He was in law school at UK, and I was at Vanderbilt. That summer, my father was upset with Rich, but that was nothing new. And I never connected what was going on with

Megan to Rich," he said. "Why would I? Megan was sixteen. Rich was twenty-two, and your quiet, shy older sister was not his usual type."

"So how did you put it together?"

"After Megan ran away, people were saying she was pregnant. I overheard my father say something to Rich about her—something about how Rich should be glad that little problem was out of the way, and that he hoped Rich learned something from the whole experience," Stephen said. "I thought Rich got Megan pregnant and asked her to leave town. The other girl I brought up to Rich—that happened later. It wasn't until then that I started wondering about Megan. If maybe he forced her, too. At that point, what could I have done, Allie? Megan was gone. And the other point? That he might have intimidated her into leaving? She left on her own. No one forced her to go. I know that because she left with me."

"So you just let it go?"

"I felt guilty as hell about what happened to her. But I still didn't know anything. I didn't see the point in asking my father or my brother—I wouldn't have believed anything they said about it. And without any evidence . . . what could I have done? She was dead."

"I don't know," she said. "All those questions . . . All those doubts . . ."

"You lived with them yourself for years," he pointed out. "And I'm not saying that to hurt you or to criticize you. I'm saying people make compromises all the time. Your mother was all you had left. You lived with the questions, you made your peace with it, for the sake of your relationship with her."

Allie closed her eyes, not quite able to bring herself to admit she'd done just that.

"This is my family," Stephen said finally. "I've been trying to find a way to co-exist with them for years. Mostly, I go my own way now. I love my mother, but I don't understand her. She stays with my father even though he treats her like shit. My father and I are like polite strangers. I tolerate him for my mother's sake, and I tolerate my brother, as well, but I don't trust him and I worry about what he's capable of doing to someone else or even to himself. We gather around the dinner table on national holidays and act as civilized as possible. I run into them every now and then when I go see my mother. But that's it. That's my big, happy family.

"Did I do the wrong thing all those years ago? I don't know. I regret a lot of things—especially the fact that your sister died. But regrets don't change anything. I've tried hard to live my life the way I see fit and be comfortable with the man I've become. But looking at it all through your eyes, I don't really like what I see. I'm afraid you won't, either."

Allie squeezed his hands more tightly, hating the bleakness of his tone. He'd been hurt, too. "Stephen—"

His hands were on her arms, gentle and soothing where his brother had no doubt left bruises. He seemed to feel the need to atone for what his family had done, so Allie let herself rest there, nearly in his arms, nearly back under the mesmerizing spell that was Stephen Whittaker.

"I'm sorry, Allie." He brought one of his hands to the side of her face. "I'm so sorry. I hate what my family's done to yours."

She leaned into him, into the luxurious warmth and reassurance of his touch. In a few short days she'd become addicted to it. She didn't protest when he shifted, bringing his body in line with hers, pulling her to him and wrapping his arms around her. He pressed her head down to his chest and gently stroked her back. She felt some of the tension seep out of her, some of the ugliness of that scene with his brother fading away and that awful, enveloping loneliness fading away. Even now, he just took it all away.

"How do you make every bad thing seem not so bad when you touch me this way?"

"I don't know, Allie. I do know life looks a whole lot better when you're in my arms."

Allie didn't know what she could say to that. She liked the whole world so much better when she was in his arms. But she didn't trust the feelings, either. Didn't trust them to last, didn't trust him not to hurt her again.

He made her feel so much, as if her heart was so full it hurt. It scared her, and she didn't understand it, and it hurt. She felt raw and utterly exposed. But she didn't know how to walk away from him, either.

He rested his chin on the top of her head, her face was buried in the sweet-smelling curve of his neck. Heat radiated from him, and she snuggled closer. After years of being so empty inside, she didn't know how she could go back to the way things had been without him in her life.

Chapter 16

Martha heard about the runaway boy during the lunch shift, and she hurried home to tell Tucker, hoping it would put his mind at ease about his silly notion that the boy could be Janet Bennett's son.

It hurt Martha that her man was still so hung up on a woman he hadn't seen in fifteen years that he was in a tizzy about this boy. Martha had been living with that kind of hurt for as long as she'd been involved with Tucker. He'd been up front with her from the start. He'd given his heart to someone else, and even if he couldn't be with that woman, he would never love anyone else. Martha heard him loud and clear. She simply hadn't believed him at the time. But it turned out to be the truest thing anyone had ever told her, and she couldn't even find it in her heart to hold it against Tucker when he'd warned her so plainly. What he didn't understand was that Martha didn't have a choice at that point, either. She was already in love with Tucker, even if he couldn't love her back.

She pulled up in front of the house. Tucker, looking grim, was waiting.

"You heard?" she said.

"Some nonsense about the boy being a runaway

from Mississippi who's been hiding out at the Bennett house."

"Alabama," she said. "The boy's from Alabama. Birmingham, I heard. The sheriff found a bulletin on him."

"Bulletin?" he said. "What did the kid do?"

"Ran away."

"Why'd he come here? Why the Bennett house?"

"I don't know. It's as good a place as any."

Tucker shook his head. "Something's not right. That boy . . . for him to be there. For him to look so much like Janet. . . . It can't be a coincidence."

"What else could it be?" Martha asked.

"I don't know. But I'm going to find out."

They were once again near downtown Lexington when Stephen turned into a street of elegant, brick town houses in a lushly landscaped, garden-like setting, pulling into the driveway of an end unit. There were wide sidewalks, a profusion of fall color from the trees and the flowers. He led her to the back of his town house to a patio that bordered a small lake. Allie stared at the water, a calm silvery blue. Some ducks paddled lazily across the water in the distance. Birds soared overhead. She was so tired, and she just wanted to forget about every ugly thing they'd found out today. She wanted to let this place soothe her, let herself have just a few more moments with Stephen.

"It's lovely here," she said. "You built this development?"

"Rebuilt it."

"I like it, Stephen."

"I was hoping you would."

He slid an arm around her waist and led her inside. It wasn't flashy or fancy, the room filled with solid pieces of furniture, the overall feeling one of understated elegance, but comfort, as well. The walls were an off-white color—a chalk-like shade that looked rich and wonderfully textured against the accents in dark green. She could see Stephen here, sprawled out on the big, striped sofa, walking down the beautiful staircase in the morning with his shirt unbuttoned, the tails untucked, his hair still wet from the shower.

"It suits you," she said.

"How is that?"

"Solid, strong, dependable." She believed he was all of those things.

He winced. "God, I'm that boring?"

"No." She shook her head. "Nothing like that."

Stephen put his keys on the foyer table. Allie followed him, admiring the massive mahogany door with its elegant cut-glass window, the antique light fixture that hung in the hallway in front of the elaborate gold-tinted mirror.

She could see them reflected in the mirror. He caught her staring and came up behind her, slipping his hands around her waist and pulling her body back to rest against his. Heat radiated from him. He spread his fingers wide, his palm flat against her abdomen. Pleasure unfurled deep inside her belly, his effect on her that potent, that instantaneous.

"I don't want to take you back just yet." He nudged her head to the side, his mouth settling on the tender skin at the side of her neck. "You scared me today. The way you looked at me. The things you were thinking about me."

Allie shivered as his teeth nipped at her neck, her body coming alive. She could feel his erection pressed against her hips. Instinctively, she arched against him, increasing the pressure, unable to stop herself from wanting him. Hours ago, she'd been crushed, thinking he'd gotten her sister pregnant, believing everything between him and her had been a lie.

"It scared me, too," she admitted.

"I'm afraid you're going to hate me before this is over," he said, through lips pressed to her skin, his mouth doing terribly erotic things to her neck.

And then she knew he'd brought her here to make love to her again, to bind them even more strongly together. She shivered at the thought. And she wanted it, too. To be bound to him to the point where nothing at all could ever come between them again.

Stephen lifted his head. His gaze met hers in the mirror. "Are you afraid of me?"

"I've never been afraid of you. Just of the way you make me feel."

He turned her in his arms until she faced him, letting her rest there against him for a minute, unashamed of his blatant arousal, letting her think of what he wanted, letting her make up her mind about what she wanted, as well.

"Come upstairs with me, Allie. I have a big, old mahogany bed with cream-colored sheets, and I've been picturing you there. I've been thinking you're going to look absolutely perfect in my bed."

Trembling at the erotic image he painted in her head, she slipped her hand into his and let him lead her upstairs. The bed was magnificent, the wood rich and positively gleaming, the mattress sitting high off the floor. He pulled back the comforter and the top sheet, lifted her up onto the mattress, and eased her back until she was lying on the bed. Then he undressed her.

Watching her the entire time, he slipped off her shoes, unbuttoned the cuffs of her sleeves, then the tiny buttons down the front of her dress. He pulled the ends of the dress open, leaving her in a lacy pair of panties and a matching bra and stockings that stopped at the top of her thighs.

The bra fastened in front, and he undid that and pulled it open as well, then slid her panties down her hips and stepped back to study her as she imagined he might study a painting in a museum.

His look alone was enough to heat her body, to have her itching to touch him, to look at him as he was looking at her. She felt her nipples bunch up, begging for his touch, until they almost hurt. She watched him watch the changes in them, nearly arched up off the bed in anticipation when he reached out a hand and slowly stroked one of her breasts, then the other.

He used one hand, five fingers, running all over her body, as if he might memorize her by touch alone. He stroked her jaw, ran the pad of his finger along her bottom lip. She touched the tip of her tongue to his thumb and was rewarded by the first, brief break in his control. He looked for a minute like he was going to devour her whole, but pulled back a second later and resumed that sweet, slow stroking of her body.

When his hand finally dipped between her thighs, there was no hiding what he'd done to her. Her body was soft and moist, ready for him. He slid one finger deep inside of her, and she cried out, wondering if he was going to do nothing but watch her. If he was going to make her writhe and beg and cry out.

She'd never seen a man more intent on learning her body, learning what she liked and how she responded to his touch. She was twisting and turning on the bed, fighting to stay still but unable to, fighting not to reach for him, not to beg for him. But she was dying to touch him.

She closed her eyes, was breathing as if she'd just ran for miles. There were tears seeping out of the corners of her eyes, and then she felt his tongue, warm and smooth and velvety soft, against the inside curve of her knee. The bed gave beneath his weight. He settled himself between her legs, a hand on either side of her legs as he leaned over her.

He slowly worked his way up her thigh, licking and sucking and biting gently. She cried out when he reached her center, at the first sweet touch of his tongue, and moments later when her whole body convulsed around him. He was merciless, going on and on when she knew she just couldn't take anymore. Sensations piled on top of sensations, overwhelming her, leaving her drained and weak and still so very needy. Until he finally stripped off his clothes and came to her, covering her body with his, filling all the empty places until she thought she would never be alone again, that she would never be afraid, and knowing she would always, always need him.

The phone rang, pulling Stephen out of a deep, satisfying sleep. He grabbed the receiver and rolled onto his back. Allie followed him, sleepily settling herself against his side, trusting him at least in her sleep.

Stephen brought the phone to his ear. "Hello."

"What the hell do you think you're doing!" a voice roared at him.

"Hello, Dad," Stephen said casually.

"Have you lost your mind?" his father said. "Knocking your brother down in a public place. Bloodying his nose. Your brother is so upset. I've never seen him like this. I don't know how I'm going to calm him down, and with the election coming up, he doesn't need this, Stephen. None of us do. I still can't believe you did it. Despite our differences, I never thought you'd forget who your family is. Or hurt your brother this way."

"What can I say? I never knew my brother had taken up raping sixteen-year-old girls as a pastime."

"Is that what that woman told you? And I know damned well it wasn't Megan Bennett. There's no way Alicia Bennett could know for sure what happened fifteen years ago. She's going fishing, Stephen, probably thinking we'd pay a fortune to keep her from running her mouth about Rich and her sister, and I can't believe you've let yourself be a part of that, of ruining your brother's career."

"I think Rich can ruin his career all by himself without any help from me. Or Allie."

"She's playing with you, Stephen. I can't believe you've been fooled so easily by a woman."

"You don't know anything about her, Dad."

"I know I trusted you to take care of this for me. I can't believe I thought you could do this for me without screwing it up."

"I can't believe you protected a rapist. Did you know he killed her, Dad? Did you protect him then, too?"

"That's nonsense. That girl died in a car accident in Georgia."

"Did she? Or did somebody run her car off the road that night."

"You don't know what you're talking about," his father said. "And if you'd just done what I told you, none of this would have come out. We could have paid that girl a nice price for that house, and she would have been gone by now. I could have handled it—"

"The way you handled Megan Bennett? You must have loved it that I was the one who helped her out of town, solving that little problem for you."

"It was convenient," his father said.

"God," Stephen groaned. He'd helped them get away with it.

"You're forgetting what's important here, son. We're your family, and family's what counts."

"I've done all I'm ever going to do in the name of family loyalty. You've shoved that concept down my throat for years, and it's not going to work anymore."

"Stephen, I swear to God I wonder if you're really my son."

"Right now I wish I wasn't."

"Stay away from Alicia Bennett."

"Tell Rich to stay away from her. If he tries to come near her, he'll have to get past me. The same goes for anybody else you might send after her."

"Don't you threaten me, Stephen."

"I mean it. I'm through looking the other way. For both of you. Stay the hell away from Allie."

"Stephen—"

He hung up the phone, none too gently, unable to listen any longer, uninterested in anything else his father might have to say. Allie stirred in his arms, and he sank back down onto the bed, pulling her closer.

He was going to lose her. If not today, then tomorrow. Maybe the day after. This was likely all the time he'd ever have with her, and it might be selfish of him to take it. But he'd take anything he could get with her at this point.

Turning onto his side, he stared down at her, her dark hair spread out on the pillow, her skin looking warm and soft against the pale sheets. There were dark smudges under her eyes—evidence of too many sleepless nights spent scared and alone in that old house. He brushed his thumb across her lips, bent to kiss her softly.

"God, Allie," he said.

He wanted to ignore everything else in the whole world and keep her here with him for a while, where no one would bother them and nothing from the past would come between them, not yet.

She was beautiful to him. Sexy. Determined. Vulnerable in a way that made him ache for her. He had a deep need to fix everything for her, to make it his mission in life to make her smile and to keep her safe. He'd never needed to do that for a woman before, and he worried that when he lost her, there'd be a huge hole in his life that no one else would ever fill. He was afraid his life would never be complete without her, and he figured he'd sealed his fate earlier today by not telling her about the little job his father had him doing.

She gave a sigh and rolled over again, her head landing on his shoulder, her entire body pressed against his. Stephen put both his arms around her and wondered how he'd ever let go.

* * *

Allie slept against the curve of his shoulder in that marvelous old bed of his, for how long, she didn't know. She thought she heard the phone, but was too sleepy to care. As she was drifting off again, clipped, angry words brought her fully awake.

Stephen hung up and kissed her softly. "Sorry about that."

She snuggled against him, feeling his arms tighten around her. "Your brother?" she guessed.

"No. My father."

Allie rolled away from him, just far enough that she could see his face. His hair was mussed, and his chest was bare, and he looked upset.

"He's angry at you?" she asked.

"Nothing unusual about that, believe me."

"Stephen . . ."

"I don't want to talk about it, Allie. Not my family and all that it's done to yours. Not while you're in my bed, all right?"

He meant it, she realized, quietly agreeing.

He propped a few pillows against the headboard and settled her against them. The sheet shifted as she moved, slipping down to her waist, leaving her breasts bare, and he was looking at her again.

"I was right." He gave her a devastating smile. "You're perfect here."

"Is that how you judge your women?" she teased. "By whether or not they look right in your bed?"

"No," he said, leaning over her, kissing her softly, sensuously. "I've got a checklist."

"You would."

He leaned over and kissed her again. "I think about how she tastes."

He ran a hand down her arm to cup her breast,

his hand big and dark on the milky white skin. "The way her body responds to my touch."

He slid his arms around her until her breasts were nestled against his chest. "Whether she fits in my arms as if she'd been made just for me."

A moment later he was nudging her thighs apart, slipping inside of her, filling her once again. Her eyes were open, and she watched him, watched the look of utter concentration on his face.

"I think about whether I go a little crazy every time I'm inside of her. Whether she's the first thing I think about every morning when I'm still half asleep, whether her face is drifting through my mind at night. Whether I can't stop thinking about her all day, and worrying about her and wishing I was with her. Whether I can't stop wishing I could stand between her and the rest of the world and make sure no one ever hurts her again, or make it plain that anyone who dares try will have to answer to me. I think about whether I want to own her, body and soul. Whether I have a thoroughly primitive urge to stake my claim, one that can never be ignored."

He started moving inside of her, in and out in long, powerful strokes, and she clung to him, her hands on the powerful muscles of his upper arms, her nipples nestled into the dark, curling hairs on his chest. His mouth came down to hers, then went to her neck.

"That's how I judge a woman, Allie. That's how I know."

"Know what?" she whispered.

"That you belong here with me."

What could a woman say to that, Allie thought as she lay in his bed a few minutes later. His cream-colored sheets still tangled around her, his bed still warm from the heat of his body, his scent still clinging to the pillow where she lay her head. It was just a bunch of pretty words, the practical side of her, worried they were moving much too fast, argued. Sweet, flattering, arousing words. He didn't have to bother with them. He didn't need words at all to seduce her. She'd fallen easily enough into his bed, and she had no desire to leave.

But it hadn't felt like empty, meaningless words, her heart argued. It had felt real. That marvelous look in his smoke-colored eyes, that mesmerizing mouth, the magical feel of him moving inside of her—all of that seemed to work to spin some kind of spell around her to make her believe everything he said.

"I don't think I want to know what's going through your head right now."

Allie looked up and saw him standing there, a mountain of smooth, wet golden skin and muscles, covered by nothing but a bath towel. He looked marvelous when he was naked. Even when he was mad.

"I was just—"

"No. I mean it. I can tell from the expression on your face that I don't want to know."

"Stephen—"

He turned his back to her and started tearing through his closet for clothes. "Don't tell me you regret this, Allie, okay? Don't tell me. Not now."

"All right. I won't."

"Don't tell me it was a mistake, either."

He dropped the towel and stepped into a pair of white briefs, then jeans, faded to a pale blue that clung to every enticing curve. He grabbed a shirt, shoving his arms through the sleeves and buttoning it.

"It's getting late," she said carefully. "And I want to get back to Casey."

"I thought you would." He gave her a bleak look. "Take a shower first, if you like. I'll find us something to eat, and then we'll get out of here."

Allie waited until he left the room, then stood up, taking the sheet with her as she walked into the bathroom, still hot and steamy and smelling of him.

She stood in front of the mirror, hardly recognizing the woman staring back at her. Her hair was a mess, and she looked very pale, except for a reddish spot on her skin here and there from where he'd nuzzled his cheek or his jaw or his mouth against her, the stubble on his face abrading her skin. She looked exactly like a woman who'd spent the early evening hours in bed with a man, one who claimed she looked perfect in his bed, that she felt perfect in his arms. She was falling head over heels in love with him.

Be smart, Allie told herself. *For once in your life, be smart.*

There'd been silly, childish dreams running through her head almost since the day she and her mother ran away, dreams about putting her family back together again. About having what most of the other kids had—a mother and a father and a brother or a sister and a home. A place to belong and feel safe and be loved. Allie hadn't had that in so long. She wasn't sure if she ever had it. Maybe it had all been some trick of her memory, like the visions she had of her sister and her mother. But she'd wanted that perfect little family, that sense of belonging. And Stephen . . . *Damn him.* Stephen had made her want that all over again. With him.

Allie dragged herself into the shower. She washed hurriedly, was dressed and back downstairs before she'd even planned what she might say to him. She found him in the kitchen. He didn't look up as she walked into the room.

"All set?" he said.

Allie nodded, and then, when he went to walk past her and out of the room, she blocked his path. "I told you I'm not very good at this, Stephen. At the trusting part. And it's not just because of what happened between Megan and your brother."

His hands came up to her shoulders, holding her lightly, rubbing at the tension in her, sending tears to her eyes from the gentleness of his touch. He'd always been so gentle with her.

"Think about my life, Stephen. Everyone I've ever trusted has lied to me."

"I know, baby."

"How am I supposed to trust anyone after that?"

"Allie, I understand." He ran a hand through his hair and sighed. "And even knowing all of that, there are so many things I want to tell you, things I have no right to say. Not now."

"What things?"

"That this is your home," he insisted. "It doesn't matter how far you go or how long you stay away, this will always be home. It gets in your blood, Allie. You can't escape it. Every time I leave, I feel it pulling at me. Every time I come back, I feel it, too. In my heart. My soul. My body recognizes this place instinctively. Something about the way the sky looks or the particular shade of green in the grass. The way the fields rise and fall, rolling one into the next. The way the air smells and the way it feels against my skin. It's my home. And yours, too."

"Stephen—"

"I want you to stay with me. It's too soon. I know

it. But I still want you right here, in my house and in my bed. I want you to give us a chance, Allie. When all this is over, and you know everything, I want you to give us some time, to figure out what's between us," he said. "I know Kentucky holds bad memories for you. But it holds good ones, too. It's your home, and I think you belong here with me. I think you could be happy here. I'd make it my mission in life to see that you're happy."

She couldn't hold back her tears then. They flooded her eyes and spilled over, running down her cheeks. Stephen pushed her face against his shoulder and held her gently. She couldn't help but think that he was a man who made things happen. That if he said he was going to make her happy, he would.

Allie closed her eyes and took a leap of faith. "I . . . I've never felt this way before. About any man."

"I'm glad to hear it."

She laughed and kissed the side of his face. He wiped away more tears, his palm coming to rest against her cheek.

"A lot of women have come in and out of my life over the years. I've never felt this way about any of them, either." He looked down into her eyes, his gaze compelling, never wavering. "Just think about it. Think about staying."

"I will."

He caught her close, held her so tightly she could barely breathe, and she had the oddest sensation. Of everything in her life falling neatly into place. Maybe he was the man who was going to give her everything she'd ever wanted.

Much as he hated taking her back to that house, where the memories were eating her alive and the past kept tearing at their present, she insisted on going. So Stephen took her.

When he had a moment alone, he pulled out his cell phone. He was rattled by the idea that his brother had mistaken Allie for her sister, despite the fact that Megan was supposed to be dead and that Rich had to know Allie was back in town. Which made Stephen wonder—did Rich have reason to think Megan might have survived?

Someone died in that car crash. They'd buried a body and put Megan's name on the tombstone. But could there have been a mistake back then?

He was reaching, he knew. However, for Allie's sake, he wanted to believe it was possible. She'd lost so much already, and one day soon, she was going to hate him. He wanted her to have someone in her life then, someone she trusted, someone she loved. It wouldn't make up for what he'd done to her. But if he could give her her nephew, she wouldn't be all alone anymore.

Casey was here. He was convinced Megan Bennett was his mother. If there was any possibility it was true, Stephen had to check it out. He called his private investigator and fired off new instructions. He wanted to know if Casey was Megan Bennett's son, and he wanted to know if his brother had her killed.

Chapter 17

Allie was coming down the stairs the next morning when she sensed something behind her.

She didn't panic. Casey was in the attic, where they'd been working, and Stephen was working downstairs at the kitchen table today. He'd refused to leave her here alone last night after that ugly scene with his brother. She'd slept quite contentedly in his arms the entire night.

She'd been coming to find him when something on the stairs caught her attention, something odd. She turned around and found herself staring at a ray of sunshine that fell at an angle across the stairs. And then she sat down on the stairs, staring at her sister's room, the one place she still hadn't been.

Ever since she'd come back, she'd been most reluctant to go there, to even be on the staircase, she realized. Had something happened on the stairs?

The hair on the back of Allie's neck quivered. She felt sick to her stomach, felt weak and foolish and crazy. This made her feel so crazy.

She closed her eyes and thought she could hear her father's voice. Yelling. She thought she must have been sitting on the stairs like this, staring at sunlight playing on the polished wood and listening to him yelling.

Allie groaned. She wanted to see him again, even if it was just in her memory. Megan's image had been startlingly clear and seemingly so close, she could have reached out and touched her. Allie wanted one vivid image of her father to carry with her, as well. She knew where he was, too. In her sister's room.

Feeling like a heroine in a gothic novel, inexplicably drawn to danger, she slowly made her way up the stairs, the voices growing louder with each step she took. As she reached the top, something shattered in one of the rooms. It sounded like something had been flung against the wall.

"I won't have this," her father shouted. "Not in my house, I won't."

"What do you mean you won't have it? You can't just wave your hand and make it go away. God, if it were that easy . . ."

That was her mother's voice. She must be in the room, too.

"I mean I won't have her in my house. Not if she insists on being so unreasonable. On making up these outlandish lies," her father roared.

"John." Her mother got very quiet. "It's our house. Our family's home. You can't just put her out on the streets."

"This is my house, and I can do anything I damned well please, Janet. It seems you've forgotten that. And a lot of other things, too. Well, I haven't."

Allie winced. She'd never heard her father talk to her mother like that.

The door to her sister's room was flung open. Her father came striding through, her mother close behind. Allie heard her sister sobbing, pitiful, heart-wrenching sobs, but her eyes were fixed on her father. He looked so young and strong as he stood in the hallway, his face hard and impassive. His hair was dark like Megan's and longer than she remembered, and there were no harsh lines in his face, no bleak look in his eyes. Those, she remembered from the time after they'd lost Megan when grief had taken its toll on all of them. This was a different vision of her father.

Her mother grabbed her father by the arm and held on to him. *"You haven't forgotten anything, have you? All those years, you swore you loved me, that you loved our daughters. But that was a lie, too, wasn't it? You never forgave me, and you'll never forget."*

"I tried," he said. *"I did my best by all of you. But there are some things a man can't forget. Especially when it's thrown back in his face like this."*

"She says he forced her," Allie's mother said. *"Are you going to discount the word of your own daughter?"*

"She's been sneaking out of this house to meet him for weeks. Does that sound like he forced her?"

They were arguing about the rape, Allie realized. Just as Richard Whittaker said, they hadn't believed Megan.

Her mother stood her ground. *"We don't know Megan was sneaking out to see him."*

Did that mean they were dating? Allie remembered Stephen saying his brother was used to getting whatever he wanted, to taking it. Date rape? Had there even been such a term for it back then?

"Megan's in trouble, and she knows it," her father said. *"She'd say anything to try to make it look like it wasn't her fault."*

Oh, no, Allie thought. How could he do this? How could he doubt his own daughter?

"She said he forced her," her mother repeated.

"And you believe her? I wonder," he said coldly, *"did you think about saying the same thing about you and Tucker Barnes? I wonder if I would have forgiven you if you had. I wonder if I would have believed you."*

Her mother went white. Allie felt as if her legs were going to give way, and she saw now that there was more. Oh, God, there was so much more she'd never known.

Her mother had tears in her eyes. *"I never lied to you. I never pushed you to marry me, John. You chose to. You said you loved me."*

"I loved the woman I thought you were. The woman I wanted you to be."

"John, I am that woman. I've been that woman for all these years. We've built a life together. I've been happy here. Haven't you?"

"I've tried to forget," he said. *"Every day of my life I've tried. But every time I look at you, every time . . ."*

Her mother whispered urgently to him. *"What are you saying? That it's over? That you're going to leave us? That you want me to leave? What?"*

"I don't know," her father said.

"I love you, John. All these years, I've loved you. You just couldn't let that be enough, could you? You just couldn't stop trying to make me pay for something that's been over for seventeen years." Her mother seemed to crumple before her eyes. *"That's what you're saying, you know? Every time you throw this back in my face. Every time you slight Megan in some way, you're showing me that the last seventeen years we spent together don't count for anything."*

With a dazed look on her face, her mother turned and walked away. Her father stood at the top of the steps, looking stunned and shattered as well, and Megan went right on sobbing.

Allie sat there, miserable and alone and shaking. How could this be? So much anger, so much hatred in this house, and she hadn't known anything about it. How could she have been so blind? She had no doubt the scene really happened. She no longer cared how her past chose to reveal itself to her, just that she finally had the answers she was so sure she wanted.

It seemed Stephen was right. Now that the truth was coming out, she decided she liked her illusions just fine. That she had a nice, happy, loving family, that her sister's death caused an irrevocable wound between her father and her mother that simply would not heal, and that Allie was deprived of her father's love because of it. It was sad and unfair. But the truth . . .

God. Her father hadn't loved her mother. And her mother . . . Her mother and Tucker Barnes. The man who'd come to the house the other day.

It was all so ugly. She couldn't imagine her father ever talking to her mother that way. Allie tried to tell herself he would have calmed down. They would have talked things out. Everything would have been okay, if Megan hadn't run away. If she hadn't died.

That had to be the reason her father felt so guilty. He and her mother argued. Megan ran away. He never forgave himself. Neither did her mother.

Suddenly the voices filled her head once again. Her father yelling, her sister sobbing. She found herself drawn to the scene, just as people stare at grizzly accidents on the roads. This was her family, falling apart at the seams. This was what she came back to understand, and the drama was playing out right in front of her, like a private performance of a play. She must have seen it all. All along, it had been inside of her. She'd simply been afraid to face it.

Her father was yelling when she looked in the room. *"You little slut! You're just like her. Just like your mother!"*

"What?" Megan said.

"Your mother. The little tramp!"

"What are you talking about?" her sister said.

"You! I did the best I could by you, Megan, and this is how you repay me?"

"Repay you for what? You hate me. You always have, and I've always known," she cried. *"What did I do, Daddy? Before this? What did I do that was so bad you couldn't love me? I'm your daughter, dammit. How could you not love me?"*

"You're not my daughter," he said bitterly.

Allie gasped, the breath leaving her body in a long, painful rush. Megan just stared, looking dazed and frightened, and her father had taken on that same pinched, painful look he wore the night Allie and her mother ran away.

She couldn't have heard him correctly. She waited for him to explain, for him to take back those ugly words, but he didn't.

"It's the truth," he said bleakly. *"You're not my daughter. You never were."*

Megan seemed to crumple onto the bed, stunned disbelief on her face. From behind her, Allie heard her mother gasp and cry out to her father. *"How could you? How could you do that? How could you tear our family apart?"*

"She's a lying little tramp, and I won't have her in my house anymore."

Suddenly Allie couldn't stand it anymore. She turned around and ran. Down the steps, out the front door.

God, she hated this house.

She couldn't stay, she realized. She couldn't breathe here. She couldn't think.

"Allie?"

She turned around, and Stephen was there. He held her at arm's length and looked her over from head to toe, then hauled her into his arms.

"What's wrong?"

"I know what happened to Megan," she said. "I know everything now."

He pushed her face against his chest, his arms strong and unyielding as they held her to him, his body a solid mass of support for her. Nothing could hurt here her, she believed. Nothing could get to her when Stephen had her.

"My father said Megan wasn't his daughter," she said. "He called her a tramp, said she was just like my mother and that she wasn't his daughter, and he told my mother he'd never been able to forgive her for that. I thought we had been a wonderful, happy family, but we weren't. It was all a lie."

"Oh, Allie. I'm sorry."

"My mother always loved Megan more. I always knew that. I thought it was because she lost her. I tried so hard to take Megan's place, but it was never enough. I think now that Megan tried to do the same thing. I think she did everything she could to make my father love her, and nothing was enough. Because she wasn't his daughter, and when she was in trouble and scared, and she needed him, he turned his back on her."

"Allie," he whispered, stroking her hair.

"That's why Megan ran away. He didn't want her here anymore, and I bet she was scared to stay, scared to be right next door to your brother. Scared because no one believed he'd raped her. Scared of letting him have anything to do with her baby. So she left, and then she died. My mother could never forgive my father for that, and to punish him, she took me away."

Allie sank against Stephen, and let him hold her while she cried. Inside, she ached, in a way she never had before. She thought bitterly of a life spent trying to please a mother who could not be pleased after her favorite child died. The years she had spent needing her father, wanting him, but still buckling under to her mother's unwritten law that they have nothing to do with him. All the time she'd wasted.

"It's so much worse than I thought."

"I'm sorry, baby. I'm so sorry." Stephen's arms tightened around her. "You just remembered all of this?"

"Yes," she whispered. "No. It's . . . it's the house. Being in this house is making me crazy. It's like someone videotaped the whole scene and is playing it back inside my head."

"You must have seen it fifteen years ago," he said.

"I know." There was no other explanation. "And I think this was it. The last piece. I did it. I figured out the last piece."

She shuddered. Stephen held her tightly and, overwhelmed, she gave herself up to the sheer reassurance that came from being in his arms. The solid bulk of him, the strength, the warmth, the particularly appealing scent that clung to his skin—all were so familiar to her now, as was the way it seemed natural to turn to him at a time like this.

She wouldn't have been able to do this before, wouldn't have let herself be so vulnerable to anyone. She'd have been too afraid.

But it was different with Stephen. He was different

than any man she'd ever met. He knew her, understood her. He would fight for her and protect her and, she thought, lend her some of his considerable strength, should she need it.

She trusted him, she realized. To be here for her. To hold onto her and show her that physically and emotionally, she wasn't alone anymore.

She'd faced the demons of her past. The truth hurt, and she hated what she'd found out, but she'd survived it, conquered it. She could learn to live with it, to put it all behind her. She had Stephen, a wonderful, charming, kindhearted, gorgeous man by her side, and she had a goal, a purpose, one that energized her and excited her. Megan's House. She was going to turn all her efforts into making it a reality.

She was aching, exhausted and all cried out, feeling like she'd climbed a mountain or come through a raging storm. She felt stronger than ever, whole.

"I'm glad I came back," she told him. "For the first time, I'm glad I'm here."

"Me, too, Allie." He kissed her softly, sweetly. "Me, too."

Tucker Barnes confirmed everything Allie overheard. Apparently, Tucker Barnes and her mother had fallen in love long ago. They had grown up together and were to be married, but Tucker had gotten drafted and gone to Vietnam. He had come home on leave one summer when his mother had died, and when he had gone back, he unknowingly left Allie's mother pregnant with Megan.

"I got hurt over there." Tucker said that afternoon, rubbing a hand to his right knee. "It looked like I was going to lose my leg, and I couldn't ask Janet to live like that, with me hardly able to work. So I wrote her, told her I'd changed my mind about wanting to get married. And by the time I made it back home, she was married and had Megan."

"You knew all along that Megan was yours?" Allie asked.

"When I found out her birthday, I knew. Your father knew, too. Janet never lied to him. Your father married her promising to love my little girl like she was his own. I never would have let him raise Megan, otherwise. But your father never forgave any of us. All those years, Janet tried so hard to make it up to him, but there was no makin' it up."

"I think he tried," Allie said. "I think they both tried. It just wasn't enough. And I'm sorry Megan never knew you."

"I would have helped her," he said sincerely. "When John turned his back on her, I would've been proud to call her mine. I would have helped Janet, too, if she'd come to me. But I was seein' somebody else by then. I didn't love her, not back then. I didn't think I'd ever love anybody the way I loved your mother. But a man gets lonely. At the time, well, I guess Janet didn't know how it was between Martha 'n' me—"

"Martha?" Allie asked. "From the drugstore?"

Tucker nodded.

"So that's why she was so startled to see me," Allie said.

"Yeah. After Megan died . . . Well, I was a mess. I ended up telling her just about everything. And the God's honest truth is that Martha was probably the best thing that ever happened to me." He looked embarrassed admitting to such a private thing. "So . . . your mother? She was happy? Once she took you away from here?"

Allie chose her words carefully, seeing little reason to hurt him further. She told him they had lived in Connecticut, that there had been no other man in her mother's life, that she never quite got over losing Megan. She offered him some of her mother's things, including some photographs of her mother and Megan. He offered again to help her in any way he could. Allie spent a few minutes telling him her hopes for the runaway shelter, for which he not only promised his support but offered to strong-arm, if necessary, several of his friends in various aspects of construction into helping also.

Tucker thanked her and was at the front door ready to leave when he said, "The boy who was here before. I heard in town he's a runaway."

"Yes, that's right."

"You know, when I saw that boy I had the strangest idea. He's the spittin' image of your mother, just like you and Megan. I thought for a while he belonged to Janet, too. That she'd found someone else after the two of you left." Tucker shrugged. "I guess I just wanted to think there was another little part of her left in this world."

Allie was puzzled. "You think Casey looks like me? And my mother?"

"Oh, yeah. I thought I was seeing things the first time I laid eyes on him. Just like I thought I was seeing your mother all over again when I saw you."

"I never noticed," Allie said. "About Casey, I mean. People tell me I look like my mother, but I never saw the resemblance there, either."

"It's true. I see Megan in that boy, too. I even wondered about that. Megan was pregnant when she left, and I thought . . . It's crazy, but I thought the boy

311

might be my grandson. That he might be Megan's son.''

Allie gaped at him, dizzy for a second. She'd been so shaken by all that they'd learned in the past twenty-four hours, that she hadn't been able to think straight. But Megan *was* pregnant when she left. Richard Whittaker's reaction confirmed that. So did what she'd overheard from her parents and now from Tucker Barnes. But the autopsy . . . Greg checked the autopsy report. Megan wasn't pregnant at the time she died. She hadn't given birth recently, either. And Tucker thought Casey might be Megan's son? How could that be?

In a daze, Allie said good-bye to Tucker and stood on the doorstep, wild thoughts running through her head. She tried to picture Casey's face, Megan's, even Richard Whittaker's.

She was reaching, she knew. But all she had was an autopsy report telling her that Megan hadn't been pregnant. Not when she died or prior to her death. But reports could be wrong. People made mistakes.

Casey was here, after all. What if he'd come to this house for a reason? What if somehow he was her sister's son?

Her heart kicked into high gear. She had lost so many people. She was a woman without blood ties to anyone in this world. To find her sister's child, after all these years . . . To have him in her life . . .

God, she wanted it to be true.

Stephen faced down the sullen-looking teenager sitting across from him in the attic and said, ''Want to try again?''

''Huh?'' Casey said.

"Your story? Want to make up another one for me? Or do you think we might try the truth this time?"

"I don't know." Casey shrugged. "Want to tell me if you're my father?"

Stephen hesitated, thinking this was not his responsibility. It was something for Casey's mother to deal with, whoever the hell she was. And in the back of his head was the nagging possibility . . . If this was somehow Megan's son, Casey's father was likely a rapist. Stephen's own brother.

How did you tell a mixed-up, already hurt kid that the father he was so desperate to find was a rapist?

Stephen wouldn't. If the price for protecting Casey from that was letting him believe Stephen was his father, Stephen was willing. Hell, if this was Megan's son, he owed it to the kid and to Megan to help Casey in any way he could.

"Well? Daddy?" Casey asked.

"We'll have to let your mother settle this, Casey. After all, she's the only one who'd know for sure."

"I told you. She's dead."

"Well, that's funny," Stephen said. "Because the last I heard—which was about two minutes ago— your mother was on a plane coming back from Rome to wring your sorry neck."

"Oh. Well . . . maybe she's not dead."

"*Maybe she's not dead?* That's all you've got to say for yourself?"

"I don't owe you anything," Casey said. "I don't even like you. I've got things I'm trying to figure out, and all you've done is try to keep me from doing that. So I don't see that you have any right to expect anything from me."

"I told you the truth earlier when I said I don't have any children—"

"Not good enough—"

"You want me to deny that I ever slept with your mother? How can I do that? I don't even know who your mother is. All I know is that you lied to me when you said she was dead."

"I didn't want you to go lookin' for her. I thought if I told you she was dead, you'd leave her alone."

"And why didn't you want me looking for your mom?"

"Because she'd come and get me, and I don't want her to do that until I figure everything out. Then you brought up that stuff about her adopting me, and I . . ." Casey had tears in his eyes. "I never thought about that. I guess she looks a little bit like Allie and like the photos of Allie's sister, but still . . . She lied to me about everything. I guess she could have lied about how she got me, too."

"I don't know anything about you being adopted," Stephen said.

"Okay. But if she is my mom, and she is Megan Bennett, then she hated it here so much she wanted these people to think she was dead. Something really awful must have happened to her here. I didn't want anybody trying to find her and bring her back here, if she didn't want to come back."

"Well, she is coming. To get you," Stephen said. "I bet she would have been here two weeks ago if you hadn't been lying to her, too."

Casey looked a little sheepish at that.

"You did that to your own mother. You somehow managed to convince her you were off on a school trip and slipped away to Kentucky instead."

He shrugged. "Wasn't that hard."

But the kid's look said otherwise. His look said he was proud of getting away with it for as long as he had. The kid was obviously very intelligent. He was determined and had absolutely no fear.

"I tried to find out what I could without coming," he said. "I—"

"You wrote the letter," Stephen said. God, he should have figured that out long before now. "From Jason Getty. You wanted to know if Megan Bennett really died in that accident. If anyone thought she might be alive."

"Yeah."

"Who's Jason Getty?"

"A friend of mine's father. I mean, I've never really met him, but we're friends. We talk in E-mail, and I wanted to write to my grandmother, but I didn't want to tell her my name or my address. I didn't want anybody to be able to find my mom through me, just in case something really bad happened to her back here. So I wrote the letter to my friend, and he mailed it using his address and his father's name. He gets home first, so he always gets the mail. I didn't think it would be any trouble, but then that private investigator came around asking all those questions. . . . It scared me."

"But not enough to keep you from coming here?"

"No."

Stephen frowned at him. "How'd you manage that?"

"I'm in this youth orchestra, and we won some big contest, and the prize was a chance to compete in a music festival in Italy last week. It's supposed to be some really *big* deal. My mom wanted to go, but she got this new job, and she had a trip scheduled for the same time. So I was supposed to go on my trip, and she was going to France, and we were going to get together in Rome for a few days before heading back."

"Okay. What else?"

"Her plane took off an hour before mine. So we went to the airport together, and I told her good-bye, and she left me at the gate. I figured all I had to do was convince her I was on the school trip, and I could have a couple of weeks to come here and find out about my dad."

"You just decided to do this?" Stephen said.

"She wouldn't tell me anything," he said angrily. "She said my father died before I was born, and that we didn't have any other relatives, and none of that was true."

"How do you know it isn't true, Casey?"

"I heard her talkin' about it to a friend of hers one night, when she was real upset. She said she'd been lying about her whole life for too long to stop now." Casey looked mad again. "So, the way I see it, I had to come here. I've got rights, too, you know. Just 'cause I'm a kid, doesn't mean I don't have rights."

"I don't think your rights extend to scaring your mother half to death and traveling across three states by yourself. But tell me the rest."

"After I said good-bye to my mom at the airport, I had a friend of mine call the orchestra director right before the plane took off and pretend to be my uncle. He told her I'd wrecked my dirt bike the night before and broken my arm. So they left without me. Mom was already gone, and I came here."

"She didn't call you while you were gone?"

"She called. My best friend—he and I were supposed to be roommates on the trip. He covered for me, told her I was out and stuff. And I called her a couple of times, before I ran out of money. Mostly, when she's away, we keep in touch by E-mail, anyway. Mom took her laptop, and I took mine. I just kept sending her E-mail and made up stuff about the trip. Jordan—he's my best friend—he sent me E-mail, too, so I knew what was going on, what to tell Mom."

"Looks like you thought of everything," Stephen admitted.

"It would have worked great except my mom bought me a nonrefundable plane ticket to Italy. I was planning on cashing it in and using the money for my trip here, but the lady at the ticket counter wouldn't give me my money back. So I ran a little short."

"And nearly starved and had to camp out in this old house."

"The man at the motel wouldn't rent me a room." Casey looked disgusted. "I told him I was eighteen, and I had my mom's credit card, but he wanted to see my driver's license. I couldn't believe it. People don't rent motel rooms to kids?"

"I don't think so. Life just isn't fair, is it?"

"No way," Casey said.

"So, why did you come here? What was it about your mother that connected her to this place?"

"She gets the newspaper from here. Always has. The Lexington paper, too. I couldn't figure out why. I asked her about it a few times, and she said she always wanted to live in a place like this. But she seemed upset that I even asked. . . . One day when she was gone, I looked through the locked drawer in her desk. She had a bunch of newspaper clippings. Obituaries. Announcements. Stuff like that. About John and Janet Bennett. And their daughter, Megan. There were pictures, too, with the stories. And I thought the girl in those newspaper pictures was my mom, which meant John and Janet Bennett were my grandparents, and Allie's my aunt."

"Did you ask your mom about that?"

"Yeah. She yelled at me. Told me to stay out of her stuff. That's when I decided I had to come here and find out for myself."

"Just like that." Stephen said. "Lie to your mother. Scare her half to death. Travel hundreds of miles by yourself."

"I had to find out," Casey smiled slyly. "And my mom . . . She'll forgive me. Moms always do."

He looked inordinately pleased with himself, and Stephen couldn't help but think what he'd do if a child of his ever put him through this kind of misery.

"So," Casey said. "Do you think my mom is Megan?"

"We'll know soon enough. Her plane's supposed to land in Lexington in about fifteen minutes," Stephen said, then frowned at the boy. "You're not planning on running off again, are you?"

"Nah, I'm busted. I just wanted to know about my father. I figure with all the trouble I've gone to to find out, she'll tell me now."

"That's it? That's all you have to say for yourself? After all you've put your mother through and all the risks you've taken, that's the bottom line. It's okay, because you'll probably get what you want. Casey, I think you're in deep shit. I think your mother's going to have a whole lot to say to you, and not just about your father."

"She'll be mad, but she'll get over it," he said smugly. "It's just the two of us, and we have to stick up for each other."

"It may not be just the two of you anymore," Stephen said.

"I hope not. I like it here. I like Allie. She's cool." Casey grinned. "You like her, too, don't you?"

"Yes, I like Allie," he said.

"So, are you guys gonna get married and stuff?"

"I don't know if she'd have me," he admitted. "If she would, that would make me your uncle, which would give me the right to kick your sorry butt if you ever do anything like this again."

Casey frowned. Stephen saw the irony—him becoming Casey's uncle through marriage when he'd bet money he already *was* Casey's uncle, by blood.

"I didn't think you liked me very much," Casey said.

"All I knew then was that you were this little punk scaring Allie, and as you said, I like Allie," Stephen explained, then decided the kid needed some reassurance. "If you want me to like you, Casey, you're going to have to show me there's something inside of you for me to like. You can't run away from your mother this way. You can't scare her like this. You can't take these kinds of chances."

"I had to find out."

"You're going to be a man soon. A man takes responsibility for his actions. He thinks things through, and he doesn't just think of himself and what he wants. He's careful and considerate of the feelings of the people he loves," Stephen said, thinking he'd failed by that test in a number of ways. He'd done what he had to do, but he was most definitely going to hurt Allie badly.

"Are you gonna tell my mom all that stuff? About me scaring Allie?"

"I think when I finally see your mother, I'm going

to have some other things on my mind, Casey. I think we all will."

"Maybe she'll be so excited seeing you and Allie again, she'll forget about punishing me."

"No way," Stephen said. "Come on. Let's go talk to Allie. We need to figure out how to tell her about this. We can't have your mother just walk in the door out of the blue."

When Stephen and Casey came downstairs, Allie studied Casey's face, looking desperately for something of herself, something of Megan, wondering if she saw it now simply because she wanted so desperately for it to be true. She wanted one last piece of her family back.

A minute later Stephen had chased Casey off into the kitchen, though he'd been reluctant to go, and Allie told Stephen what she'd learned.

"Tucker knew all about the scene with Megan and my parents. My mother told him. And he said the oddest thing. He wondered if Casey might be Megan's son. He thinks he sees a family resemblance."

"Allie, come in here and sit down."

"I know it's crazy," she said. "Wanting to believe it, just because he thinks he sees a resemblance. But Megan *was* pregnant when she left here fifteen years ago. If her child survived, he would be thirteen now."

"Allie, listen to me." Stephen sat down beside her and took both of her hands in his. "I don't know who Casey's mother is, but she's on her way here. Right now."

"He said she was dead."

"I know. He lied," Stephen said.

"Is it . . . Are you trying to tell me my sister's alive, and she's coming here?"

"The woman who raised him is coming. But I don't know if she's the woman who gave birth to him, and I don't know if she's Megan."

"But it could be? She could have survived?"

"Allie, I don't want you to get your heart broken again. I told you—the kid lies. He's lied to us about so many things."

"Okay. He's lied. But . . . you think it's possible? You think my sister might be alive?"

"Yes," he said.

"Oh, my God." Allie started to cry. She started smiling and crying and laughing. "I never even imagined that."

"I know."

"Tell me," she said. "Tell me everything."

"The detective you hired told you Megan was with a group of runaways in Macon that winter, and that one of them was pregnant."

"Yes, he did."

"This morning I talked to the man I hired. The other runaway girl was named Margaret Addison."

"Addison?" she whispered. "Casey's mother?"

Stephen nodded. "My guy had also gone back to the trooper and asked some more questions. The trooper said when he got to the scene, four people were there—the doctor, two boys in their twenties, and the girl. A pregnant girl."

"A pregnant girl?" Allie couldn't breathe. "Megan."

"The trooper didn't hear anything about a second girl being in the car. He thought she showed up after the accident and was nothing but a witness. In fact, he hardly talked to her or even saw her. The doctor had her in his car, all wrapped up in a blanket. They were all soaked from being out in the rain, and the doctor said the girl was too upset to talk. But we found people in town who think they saw the two runaway girls together that day. The accident happened on the road between the town and the place they were staying. I think they were both in the car, and only one of them survived. The pregnant one."

"And she wanted to stay dead, so she took her friend's name."

Stephen nodded. "I looked at the reports. The girl who died had been in the water for three days before they found her, and three days in the water . . . They didn't have DNA tests in those days. They would have relied on generalities. Height, weight, age, hair color, and the things they found in the car. Megan's things. A learner's permit, a school ID card, some photographs. A necklace. Your father went there to make the ID, but maybe he was convinced it was Megan before he ever looked at the body."

"The girl we buried wasn't pregnant. She hadn't given birth recently. Greg checked," Allie said, a big, broad smile spreading across her face. Her sister was alive. "Tell me about her. About Casey's mother."

"Casey said she claimed his father died before Casey was born, that they had no other living relatives. But Casey didn't believe that. She had old newspaper clippings about your mother and father and Megan, things she kept locked away, and when he saw Megan's picture, he thought that was his mother, which meant he had grandparents here and he hoped, a father."

"Oh, God. He's your nephew, too."

Stephen nodded.

"I can't believe it." She'd stopped asking for miracles a long time ago. She'd stopped believing, and she'd gotten used to the idea that she had no one but herself. But now . . . "Oh, Stephen. Tell me everything you know about her."

"Casey says everybody calls her Meggie."

"My mother called her that sometimes."

"I know," Stephen said. "She's supposed to be thirty-three years old."

"Megan would be thirty-one."

"She's a freelance graphic artist, supposedly born in Arizona, no family. She went to Ole Miss, working her way through a four-year program in a little over six years, because she had Casey. Left an established firm two years ago to go out on her own. She's won several awards. Casey's never really been in trouble before now. He's very intelligent. He goes to an expensive prep school in town, and he was supposed to be on a class trip for the past two weeks."

Stephen told her all about it. Allie decided she liked Casey even more.

"I want to believe it. That Megan's alive, and she's coming here," Allie said. "But really good things never seem to happen to me."

"Maybe your luck's starting to change," he said. "Maybe it's all going to be good from here on out."

"I don't think anyone leads a truly charmed life."

"No, but people do find happiness. Sure, there are going to be disappointments along the way. But life can be good, too, Allie." He stared down at her. "It can be so good."

Chapter 18

Allie had never known time to drag by so slowly. She climbed the steps to her sister's room, and Casey, who was just as nervous as she was, went with her. They picked through Megan's old things, and she told Casey the bits and pieces of their childhood she remembered. He apologized solemnly for breaking into the house and for scaring her. Allie gave him a long hug and promised him, no matter what they found out after his mother arrived, that she would help him. She made him promise that he'd never run away again.

"I think I'd like it if you were my aunt, Allie."

"I'd like it, too."

"My mom's probably gonna yell a lot when she gets there, and she'll threaten to ground me and do all sorts of stuff. But she's really pretty nice most of the time."

"I'm sure she is." Sighing, Allie looked at her watch one last time, then looked back at Casey. "I can't believe you came all this way by yourself."

"It wasn't so bad," he insisted. "It didn't work out exactly the way I planned, but I got my mom to come back here. She's gonna tell me I was wrong to lie to her and take off by myself, but I'm still glad I did it. 'Cause she'll tell me about my father now." He stopped to think for a minute. "I'm not gonna tell her the part about being glad I came here."

"I wouldn't if I were you," Allie said, thinking it must be hell to raise a teenager.

Allie grew more nervous with every passing moment. Finally, she heard a car coming down the road. Casey looked scared once again.

"Want to go down together?" she asked.

They went. Halfway down, the front door opened. "Allie?"

Stephen stood in the doorway, his arm around a woman with long, dark hair and a hesitant smile that took her back fifteen years.

Casey yelled, "Mom!" and started running.

Allie moved more slowly, hanging onto the banister for support.

The woman enveloped Casey in a bear hug. He started to speak, but she interrupted him. "Casey, if you're half as smart as your SAT scores claim, you won't say a word right now."

Then she just held him, the look on her face one of sheer relief.

Allie waited until the embrace wasn't so fierce, until she sensed that the woman's equilibrium had been somewhat restored by the feel of her son, safe and whole, in her arms once again.

The hesitant smile reappeared, familiar smiling eyes with faint lines at the corners now and hair that had been tamed over the years. She was close enough to touch, and so different from the girl Allie had seen sitting at the piano, playing out her sorrows with the bruises on her arms.

Finally Allie said, "Megan?"

"Oh, Allie." The woman smiled broadly and held

out her arms. Allie fell into them, felt them close tightly around her. "I'm sorry. I'm so sorry."

And then neither one of them could do anything but cry and hang onto each other.

"I never meant to do it," Megan said later. "I never thought anyone would think it was me in the car. But once it happened, it seemed smarter to let everyone believe I was dead."

Allie and her sister sat on the floor of Megan's old bedroom, a place where they'd had many long, serious talks in previous years. Stephen had promised to keep Casey downstairs to give the two women some privacy.

Allie told Megan she knew about the argument Megan had with their parents, about the fact that John Bennett wasn't Megan's biological father. She knew Stephen helped Megan out of town that day and that Megan ended up living with a group of runaways in a barn in Macon, Georgia.

"Tell me the rest," Allie said.

"Casey was due any day, and I was getting scared about how I was going to take care of him. I thought I owed it to him to try to go back home. A friend of mine, one of the kids I met on the streets, a boy named Mitch—"

"Mitch Wilson is here," Allie said. "He lives in Lexington."

"You're kidding?"

"No. He came here after you died. Looking for answers. Looking to punish someone, maybe."

"Mitch." She sighed. "I thought he'd forget all about me."

"I don't think he ever did," Allie said, thinking by the look of things, her sister hadn't forgotten much about Mitch Wilson, either. "He looks wonderful, by the way. Just in case you might be wondering . . ."

"I can't believe he's here."

"I'll take you to him. Later," Allie promised. "Tell me what you did."

"We scraped together some money and came back here. We were about a mile from the house when Rich saw us. He looked furious, and I was so scared of him. I decided it was too much of a risk—to come back. So Mitch and I just took off, and Rich must have followed us somehow. Or maybe he knew where we were all along. I don't know. I always felt like he was out there, watching me, to make sure I wasn't going to make trouble for him by telling anyone what he'd done or by claiming my baby was his.

"A few days later, we were back in Macon. My friend Meg—the real Margaret Addison—was with me. I was coming out of the clinic when I thought I saw Rich. We just took off. I was so scared. And then the storm hit. It was awful. The rain was coming down so hard, we could hardly see. The wind was blowing. I didn't even see the car coming. It was so big and so fast. It rammed us, and I screamed, and we started sliding. The next thing I knew, we were in the water."

"So he did try to kill you," Allie said.

Megan nodded. "I was more worried about Rich than anything else. I got out of the car and made it to the bank. I grabbed onto a tree branch that hung out over the water. I don't know if he meant to kill us or just to scare us, but I heard a car back up. It stopped on the side of the road, and a man got out. There was a flash of lightning, and I saw his face. It was Rich.

"I didn't even think of Meg at first. I was too

scared of him. It wasn't until he got back in his car and left that I panicked and realized I hadn't seen her since the car went into the water. By then, it was too late. I looked for her, but the water was cold, and it was moving so fast. I never saw her again." Megan's voice shook. "I'm not really clear on what happened next. A couple of cars came along and stopped. One of them was the doctor I knew from the free clinic, a man named Jim. He wrapped me up in a blanket and made me sit down inside a car, out of the rain. He and a couple of guys went into the water after Meg, but it was too late. They couldn't find her.

"The police showed up, and I was still sitting in Jim's car. When the police came over to question me, they assumed I was just someone who'd come along and seen the car and stopped to try to help. I begged Jim not to say anything else. I told him I couldn't go back home, that the man who raped me was there. That I was scared, and I had to protect my baby.

"He helped me get into a home for teenage mothers in Alabama," she said. "The police identified the body in the creek as mine, and it just seemed right. Meg didn't have anyone. The only person left who cared about her was her grandmother, and when her grandmother died, she ran away. And when Meg died, I became her. It's not even that hard, at least not on paper. You can find books on how to do it. They tell you to find someone who's about your age who died, and assume her identity, and I already had someone's identity.

"I almost gave Casey up. I wanted so much more for him than I could give him, but when it came time to sign the papers . . . He was all I had left in the world, and I wanted him, even though . . ."

"Rich raped you?"

"Some people might call it that today. Back then . . . There was no term that really applied. I was sneaking out to see him. I let him kiss me, but he wanted more than that, and he didn't listen when I told him no. Afterward, he got up and went right on, like nothing happened. Like I wanted it, and I liked it. Like he was entitled to have sex with me if he wanted to."

"It was rape," Allie said.

"It took me a long time to understand that. At the time, it was more like a date gone bad, and I felt like I was as much to blame as he was. He was so nice to me in the beginning, Allie. He acted like he really liked me. Nobody had ever treated me like that. Nobody ever made me feel special. And that one night, he just started kissing me, and he wouldn't stop. He'd been drinking, and he was so much stronger than I was. All of a sudden, he was like a stranger. I kept thinking I was going to wake up, and it would all be a nightmare. He said girls didn't like sex the first time. That we'd do it again and again, and eventually, I'd like it.

"I was terrified of him. He was right next door, and his father was a judge. I knew he'd never be arrested, much less go to jail for what he'd done. So I hid the bruises, and I kept to myself. I tried to stay out of his way. But he caught me two more times, and I swear he enjoyed it," she said. "I never said a word to anyone until I hadn't had my period in two months, and when I told Mom and Dad, they didn't believe me. My own father told me that he wasn't my father and he didn't want me in his house any longer. So I left. I didn't want Rich to have anything to do with the baby. I didn't want Casey to ever know."

"Megan, what are you going to tell Casey?"

"I don't know. I know what it's like to have someone lie to you about who your father is. But rape . . . How can I tell him that? How can I tell him the best thing in my life, the person I love more than anyone or anything, came to me through such an ugly act? And if I tell him that, do I tell him who did it? What if Casey doesn't even believe me? What if he wants to have a father so badly that he wants a relationship with Rich? It scares me to death. It scares me to think of what Rich might do, even now, to try to keep us quiet about what he did all those years ago."

They sat there for a moment.

Megan said, "I don't want to think about that now. I want to think about happy things. I want to know all about you. And Stephen? I saw the way he looks at you. God, if I was sixteen again and he looked at me like that, I would have melted right on the spot."

Allie laughed. Megan did, too.

"He knew how I felt about him," Megan said. "But he was so nice about it. He was a good friend to me that summer. I almost told him everything."

"I wonder what would have happened if you had?"

"I don't know. I try hard not to second-guess anything. There's no point. I made mistakes. I did things I regret, but I have Casey and my business, and I've managed to stay fairly happy most of the time. It's not perfect, but it's my life, and I like it. I'm certainly not going to waste my life feeling sorry for myself or feeling like a victim."

"Me, either," Allie said. "I think it took me longer than it did you to see that. But I finally made peace with it myself. With the whole mess. Later, after everything calms down, we have to talk about the house. Mom left it to me, but by rights, half of it should be yours—"

"Allie, I don't want any part of this house. If I hadn't had to come back here, to find Casey and to see you, I wouldn't have ever wanted to set foot inside these doors again. There are too many bad memories here for me."

"What if we made some good ones?"

"I don't think that's possible."

"I do." She quickly told her sister about her hopes for the shelter.

"It's something to think about." Megan looked around the room, a glint of tears in her eyes. "I spent some time in shelters. Some that were very good. Some that even made me think about trying to come back home."

"We could make it one of those," Allie said, her throat tight with tears. "You and me. Together. You'd know just what it needed to be, and I . . . Well, I have work to do, too. Stephen's insisting there are a dozen practical reasons it would never work. Not here. But if you and I were working together, I think somehow we could do it."

"Here? In Kentucky? You're going to stay?"

"I'm not sure."

"Are you and Stephen getting married?"

"No."

"You turned him down?"

"He hasn't asked," she said. "I don't know if he will."

"Of course he will. He's a good man, Allie."

"I know."

"And you're in love with him." Megan grinned.

"I think I am. It scares me. But I think I am."

Stephen came upstairs a few minutes later and something about the way he carried himself, the pinched, painful look on his face had Allie compelled to suddenly be by his side. She slid close, putting her arm around him, leaning into him, thinking this had to be so hard on him. His brother was a rapist, a murderer.

"I heard what you were saying," Stephen told Megan. "Trying to talk Allie into moving back to Alabama with you?"

"I haven't seen her in a long time," Megan said. "I miss her."

"So stay here with her," he said.

"We can't do that," Megan said.

"Of course you can."

"We have a home, Stephen. In Alabama."

"You have a family," he said. "In Kentucky."

"I have my reasons for staying away from Kentucky," Megan said. "I think you can guess what they are."

"You don't have to worry about Rich," he said softly.

"I'll always have to worry about Rich. He's always held all the power. He still does. Who's going to believe me, even now? DNA would prove he fathered my son, but it wouldn't prove he raped me or that he killed my friend fifteen years ago. It would still be my word against his, and I don't want to put myself or my son through the kind of fight it would take to bring your brother down."

"Megan, you don't have to fight him anymore."

"Of course I do—"

"He's dead," Stephen said.

"What?"

"He's dead."

Megan gasped. Allie did, too. She moved to stand in front of Stephen, putting her palm against his cheek, making him look at her. He seemed truly stunned and hurt and for once, not quite sure of himself.

"What happened?" she asked.

"He was upset after we talked." Stephen laughed bitterly. "Upset is an understatement where Rich is concerned. Out of control. In a rage. Maybe because he thought he was going to get caught, that he'd finally have to pay for one of the wrongs he'd committed. Maybe he'd finally gotten himself into a mess our father couldn't fix. I don't know. I suppose we'll never know. But he had too much to drink and never made it home. Turns out he drove his car off one of those big bridges off I-64 near Frankfort and went into the river. They just found his car about an hour ago. He was inside. He won't be hurting you or anyone else anymore."

Shocked, Allie slid both her arms around Stephen and held on tight. He stood stiffly in her embrace, breathing hard and trembling. Megan left at some point, and Allie felt tears filling her eyes. Stephen had been so good to her when everything was falling apart around her, and now he was hurting.

"I'm so sorry," she said. "What can I do?"

"I don't think there's anything anyone else can do, and I have to go. I have to call my parents. I have to go to his wife. She . . . I know she loved him at one time, even if she probably came to hate him as much as I did over the years. But he was her husband, and they have two little girls. Two beautiful little girls."

"You don't have to do this alone," Allie said. "Let me help you. The way you've helped me. I wouldn't have survived the past few days without you, Stephen. I love you."

"Don't say that." He tried to pull away from her. When she wouldn't let him go, he took her hands and pried them loose.

Puzzled, she said, "I wasn't supposed to fall in love with you?"

"I don't deserve that, Allie."

"Of course you do—"

"No, I don't," he insisted. "And I can't talk about this now, all right?"

"Talk about what?"

"Any of this," he said bleakly. "There's no pretense left inside of me. There's nothing."

It was her first inkling that something was going on besides the fact that his brother was dead. She backed away from him. Not sure she wanted to hear any more.

"I'm sorry," he said. "I am so sorry."

Allie started to cry. She couldn't have said where the tears came from, or what warned her how very close to disaster they were in this moment. But there it was. Intuition, or maybe what she could see in his eyes. His painfully sad eyes. Nothing left inside of him, he'd said. Nothing.

Not even for her?

"I don't understand."

"Allie, I haven't told you everything," he said bleakly.

"You kept things from me. Things you suspected, things you feared. I know that. You told me that," she said, trying to make excuses for him now. It was so ridiculous. She found she couldn't help herself. She knew all about catastrophes, about everything in her life changing in an instant. Megan seemingly dying. Allie's mother taking her away. And now Stephen, the man she loved. They were one step away from disaster. She knew it.

She was scared, backing away from him, when he said, "I lied to you."

"No," she whispered.

"I wanted to tell you. I promised myself, the first moment I could, I would, and I suppose this is it. I don't have any words to make this easier. I couldn't put together a coherent thought right now. Not that it matters. There aren't any words."

"I don't understand at all," she whispered.

"I know. I always thought when this moment came, I would stand here one more time and say there were things I hadn't told you, that I still hadn't lied to you. But it's just not true, Allie. I've been lying."

"All along?" she choked out.

He nodded. "I knew you were coming back here. My father knew, and he told me. He was worried about what you were going to do, about what you were going to find out. He wanted someone to keep an eye on you, and he wanted you gone as quickly as possible."

Allie stared at him as if she truly didn't know him. He'd told her that all along. *You don't know me.* And she hadn't believed him. He'd told her she'd regret making love to him, too, and she hadn't believed that, either. Turns out, he was right. Stephen was always right.

"You've been spying on me?" she said when she

could put together the words. "You've been reporting back to your father about me?"

He nodded.

She nearly doubled over from the pain that knifed through her, through her stomach, her heart, her lungs. A glutton for punishment, she whispered, "What else?"

"I had someone digging into your background, your financial records, your employment records and your mother's, before you ever got here. I knew you couldn't afford to keep the house, and I thought I'd make it easy for you to leave by offering to buy the house from you."

"I don't believe that," she said.

"It's true. I was waiting for you the night you arrived. It was no chance meeting."

Allie thought about the first time she saw him, standing there on the porch in the darkness. She thought about the dinner by candlelight and the way he'd utterly charmed her, thought about the way he'd held her when she cried and kissed her on the porch the next night. She thought about agonizing over the idea that he might be looking at her and still seeing her sister, that there might have been something between them and that he might be trying to relive those days with her now. But she never imagined anything like this.

"It was all a lie?" she cried.

"No." He shook his head, not quite meeting her eyes. "No, it wasn't."

She slapped him then, slapped him hard across the face for the second time in two days. He just stood there and took it. She watched as her handprint rose up red against his cheek and his jaw went even tighter.

"I can't believe this," she said, a fine trembling rolling through her entire body. She wasn't sure how she was still on her feet, she was so shaken. "I can't believe you'd do this to me."

"I'm sorry," he said.

She staggered back a step, thinking of the things he'd done to her, the things he'd said to her, and the things she'd said to him. Like *I love you*. She'd just told him she loved him, something she'd never said to another man in her entire life, and likely never would again.

"Don't you even have a conscience? I trusted you—"

"I had to have you trust me," he said. "I had to have you close, because I didn't know what my brother or my father had done all those years ago, and I didn't know what they might do to keep the truth from coming out now. I was afraid of what they might do to you, especially once you made it clear that you weren't leaving here without all the answers you thought you had to have."

"You're trying to tell me you did all this for me now? That you just wanted to protect me?"

"I did," he insisted.

"No—"

"Fifteen years ago, I did a lousy job of protecting your sister from my family. I sat back and did nothing, because this was my family and I thought I needed to find a way to coexist with them. Which I did by looking the other way, by being afraid to ask those really hard questions. Like *What did you do to Megan?* I was afraid of the truth. I thought I could slide all around it and somehow manage all these little problems without any of them blowing up in my face. But then that's just me," he said bitterly. "I always think I can handle any situation."

"That's what I am? A situation? Someone to be handled?"

He didn't say anything to that.

She felt the anger start to burn its way through every other emotion and decided to go with that. It was easier than anything else at the moment.

"So you decided to do a little job for your father? This man that you're not like at all? The one you can't stand?"

"I thought I could handle him, too. I thought I could feed him enough information to satisfy him so he'd leave you to me, so he wouldn't send anyone else to spy on you, and I thought I could stick close enough to you to make sure nobody hurt you," he said. "Which meant I had to get you to trust me, and to do that, I had to lie to you."

"And tell me that you were just so lonely," she sobbed. "That you just never quite fit in with the rest of your family, and you knew how I'd always felt. That we had so much in common."

It sickened her now, and he said nothing, which infuriated her even more.

"And yesterday morning? Yesterday afternoon? Last night? When you and I . . . When . . ." She couldn't even say it. He'd made love to her. At least she thought it had been love. "I can't believe this. You said you were afraid I'd hate you before this was over—"

"And now you do—"

"You said all those things about me belonging here. About this being my home, and the two of us being happy here."

"I want that. I still do."

"You made love to me," she cried. "And you made me fall in love with you. Why would you ever take things that far between us?"

"I never meant to," he said.

"So it was just one of those things?" she cried. "Is this the part where you try to tell me that was real? That everything else was a lie, but that part was real?"

"No." He shook his head and looked away. "I don't suppose I will."

"Why didn't you just tell me? Why not tell me the truth?"

"I couldn't take that chance, Allie."

"The chance that I wouldn't believe you?"

"That you'd be so angry and so hurt, you wouldn't let me anywhere near you, and my father or my brother would come after you," he said. "Think about what we just found out. My brother tried to kill your sister fifteen years ago. You saw him yesterday. You saw how angry he was. Do you think he wouldn't try to do something now to keep you from finding out exactly what happened to her? Maybe you'd take that kind of chance with your own safety, but I wouldn't."

"Because I mean so much to you," she said sarcastically.

He closed his eyes and backed away. A tense, deep silence stretched between them, and she had to concentrate hard just to breathe in and out and not scream at him or collapse on the floor in a heap.

Finally he said, "I never wanted to hurt you."

She laughed bitterly. "The people I love always end up hurting me."

"I never expected to feel this way about you, Allie. I never thought you'd come to mean so much to me, and by the time I figured out that you did, I was in way too deep. I was afraid they were going to hurt you. When it came down to making a choice—between hurting you emotionally or the possibility of you being hurt physically—I didn't see anything else I could do but protect you."

"Even if it meant I'd hate you for it?"

"I suspected that's exactly what it would mean," he said, obviously resigned to it. "And even knowing what I know now, if I had it to do all over again, I'd lie to you still. Because you're here. You're safe. You have your sister back and a nephew and all the answers you just had to have. I'd just try my damnedest not to fall in love with you, not to touch you, until I could tell you the truth."

"When you truly care about someone, you don't lie to them every time you see them, Stephen."

"I wouldn't know about that. My family lives on polite, little lies."

"Don't," she said. "Don't you dare."

"All right." He squared his shoulders and took a breath, looking every bit as bad as she felt. "I have to go. Rich . . . There are things I have to take care of, but you and Megan and Casey should be fine. Rich can't hurt you anymore, and I think my father's going to be too busy burying his son to give you and your sister a second thought. Just in case, I left the guards on duty outside."

Allie shivered and let miserable tears fall down her cheeks, and she wouldn't even look at him. She couldn't.

"I'm sorry, Allie," he said.

And then he was gone.

Chapter 19

Four days later, Allie and her sister stood on a pretty hillside beneath the sprawling branches of a willow tree, beside Allie's father's grave and the one that held Margaret Addison's body.

Allie and Megan had spent the last few days talking about everything imaginable and cleaning out the house. Allie found a letter addressed to her from her father, one he never mailed. It seemed fitting to read it at his grave.

It was dated nearly three years ago, right before her father died.

> *My dearest Allie,*
> *If you've found this, I can only assume you've finally come home, because I'll never quite find the courage to mail it. I wish I could be there to say these things to you in person. I wish I had the right. But the truth is that I've been a coward for much of my life, and before that I was a fool.*
> *I'm assuming you know everything now, that I married your mother and made promises to her and to Megan that I didn't keep. I honestly thought I could. I tried, but it just wasn't enough, and we've all suffered for that, for all my shortcomings. And for everything, I'm truly sorry.*

I should have been kinder, more forgiving, more loving. I should have been more appreciative of all the precious gifts God gave me—most of all for you and your mother and Megan.

Bitterness is an ugly thing in a person, my darling. The roots can sink down so deeply, it can be almost impossible to dislodge. The truth is that the people we love are seldom perfect. We all make mistakes. Even good people sometimes make terribly hurtful mistakes, and then we have to choose. To forgive them and to move on, or to hold onto all those old hurts and let them ruin not only the present, but the future as well.

That's what I did. I can see that now, but at the time I was blind to it all. I did this to all of us. I knew it from the moment we woke up that morning and Megan was gone. I knew something terrible was going to happen, and I knew it was my fault.

Finding out that Megan was dead, and having to tell your mother and you, having to go to the cemetery that day and put her into the ground—it was the hardest thing I've ever had to do. And I don't think I realized until Megan was gone how very much she meant to me. She may have been another man's child, but in truth she was more mine than his. I was there the day she was born. I was there for nearly every day of her life, and I didn't see what a blessing that was until it was too late. I did love her, even if I didn't show her that love, not the way a father should have. But I loved her, and I hope that I'll see her again someday, somewhere, and that I'll have a chance to beg her forgiveness, just as I beg now for yours.

You were the absolute light of my life, and I hope

*that after you and your mother left here, you found
all the happiness you deserve.*

*I hated to see you go. I missed you desperately, but
your mother was right to take you from me. I don't
deserve to have you in my life, not after what I'd
done to tear our family apart.*

*So I've been here, all by myself in this house that
was once filled with so much joy. I've had more time
than I could ever need to examine the mistakes I've
made along the way, and I suppose that's a fitting
punishment for what I've done.*

*I can only tell you that I wish I'd been a better
man, a kinder, more forgiving, more generous man.
I wish I'd been the father you and your sister deserved, and I hope you'll never doubt that I truly
loved you. I wish you all the happiness in the world,
all the good things life has to offer, my precious, precious girl.*

Allie swiped at her own tears and passed the letter
to her sister. "Read it. It's about you, too."

She stood there while her sister read, while her
sister wiped away tears of her own.

"God, what a mess," Megan said.

Allie nodded and had to remind herself that this
was what she wanted. The whole, ugly truth. All her
family's failings, all their faults, all their mistakes, all
the answers. Uncovering them had cost her a great
deal, but it had given her so much, as well. She had
her sister, her nephew, and she was truly free to start
her life all over, to do anything she wanted.

Megan had made her decision. She was coming
back to Kentucky, back home. Mitch Wilson had
shown up on their doorstep the first night she was
in town and grabbed onto her like he would never

let her go. He'd always had trouble accepting the idea that she was dead. All these years, he'd been looking for her, waiting for her, loving her. Allie thought her sister loved Mitch just as deeply.

Megan had chosen to tell Casey the whole, painful truth about his biological father, because Rich was gone now and couldn't hurt him anymore, and because Casey had an uncle, a grandmother, two grandfathers. She suspected Tucker might be marrying Martha soon, giving Casey a step-grandmother, as well. There were also his two half sisters. Casey had taken to his grandmother right away, and he was fascinated by the two little girls, who were two and four and absolutely bewildered to find their daddy gone.

Mrs. Whittaker had decided to end her forty-year marriage to Stephen's father. She'd kicked her husband out of their home and taken her daughter-in-law and two granddaughters in instead, and made it clear that Casey would always be welcomed there. She'd made a heartfelt apology to Megan and Allie for everything her family had done to theirs.

Casey had been with her and the girls today, in an overflowing church for Rich's very public funeral and now for what the family had decided would be a very small, private graveside service. Allie and Megan watched and waited from a distance, taking this time to say good-bye to John Bennett and to simply be with each other.

The emotional roller coaster of the last week seemed to have consumed Allie with a vengeance. She was tired, and felt like she still had so much to do. At the moment she simply felt incapable of doing anything.

Megan slipped her arm around Allie's waist, and

they leaned on each other for a moment. "You haven't told me what you've decided to do," Megan said.

"I just don't know." She felt that awful sense of rootlessness once again. Before, she'd thought to stay here. To make the runaway shelter a reality and to be with Stephen.

"Casey and I are going to be here. With Mitch, and I want you here, Allie. You were all set to stay before."

"I know." But Allie didn't know if she could be here anymore. Stephen was going to be a part of Casey's family, too, and they were bound to run into each other from time to time. It would be so painful.

"What about the shelter? You were so excited about it, and it's a good idea," Megan said. "It's important."

Allie sighed. "It was important to me, but the more I've thought about it, the more I see that I wanted it for all the wrong reasons. I think it was about me wanting a place to belong. I wanted a way to stay in the house we grew up in. I wanted to have a family around me, even if it was a family of teenage runaways. Which is a purely selfish reason to build a runaway shelter."

"Maybe that was part of it. But I think underneath all the hurt and the natural reserve that comes from the way you were raised, lurks the heart of a closet idealist, Allie. Someone who honestly wants to make the world a better place." Megan smiled gently. "We all have a choice about how we spend our lives. You want to take your time and energy and use it to help people, and I admire that about you so much. The world needs people like you. There are a bunch of lost teenagers who need you, too."

Allie fought back more tears. "You really think so?"

"I know so. You'll be so good with them. You know exactly what it's like to feel lost. But you're not anymore. I'm here, and I want to help you with the shelter. I want us to find a way to make it work."

"I'd like for us to do it together. I don't want to leave, but . . ."

"Stephen?" Megan guessed.

"Yes."

"Have you talked to him yet?"

"No." But her eyes were automatically drawn to him. He stood straight and tall between his sister-in-law and his mother—who was as devastated by facing up to the truth of who her son was, as by the fact that he was dead. His two little nieces were in front of him, Casey behind his right shoulder, his father standing conspicuously alone.

"Stephen made the most generous offer," Megan said. "He came to see me, in the middle of making his brother's funeral arrangements, to tell me he knew how much Casey wants and needs a father. He said he was willing to step in and take whatever role in Casey's life that Casey and I would like. And he means it, Allie. He's already been so good with Casey, trying to help him now with all that he's feeling about Rich. He told Casey there's good and bad in most everyone. That it's okay, especially with family, to love them for the good, even if you despise the bad things they've done."

Allie couldn't say anything to that. Her father's eloquent plea, his bitter lesson, was running through her head. But she was still so angry, so hurt. She was trying very hard to convince herself that Stephen Whittaker had never truly loved her, and that she couldn't love him, though she still couldn't pry her eyes away from him right now.

He stood by his brother's grave, the rock at the center of what was left of his family, the one holding everyone together, the one everyone depended upon. He'd done the same thing for her. Even when he'd lied to her, he'd been a rock. She had no doubts that if she or Megan or Casey ever truly needed anything from him, he would help them and protect them. And she hated seeing him like this, wondering if everyone was taking comfort from him, drawing strength from him, while at the same time no one was giving anything to him in return.

He was just a man, after all. Complex, driven, stubborn to the point of being arrogant, always thinking he was right, always thinking he could manage any situation that came along.

And he'd managed her. . . . The little problem. She hated thinking of herself that way, hated thinking of him seeing her like that.

He couldn't truly love her and do that to her, she'd told herself over and over again, even as she missed him more than she could ever imagine missing anyone.

"I know he hurt you, but I also think he loves you," Megan said. "Sometimes we end up hurting the people we love the most, Allie. Look at what our parents did to each other. Think about how much I hurt you by staying away, by letting everyone believe I was dead."

"You did that to protect yourself and your son."

"And Stephen says he did this to protect you from his father and his brother. He did it even when he knew he might well lose you over it. He put his own feelings aside to protect you at all costs," Megan said.

"Think about what that says about him, about the kind of man he really is. Think about what you'd do to protect him, if you thought he was truly in danger. You'd do anything. You'd say anything. Because you love him."

But Allie said nothing. She couldn't. It hurt just to stand here and look at him. Did they know how alone he felt at times? Did anyone even think that he might need someone, too? Surely there was someone who could look past the facade and see the man underneath.

"I'm going to Casey," Megan said. "We'll see you back at the house."

Allie realized the service was over. People were leaving. Stephen walked his mother and his sister-in-law to the waiting limousine, then stepped back, watching them drive away. Then he stood by the casket by the open grave, his back every bit as straight as it had been the entire time she'd watched. He never wavered.

What was he thinking, she wondered? Of the waste it was for a man to have died so young and to have done so much wrong with his life? To have left behind two beautiful little girls and a wealth of unfulfilled potential? That his family had been torn apart, his parents separating after forty years and his brother gone, the whole foundation of his life shaken.

Allie knew what that was like. He'd given her back her family. It didn't seem right that he'd lost so much of his in the process. It didn't seem right that he was standing there by his brother's grave all alone.

She was walking toward him even before she made any conscious decision to do so. He turned at the last minute, hearing her approach, and for a second, his expression was utterly bleak, before he carefully schooled his features into a cool, impersonal mask.

"Allie," he said.

She slipped her left hand into his right. He stiffened at the touch but still said nothing. He just watched her with those beautiful dark eyes of his.

"I'm sorry," she said.

"For what?"

"That you've lost your brother."

"He was a terrible human being, Allie. He tried to kill your sister. He did kill Margaret Addison."

"He was still your brother."

Stephen shook his head back and forth. "I wanted to kill him myself for what he did to Megan. I hated the idea that we had the same blood running through our veins."

"I can understand that. But you still didn't want him to die. It had to be a shock. Maybe even worse because of how angry you were at him."

"You must despise me," he said, even as she stood there holding his hand. "You must despise my entire family."

"I don't hold your brother's actions against you," she said. "And I hate seeing you like this. Hurting and all alone."

It was true. All of it. Once again, she couldn't help herself where he was concerned. She came to stand directly in front of him, wrapping her arms tightly around him and feeling his whole body stiffen, feeling his quickly indrawn breath, finally his arms slowly closing around her.

She held him for a long time, thinking it shouldn't be this hard to let go of him, given how angry she still was and how hurt. Thinking that she shouldn't still feel so much for him, that she should be able to stay away, but she couldn't. She just couldn't. Not today.

"Allie, you don't owe me anything," he said.

"Yes, I do. You wouldn't have left me alone if I was feeling like this. You didn't."

She felt a shudder run through him, felt an answering one run through her entire body and held him more tightly, for as long as she dared. Then she slipped away from him and left him there all alone once again.

He stayed away for three and a half weeks.

Allie and Megan cleaned out the house. Megan went back to Birmingham temporarily, to put her house on the market and prepare to move her business to Lexington. Mitch Wilson had proposed, and she'd accepted. He'd been tempted to marry her before she left, not wanting to let her go again, but she'd talked him into a quiet ceremony in front of a justice of the peace when she returned and a roaring party afterward at his restaurant. She was shopping for office space downtown, near him, and they were house hunting.

Megan's reappearance had caused quite a stir in Dublin. But luckily, so far no one had linked her disappearance or return to Stephen's brother, which was fine with everyone. Rich was dead. No one saw any reason to make the events of the last fifteen years public. Stephen's mother intended to claim Casey as her grandson, as Rich's son, but not right away. Rich was still news, and no one wanted to see their stories plastered all over the local papers.

Allie was starting to think Stephen was right—that she did belong here, that there was no escaping this place she'd always considered her home. Good mem-

ories and bad, they were all here. So was all that was
left of her family.

She'd gone to Connecticut briefly to arrange the
sale of her mother's house and pack her things, and
when she returned to Kentucky, she'd received an
unsolicited offer on her parents' house—a generous
one, she thought. If she accepted it, she and Megan
and Casey had agreed to set the money aside either
as a donation to a charitable organization or as seed
money for a shelter in central Kentucky.

Allie had buried herself in the nitty-gritty details
for weeks, and after talking with dozens of people,
she had to admit, the shelter as she originally con-
ceived of the idea was never going to fly. Dublin was
too small, which complicated funding and volunteer
issues, and a majority of the town's zoning board
had told her in no uncertain terms they'd never vote
to allow such a place on Willow Lane.

Which meant she had some hard decisions to make
about where she was going to live and what she was
going to do with her life. She thought perhaps Megan
was right. Allie was an idealist. She still wanted to
believe she could make a difference. She had a deep-
seated need to feel her life was worthwhile, and she
thought the most personally satisfying thing she
could do was to help others somehow. She just had
to figure out how.

At the moment she hadn't figured out anything,
and she couldn't have been more surprised to find
Stephen at her front door one day, looking so tall
and so solid, so heartbreakingly gorgeous, if a bit
reserved and probably unsure of his welcome.

"Hi," she said tentatively.

"Hi. I was wondering if you had a few minutes.
There's something I'd like to show you."

She hesitated. She'd missed him so.

"Please," he said.

"All right."

She got her sweater, because there was a chill in the air this morning, and let him lead her to his car, the big four-wheeler this time. She was conscious of every move he made, every little brush of his body against hers, even the hand at her back as she walked.

She didn't ask where they were going. She'd always been willing to go anywhere with him. Her first instincts had been to trust him, even when he gave her cause to think she shouldn't.

He took her back to Dublin, down a road just off Main Street, a place of older houses, many of which had been converted into business offices. There at the end of the street was an oversize lot amid towering trees. He parked at the curb and helped her out of the car, his hand falling to his side the minute she had her feet on the ground.

He had a canister with him, a long white one, from which he pulled a sheath of papers he unrolled on the hood of the car.

"What do you think?" he said.

Allie stared at the pen and ink sketch, an artist's rendering of a house. She looked back at the empty lot. A house on this site.

"It looks like my house," she said. "On this lot?"

He nodded.

"I was talking to my mother and mentioned that you wanted to turn your house into a runaway shelter. She liked the idea. She's also an excellent fundraiser. She raised a half million dollars for the new library last year. But even with all the clout she has in this town, she didn't think she could get her neigh-

bors behind the idea of a shelter in their neighborhood. All those things I told you about the shelter,
Allie, self-serving as all it was at the time, it was still
good advice. I don't think you'd ever overcome all
those obstacles and make a go of a shelter on Willow
Lane. But this . . . You could make this work."

Allie stared at the sketches, noticed the lettering
along the bottom. *Meg's House.*

"Your sister didn't think her name should be on
the project. She suggested Meg's."

"You never give up, do you?" Allie said, not sure
if she was complaining about that or admiring him
for it.

"So far . . . No, I've never given up on anything I
truly wanted. You don't either," he said. "It's one of
the first things I admired about you."

"Stephen—"

"Just look at this. Think about it," he said. "I
should probably tell you, I thought about just going
ahead and doing it—"

"Doing it?"

"I actually made an offer on the lot," he said. "My
mother and my sister-in-law want to help, too. I
know you have an offer on the house—they're low-
balling you, by the way—and my mother and Renee
want to buy the house from you and donate it, for
the shelter. Or you donate it, and take their money
to get the project going," he said.

"Wait a minute. What do you mean—you thought
about just doing it?"

"Letting them buy it without saying anything to
you. Having a real set of blueprints for the renovations drawn up, going ahead and moving your house
to the site. I thought I'd have it sitting here waiting
for you. A done deal. And then I decided I'd better

wait a minute and think about it first." He honestly looked chagrined, then admitted, "Maybe that would have been a little . . ."

"Controlling?" she suggested. "Arrogant? The actions of a man who's sure he always knows what's best?"

"I did stop," he pointed out. "And just because I thought of it doesn't mean it's a bad idea. I know it isn't exactly what you wanted, but we can bring your house here. I've been all over it with an engineer, and it can be done."

"You've been there with an engineer?"

"Megan let us in," he said.

"Of course."

"Look at this neighborhood, Allie. It's mostly businesses now. I don't think anyone would fight you on the zoning. It's close to the hospital, so there are lots of health professionals. I bet you could round up a lot of volunteer medical professionals from the neighborhood. My mother and Renee honestly want to do this. I can find somebody to move the house. As for the renovations that would be necessary, the architect's a friend of mine. He owes me a favor. So you don't have to worry about his fee. I can twist a few arms, and get a good bit of the renovation work donated or done at cost. It could work."

She folded her arms across her chest and stared up at him, fighting the urge to grin. Or to cry. "You have it all figured out, don't you?"

"Why don't you give me a clue here." He looked a bit worried. "I'm not sure if I'm being manipulative or helpful."

"Both, I'd say." It was so like him to just push forward like this. "Why did you do this, Stephen?"

"I thought about what I had to offer you." He

frowned, looking quite serious and sincere. "What I wanted to *give* you. I thought it was fitting that it come from my family, because of all that we took from yours."

"So this is guilt?"

"It's me trying, to give you something you want, something I thought was important to you, and . . . Oh, hell, I can't change the man that I am. I still want you," he confessed. "I want to give you this because I know it's important to you. I want you to have everything you want, Allie. Everything you need. But I also want to give you a reason to stay."

Through great force of will, Allie managed to say nothing. Not yet. And she couldn't quite bring herself to look at him anymore. She didn't think she could hide what was in her eyes, and she liked too much what she saw in his.

"So . . . what does that make me?" he asked. "Someone who hasn't learned a thing by losing you? Someone you don't want anything to do with? Someone you could never live with? Never trust? Never forgive?"

She knew exactly who he was. She knew. He was a man who got things done, one who seemed incredibly adept at bending the world to his will—just as his father and brother did. Except he wasn't like them in so many of the ways that counted. He wasn't evil. He wasn't selfish. He didn't see himself as a man entitled to exactly what he wanted, either by virtue of his birth or the fortune that came with the Whittaker name. He earned it through hard work and perseverance, and she thought at the core, he was a genuinely kind, caring man, that the vast majority of the time, he put his time and talents and incredible drive to work for good.

"I think all of that makes you the man that you are," she said simply. "Determined, hardworking, someone capable of making things happen, someone who likes to take charge, someone who thinks he can handle anything."

"I don't think I could handle losing you," he said. "I don't know how to handle the idea that you might walk away from me right now and I might never see you again."

"I have a feeling you'd come find me," she said.

"I hadn't planned on giving up anytime soon. If that was a question of my intentions."

"So . . ." She looked back down at the plans. "This is an apology?"

"I was thinking more along the lines of a gift," he said, coming close enough to touch her, to take the hand hanging by her side in his and look down at her with glittering, dark eyes that had always seen too much.

She had tears on her cheeks, tears he gently wiped away.

"I wanted you to understand that the things which are important to you are important to me, too, and that if you were mine, Allie, I would do anything in this world to see that you're happy."

He framed her face with his hands, brought his lips down to hers for a long, slow, sweet, hungry kiss.

"I love you," he said. "And I'm so sorry. For everything. I wanted to protect you from every bad thing in this world, from everything that ever hurt you, and I ended up hurting you even more myself. Do you think you might be able to forgive me for that someday?"

"I think it's a distinct possibility."

"I will never lie to you again. I will never keep

anything from you." He kissed her again, deeper, harder, with more hunger this time. "I've never wanted anything as much as I want you. And I want forever, Allie. I want you to marry me, and live here with me, and make a family with me. Forever."

She closed her eyes, buried her face against his neck, and breathed in the scent of him, absorbed the incredible feel of his arms securely around her once again, his heart beating solidly against her palm.

"I know you. I know what you want," he said. "You want a refuge, a sanctuary. One place in this whole, big, scary world where you feel absolutely safe and wanted and needed and loved, and that place is with me. I know what it means to you to have that. I know what it cost you all those years you did without it, all the time you were alone. But you don't ever have to be alone again, because I'm here, and I love you. I can't imagine that you need me half as much as I need you."

"I've never quite understood why you would need me."

"You want a list? A dozen reasons, maybe?" he suggested, then started rattling them off, punctuating each one with a kiss. "Maybe because you made me realize how lonely I was, how empty my life had become. Because you filled up all those empty spots. Because I'm much too cynical, and you reminded me what optimism and what hope is all about. Because you reminded me of what's important in life. That I love this place, and that it's my home, and that I want to share it with a woman who loves completely, with her whole heart, and forever. Someone who hangs on tight to the people she loves."

Allie stood there in his arms, unable to say anything at all. The sun was streaming through the tops of the trees. The sky was a surreal blue with big, puffy clouds ambling along within it. Birds were singing, she realized. There was a slight breeze blowing, and she could smell the river that flowed through town. She could almost hear it.

There were times, between all the worry and all the little revelations, that this place called to her, when a part of her recognized it and felt like it was right to be here, yet never more so than in this moment with him.

There was vibrant color spreading through the tall trees, and she had to admit it was beautiful here, that she'd found the sense of belonging she'd always craved. Somehow, deep inside, she recognized this place. This was her home, the one she'd always wanted, and it was here with him.

"Is that enough?" he whispered. "I have a half a dozen more reasons—"

"It's enough," she said as he kissed her through her tears.

Penguin Putnam Inc.
Online

Your Internet gateway to a virtual environment with hundreds of entertaining and enlightening books from Penguin Putnam Inc.

While you're there, get the latest buzz on the best authors and books around—

Tom Clancy, Patricia Cornwell, W.E.B. Griffin, Nora Roberts, William Gibson, Robin Cook, Brian Jacques, Catherine Coulter, Stephen King, Jacquelyn Mitchard, and many more!

Penguin Putnam Online is located at http://www.penguinputnam.com

PENGUIN PUTNAM NEWS

Every month you'll get an inside look at our upcoming books and new features on our site. This is an ongoing effort to provide you with the most up-to-date information about our books and authors.

Subscribe to Penguin Putnam News at http://www.penguinputnam.com/ClubPPI